Shy
Creatures

Also by Clare Chambers

Uncertain Terms
Back Trouble
Learning to Swim
A Dry Spell
In A Good Light
The Editor's Wife
Small Pleasures

SHY CREATURES

Clare Chambers

WEIDENFELD & NICOLSON

First published in Great Britain in 2024 by Weidenfeld & Nicolson,
an imprint of The Orion Publishing Group Ltd
Carmelite House, 50 Victoria Embankment
London EC4Y 0DZ

An Hachette UK Company

1 3 5 7 9 10 8 6 4 2

A CIP catalogue record for this book is
available from the British Library.

ISBN (Hardback) 978 1 3996 0255 6
ISBN (Export Trade Paperback) 978 1 3996 0262 4
ISBN (eBook) 978 1 3996 0257 0
ISBN (Audio) 978 1 3996 0258 7

Typeset by Born Group
Printed and bound in Great Britain by Clays Ltd, Elcograf S.p.A.

www.weidenfeldandnicolson.co.uk
www.orionbooks.co.uk

To Peter

Chapter 1

— 1964 —

In all failed relationships there is a point that passes unnoticed at the time, which can later be identified as the beginning of the decline. For Helen, it was the weekend that the Hidden Man came to Westbury Park.

On Friday, she had been preparing the art therapy room for her favourite group of the week – Male Alcoholics – when Gil put his head around the door. Seeing that she was alone, he came in and sat on the corner of her desk, watching as she laid out paper, pencils, charcoal and paints. A semicircle of easels was arranged around a still life – a wicker chair, draped in velvet cloth, beside a table on which sat a vase of tulips, a milk jug and a bowl of eggs. The doors to the two small side rooms, used by patients who preferred to work in privacy, were half open and he sent a glance of enquiry in their direction, which Helen answered with a reassuring shake of the head before he spoke.

'Kath is going down to Deal for the weekend with the children.'

'Really?' There had been false alarms of this nature before and Helen had learnt not to give in to optimism too far in advance.

He nodded. 'Her god-daughter has just had a baby and she's going down there tomorrow to . . . do whatever it is women do on these occasions. So . . .'

He stared at her with that burning look that he turned quite unconsciously on women of all ages, and his patients, both male and female. Helen had seen this phenomenon at work, but she liked to imagine that it contained a little extra intensity when it was directed at her.

'You could stay at mine?' she ventured. Even though they had been lovers for three years and he had found her a suitable flat and contributed to her rent with just this kind of opportunity in mind, it had been possible no more than half a dozen times.

'If you'll have me.'

'Well, I suppose. If you don't make a nuisance of yourself.'

This conversation took place across the width of the room and Helen had continued all the while to sort out materials for the forthcoming class. No one walking in on the scene would have suspected anything unprofessional in their manner. In the early days of their relationship, when passion made them more reckless, the art therapy studio and its side rooms were often used for assignations. Now, they were more careful, or perhaps less passionate. None of their colleagues, from the medical superintendent to the ward orderlies, had any inkling of the affair and if Helen had ever blushed or smiled more than somewhat in his presence, well, so did everyone else favoured by the full beam of Gil's attention.

'I'll be over after lunch tomorrow, then. Kath will have the car, so I suppose I'll have to walk.'

He was thinking aloud, not fishing for a lift. Helen had no car – just a second-hand scooter, on which she rode the four miles from her flat in South Croydon to Westbury Park each day.

'Good. I'll cook something nice, then. You'd better go. My men will be here in a minute.'

Gil nodded, raking his hand through his thick hair, which was mostly dark but streaked here and there with grey. By some sorcery of nature or grooming, it was always the same untidy length, just below the collar, but never seemed to grow longer or have been cut suddenly shorter.

'I love you,' he said and was gone, his footsteps echoing down the long corridor.

Helen tuned the radio to the Third Programme. A background of classical music, at a volume to soothe rather than stir, had proved to be the most conducive to an atmosphere of calm and concentration.

The room, thanks to her little touches, was the pleasantest in the entire hospital. The colourful mobiles, stirring gently on their fishing-line frames, the prints by old masters on the wall alongside paintings by the residents of Westbury Park past and present, dried flowers in a vase, screen-printed cushions and an atmosphere of harmony and order were all her doing.

She put on her overall, a white coat just like the doctors wore, but smeared with paint and charcoal dust. The alcoholics were arriving in a pack, as they always did, to avoid confronting art alone. They were quite talentless with pencil or paint and had originally signed up, Helen suspected, in the hope of nudes. The still life with milk jug and eggs had been a disappointment, but better than falling back on the imagination, which was treacherous terrain indeed. The chief attraction of the class was as a respite from the hours of group therapy which, along with disulfiram, formed the body of their treatment. In the art room there was no requirement to reflect on their addiction or talk about the misfortunes that had brought them low. Instead, they cheerfully mocked each other's and their own efforts and were generous in their praise of anything more or less resembling its subject.

Helen's purpose, as had been made clear at her interview, was to provide them with materials and space and to encourage free expression, but not to teach or diagnose or psychoanalyse

3

or trespass in any way on the work of the medically trained professionals, like Gil. Today, she was distracted from performing even this modest service by thoughts of the weekend ahead. She had failed to share with Gil the complication that was now casting a considerable shadow over their plans.

Three weeks ago, she had accepted an invitation to a family dinner on Saturday night from her brother, Clive, and his wife. The event was to celebrate their daughter's sixteenth birthday and had been in her diary and on her mind as something to look forward to. She was fond of her niece, Lorraine, who was gawky and lacking in confidence, and of Clive, too, up to a point. His wife, June, she just tolerated. Clive had even taken the unusual and thoughtful step of phoning her earlier in the week to ask if she would like their parents to pick her up on their way. She had refused the lift – her father was an erratic driver with a furious temper behind the wheel, and away from it – but confirmed her attendance. Now, she would have to pull out. It was always the way: Gil's availability could never be counted on until the very last minute; hers was simply assumed. Only sickness would suffice as an excuse at such late notice and it would have to be something significant to justify cancellation.

In contemplating the deception that would soon be necessary, Helen started to feel the intestinal cramping and queasiness that often accompanied the contemplation of her moral failings. By the time she came to make the fateful call, it might very well not be a lie at all. The other possibility, that she should honour her original commitment and forgo the weekend with Gil, did not even occur to her.

Roland, one of the more diligent members of the group, beckoned her over, rousing her from her brooding. He had started his sketch without considering the layout of the page. Although the vase, jug and bowl were arranged in a cluster on the table, on paper the same elements were spread out in a

4

straight line, evenly spaced and untethered to any background. The eggs – tiny, flattened pebbles – floated freely above the two-dimensional bowl. It was like the work of a six-year-old, and yet this was a man who could operate a metal lathe in a workshop, fix every kind of motorcar engine and bang out the chords of any tune you could sing on a pub piano.

'It doesn't look anything like it,' he said, shaking his head. 'What am I doing wrong?'

'You're not doing anything wrong,' Helen said. 'There's no right or wrong about it.'

'But I want to get better or what's the point?'

For a moment she wondered whether he was talking about his drawing or his addiction. If only he could be cured of the latter, it hardly mattered whether he could draw tulips or milk jugs.

'If it's the composition that you find difficult, perhaps you could focus on just one item.'

'Can I start again?'

'Of course,' said Helen, retrieving the sketch before he could crumple it into a ball. 'Don't destroy this one. We'll put it in your folder.'

She was scrupulous and superstitious about preserving her patients' work, keeping it long after they had been discharged. It was both respectful of their efforts and provided evidence of the value of the therapy. Her mentor at the hospital where she had worked previously as a volunteer had been emphatic on this point. 'You are not here to teach art and your patients are not here to produce art. They are here to get well. It is the *process* of painting or drawing or sculpting that can help with that. But you must still treat the outcome of that process with respect.'

It was an argument on this theme that had first brought her to Gil's attention soon after her arrival at Westbury Park three years previously. Full of enthusiasm for her new role, she had begun by working long after her prescribed hours, cleaning

5

brushes and palettes, sharpening pencils, wiping tables, decorating the studio in readiness for the next day. One evening, returning a rinsed coffee mug to the small room in a distant wing of the hospital where staff could go to make hot drinks or play cards on their break, she walked in on three orderlies sitting together weaving a rug.

They had arrived early for their evening shift and were filling the last few precious minutes before they were due on the wards. They glanced up as Helen came in and, seeing from her painting overall that she was not a doctor and needed no special deference, ignored her and carried on their conversation.

Rug-making was one of the popular occupational therapies for patients and for a moment Helen smiled at the notion of the staff choosing to relax in just this way. There was something touching in it that spoke of shared humanity. These elevated thoughts withered abruptly as Helen realised that what they were doing was not *making* a rug, but unmaking one, pulling out the strands of wool with metal hooks and tossing them into a bag at their feet.

'What *are* you doing?' she asked, failing to keep a note of astonishment from her voice.

They turned as one and the spokesperson of the three, a solidly built woman with tightly permed curls, said, 'We're just unpicking this blessed carpet, so they can do it all again tomorrow.'

The other two laughed, not maliciously, but it was still a jangling affront to Helen.

'Why on earth would you do that?' Helen asked. She had promised herself she would keep her head down as a new member of staff, fit in, make friends and avoid conflict, and already she was on the edge of a quarrel.

'We haven't got enough wool for them to keep making more and more rugs. And where would we put them all? Anyway, they don't care.'

Helen didn't need to ask who 'they' were. 'Who told you to do this?'

'We've always done it,' one of the other women said, with slightly less confidence. 'We just haven't got the wool.'

'Right.' Helen took a breath and composed herself. In the uncodified but nonetheless unchallengeable hierarchy of Westbury Park, ward orderlies were (just) below her and it would therefore be unconscionable to berate them for doing no more than their job. She needed to go higher. 'May I borrow this?' She indicated the bag of wool scraps. 'I'll return it.'

The three women nodded, humouring her. Helen could imagine the exchange of tutting and eye-rolling that would ensue as soon as she departed.

It so happened that Dr Rudden's office was the first that she came to as she stalked the corridors looking for somewhere to vent her frustration. They had not been properly introduced at this point, although she had attended a staff meeting at which he was present, along with the medical superintendent, psychotherapists, social workers, nurses and occupational and physical therapists. She had noticed him only to the extent that he was the most handsome man in the room, from a field offering no serious competition, but he had mostly kept his head down, writing or doodling on a pad.

She knocked firmly – there was no point in timidity now; she needed to keep things on the boil if she was to carry this through – and a voice said, 'Come in.'

He was sitting behind his desk, with his chair angled towards the tall windows, looking out onto the green lawns, where patients still wandered in the early evening sunshine. A cigarette smouldered in an overflowing ashtray, sending a column of smoke up to an already overcast ceiling. On the wall behind him was a print of Richard Dadd's *Titania Sleeping* – a painting Helen knew well and would have remarked on, in other circumstances.

7

He swung his feet off the window ledge and stood up, raising his eyebrows in welcome. 'Hello . . .?'

'Helen Hansford.'

'Helen Hansford. The new art therapist. What can I do for you?' His voice was attractive, soothing, but she didn't want to be soothed – yet.

'I'm in a bit of a rage, actually.' She held up the bag of wool. 'I've just come across a group of orderlies unpicking a rug made by patients in OT so that they can do it all over again tomorrow. Were you aware of this?' She dropped the bag on an expanse of leather desktop undisturbed by paperwork of any kind.

He avoided the question, asking instead, 'This offends you?'

'Yes. It offends me. It's disrespectful to the patients; it belittles their efforts and it's just poor practice.'

He nodded slowly. 'But if it's the process rather than the outcome that is therapeutic . . .'

'Even so, they should be able to see and enjoy the product of their work.'

With a motion of his hand, he invited her to sit down, but she shook her head. It was easier to remain indignant when standing.

'Perhaps if you think of it in the same light as doing a jigsaw or building a house of cards, where the satisfaction doesn't come from the idea of creating something permanent—'

'It's not the same at all!' She could feel her voice rising up the scale. 'No one expects those things to last. But rug-making is a craft and a rug is a useful thing. It would look very nice in the day room.'

He looked at her through narrowed eyes for a long moment, as though her words warranted deep and considered reflection. The pause grew intimidating and Helen was the first to crack.

'And they were taking it apart with such relish. It made me wonder who was mad and who was sane around here.'

'Well, that's a very healthy attitude to hold,' he said. 'Though we don't use the word mad any more. Not of the patients, anyway.' He seemed to be enjoying himself. 'If I can't persuade you to sit down, do you mind if I do? My back is playing up.'

'Please, go ahead.'

He resettled himself in his chair, without releasing her from his gaze. 'You're quite right, of course. I agree with you.'

'In any case,' said Helen, who had not caught up with this surrender and didn't want a valid point to go to waste, 'has anyone bothered to ask the patients what they think?'

'You're right. I agree with you,' he repeated. 'What would you have me do? I suppose the problem is materials?'

'Yes. That's what they said. I'm sure they were only trying to help,' Helen conceded, disarmed now in spite of herself.

'Always money,' he sighed. 'Well, leave it with me.'

'Thank you . . . Dr Rudden.'

'Gil, please.'

She left the office with a strange fluttering in her ears, her heart beating a little faster in her triumph. Already there was between them that invisible thread that joins two people who have noticed each other for the first time.

It was only a week later that Helen rode into the car park to find a green van with its back doors thrown open and a man unloading three-foot-square cardboard boxes onto the forecourt. She parked her scooter in its usual space and as she approached the van, she could see that one of the boxes had burst open to reveal bulging packets of woollen yarn. Charlie, the caretaker's assistant, arrived dragging a porter's trolley.

'Delivery for Dr Rudden,' the driver said, pushing the last box off the back of the van.

'I don't know where he's going to keep it all,' said Charlie. 'He's not got a big office.'

'Take it to Occupational Therapy,' Helen said. 'I'll tell him.'

Although she had seen him from a distance in the mornings, sweeping up the drive in his Ford Zephyr – the mark of a spiv, according to her father – they hadn't spoken since that exchange in his consulting room. Now, she made her way straight there to thank him, checking her appearance in the glass panel of the day room door as she passed. There was no reply to her knock, so she returned to the art room, disappointed.

He was already there, ahead of her, standing in front of a print of Dürer's *Melencolia I*, which she had hung above her desk. It had come with her from her room at college to her lodgings in Hertfordshire and now here. He turned at the sound of the door.

'You've made this place lovely,' he said, the first person to acknowledge that the transformation was her doing alone.

'If you have to spend all day somewhere, it may as well be pleasant,' she said, adding, before the conversation could run along a different course, 'I came to find you to thank you for the wool. I saw it being unloaded just now. Mountains of it. That was quick work.'

He shrugged. 'Oh, it took very little effort on my part, really. I have some private clients who have these philanthropic urges. I only had to mention our problem. It's you I should thank for noticing it. Sometimes it takes a fresh pair of eyes.'

They locked eyes for a moment and the circuit was only broken by the hesitant tapping that heralded the arrival of the first patients of the day.

'You mean a mental asylum?' her mother had said when Helen called to tell her about her new appointment at Westbury Park. 'Oh, Helen.'

She had not expected congratulations; her parents were not the sort of people who took much pleasure in others' success.

In any case, her mother had an aversion amounting to phobia of any kind of disability. 'Don't look at him; he's a bit peculiar,' she would hiss, dragging Helen across the road to avoid a mumbling old man or a child in callipers. She had stopped going to church because a woman who sat at the back in a wheelchair used to moan and thrash her head during silent prayers.

'It's not actually called that any more,' Helen replied with some asperity.

'You can call it what you like. It's still going to be full of very odd people.'

The shudder was audible down the telephone line. This had been more or less her objection to Helen going to art college, which she imagined to be peopled with bohemians, communists and other degenerates. She had been slightly mollified when Helen emerged from the establishment, apparently uncorrupted, to take a teaching job in a girls' grammar school in Hertfordshire. This she regarded as a perfectly respectable stopgap until a husband came along, but this latest move was beyond all understanding.

'Weren't you happy at the school? I thought you liked it.'

'I did. But now I want to do something different.'

'It'll be different all right. People in straitjackets thinking they're Napoleon.'

'You have such a Victorian view of these things.' Helen couldn't help laughing. 'People get sick; we try to make them better, like any other hospital. In any case, it means I'll be moving to Croydon, much nearer to you and Clive.' She offered this up as though greater proximity to her family had been a motivating factor, when it had in fact been rather the opposite.

'Croydon?' her mother mused, having raided her imagination for further psychiatric disorders and come away empty-handed. 'I've an idea our Kathleen's husband works in a mental hospital in that part of the world. I wonder if it's the same one.'

'Who's "our Kathleen"?' asked Helen. Her mother came from a large family, its members estranged by distance and contrasting fortunes, and the name rang only the faintest of bells.

'My cousin Mary's youngest. Yes, I believe they live not far from Clive and June.'

'And yet you never see them.'

'Well, she's much younger than us. Closer to your age than mine. And we had a bit of a falling out with Mary when we didn't have Kathleen as a bridesmaid.'

'But that was over forty years ago,' Helen protested. 'Surely they don't still bear a grudge.'

'Oh, I'm sure it's all forgotten now. Although we weren't invited to Kathleen's wedding. We still sent a gift — a Royal Worcester cruet set from Selfridges. Not cheap.' There was a pause. 'We never got a thank you.'

If Helen remembered this conversation, it was only for her mother's talent for nursing ancient slights and not for the original matter of her cousin's daughter's husband being a potential colleague at Westbury Park. By the time she started her new job, it had completely slipped her mind and so when she had a telephone call one evening at her lodgings from a Kathleen Rudden, inviting her to dinner, it took more than a moment to make the connection.

The Ruddens lived in a Victorian villa in a suburban street backing onto the playing fields of a boys' school. A cricket match was in progress and Helen could hear the clop of a struck ball and the crackle of applause as she walked up the driveway, carrying a box of fruit jellies. The sweets had been a farewell gift from a pupil, kept for just such an opportunity as this. She had not pictured Gil, with his air of weary contempt for convention, in quite such genteel surroundings and it gave her courage. The discovery that he was not only married, but to a distant relative, had unsettled her.

Helen knew, without vanity, that she was good-looking. The evidence was there in the mirror and in the attention, wanted and unwanted, that she regularly attracted from men. It was rare, though, for her to feel any interest in return. She had never been short of potential partners, but these relationships had always foundered at the point where the man proposed marriage, prompting a wave of claustrophobia and a determination to escape. She was sure she had not imagined the tiny electrical charge that had passed between her and Gil at their first proper meeting in his office but, as things stood, he could hardly be more unavailable. It was disappointing, but having dismissed him as a romantic proposition, she resolved to take a purely anthropological interest in studying him in his domestic habitat.

The doorbell growled and a moment later a blurred figure appeared in the stained-glass panel of the front door, which was opened to reveal a slender woman in her mid-forties with blonde hair and a pink complexion, not quite tamed by powder.

'Hello,' she said, sticking out one leg to impede, momentarily, the escape of a tabby cat. 'I'm Kathleen. Come in.' She held up a glass, empty apart from a chewed semicircle of lemon rind. 'We're already on the gin.' Looking over Helen's shoulder, she took in the scooter parked at the kerb. 'You came on a motorbike!' she said in admiring tones.

'Oh, hardly. Just a little Vespa. Goes about as fast as a milk float.'

'Handy for nipping about, I should think. Better than our car. It's such a beast to park. I can't see over the bonnet.'

In the hallway, Helen handed over the jellies and Kathleen thanked her so effusively she suspected they would again end up in the back of a cupboard until they could be safely passed on. On the shallow shelf unit running along the wall was an assortment of ornaments and figurines without any organising principle. Chinese dragons rubbed shoulders with porcelain flower girls, commemorative coronation teacups and carved wooden elephants. A spicy, savoury smell of meat and onions gave Helen hopes of something more appetising than the pork chop and tinned spaghetti casserole that her landlady, Mrs Gordon, had been preparing as she'd left.

Gil was sitting in an armchair in the front room, reading *The Times* and rattling the ice in his glass. He was listening to 'The Rite of Spring' – music of a style and at a volume belligerently unsuitable as background to a dinner party. He stood up in polite readiness and then gave a start at the sight of Helen and glanced uncertainly at his wife for enlightenment.

'Oh, Gil, don't stand there gaping or Helen will think you weren't expecting her. This is Mum's cousin Nancy's daughter. She works at the Park. I *told* you.'

She strode across to the record player and yanked the arm off with a screech that made Helen and Gil wince. The silence that followed was abrupt, brutal.

'Yes, I'm sorry. You did. I must have just switched off at the word "cousin".' He turned back to Helen. 'Well, this is a nice surprise.'

'Have you already met?' Kathleen asked, looking from one to the other.

'Yes. Helen came storming into my office in her first week to harangue me about rug-making.'

'Oh, well.' Helen laughed at this version of the event but could hardly deny it. 'It worked, anyway. Your rich clients came up trumps with the wool.'

This was an anecdote that had clearly not merited a retelling at home, as Kathleen looked blank and needed the whole story explaining while Gil went to the kitchen to fix drinks.

'Yes, my husband has no end of obliging lady clients,' she was saying, when he returned with three clinking tumblers of gin.

It was suspiciously bluish and viscous, and Helen could feel a burning in her nose and the punch of alcohol from the first sip. She was still convalescing, when there was a scuffling from the hallway and a boy and a girl, both in pyjamas, appeared at the door.

'They wanted to say hello before bed,' said Kathleen, beckoning them inside.

The girl, who looked about ten, was thin and pale and almost paralysed by shyness, and the boy, a few years younger, was shiny-faced with a cheeky expression. He had a US Marshal's badge pinned to his chest pocket and a long-barrelled silver pistol tucked into his dressing-gown cord.

'This is Susan and Colin. This is Helen, your second cousin once removed or something like that. Say hello.'

'Hello,' they mumbled, writhing with embarrassment.

'Hello,' said Helen, uncomfortable on their behalf.

It was too bad, being made to perform for strangers. She wished now she had thought to bring a gift for them – colouring pencils or a tin of paints. Something that might make them remember her kindly.

'That's a very realistic gun you've got there, Colin,' she said, feeling that it demanded some acknowledgement.

'It's a Buntline Special,' the boy replied, blushing fiercely. 'I won it in a Wyatt Earp competition.'

'How exciting. What did you have to do to win?'

'Colour in a picture and send it off.'

'Goodness – it must have been quite a day when that arrived.'

'I'll say,' Gil said. 'He's been lying in ambush and shooting at us more or less constantly ever since.'

'Off you go, then,' Kathleen said, dismissing the children with a nod. 'You can read for a bit, but no tearing about up there.'

They slouched out, disappointed to be exiled from whatever fun the grown-ups had planned. It seemed early to be sent to bed, Helen thought, with the sun still over the trees and boys out on the field playing cricket. How utterly powerless children were, at the mercy of the whims of their parents. No wonder they clung to their toy pistols.

'I'm sorry if I've interrupted their bedtime routine,' she said.

'Oh, don't worry. They'll take full advantage.'

'They'll probably be playing Monopoly all evening while we're down here,' Gil agreed. 'Ruthless little capitalists, the pair of them.'

They ate in the dining room overlooking the garden, at a polished oak table, using what Helen imagined to be the 'best' Royal Worcester. She noted that the infamous cruet set did not put in an appearance, casualties no doubt of the usual attrition that depletes wedding presents over the years. In the Hansford household, salt and pepper pots, making convenient missiles, were sometimes flung at the wall by Helen's father during flashes of temper at mealtimes, but it was hard to imagine the Ruddens indulging in that kind of behaviour.

The goulash – for that was the source of the tempting smell in the hallway – looked promising in the serving dish but grew less so on nearer acquaintance. The cubes of meat were undercooked and resistant to attack by fork or teeth. They were accompanied by mashed potato and tinned French beans, which were tasteless but perfectly edible. Having chewed with polite determination at a chunk of beef and forced it whole down her bulging throat, Helen noticed through watering eyes that her hosts had abandoned theirs entirely and without comment, so followed suit with some relief. The conversation settled inevitably on the two modest patches of common ground: shared relatives and Westbury Park.

'I'm sorry your parents couldn't come tonight,' Kathleen was saying. 'It was such a nice surprise to hear from your mother. I did invite them, but I got the impression that they don't get out much.'

She helped herself to another glass of claret with an unsteady hand. Helen observed that Gil had poured but not touched his. To stop her drinking it all, she thought, with a flash of intuition.

'It's my father. He can just about be persuaded to drive over and see my brother, Clive, once in a while, but apart from that he hardly leaves the house. Or the chair, in fact.'

'It's hard on your mother. Can't she go out without him?'

'Can't. Won't. Who really knows?'

'I expect they're happy in their way,' Kathleen declared.

'No, I wouldn't say that. They just sort of co-exist.' Helen had never discussed her parents' marriage before. There was no one who knew them well enough to be interested, apart from Clive, who knew them too well to relish any further expatiation, and had, in any case, odd notions of loyalty and discretion. His wife, June, would have been very ready to dissect the failings of her in-laws, but Helen didn't much care for her opinions, so didn't ask.

Helen's parents had been happy once in her lifetime, during the war, but only separately; not as a couple. Her father had volunteered as soon as possible and gone into the Royal Engineers – an abandonment that his wife still recalled with bitterness. He had had the time of his life, a man among men, doing real work. And her mother had been happier too, in a way, having Helen to herself, down in the New Forest at her sister's, out of the range of Hitler's bombs and her husband's temper.

'Perhaps I should just drop in one day. Would that be all right, do you think?' Kathleen said, collecting up the plates of uneaten beef.

'Yes. Mother would love to see you. Dad will just go down to his shed. He doesn't like the sound of women enjoying themselves.'

Gil laughed at this – almost in sympathy, it seemed to Helen.

'He sounds quite a tyrant,' said Kathleen.

'Oh, just the regular kind,' Helen replied hastily, in case she might already be regretting her offer to visit. 'I think a lot of men are suspicious of any female enjoyment if they aren't the source of it.' She avoided looking at Gil as she said this in case he thought she was challenging him to respond, but he did anyway.

'You are severe on us, Helen,' he said without a trace of rancour. 'I shall have to tread carefully.'

'Yes, do,' said Kath, carrying the plates to the door. 'You're outnumbered.'

'I know. I can sense the alliance against me building.'

'The loyalties of a wife and a colleague are nothing compared to the bonds of womanhood, I'm afraid,' said Helen with a smile.

'Exactly,' said Kath. 'Excuse me while I get the pud.'

Gil turned to Helen. 'Who interviewed you for your job? I only ask because it's usually me, and in this case it obviously wasn't.'

'The superintendent and someone called Dr Frant.'

'Ah, Lionel.' His voice was carefully neutral. 'What did you make of him?'

'I'm not sure. I was more concerned with what he was making of me. He seemed distant, not terribly warm.'

'Yes, that's him.'

'But the superintendent was lovely. Super, in fact.'

Dr Morley Holt had taken Helen on a tour of the hospital and grounds himself and shown her the greenhouses and the vegetable garden; the workshop and the print room; the day rooms and the recreation hall with its wooden floor scarred with the indentations of high heels. Everywhere they went, patients would turn like sunflowers to catch the rays of his attention and he would stop to dispense encouraging words. Helen had felt like a courtier accompanying the monarch on a royal walkabout.

'He's a good man. Legend has it that the first thing he did when he started here in the forties was to open the big iron gates at the entrance. They've not been closed since. As long as he's at the helm, the place will be fine. He's done away with a lot of the bad practices. Dragged us out of the dark ages.'

Helen knew exactly which practices Gil meant. She recalled clearly her first visit to an insulin ward. The sight of patients lying in the dark in induced comas in an all too realistic approximation of death had seemed to her closer to torture than therapy and everything in her revolted against it. At the doctors' bidding, they would be resurrected by the adminis- tration of glucose through a feeding tube. The horror of this had never left her.

'That's partly why I applied for the job. I'd heard such good things about Westbury Park and when I walked around the grounds for the first time, it looked more like a university than a hospital.' There had been people sitting out on the lawns reading or just enjoying the sunshine. At a careless glance they might have been students but for the variety of ages and the dishevelment of some. Patients worked unsupervised in the vegetable allotment or weeded the flower beds. As she'd passed an open window, she had heard the trickle of a piano.

'Would you like a cigarette?' Gil asked, patting his pockets and producing a crushed packet of Players. 'I don't smoke in the house because Susan has asthma, but we can loiter in the garden.'

'I don't smoke, actually, but go ahead. My father has a sixty-a-day habit and it rather put me off.'

'No. If you don't then I'll do without.'

Kath returned from the kitchen with a brick-sized jelly in which a jumble of strawberries and raspberries was suspended. 'Ta-da!' she announced.

'Oh, well done,' said Gil dutifully.

It looked like nursery food to Helen, but the fruit had been soused in cherry brandy and delivered more than a hint of alcohol. It was served in slabs with thin cream and a fan-shaped wafer.

'How did you get into this line of work?' Kathleen asked. 'Your mother said you were a schoolteacher until recently.'

'I was teaching art at a girls' school in Hertfordshire. Then I started to do some volunteering at a psychiatric hospital, working with ex-servicemen. There was a rather amazing woman there called Pam Hickey who ran art therapy classes.'

'I know her,' said Gil, suddenly animated. 'Was it at Napsbury?'

'Yes. It was Pam who encouraged me to go for the job at Westbury Park. She said it had a similar ethos to Napsbury and I'd be able to do good work there. I'd been volunteering every school holiday for three years and I'd come to enjoy it more than teaching.'

'You must have met Ronnie Laing, then,' Gil said.

'Barely. He was in a somewhat rarefied realm. I was just a volunteer. I don't think he noticed me.'

'Oh, he'd have noticed you all right,' said Kathleen.

'I'm rather an admirer of Laing,' Gil said. 'I feel he's on to something. You should read *The Divided Self*. He has some interesting things to say.'

'I already have,' said Helen.

He looked up, as though aware that a point had been scored against him. 'What did you make of it?'

'I thought it was difficult,' she admitted. 'I mean both the language and the ideas. But also exciting.'

'I didn't get past the preface,' said Kathleen cheerfully.

'He has his detractors,' Gil conceded. 'Lionel Frant's not a fan. But I'm inclined to agree with Helen. I found it exciting, too.'

'If you have any other reading recommendations, I'd be glad to hear them,' Helen said, flattered by this talk of shared enthusiasm. He could have found no surer way to make her his disciple than to treat her as his intellectual equal.

'You can browse the shelves in my consulting room. Borrow anything you fancy.'

They continued to discuss those former colleagues they had in common until there was a creaking on the stairs and Colin appeared, grinding his knuckles into his eyes and saying he had had a nightmare.

'Go back to bed and I'll be up in a minute,' his mother promised, and this seemed to Helen a cue to depart.

It had been a pleasant evening and interesting to see Gil *en famille*, where he appeared much less formidable, tamed by the trappings of suburban life, the best china, the three-piece suite and the fussy little ornaments. Somehow, though, she felt all that was Kathleen's doing and nothing to do with Gil, who was aloof from his surroundings.

She couldn't imagine the invitation being repeated. There was no chance of asking anyone back to her lodgings in Croydon with Mrs Gordon – all meals provided and no visitors after 10 p.m. – but without some element of reciprocation, it was hard to see how the relationship could proceed. She felt sure that now that family obligation had been discharged and curiosity satisfied, she would not hear from Kathleen again.

The following day, Saturday, Helen wrote a brief thank-you note, praising the food (with no mention of the inedible beef), the conversation and the children. The proper course would have been to post it to arrive on Monday, but instead Helen put it in her bag to give it to Gil by hand, telling herself that a stamp was a stamp, after all.

This stratagem – even if unacknowledged as such – was unnecessary, as Gil was again ensconced in the art room when she arrived. He was sprawled in the wicker chair that formed part of her still-life arrangement, one leg bent, the ankle resting on his knee. He didn't stand as she came in.

'Hullo,' she said, producing the card and handing it to him. 'Thank you for having me on Friday. It was a very jolly evening.'

He snorted at this. 'It must have been dull for you.'

'Not at all.'

'I wasn't expecting you. I thought it was going to be one of Kath's horde of awful relatives.'

'Well, it was in a way.'

He smiled, picked up the apple from the fruit bowl beside him as if about to eat it and seemed surprised to discover that it was made of wax.

'If I'd known it was you, I'd have made more effort.'

Helen felt her cheeks growing warm at this compliment that seemed to cross a line. To hide her discomfiture, she took off her jacket and hung it on a wooden hanger, swapping it for her painting overall. Gil seemed perfectly comfortable and in no hurry to leave.

'In what way?' she asked, amused by this display of bourgeois anxiety.

'Oh, I don't know. Invited some more entertaining company for you.'

She was aware of him watching her buttoning her overall and pocketing round-ended scissors, a rubber and her favourite charcoal pencil, all items that would disappear if not guarded. In the few weeks since her arrival at Westbury Park, Helen had observed that, in the absence of other clues, it was possible to discern a person's status from the contents of their breast pocket. Doctors carried a fountain pen; nurses, a thermometer; patients, a toothbrush.

'I was perfectly well entertained,' Helen said, her preparations complete. 'I would just have spent the evening in my digs otherwise, with only Mrs Gordon's poodle for company.'

'Mrs Gordon's poodle. It sounds like a song by Noël Coward. I suppose I should get to work.' He hauled himself up. 'But I find this room very soothing.'

'Well, it's usually free from one until two while I'm in the canteen. You're welcome to it.'

'Thank you. But it doesn't have the same effect if you're not here.'

Once the door clicked shut behind him, Helen let out a slow breath. She realised she was gripping the back of her chair and her pulse was racing as though from a sudden awakening, a combination of physical excitement with a hint of danger. This sensation was new and quite unlike the placid affection she had felt for her former lover and would-be fiancé. She must avoid Gil at all costs, she told herself, knowing that she wouldn't and that she was already looking forward to their next encounter.

The following week, at the end of a full day of classes and an upsetting incident with a patient, Helen left the art room later than usual to discover that her scooter wouldn't start. Treading on the kickstart failed to produce even a tremor. This was a setback. When she lived in Hertfordshire, she had cultivated a local garage who did all of her repairs and could be relied upon to send out a pick-up truck in this kind of emergency. She had moved to Croydon too recently to make those useful connections and was now quite at a loss. It was at times like this that Helen felt the want of a husband. Romance was, of course, wonderful while it lasted, but it was for assistance of a practical nature, involving spanners, that a man was worth ten women.

For a second she considered ringing Clive and then dismissed the idea. It was six o'clock; June would have his dinner on the table and the claims of a wife trumped those of a sister. She would have to get the bus home and call out a mechanic in the morning, chosen at random from the telephone directory – a dicey business.

A fine drizzle was falling and she could feel her hair, so carefully set the day before, beginning to kink, so she headed back to the hospital to borrow one of the abandoned umbrellas from the lost property office. At the entrance she ran into Gil, lighting one cigarette from the stub of another, blinking against the billowing smoke.

Her frustration must have been written on her face as he stopped and said, 'Are you all right?'

'Yes. No. My stupid scooter has packed up.'

'Can I give you a lift somewhere?'

'No, it's all right, really. I'll get the bus and sort it out in the morning.'

Ignoring this, he took her elbow and steered her towards his car, parked in its usual space near the entrance. 'I insist. Where do you live?'

'Addiscombe.'

'Oh, well, practically on my way. Then we'll get Arthur to have a look at your scooter in the morning.'

'Who's Arthur?'

'The handyman. Does all the repairs here. There's nothing he can't fix.'

Helen had a vague recollection of a white-haired man in tan overalls tackling a blocked sink in the staffroom with a plunger and some choice language. He hadn't seemed particularly sunny-tempered then and she wondered how amenable he would be to taking on motorcycle maintenance, a task far beyond his remit.

'It's hardly his job,' she protested as Gil opened the door for her and tossed a pair of pumps and an A–Z roadmap into the back.

The interior smelt of stale smoke and was chaotically untidy, the rear seat taken up with children's gym bags, crippled tennis rackets with broken strings, men's dress shoes and a bundle of magazines tied up with string – evidence of chores parked and awaiting completion. She had imagined him to be proud and possessive of his car, as men so often were, but again she had misread him.

'No, it's not his job, but if you keep him sweet, he's surprisingly obliging. I slip him a bottle of whisky now and then.'

'Ah. You have everyone eating out of the palm of your hand,' said Helen.

He shot her a sideways glance. 'Not quite.'

The rain was coming down harder now, so he crushed the cigarette out in the full ashtray and wound up the window. They drove out of the Park and were immediately on quiet roads with dripping hedgerows and farmland on either side. Twenty minutes from the building sites of central Croydon – a little city in the making – you could be in open countryside. For Helen, the journey to work, the red-brick and concrete gradually thinning out and giving way to fields and trees, was one of the pleasures of the job.

The issue of the faulty scooter now resolved, she was aware of another niggling problem at the edge of her consciousness, still to be confronted. It came back to her now, in all its unpleasantness, and a gusty sigh escaped her.

'Anything wrong?' Gil asked.

'I haven't had the best day,' Helen admitted. 'There was a scene in one of my classes. I didn't handle it well. That's all.'

'Are you going to tell me about it?'

'One of my male patients, Perry – I've seen him before and he's usually fine – was being a bit . . . disinhibited today. Painting sexually explicit pictures, to try to shock me, I think, and then talking loudly about what he'd like to do, getting quite aggressive. Ignoring him seemed to make him shout louder and engaging with him only seemed to encourage him. I didn't feel in any real danger, but one of the other patients who thought Perry was threatening me tried to intervene and swung a punch, and it all got a bit out of control. I had to call for help and four orderlies came in and put Perry in restraints and took him off. I've seen it done before – not here – and it always disturbs me. It looks so brutal.'

'I know.'

'He was screaming, "I'm co-operating, I'm co-operating," but he was thrashing around and they could hardly hold him. I went to see him later to check that he was all right, but he'd been sedated. It made me feel I'd completely failed.'

'Sometimes you have to put the safety of the other patients – and yourself – first.'

'Has that kind of thing ever happened to you?'

'Of course. And, like you, I always feel it as a failure. But, over the years, I've started to feel a lot less uncomfortable about the occasional use of restraint for the control of a patient who is acting violently than about routinely medicating non-violent patients.'

'You don't think the drugs work?'

'It depends what you mean by work. At best, they may temporarily ease certain symptoms – while causing others. My scepticism goes deeper than that. I think we should be asking what we really mean by sickness and wellness.'

'So, you're one of those psychiatrists who doesn't really believe in mental illness?'

'I certainly don't agree that everything in the DSM can be considered a mental disorder. Homosexuality, for example.

Most so-called mental disorders are just behaviour that society doesn't approve of.'

The windscreen was starting to mist over. Gil leant forwards impatiently and wiped it with the sleeve of his jacket, leaving behind a film of tiny fibres.

'I agree with you. We talked about this endlessly at Napsbury. But how does that kind of theorising help an individual patient who is suffering? How do you actually treat them?'

'Well, with their consent firstly. Anything else is abuse. And with a little more restraint when it comes to putting labels on people. "This patient has symptoms A, B and C." *Ah! Then he must be schizophrenic.* "And what is schizophrenia?" *It's a condition characterised by symptoms A, B and C.* It doesn't tell us anything.'

'You sound as though you hardly approve of your own profession.'

'Oh, we do all right for some. They come in, in a state of some distress – not usually, it has to be said, on their own initiative, but because they have become too much for their family. And we medicate them and medicate them some more. After a period of weeks or months, they learn how to pass as "normal" again and we send them out.'

'What else is there?'

'I'm not saying we haven't made strides. When I first qualified, women on long-stay wards, who had been there decades, sat around all day with nothing to do. There was a lot of friction between patients and staff. Now, they have their day rooms with knitting and magazines and music. They can do their hair and bake cakes. The atmosphere changed almost overnight. All that "us and them" antagonism has mostly gone.'

When he started to warm to a topic, his voice lost some of its polish, as though in talking about matters of belief he became his truer self. 'But these are small gains. What I'd like to see is a proper community, living together as equals, with no distinction between doctor and patient. There would be no mad and sane; no sick and well, no normal and abnormal. There would be no need for all those worn-out labels.'

Listening to Gil, Helen felt like a student again, in the presence of some charismatic professor, awakened to new possibilities by his superior understanding. It was impossible not to be caught up in his utopian dreams.

'Don't you think it all comes down to the relationship between therapist and patient in the end?' she said.

He was quiet for a while and then, instead of answering her question, he said, 'I like talking to you.'

He seemed to be taking a route she didn't know, down narrow lanes with few passing places, the road surface crumbling and potholed. They passed a boarding kennels and, a little further along, a wooden shack in which an old woman was sitting selling cherries and bundles of rhubarb.

'Poor woman. What kind of custom is she going to get out here?' Helen said. 'Perhaps I should have bought some for Mrs Gordon.'

'Mrs Gordon's rhubarb cobbler. I can see it now.'

'No, you really can't. She's a terrible cook.'

As Helen described the pork chops in tinned spaghetti and other atrocities, she felt the spectre of Kathleen's goulash had inadvertently been summoned and wished she had avoided the subject of food, but Gil just laughed.

'I'll pick you up tomorrow morning,' he said. 'Is eight fifteen all right? I have nine o'clock ward rounds. Then I'll get Arthur to look over your bike.'

'I don't need a lift in,' she protested. 'I can pick up the 403 so easily.'

He clicked his tongue impatiently. 'Helen. It's not a sacrifice. A twenty-minute car journey with you is almost certainly going to be the best part of my day.'

She felt herself grow hot from this compliment. Later, she would think to herself, that was the moment to stop it, when it could easily have been batted aside without too much awkwardness and never mentioned again. But she didn't and there was a moment or two of electric silence, then the car gave a terrific jolt as it hit one of the water-filled craters in the road and they both started.

'Oh, God, don't say I've burst a tyre,' Gil said, pulling into the gated entrance to a paddock and getting out to inspect the damage.

Helen sat, rigid with anticipation.

He got back in but made no move to restart the engine. 'Seems all right, thank God.'

'That's a relief.'

Through the windscreen the view of cropped grass, ploughed fields, squat hedgerows and distant clumps of trees was scattered into thousands of droplets. Within a few seconds the glass had misted over again from the damp of Gil's wool jacket, sealing them off from the landscape outside. They sat listening to the clatter of the rain without speaking or moving. This moment of quiet communion went on too long; it was not natural. Something had to happen, but Helen felt powerless to act and unable to think of the form of words that would release them from this dangerous intimacy without embarrassment. It was too late anyway: by her silence, she had already declared herself.

At last, he spoke. 'Ah, Helen. You know what I'm going to say.'

'Yes, I think so. But say it anyway.' The moment of confession, when it came, was the high point in any relationship and could be experienced only once.

He leant towards her and whispered in her ear. Then he turned her face to his and they looked into each other's eyes for a long, expectant moment before their lips touched.

Within three weeks, Gil had found her a furnished flat in South Croydon and paid off Mrs Gordon with a month's rent. His family home was naturally out of bounds as a meeting place and Mrs Gordon had old-fashioned views about male visitors.

The new flat was at the top of a large Edwardian house and had a bedroom, sitting room, tiny kitchen and a long, narrow bathroom, all with sloping roofs and crooked floors. The fireplace in the bedroom was scarcely large enough to hold more than a few twigs, suggesting this must once have been the housemaid's quarters, but even so, the rent was twice what Helen had been used to paying or could afford.

Gil insisted on making up the difference, arranging everything with the speed and expertise that hinted at previous experience. When Helen questioned him on this point he denied it, without any particular force. Curiously, she felt more guilty about the diversion of funds – money that rightly belonged to Kathleen and the children – than about the betrayal of loyalties. Though not guilty enough to call a halt to the affair.

The décor was an unappealing mixture of ancient and modern: Formica in the kitchen; a new divan bed from Allders of Croydon in the bedroom; an art deco compactum wardrobe on the landing; an ornate Victorian sideboard and a plywood coffee table from Heal's in the sitting room. It took all of Helen's ingenuity and artistry with fabric and paintings and rugs to disguise this baleful collision of styles, but she had a gift for making the ugly beautiful.

The pillars of their relationship, Gil made clear at the outset, were solid, indestructible, eternal – not things that could be put to the test or negotiated away. 1) She was the love of his life, the keeper of his heart, the one above all others. 2) He would not leave Kathleen until both the children had left school for work or college. As his youngest was only seven years old, this day was so far off as to make the promise all but worthless. He was not opposed to divorce in principle; sometimes it could be seen as the remedying of error, but when children were involved, the remedy had to be deferred.

Helen understood, of course, accepting just what he could spare her and no more. Sometimes in the lean hours of the night when woken by the creaks and knocks of the resting house, she imagined these two pillars, vast, sand-coloured, rising up into a cool blue sky. It was a troubling image, for what possible structure could be supported by just two pillars?

Early on, when mutual fascination meant anything was permitted, Helen asked him why he had married Kathleen. They had left work separately and reconvened at a pub car park a few miles away in the countryside, from where Gil had led her through fields and along footpaths to an ideal place, completely screened from the path, where they could make love in the open air. The fact that he found the perfect spot without any hunting seemed evidence of the universe falling into line to accommodate them.

'It was just the end of the war,' he said, winding a tress of her hair around his finger. 'She was in the Wrens. We'd met in Naples where I was serving. I was seeing a friend of hers at the time – Belinda. I don't know what happened to her. Then when the war was over, I was back in London and I bumped into Kath just by chance in Shaftesbury Avenue. We went for a drink and started seeing one another. Within a month she was pregnant, so we had to get married pretty swiftly. She wasn't keen on the alternative, not surprisingly. And then on the "honeymoon"' – he gave the word a leaden emphasis – 'she had a miscarriage.'

Neither of them said anything for a while, the only sound the rustle of wind in the treetops and the seething of insects in the long dry grass at the edge of the field.

Chapter 2

Helen would rather have given her excuses to Clive, but after a long wait it was June who answered the phone on the Saturday morning.

'Sorry, I'm in the middle of making pastry – my hands are all floury,' she said, dropping the receiver with a clunk.

Helen swallowed. Pastry for the party tonight, which she would now not be there to appreciate.

'Hello, June.' She drew the line at faking the watery croak of an invalid, and the note of regret in her voice was genuine. 'I'm so sorry, but I won't be able to make it this evening. I've gone down with a stomach bug and I'm feeling lousy.'

'Oh no, what a pity! Lorraine will be so disappointed.'

Helen accepted the lack of sympathy as no more than her due. 'I know. I've been looking forward to it, too.'

'You don't think you might be feeling better by this evening?' June asked.

'No.' Helen was firm. 'In any case, I wouldn't want to spread it about to the rest of you.'

'Ah, it's a shame for you, Helen. Maybe you can pop round one evening in the week for a cup of tea instead. We'll save you a piece of birthday cake.'

'Yes, I'll do that. As soon as I'm up and about. Give Lorraine my love. And Clive.'

She replaced the receiver in its cradle, swamped by relief and self-disgust, hoping that no one had overheard her. The telephone, shared by all three flats, was on a hallstand by the front door. Tenants wrote the number and duration of the call in a notebook and the landlord would somehow divine their share of the bill and collect it in cash quarterly.

So persuasive was her performance that it was a minute before Helen remembered that she was not in fact sick at all and could bound rather than totter back up the two flights of stairs to begin her preparations for Gil's arrival.

The evening before, she had made a boeuf bourguignon from her Elizabeth David cookbook and it was now maturing in the fridge in a Pyrex dish. She would serve it with a potato gratin and some braised celery. Gil was not, she had discovered, a great lover of sweet things and so elaborate puddings were wasted on him. However, the occasion merited some effort, so she was planning to make a chocolate mousse – a chore, as she had only a balloon whisk for beating the egg whites.

By lunchtime she had changed the bed linen, taken the sheets to the laundry on the Brighton Road for a service wash; made the mousse twice (the first time the chocolate had seized as it melted, resulting in a further trip out for new ingredients); tidied the flat; had a bath and painted her nails – fingers and toes. There was a full ice tray in the tiny freezer box at the top of the fridge and a lemon in the fruit bowl for gin and tonics. Gil would bring some decent wine and there was half a bottle of red left over from the bourguignon.

They would spend the afternoon in bed, inevitably, and then maybe drag themselves out for a walk over Shirley Hills or Lloyd Park. After dinner he might read to her. He had a deep, mesmerising voice like Richard Burton, which made everything seem both rich with significance and easy to understand, even Shelley.

Recently, he had tried to convert her to modern poetry and had some success with *The Whitsun Weddings*. She was coming round to Larkin, although privately she preferred Betjeman, whom Gil considered a 'silly old maid'. He had other robust opinions: Andy Warhol was a fraud, Virginia Woolf was 'mostly unreadable', D. H. Lawrence was a genius, Graham Greene was 'fiction not literature', television was an abomination, the opium of the masses. He liked the idea of cinema in principle, but never went. Kathleen had dragged him to see *Tammy and the Bachelor* in 1957 and he had not been back since.

They preferred opera to pop music and he had bought Helen several gramophone records, including Callas singing *Norma* and Elisabeth Schwarzkopf in *Der Rosenkavalier*, which could always move them to tears. If tears were not required, they might have another stab at modern jazz, which they approached with gritted teeth, as something that must, surely, be doing them good.

They didn't like the idea of being stranded in the past and distrusted nostalgia and anyone who resisted change, so they had recently made a diligent attempt to understand the Beatles phenomenon. Gil felt he could hardly be a useful practitioner of psychiatry to young people if he didn't. They both liked what they had seen of the four cheerful and unpretentious young men. Gil admired John Lennon's wit and irreverence, and Helen thought Paul McCartney charming. But when they listened attentively to all the tracks on *Please Please Me*, like anthropologists studying the rites of a newly discovered tribe, they found the songs corny and simplistic.

'Perhaps it sounds better with the screaming?' Helen suggested.

'We're just too old,' said Gil.

There was a certain sort of popular music, a staple of *Two-Way Family Favourites*, typified by Jim Reeves and Kitty Kallen, which Helen used to like until Gil told her it was mush. Now, she couldn't help hearing it through the filter of his disdain and wished he had left her to her harmless pleasure.

Chores completed, Helen changed into a yellow shift dress that she knew Gil liked, and the cream suede pumps he had bought her in the early days of their affair. He had found out her shoe size by stealth and surprised her with the gift, which had seemed more intimate and romantic even than jewellery.

Lunchtime came and went and with it the hour appointed for Gil's arrival. She wasn't hungry; food preparation always robbed her of an appetite and, in any case, the usual anticipation of being alone with him made her queasy. The metal gate clanged and she leapt up and hurried to the gable window, but it was just Mr Rafferty from the ground-floor flat taking his whippet out for a walk.

She picked up her library book – *The L-shaped Room* – but the predicament of its heroine, lonely and abandoned, did not provide quite the distraction she needed. Instead, she put on *A Kind of Blue*, convinced that if she listened attentively and with due reverence she would be rewarded by Gil's appearance.

Closing her eyes, she allowed the plangent notes of trumpet and piano to break over her in a series of waves, rhythmic but not regular, until she felt almost on the threshold of some new appreciation. Beneath the waves was the sound of shingle, perhaps a snare or the hiss and crackle of the recording – and even fainter and more distant, another less welcome sound: a ringing telephone.

'Darling, I'm sorry.'

His words fell like hammer blows, leaving her hopes for the weekend in smithereens.

'Why? What?' she asked, unable to keep the tremor of dismay from her voice.

35

'Kath's crashed the car. I'll have to go and rescue them. They're all OK, but obviously stranded and a bit shaken.'

'Oh, God. How awful.'

Even at her most jealous and rivalrous, she had never wished for any harm to come to Kathleen, and yet she felt a sort of furious resentment that smothered every sympathetic instinct.

'Yes, I know. Bloody unfortunate timing.'

'It can't be helped,' she said, trying to be the selfless, uncomplaining woman he thought her. 'I hope the children are OK.'

'Yes, all fine. Car's taken a bit of a bashing. Anyway, I'm sorry it's ruined our plans. I'm going to miss you desperately.'

'Same here. How will you get to them without a car?'

'My neighbour's going to drive me down to Sevenoaks. They'd hardly gone any distance, luckily.'

Helen wondered but didn't ask if Kathleen had been drinking. Surely even she drew the line when she had the children in the car. It was no secret between her and Gil that Kath drank too much, sometimes to the point of unconsciousness, but it was a subject that only he could raise.

'I'll see you on Monday then, I suppose,' Helen said. The rest of the weekend unrolled joylessly ahead of her, a long, empty road.

'Yes, Monday. I love you.'

There was a click and silence. She sat for a while, marinating in her own disappointment. All of her preparations and scheming had been for nothing and her excuses to June so efficient and final that there was no retracting them. Slowly, she hauled herself back upstairs and peeled off the yellow dress, changing instead into a pair of unflattering trousers and a sweater with a moth hole the size of a shilling on the front. There was no point in looking her best now.

It occurred to her that she experienced their relationship as a series of peaks and troughs; for every high, a corresponding low; the thrill of anticipation inevitably followed by an equivalent plunge in spirits. There was always a reckoning: fate had to balance its books.

She wished she could imagine some distant future in which she could hear his name and feel nothing. There had been one occasion, about six months into their affair, when she had been surprised into seeing him through momentarily unclouded eyes. She had been walking through Surrey Street market on a Saturday buying fruit and vegetables for the week ahead. Gil had been a few stalls ahead of her, his daughter, Susan, by his side. He was wearing his tweed overcoat and corduroy trousers, and his dark hair was shot through with grey. For more than a moment Helen didn't recognise him. Away from the hospital he looked so ordinary – just a tired, middle-aged man buying potatoes. No heads turned as he passed and Helen had experienced the curious sensation of seeing him as everyone else must; as he really was, perhaps. She had ducked out of sight behind a stall selling trays of white eggs, her heart thumping in protest at this unwanted awakening.

The feeling of estrangement lasted the rest of that day, but when she woke the following morning, it had worn off, to her great relief, and the next time they met, in her storeroom off the art studio, he had reacquired all of his old powers.

On normal weekends, with no expectation of seeing Gil, Helen had no trouble filling her time, but now, robbed of all agency, she was at a loss. There was always correspondence due – she owed letters to an old friend from college and to Pam. Library books needed returning or renewing and it was pleasant to browse the shelf of new acquisitions and exchange a whispered word with the librarian. There were, besides, books on psychiatry and papers in learned journals – donated by Gil – to be read. A laundry bag full of nylons and underwear that she had stuffed in the wardrobe out of sight could be handwashed and hung over the bath on the wooden airer, now that the bathroom would not be needed. She could listen to *Afternoon Theatre* or take a walk to the ornamental gardens. None of these activities held any appeal.

It might have helped if she could have poured out her frustration to a female confidante who would be able to sympathise without judgement, but since moving to Croydon and taking up with Gil, she had neglected her old friends in Hertfordshire, choosing instead to keep weekends free in case he should be unexpectedly available. A certain reticence about their predicament had also discouraged her from making friendly approaches to her new colleagues. There had been opportunities, but she had squandered them. One of the occupational therapists, a woman called Babs, had invited her to supper once, soon after she had started at Westbury Park. She was lively and vivacious, and Helen had taken an immediate liking to her. Babs was single, in her late twenties and energetically searching for a husband. She had seen Helen as a possible partner in this enterprise; someone to make up foursomes at tennis or bridge, an ally in the awkward business of walking into bars and clubs and other places where single men were said to lurk. In other circumstances they might have become close, but Helen couldn't confide in her about Gil and didn't want to lie. Her resulting lack of openness seemed to starve the relationship of the oxygen it needed to grow. Helen had no interest in chasing men, even for sport, and felt uncomfortable repaying Babs' candid confessions with evasions, so the friendship had been unable to flourish. The need for secrecy had made real intimacy impossible; the benefits were nothing when weighed against the risk of gossip reaching her family, her colleagues or Kathleen herself. Helen knew only too well the vitriol her parents reserved for women who took up with married men.

She had hardly envisaged their approval, but nevertheless it gave her a jolt to hear the venom they directed at Christine Keeler, who was 'no better than a tart', and Stephen Ward – 'a ghastly little man, a pimp'. For the adulterer himself, 'poor Profumo', there was just a sorrowful click of the tongue for his tarnished reputation. It seemed monstrously unfair.

Instead of trying to rescue something from the wreckage of the day, Helen surrendered to it, falling asleep on the couch and waking stiff-necked in the early evening with the cushion's tapestry pattern embossed on her cheek.

For dinner she ate half the potato gratin, a quarter of the bourguignon and a chocolate mousse, mocked by their unnecessary luxury. She eyed the half bottle of red wine on the draining board, but thought of Kathleen and left it untouched. At Clive and June's they would have finished dinner, and cake, and be playing Nap, while Lorraine lay on her bed listening to her transistor radio. There was nothing interesting on television – a documentary about the inventions of Buckminster Fuller didn't tempt her – so at nine o'clock she took her contraceptive pill, acquired for her extra-legally by Gil, and sat in bed reading *The L-Shaped Room*.

Perhaps the worst part of the experience was the certainty that there was nothing to be learnt from it and if she found herself in similar circumstances a week or a month from now, she would only do exactly the same.

Chapter 3

Helen had another helping of boeuf bourguignon on Sunday afternoon, decided that she had never much liked it anyway and took the rest downstairs to Mr Rafferty. In the three years they had lived in the same building, they had exchanged no more than cordial greetings in the hallway, so this offering represented a significant advance in neighbourly relations.

'Oh, a stew, how lovely,' Mr Rafferty said, his eyes watering with gratitude. 'I was going to have a boiled egg.'

Beside him in the doorway, the whippet looked up at Helen with a mournful expression. She had never heard it bark.

'Well, I made rather too much,' Helen said, glancing over his shoulder into the hall, which had bare, nicotine-stained walls, brown paintwork and blue lino that was blistered and cracked. An open door revealed a slice of kitchen from which the chatter of a radio issued.

'Would you like to come in for a moment?' Mr Rafferty made a sweeping movement of welcome with one arm. 'I could put this into a saucepan and give you your dish back.'

Helen had a sudden and strong determination not to cross the threshold and be a witness to the spartan comforts within. She was saved by the ringing of the telephone on the hallstand behind her.

'Oh no – keep it for now. I'll pick it up another day,' she said, convinced that it was Gil calling.

'Hello?' she said. 'Is that you?'

'Yes,' came the puzzled reply. 'How did you know?'

'It makes a different ringing sound when it's you. Deeper. More imperious.'

He laughed. 'Listen. Are you busy? Something's come up that might interest you.'

'Of course.' The weekend was redeemed and her spirits restored.

'I've been called out to a house opposite Lloyd Park. About five minutes from you. I'm calling from there now while I wait for the GP to arrive.'

'Why do you want me?'

'Because I've never seen anything like this in my entire career.'

'What? Stop being so mysterious.'

'Can you be here in five minutes?' He rattled off the address. 'If not, meet me at the hospital in an hour. There's a man in this house who hasn't seen the light of day for at least ten years.'

The house was a three-storey Edwardian villa on the corner plot of a main road, surrounded by a high wall, with a neglected front garden of tall trees and matted brambles. An alder was growing so close to the front of the building that its branches brushed the brickwork and obscured one of the second-storey windows. Caught up in the tree, and snagged on the shrubs and brambles below, were various items of clothing. A silk dressing gown rippled and snapped in the breeze and a corset swung stiffly from a branch like an inn sign.

A heavy iron gate with spear-topped railings gestured in a futile way to security, while beside it a collapsed portion of wall offered alternative access. Helen had driven past the house frequently over the past three years without paying it any special attention. It wasn't the only overgrown and shabby property in the area, but now that she came to look at it, she could see that the dereliction was more than merely superficial.

The lower windows were black with soot, the curtains yellowing rags. A forked crack in the brickwork, which reached from the eaves to the ground like a bolt of lightning, was an inch wide. It looked as though the strategic application of a crowbar could split the entire house in two.

An ambulance was parked at the kerb, the driver standing on the pavement smoking a Woodbine. He winked at Helen as she passed.

Gil met her at the front door and ushered her inside a long, dark hallway with bulging wallpaper the colour of raw liver. Even though it was bright daylight outside, the gloom within was relieved only partially by a single sallow bulb. In the large drawing room, cluttered with ancient furniture, including armchairs, spindly tables, footstools and a baby grand piano, sat an elderly woman, considerably dishevelled, being examined by the GP. From above the mantelpiece, an oil painting of an Edwardian gentleman, portly and prosperous, surveyed the shabbiness.

'More people!' the woman exclaimed in a rasping voice at the sight of Gil and Helen. 'I shall never be able to feed you all!'

The GP straightened up, detaching himself from the prongs of his stethoscope. 'Chest's got a bit of a rattle,' he said. 'Not in bad shape apart from that. Physically, I mean. But she needs to go in, obviously.' He addressed these words, without lowering his voice, to Gil, who frowned and gestured to him to withdraw. 'It's all right – she's quite deaf,' he said, refusing to accept the rebuke.

'Nevertheless,' said Gil coldly, walking out of the room so that the doctor had no option but to follow.

'Who's deaf?' called the old woman.

Helen approached her. 'I'm a colleague of Dr Rudden,' she said gently. 'Can I get you anything?'

The woman was craning to left and right, searching for something. Her hair, a dead grey skein twisted and pinned into a baggy bun, had slumped over one ear.

'My handbag. Who's taken my handbag?'

Helen located it under one of the tables and returned it to the owner, who wound the cracked leather strap twice round her fist like the leash of a dog that was liable to bolt.

'Is William all right?' she asked presently. 'I hope he's not being any trouble. He's a good boy really.'

'Is William your . . . son?'

'No, no. My nephew. We had a bit of a set-to, but it was nothing really. We rub along all right.'

The ambulance driver and his colleague appeared in the doorway carrying a canvas stretcher chair.

'All right, Grandma,' the driver said in a cheerful voice. 'Let's get you off to hospital. Shall we get you in the chair?'

'I can't leave without William,' she protested. 'He'll not manage without me.'

'He'll be coming with you,' the driver replied. 'They're just seeing to him now.'

Helen left them to their manoeuvres, which were somewhat hampered by the old woman's refusal to slacken her grip on the handbag even for a second as they transferred her into the stretcher chair. She followed the sound of voices towards the top of the house, ascending a staircase to which a threadbare runner, worn down to string in places, was only loosely attached by a few broken rods. It shifted and slipped underfoot and snagged at her heels with each step. On the top landing, consisting of bare floorboards and protruding nails to which some scraps of felted material still clung, she found Gil conferring with a police constable and the GP.

43

'No, I very much don't want to use restraints at this stage,' Gil was saying. 'I should just like to talk to him and persuade him to come with us to hospital voluntarily. It may take a little longer that way, but . . .'

'Me and the sergeant couldn't get a word out of him,' the policeman said. 'The old lady says he's her nephew, William Tapping.'

'How did you get involved?' Gil asked.

'The neighbours reported a commotion. Shouting and stuff being thrown out of the windows. We get here and find the old girl in hysterics and a naked man with a great long beard and hair down to here, who bolts up to the attic and barricades himself inside.'

'Have the neighbours made any complaints before?'

'They say they've been here ten years and weren't aware of any man living at the property.'

'Do you mind if I try to talk to him alone?' Gil said to the assembled company.

'Be my guest,' said the GP. 'I've already signed the forms if you need them.'

'But you haven't assessed him?' Gil said with rising impatience.

'It's hardly necessary. He's unquestionably one for the Park.'

Gil knocked at the door. 'Mr Tapping,' he said in his professional voice, full of calm reassurance. 'I'm Doctor Rudden. May I come in? You're not in any trouble.'

After a moment or two there was the shriek of wood on wood as a heavy piece of furniture was dragged across the floor.

'Perhaps if you kept out of sight,' Gil whispered to the police constable, who moved to the furthest corner of the landing.

The door handle rattled and turned slowly. The door opened just wide enough for Helen to see the upper half of a man's face, pale against a matted thatch of dull brown hair and a beard that hung down like shaggy bell ropes to his waist. He was

44

wrapped in a tartan blanket and the hand that clasped it closed at his chest had long, ridged fingernails. He could have been any age from twenty to eighty; all the usual identifying markers were obscured by that hair, and the overpowering impression of wildness and neglect.

'May I?' Gil asked, without taking a step forwards.

The man withdrew silently into the shadows of the room and Gil followed, leaving the door just ajar behind him.

On the landing, the minutes passed; the young police constable fidgeted and looked at his watch. Helen smiled at him with some sympathy; she knew Gil was not a man to be hurried where a patient was concerned and recognised no authority but his own.

'I expect he knows what he's doing,' the PC muttered.

'He's very experienced.'

'I'll bet,' he said with a wink.

Helen gave him her frostiest look.

The ambulance driver appeared at the bottom of the stairs.

'Any progress?' he called.

The GP clumped back down to him and they conferred in low voices.

After ten minutes the door opened and Gil appeared, followed by William Tapping, clad now in a curious ensemble of flannel trousers, pyjama jacket and sandals. Perhaps at Gil's suggestion, the jacket had been fastened over his hair, which hung several inches south of the hem. In one clawed hand he clasped something round and metallic, his knuckles glowing white.

Helen and the constable moved aside to let him pass and because she knew her mother would have turned her face away, cringing at the sight, Helen looked him directly in the face and smiled. The man's eyes skated over her with the merest flicker of acknowledgement and he followed Gil downstairs, not unsteadily or reluctantly but with a straight back and a dignified tread. Like a deposed king going into exile, as Gil put it later.

45

Chapter 4

Patient: Louisa Tapping

Age: 74

Admission: first admission

Psychiatric history: unknown

Suicide: The patient denies suicidal thoughts.

Violence: The patient denies thoughts of violence towards self or others.

Trauma: unknown

Medical history: In 1956, the patient was admitted to Mayday Hospital with a head injury following collapse at Croydon Crematorium. Concussion, confusion, possible stroke. Patient discharged self against advice.

Medication: none

Family history: unknown

Residence: Coombe Road, Croydon. Patient is unmarried, financially self-supporting, has never worked. Has no living relatives apart from nephew, William Tapping, resident at same address.

General appearance: unkempt

Behaviour: co-operative

Consciousness: alert

Speech: normal

Attention: Unable to count backwards from 100.

Language: Patient can repeat back simple phrases.

Memory: Impaired. Patient unable to remember five words after five minutes.

Orientation: Patient knows name and address but not day, month or year.

Mood: relaxed, occasionally agitated

Affect: even

Thought process: confused, non-linear

Insight: Poor – when asked what she would do if a parcel addressed to a neighbour was left on her doorstep, was unable to formulate reply.

Initial assessment: The patient is an elderly lady with symptoms of moderate senile dementia. She is living with a younger adult relative who seems to be suffering from neglect. Police called after altercation at house reported by neighbours – shouting, defenestration of clothing and effects. Patient exhibits distress at possibility of being separated from nephew.

Patient: William Tapping

Age: 37

Admission: first admission

Psychiatric history: unknown

Suicide: unknown

Violence: unknown

Trauma: unknown

Medical history: Last recorded visit to doctor in 1936 for tonsillitis.

Family history: The patient has one living aunt with moderate senile dementia.

Residence: Coombe Road, Croydon. The patient has been sequestered at this address for at least ten years, probably more. He lives with his aunt.

General appearance: Neglected, underweight, pale. The patient has long, unkempt hair and beard, and long fingernails.

Behaviour: Physically co-operative. Responds to instructions. Mute.

Psychomotor: normal

Consciousness: alert

Speech: mute

Language: unknown

Memory: unknown

Orientation: unknown

Mood: calm

Affect: flattened

Thought process: unknown

Thought content: unknown

Insight: unknown

Initial assessment: The patient was discovered semi-naked and in a neglected state in a house in Croydon in which he has been sequestered, voluntarily or otherwise, for some years. The only other occupant is his aunt of 74 who has dementia. The neighbour of some ten years was unaware of his existence. He is currently mute, although his aunt reports he can communicate normally. The nature of their relationship is unclear.

Chapter 5

— *1964* —

William was not religious, but on Sunday mornings he liked to listen to the church bells and remember the dead: his parents Selwyn and Alma, Aunt Elsie, Aunt Rose, Myrtle, Philly, Ada, Goldie and Tiny who was taken by the fox, Boswell the stray cat – and the one he was never to mention or think about. That done, he could dismiss them from his mind for another week and keep a clear head as far as possible.

After rising late, he washed at the bathroom sink and raked the spots on his back and chest. The advantage of having such long fingernails was that there was no part of him that could not be reached and scratched. Of course, this was only an advantage with regard to the temporary relief of itching. In the matter of longer-term comfort and the healing of sores, the long nails had to be considered an aggravating factor.

He rubbed Germolene into the worst of the lesions with the palm of his hand and then dressed himself in yesterday's clothes, which were folded over the back of his chair: dun-coloured trousers, vest, shirt, pullover, socks, sandals. This was one of only three similar outfits worn in rotation and laundered on the rare and unpredictable occasions when Aunt Louisa decided that it was washday and raided his room.

49

It took him only four throws of the dice to score a double six – an auspicious start that put him in a positive mood – and he completed the next crossword puzzle in his book, then played two games of chess against himself, both ending in stalemate.

For lunch there was roast beef, cooked by Aunt Louisa, the joint pulled apart with two forks because of the matter of the missing knives, served with cabbage and mashed potato. For pudding it was whole baked apples with demerara sugar, as it had been every week since the previous autumn, complete with skin, core, stalk and sometimes twig. It was his job to pump the handle of the Bel cream maker, which was screwed to the edge of the kitchen table, until the mixture of warm milk and unsalted butter extruded from the nozzle in thick white spurts.

In the afternoon, Aunt Louisa hunted for things she had lost, misplacing other items in the process, which would then become the object of the next day's search. Distracted by the discovery of a half-finished tapestry, begun some years ago when she could still embroider, she sat and looked at it in wonderment until she fell asleep.

While the light held, William decided to finish his drawing of the magpie that he had started the previous day. He had found the bird injured and twitching on the ledge outside the kitchen window and brought it inside to nurse it back to health. He had kept it in one of the wooden crates they used for storing apples, which he lined with what looked like rags from the mending basket.

It had seemed uninterested in his offerings of milk and breadcrumbs, so he had crept out under cover of darkness to harvest slugs from the wet garden path. He rather regretted the absence of knives, as it would be no easy task cutting them up with a spoon. For a moment he considered and then dismissed the idea of putting them through the mincer. In the end, he put them into the crate alive, but in the morning the bird was stiff and dead, and the slugs had escaped as far as the landing, leaving trails of silver slime on the carpet. Even lifeless, the magpie was still glossy and noble and a much more compliant model, so William had spent most of the day drawing until the close work and poor light gave him a headache, when he put the corpse in the fridge on a plate, covered with an upturned mixing bowl.

Now he stood before the open fridge, shaking, unable for a moment or two to process the sight of the empty shelf, the unequivocal absence of magpie. From the front parlour he could hear the chirping of the wireless and the rumbling snores of Aunt Louisa. He strode in and stood over her, clenching and unclenching his fists. It was a long time, years, since their last row and he was out of practice, but he was riled now and a scene of some kind was inevitable.

Something, perhaps the pungent, unclean smell of his beard, or the heat of agitation radiating from him, caused Aunt Louisa to wrinkle her nose, twitch and open her eyes. She flinched to find him looming above her.

'What have you done with my magpie?' he demanded, his voice hoarse from lack of use.

Sometimes, without any animosity, a whole day could pass without either of them speaking.

'I threw it out,' she croaked, only half awake but still defiant. 'You can't keep a dead bird in the fridge. It's unhygienic.'

This exchange of accusations was unusually direct. In the normal run of things, grievances were framed so as to implicate a fictitious third party. 'Who's left the hall light on?' Louisa might squawk from her armchair in apparent bafflement. 'Who's used up all the margarine?' William might wonder aloud at breakfast. This approach avoided the unpleasantness of a confrontation and might even prompt a grunted admission from the guilty party.

'You keep chicken in the fridge. Chickens are birds,' he retorted.

'Chickens are food. This wasn't food. It'll go all maggoty.'

'Not in the fridge. That's why I put it there. What have you done with it?'

'I put it on the compost heap.'

William made for the door as if to retrieve it in broad daylight. Aunt Louisa called his bluff, successfully. He halted, quivering with rage.

'The foxes'll have it by now,' she said, not cruelly but to put an end to any ideas of salvage.

'How would you like it if I threw out your things? You keep all that stuff upstairs for years and years but I can't even keep something long enough to finish drawing it. It's not fair.'

It was not easy to stalk out with his flapping sandals restricting him to a shuffle, so he slammed the door for emphasis, causing the pictures on the wall to rattle in their frames.

Upstairs, he made for Aunt Rose's room – the shrine – and threw himself on the bed without taking his sandals off, a sacrilegious act. He had no desire to take out his frustration on Rose, the sweetest of all the sisters, dead twenty years and blameless, but he knew it would infuriate Aunt Louisa if he riffled through these precious relics.

He opened the wardrobe door, batting away the flurry of moths that blew into his face. There was her olive suit, peppered with holes, a fox fur stole with muzzle and feet, a dark blue satin evening gown with a pattern of pale pink roses that she must have last worn before he had even come into the world. Rows of dresses, the fabric faded and bearing the scars of amateur mending, the armpits crisp with dried sweat, shivered on the rails as he ran his hands across their surface. Even now if he put his face in the folds he could smell her powdery rose-petal scent.

Pooling on the wardrobe floor was a satin dressing gown in Germolene pink. It was cool and slippery to the touch, and he thought how soothing it would feel next to his angry skin. His own dressing gown was made of Shetland wool; warm but prickly as briars.

He stripped off to his underpants and slipped his arms into the wide sleeves, tugging his bell ropes of hair free so that he could feel the gentle kiss of the fabric against his back. It was tight across his shoulders; the seams strained and puckered as he flipped his hair and beard out of the way. Any sudden movement and it would tear.

He envied women the softness of their dresses, the silks, satins and fine angora, while men's clothes were made of serge and tweed and flannel, coarse and unyielding. Of course, women had their own discomforts in the form of corsetry, straps and tapes and their foolish shoes, deliberately built to pinch and deform their delicate toes. His own sandals were models of comfort and utility. Adjustable as to width and accommodating as to the length of his toenails, they could hardly be bettered.

There were several dainty pairs of Rose's pumps, standing in line on a rack on the dusty wardrobe floor, wooden shoe trees holding them in shape. They were quite useless to Aunt Louisa, who had large, manly feet, but she kept them anyway. Not as a conscious effort to create a museum of Rose, but because they were all perfectly good and it wasn't done to throw away anything that was perfectly good, just because one had no use for it.

'What are you doing?' Aunt Louisa's voice, shrill with fury, made him start guiltily, though he had done nothing wrong. 'Take that off!'

He had been about to take it off anyway, as it was too small, but her tone of outrage annoyed him. What was the point of keeping all these things if they were never to be

53

used? Where was the harm in wrapping himself in Rose's dressing gown? He faced her down, drawing the edges of the robe more firmly together. She flew at him and tried to tug it off his shoulders and as he drew away there was a rending sound of breaking threads.

'Look what you've done!' she wailed, her hand over her mouth.

'Look what *you've* done!' he cried back, the unaccustomed loudness tearing at his throat.

'Take it off!' she commanded. 'It's not yours. It's a *lady*'s gown.'

'Why are you keeping all this stuff? She's never coming back.'

He let it fall to the floor and stood before her in his frayed underpants. His aunt recoiled, though his naked flesh was mostly concealed behind thickets of hair and beard. For a second he considered handing the dressing gown over and letting her have her victory, and one more piece for the mending basket, but then he remembered his magpie, flung onto the compost heap to be mauled by foxes.

He turned his back on her, tugged the net curtains aside and forced up the sash window, which shuddered and screeched in its tracks from decades of disuse, showering the sill with flakes of paint and rotten wood. The cool air streamed in, smelling of spring and fresh new growth. He snatched the robe, rolled it up and threw it out of the window. It ballooned briefly and then snagged in the branches of the alder.

'You wicked boy!' Aunt Louisa cried, taking a step back as though she might be next.

He strode to the wardrobe and seized an armful of hangers. Out went the olive suit and the fox fur and the navy dress. Out went a whole drawer of vests and camisoles and knitted cardigans shredded by hungry moths.

Aunt Louisa crumpled onto the velvet slipper chair, wailing. He left her there, uncomforted, and went to get a glass of water to soothe his sore throat, which he had strained by shouting. He knew that within minutes she would have forgotten the argument and be downstairs making him bread and dripping for tea.

Chapter 6

Helen missed the hurriedly convened conference on Monday morning to discuss the case of the Tappings – aunt and nephew – as she had a class and no reason beyond curiosity to be included. Gil had promised to brief her later. Unless there were pressing reasons against, it was established practice at the Park for the senior psychiatrist admitting a patient to assume responsibility for their care. Having been present at the moment of William's re-emergence into the world, Helen felt a tender sympathy towards him and was keen to be kept informed of his progress. As soon as her morning sessions were over, she cleared up with uncharacteristic haste, throwing brushes into the sink and leaving tables unwiped, and hurried to Gil's office.

Mistaking the reason for her urgency, he drew her inside and pressed her against the closed door, murmuring apologies for her spoilt weekend.

'Oh, that's all right,' she said, pulling away fractionally and glancing at the tall, uncurtained windows that gave onto the lawn. 'Tell me about the meeting.'

'Ah, well, Lionel was seething with envy, which was very gratifying. He'd love to get his hands on my hidden man.'

'Yes, yes, never mind your playground rivalries, what have you discovered?'

'Not much. We've got an old lady with dementia who won't stop talking and a man who can't or won't communicate at all. So, it's difficult to get an accurate picture of their life together. Was he a prisoner or a recluse? Was she? It's hard to say.'

'The house didn't look especially fortified,' said Helen, remembering the crumbling front wall, the rotten window frames. 'And it's hard to see the old lady as any kind of gaoler.'

'There are other kinds of imprisonment.'

'I couldn't sleep last night for thinking about him. He looked like that painting by Blake.'

'Yes, I thought of that, too. But it was just the hair. He wasn't crawling naked on all fours. At least not when I got to him.'

'According to the police constable, the next-door neighbour had no idea there was a man living in the house.'

It seemed astonishing, a terrible indictment of modern ways of living, but then Helen remembered Mr Rafferty, about whom she knew so little, and the other inhabitants of the flats, strangers all.

'The GP's records at least give us a year of birth for William – 1927 – and his last visit to a doctor, for tonsillitis, was before the war. Since then, nothing.'

'How can you diagnose him if he won't speak?'

'It's a good question. I'm not convinced he can be given a diagnosis of schizophrenia – he may have sound reasons for not talking. And I'm not prepared to prescribe Largactil just because it makes life easier for the ward sister.'

'What about the aunt?'

'I'm going to talk to her now. Want to come?'

'Yes, please.'

'Listen,' he said, catching her hand and squeezing it. 'I'm sorry about Saturday.'

'Never mind. Another time. Was everyone all right? I should have asked.'

It seemed a long time ago now, her eager preparations and subsequent despondency. They were just moods; they changed and changed again.

'Yes, no damage, apart from the car.'

Gil slipped out of the office first to check that the corridor was clear and Helen followed him to the geriatric ward where female dementia patients were accommodated. They passed the occupational therapy room, where a group of men and women were sitting at a wooden bench assembling ballpoint pens, tossing the finished articles into a crate. Some worked at a frantic rate, handling the ink cartridge, spring, barrel and lid with tremendous speed and dexterity. Others moved laboriously as though taxed to the very limits of their skill, but in spite of this inequality of output, there was a convivial atmosphere of concentration and industry. Further along they passed a day room, where four men were playing cribbage. One of them looked up and gave Gil a wave.

'Afternoon, Dr Rudden,' he called.

'Afternoon, Jim,' Gil replied without breaking his stride.

He was good with names; he never had to stand clicking his fingers while the ratchets of memory aligned or fall back on 'young lady' or 'my good man' to cover a blank.

They found Louisa Tapping sitting up in bed on the ward, peeling through a woman's magazine while looking anywhere but at its pages. Tucked beside her was the crocodile-skin handbag. She seemed to be finding much to enjoy in the drama of shared accommodation.

The woman in the bed opposite, who had been staring placidly ahead, on seeing Gil became suddenly animated, pointing and shouting, 'That's my husband! Nurse! That's my husband!'

Gil fetched chairs for himself and Helen and drew the curtain around the bed. Calls of 'Nurse!' continued to rake the air.

'Are you the doctor?' Louisa Tapping asked. She was wearing a hospital gown and the green cardigan from the day before.

'I am Dr Rudden,' said Gil. 'And this is my colleague, Miss Hansford.'

'Well, perhaps you can tell me what they've done with Mother. She'll be wondering why I haven't been to visit.'

'I don't know about your mother. It's William I have come to talk about, actually.'

Gil sat back in his chair, one leg resting across his knee, in an attitude of complete relaxation. Helen had never seen him in a professional situation in less than perfect command.

'Is he here?'

'Yes. Would you like to see him?'

'Well, I think I ought to. He'll think it a bit odd if I don't.'

'You're very close, aren't you?'

'Oh yes, he's a good boy, really.'

'I'd like to talk to you about William. Does he ever go out?'

'Oh no. He never goes out, except into the garden now and then.'

'Why is that?'

'He doesn't like going out any more. He's a homebody.'

'When you say, "any more", do you mean he used to go out?'

'Yes, he used to go out. Once, a fox took one of the hens and he chased it all round the houses.'

'When was that?'

'Nineteen forty-four.'

'That's very precise.'

'I'm not going to forget that day in a hurry.'

'Do you go out yourself?'

'Oh yes, I go out. I go to the shops and the bank and the library and to pay the electric light.'

'Can William talk?'

'Of course he can. But he doesn't chatter like I do.'

'What was the last thing he said to you?'

'He said some terrible things. I couldn't repeat them.'

'So there was a quarrel yesterday. Just before the police arrived.'

'What day was yesterday?'

'Sunday.'

'Is it Monday today?'

'Yes.'

Louisa Tapping gave in to a fit of coughing that left her quite breathless.

Gil allowed her to recover for a few minutes before persisting. 'The neighbours said that someone was throwing things out of the window.'

At this mention of neighbours, the old lady rolled her eyes.

'We don't have anything to do with them,' she wheezed. 'They're new. I expect the police came because they threw dog mess over the fence into our garden. I expect that's why.'

They seemed to be getting further and further from the heart of the matter, but Gil's patience was infinite.

'Did you and William have a quarrel?'

'Oh, I wouldn't call it a quarrel. He lost his temper because I put his magpie in the dustbin.'

Gil glanced at Helen. Finally, they were getting somewhere.

'He was keeping it in the refrigerator. It was dead, but you can't keep a dead bird in a refrigerator, with the butter and cheese.'

'Why was he keeping it there?'

'To preserve it, I imagine.'

'So, he started to throw things out of the window, because he was angry about the magpie.'

'My sister Rose's things. She had some nice pieces.'

Gil turned to Helen. 'Would you like to ask anything?'

She had dozens of questions, but no confidence that Louisa was a reliable source of information. Much of what she said seemed delusional. 'Can William read and write?'

'Of course he can. He's got *very* neat writing. And he reads adventure stories. Sea stories. I get them from the library. And the bird book. You know, with pictures of birds.'

'Was it his idea to grow his hair and beard long?'

'I don't know that you'd call it an idea. It just grew. I can't shave him. He's a grown man.'

Of all the conversations that Helen had overheard or taken part in since her arrival at Westbury Park, this one haunted her most. The answers were so matter-of-fact, so cheerfully delivered, so very nearly rational, and yet somewhere beneath them lay the wreckage of a man's life.

As they stood up to leave, Louisa Tapping suddenly grasped Helen's hand with surprising strength so that she sat down abruptly.

'Am I going home today?' she asked.

'No,' said Gil. 'We have to get that cough under control.'

'Have you seen my mother?'

'I don't believe I have.'

'What about William?'

'William's here.'

'Then who's at home?'

'No one.'

The gasp that greeted this news triggered another spasm of coughing.

'I can't leave the house empty. Thieves will get in and clear the place out. Where's my box? What have you done with my box?'

'What kind of box?' asked Helen gently, wishing that Miss Tapping would relinquish her grip.

'My box of things!' With her free hand she began to rootle in her handbag, which was still nestled at her side, pulling out handkerchiefs, empty envelopes, several pairs of spectacles and finally a bunch of keys on a ribbon. 'You need to fetch it. This' – she held up a heavy iron key six inches long – 'is for the gate. This' – a smaller version – 'is for the front door.'

The smallest, she did not bother to identify.

'It's probably too late. They'll be in there already, helping themselves.'

She was working herself up into a state of agitation that was painful to witness.

'Where can I find it?' Helen asked, accepting the keys with her free hand.

'Oh, it's well hidden,' Louisa said with a touch of pride. 'But they are artful.' She beckoned Helen close and whispered in her ear with hot breath. 'It's in the larder in the flour barrel.'

'It's curious the way some dementia patients become fixated on finding their mothers. Like lost children,' Gil said as they made their way back to their afternoon sessions, past the occupational therapy room and the men's day room, identifiable at a distance by the wraith of cigarette smoke drifting through the open door. 'Fathers not so much.'

For Helen, imagining this was a feat of empathy too far.

'What do you make of that stuff about the box and the flour barrel?' She jangled the keys on their tatty ribbon.

'I was going to ask you if you'd mind going to investigate,' Gil said. 'I'm a bit stuck without a car.'

'Do you think it's all right? I mean ethical? She hardly has capacity.'

'You'll be doing her a kindness. If this box exists. My guess is it's as much a delusion as the magpie.'

'You don't believe that, either?' asked Helen, who had felt that part of the story too strange to be anything but true.

'One thing I do believe is that William communicates perfectly well with his aunt, if not with other people. I'll be interested to get them together, to see whether he'll talk to her in my hearing. That would be a start.'

'Did you hear her say he last went out in 1944? I mean *twenty years*? Can that be true?'

'Her memory's obviously not reliable, but I wouldn't dismiss it out of hand. She was very specific.'

'Poor man.' Helen shook her head. 'What a strange, lonely life he must have lived.'

'Come in the garden a minute – I want to show you something.'

The long, arterial corridor was cool and scented with rubber, disinfectant and the pungent, vinegary odour of paraldehyde, but outside the air was warm, rinsed clean by overnight rain. Gil and Helen walked along the path towards the vegetable garden, side by side but at a professional distance. On the games field a five-a-side football match was in progress. Helen recognised one of the patients from her Friday morning class, Roland, the lathe operator, dressed in long white shorts and studded boots, an approximation of kit. Most were in shirts, trousers and gym shoes.

They played with a curious lack of teamwork, pursuing the ball in a pack rather than spreading out and passing to each other. A row of spectators in wheelchairs, blankets over their knees, sat watching the game attended by orderlies. A self-appointed referee ran up and down the pitch waving his arms and blowing a whistle, ignored by the players, who proceeded according to their own rules.

On a terrace outside the refectory an arrangement of benches gave a view of sweeping lawns, cherry trees in full bloom and a working party of garden patients weeding the rose beds. The hospital cat, Smokey, was winding in and out of the wooden chair legs as though to relieve an itch, watched by a man in dark glasses. He was wearing a checked shirt, knitted pullover and flannel trousers that showed slightly too much ankle – unmistakably the spoils of a visit to lost and found, where abandoned clothes were repurposed for inmates without their own apparel. His dark hair was cut short, above the collar, the way all right-thinking men still wore it, unless they were trying to annoy their elders or make some political point, and his pale cheeks bore the nicks and spots of inexpert shaving.

'You didn't recognise him,' said Gil, when they had passed out of earshot. He laughed at her look of astonishment. 'Amazing what a visit from the barber can do.'

'My God,' she said, resisting the temptation to turn back and gawp. 'What a transformation. He looked so . . .' She nearly said 'normal' and then thought better of it. 'Didn't he put up resistance to being shorn like that?'

'Apparently not. He seemed to welcome it. In his silent way.'

'Aren't you worried he'll just abscond?'

Gil shrugged. 'There's no need for him to escape; he's not a prisoner. And his aunt is here.'

'Perhaps just being outdoors is a novelty.'

'It's certainly that. We've had to give him the strongest dark glasses we could find – his eyes can't cope with bright sunlight.'

Helen, remembering the filthy windows and half-curtained gloom of the house in which William Tapping had been immured, shivered despite the heat.

Chapter 7

Helen had arranged to arrive at Clive and June's at seven o'clock, by which time the evening meal would be safely eaten and cleared away. They were not the sort of people who encouraged droppers-in, especially midweek, and having already let them down once, Helen had no wish to disturb their routine.

As usual, the house – a 1930s semi in Shirley, a ten-minute ride from central Croydon – was in its state of pristine readiness for any visitor, up to and including royalty. The only way these standards could be maintained, Helen decided, was by a daily regime of cleaning already spotless rooms. June would not consider it a waste of time to take a J-cloth to sparkling windows or to beat a carpet that had seen no footfall since the last beating.

This mania for hygiene could not have been driven by Clive, whom Helen remembered from their brief period of shared childhood as someone oblivious to his surroundings, through a combination of short sight and lack of interest. His focus was always on whatever task or gadget was inches from his face: his stamp collection, the interior workings of a clock, his crystal radio set.

Somewhat distanced as children by an eight-year age gap, they had grown closer in adulthood, perhaps united by a determination not to settle for a relationship in their parents' loveless mould. Instead of blazing rages and frozen, wounded silences, June and Clive favoured a lower-wattage exchange of nagging and chuntering, which never seemed to escalate into a proper quarrel. They were, after nearly twenty years of marriage, still evidently content with one another. It was, Helen decided, something to do with each having clearly delineated spheres of responsibility onto which the other would not dare to trespass. Clive's department was paying the bills, keeping the cars on the road, paperwork, household repairs, the lawn. June was in charge of cooking, shopping, cleaning, laundry, Lorraine and the flower beds. The money she earnt from her part-time job in the perfume department at Allders was hers to spend. Helen and Clive's parents operated a similar division of duties, but in their case without the lubrication of gratitude and affection that made the machine run smoothly. Helen's own solution to the problem of marital conflict was something that she analysed only occasionally, in the cruel hours before dawn.

It was Clive who let her in, holding in his hand a new toy, a cine camera, which he was pointing in her direction, so that she instinctively raised one arm to cover her face. Then, realising she was being a spoilsport and was moreover caught for ever as such on celluloid, she relented and gave a proper film star smile and wave as she passed him into the kitchen, where June was giving the surfaces a last quick wipe.

'It's his latest hobby,' June said, filling the kettle and putting it on the hob by way of welcome. They never greeted each other with a hug or kiss; any sort of physical intimacy would have been unthinkable. 'He tried it out on your mum and dad on Saturday night. You should have seen your dad's face.'

'It's an Admira 8F,' Clive explained, following Helen into the kitchen, still filming. 'Eight millimetre. I'll be able to get all the big family occasions now. Holidays, weddings, christenings. Something to look back on when we're old and senile.'

'Speak for yourself,' June retorted.

Helen refrained from pointing out that, as a family, they hardly went in for Big Occasions. Perhaps the arrival of the camera would usher in a new era of celebration.

'So, how did the party go?' she asked, taking off her coat and slinging it over the back of the chair.

Almost before it had landed, June whisked it away to the cupboard under the stairs. From the front room came the sound of *Double Your Money*, the television left on as a reminder of all that they were missing.

'It was quiet – just the five of us. We had dinner, played Nap. I think Lorraine enjoyed it. Hard to tell with teenagers – they don't say much.'

The kettle began to shriek and June spooned tea leaves into a yellow china pot and poured on the water, which bubbled and spat as it gushed from the wide-necked spout. From a tin she produced the leftover slice of birthday cake, by now a little dry, and slid it onto a plate.

'Saved it for you,' she said. 'Oh, that reminds me . . .'

She hurried out and returned a moment later with a bottle of L'Interdit by Givenchy bearing the label TESTER: NOT FOR SALE – empty but for half an inch of amber liquid – the spoils of her job on the perfume counter. Once the contents fell below a certain level, they were replaced and the discards claimed by the staff.

'Audrey Hepburn wears it, apparently,' said June. 'But it's a bit too heavy for me.'

'Thank you,' said Helen, opening the bottle and sniffing the glass stopper, not altogether sure it was a compliment to be considered somehow equipped to bear its weight. It was not the first time she had been the beneficiary of samples deemed too 'heavy' or 'musky' for June's taste. 'Where's Lorraine, anyway?' Helen asked, sitting at the kitchen table and beginning to eat her cake. 'I've brought her present, better late than never.' She indicated the bag at her side, from its dimensions obviously containing an LP.

It had taken some stiffening of resolve for Helen to enter the alien precincts of a record shop, where she felt herself to be at least fifteen years older than the rest of the clientele and more than somewhat out of her depth. There was a group of youngsters browsing the racks and squashed into the booths in pairs trying out the latest discs, calling to each other in loud, confident voices. She could feel their eyes on her as she walked in and knew they were dismissing her as someone, if not quite of their parents' generation, still irredeemably past it, square and of no account.

She approached the counter where the shopkeeper sat, smoking a roll-up and turning the pages of *Melody Maker*. He at least looked older than her, with his leathery complexion and the greasy threads of his nicotine-stained moustache.

'I need a gift for a sixteen-year-old girl. What would you recommend?'

'Depends what she's into,' he said, squinting at her through the smoke.

'Well, I don't know what she's *into*,' Helen replied, hesitating momentarily over the term.

'Can't go far wrong with The Beatles. Ha – *With The Beatles*!' He laughed at his own joke.

'Something else, perhaps,' said Helen, remembering an incident from the previous April.

After much wheedling and pleading, Lorraine had been allowed to go to Fairfield Halls with her friend, Wendy, to hear the Merseybeat Showcase: Gerry and the Pacemakers; Billy J. Kramer and the Dakotas, and The Beatles in support. It had been her first ever concert and June had been excessively anxious about letting her go, imagining the audience to be full of rowdy undesirables.

Support for the scheme had come from an unexpected direction. As a clerk at the new Location of Offices Bureau in Chancery Lane, it was Clive's job to promote the benefits of Croydon to businesses looking to move out of London and he felt rather defensive about the town's attractions. The Fairfield Halls was a perfectly respectable venue, he insisted, the equal of the Royal Festival Hall, not a bear pit, and they were lucky to have it on their doorstep. Civic pride had been allowed to carry the day.

Lorraine was elated, and the anticipation of the event had provided the two friends with hours of excited discussion and the planning of outfits and hairstyles. It had been the best evening of her life – George had looked straight at her, she was sure of it – until the bus ride home, a ten-minute journey at most, when a drunk man on the 166 had put his hand up her skirt as she stood up to ring the bell. In her haste to get away from him, she had dropped her precious ticket stub – a treasure beyond price and irreplaceable. She arrived home in hysterics and that was the end of pop concerts and nights out with friends and taking the bus after dark. It seemed a little unfair to Helen that the reputations of Gerry and the Pacemakers, Billy J. Kramer and The Beatles had all been tainted by association with this unpleasant event, but their names were no longer mentioned by June without an accompanying roll of the eyes.

In the end, at the shopkeeper's prompting, she settled on *Stay with The Hollies*, which was sufficiently recent that there was a chance Lorraine would not already have it. The five young men on the cover looked harmless enough, with their collars and ties and smiles that were more awkward than dazzling, and not likely to excite parental disapproval.

She took it home and played it through before wrapping it, partly to check for jumps and scratches and partly out of curiosity. It was just as before with those experiments in listening to the Oh Yeahs, as Gil called them. The hoped-for moment of epiphany, when she would hear and feel in the simple jaunty tunes and soothing harmonies something to stir her soul, never came. At thirty-four, she was already deaf to the call to throw off her chains.

She had even tried the peculiar unstructured writhing that seemed to have replaced the formal dancing of her generation, to see if it brought any benefits. She would have been convinced that embarrassment depended on the presence of witnesses, until she caught sight of herself in the mirror above the fireplace, twitching gracelessly. It was as if there were two Helens in the room: one dancing, the other looking on in horror. If only young people realised how comical their cavorting looked, they surely wouldn't do it, she thought, and yet, from their rapt expressions, they seemed to have no such self-doubt.

She remembered her own dancing lessons with a Miss Gem Mouflet in Knightsbridge after the war. It had taken more than an hour from Lewisham by train and bus and was quite a stretch for the family budget, but her mother had insisted. Helen could recall the musty smell of the hall, the saloon bar plink of the old piano and the pressure of a damp hand in the middle of her back as she and a blushing public schoolboy stumbled through a quickstep or foxtrot without ever making eye contact. In another generation, she thought, that kind of dancing will be as stiff and dead as the quadrille and the cotillion.

'Lorraine!' Clive bellowed from the bottom of the stairs. 'Your Aunty Helen's here. Come down and say hello.'

A moment later came the soft padding of shoeless feet on carpet and Lorraine appeared in the kitchen. She was dressed up, as if to go out, in a pale blue minidress and a white cardigan that showed her skinny wrists. Her hair was set, styled and sprayed into a more compact version of her mother's helmet of stiff waves. Her eyes, neatly lined in upswept wings of black, stood out in her pale face.

'Hello you. Happy birthday for last weekend,' Helen said, taking the opportunity to lay aside her dry cake as she half stood and passed her gift across the table.

'Thank you,' said Lorraine, momentarily animated as she began picking at the wrapping with a nibbled fingernail.

'You look very glamorous tonight. Are you on your way out?' Helen asked.

Lorraine shook her head. 'No. I was trying things on in my room.'

'Lorraine doesn't like going out,' said June, coaxing a last well-stewed cup of tea from the dregs of the pot. 'She's a homebody.'

'I do like going out,' her daughter corrected her without much force.

'You *don't* like going out, Lorraine,' June insisted, stirring sugar into the tea and tapping the spoon against the rim of the mug as though ringing a little bell. 'She doesn't.'

Helen was spared having to reply by a murmur of gratitude from her niece, who had at last breached the wrapping paper.

'Well, say thank you, Lorraine,' said June, rolling her eyes.

'She just did,' Helen protested.

'Not very loudly,' June replied.

'*Thank you!*' Lorraine's voice, suddenly amplified, rang out in the quiet kitchen.

Helen felt the girl's mortification as both parents turned on her.

'There's no need to be rude!'

'Say sorry to Aunty Helen!'

'Really, there's no need,' Helen said. 'I heard her thanks the first time.'

Beneath her pale foundation, the girl's cheeks were pink with rage. She gave her aunt a watery smile of gratitude.

'I don't know a thing about The Hollies,' Helen went on, trying to steer the conversation back to safe waters. 'The man in the shop recommended it.'

Lorraine nodded. 'They're all right. Can I go and listen to it now?' She addressed this request to the patch of wall at the midpoint between her parents' frowning faces. 'I won't play it loud.'

'Oh, go on, then,' said June. 'But don't play it loud.'

Lorraine opened her mouth but then thought better of it and scuttled out of the kitchen. A minute later they heard the bedroom door click shut and soon after a quick, defiant blast of music, and then silence.

'I don't know what's got into her. You can see what I'm dealing with!' June appealed to Helen, who laughed pitilessly.

'All I can see is a delightful young woman.'

'I keep well out of it,' said Clive, as though disengagement from family life was a virtue.

He stood with his feet apart — braced, perhaps, to withstand the constant buffeting by female wills.

'I don't know what to do with her,' June went on, gathering the teacups and plunging them into the washing-up bowl of soapy water. 'She was always such a good little girl. Never any trouble.' She began to attack the cups with a plastic brush, sending suds flying. 'Do you remember when I had to bandage her toes with sticking plasters every day because they were all crooked. She lay there good as gold and let me do it, never a murmur.'

'Well, she was only about two years old then,' Helen laughed, picking up a tea towel to join in with the clear-up. 'You've got to expect *some* changes.'

Privately, she thought Lorraine was still more than usually compliant and June, in this as so much else, impossible to please.

'You don't see what I see. She's not like my Lorraine any more. She just lies on her bed all the time, listening to music.

72

She doesn't want to go anywhere or do anything. And she hangs around with some peculiar people.'

'Does she?' said Clive, waking up to this last accusation. 'I hadn't noticed that.'

'Oh, you don't notice anything.'

'Would you like me to talk to her before I go?' Helen asked. 'I mean, I didn't always feel like talking to my mother when I was sixteen. Still don't, really,' she added, realising that June would hardly be flattered by being aligned with her mother-in-law.

June peeled off her rubber gloves with a snap. 'If you wouldn't mind. I can't get through to her. She used to be such a good girl.'

She still is good, thought Helen, but she's no longer quite a girl and that is the beginning and end of the problem.

At nine o'clock, Helen left Clive and June to their nightly ritual of tea and Ritz crackers in front of the BBC news and went upstairs. She found Lorraine lying on her bed, picking at the fluffy ridges of her candlewick counterpane and listening to her transistor radio, which was pressed against one ear. The powder-pink furnishings of the room had barely changed since Lorraine was a child, but there were a few traces of the teenager she had become. Beside the arrangement of miniature porcelain animals on the chest of drawers that served as a dressing table was a cosmetic bag spilling its riches: nail polish, lipstick and powder. An embroidered sampler of a teddy bear recording the birth of Lorraine Sheila Hansford 7lb 3oz on 18th April 1948 shared the wall above her bed with pictures of George Harrison and The Beach Boys, clipped from the pages of *Fabulous*.

On one side of her cheval mirror hung ropes of plastic beads, coral and fake pearls; from the other dangled a string puppet of Muffin the Mule. The doll's house had been replaced by a record player, which occupied one corner of the room in the manner of a shrine, the walls above decorated with more icons cut from magazines, the few LPs arranged like offerings around the plywood altar on which it stood.

Lorraine switched off the radio and drew her legs up to allow Helen to perch on the bed, which also accommodated a number of stuffed animals and a glassy-eyed Victorian doll.

'Did you get any nice presents?'

Helen knew that Lorraine had been coveting a pair of Anello & Davide shoes for some time because they had talked about it the last time they met. It was the dove-grey Mary Janes that she was after and it was imperative that she got them before Wendy.

Lorraine extended a skinny wrist, from which a gold watch dangled loosely. 'From Mum and Dad,' she said, her voice bright with swallowed disappointment.

'Very nice,' Helen agreed in the same tone. 'I'm sorry I didn't make it to your birthday do,' she added, trying to get comfortable with the windowsill digging into her back.

'You didn't miss much.'

'I expect Granny and Grandpa were pleased to see you, though. They don't get out much otherwise.'

'I don't see why. There's nothing stopping them.' The emphasis fell lightly on the word *them*.

'Do you feel there's something or someone stopping you from doing the things you want?' Helen asked gently. She did not particularly want to stir up conflict between the generations, but June had asked her to intervene, so she would.

Lorraine looked wary. 'No. Yes. I don't know. I go to school every day. That's enough.'

'How is school going?' Helen recalled that Lorraine would be leaving in the summer to begin a secretarial course in Croydon at Clive's suggestion. She had wanted to do hairdressing at one point but had been overruled for some reason.

The girl pulled a face. 'Some of it is all right, but I'll be glad to leave.'

'I can imagine.' Helen smiled at her.

'Maths is the worst thing.'

'And then you're off to secretarial college?'

Lorraine nodded without enthusiasm. 'Typing and shorthand will be all right. But bookkeeping? That sounds just like maths to me.' She mimed puking.

'Useful skills, though. Companies always need good secretaries. And once you've got your toe in the door . . .' She realised she sounded like Clive now, insufferably complacent, and corrected herself. 'Is there something else you'd rather be doing?'

Lorraine's expression lightened. 'I'd quite like to go to art school.' *Like you* remained unspoken, but it was there and Helen was flattered. As the younger party in every significant relationship, she had always been the disciple. Her niece was the only person who looked up to her.

'I didn't know that. I could have helped.'

She couldn't recall ever having seen a painting or drawing of Lorraine's on display in the house, even a childish scrawl. It wouldn't have occurred to June to put them up on the wall; she would have considered it both untidy and conceited.

'I like art at school. It's my favourite lesson,' Lorraine was saying. 'But Mum and Dad said it's not a proper subject.' She stopped, flustered.

I bet they did, thought Helen. Instead, she said, 'Have you got any drawings I can look at?'

Lorraine rolled onto her stomach and foraged beneath the bed, producing an A3 sketch pad from its shadowy reaches and passing it across to Helen with the words, 'It's mostly rubbish.'

'I'm sure it isn't,' Helen replied.

The book was only half filled, but contained some unexpectedly confident and uninhibited pastel drawings, quite at odds with Lorraine's timid demeanour. She had not been afraid to fill the space with bold colours.

'I like these very much,' said Helen, turning the stiff pages.

Most of the subjects were taken from Lorraine's immediate surroundings: self-portraits; the view from the window; a pile of shoes; a chair. Prisoner's art, she thought.

'You need to keep practising; it's like learning a musical instrument. Take a small sketchbook to school with you and go out at lunchtime, find a bench and sit and draw what you see. Trees, buildings, people at the bus stop, anything.'

It occurred to her that she herself had not done anything like this since she'd left college. It was as though by taking a job as a teacher she had accepted overnight the world's estimation that she was not, nor ever would be, an artist. She resolved to pick it up again, to relearn those habits of observation and composition that she had lost.

'I'd feel a right Charlie,' Lorraine said. 'People looking at you, wondering what you're doing.'

'Oh, well, who cares what other people think?' Helen retorted.

From Lorraine's expression, it was clear that worrying what other people thought occupied most of her waking hours.

'How's that friend of yours – Wendy?' Helen asked, thinking that perhaps she had done enough counselling for one night. 'Do you still see her?'

Lorraine shook her head. 'She's got a new boyfriend and she's too busy with him.'

'Ah, it's a shame when that happens.' For a second or two she felt indignant towards this Wendy and then remembered that she herself, a grown woman of thirty-four, had treated Lorraine no better. 'You don't have a boyfriend of your own, then?'

'Not really.'

This seemed to Helen an ambiguous denial at best, so she waited patiently for further elaboration, a trick she had learnt from Gil, who could draw out confidences by maintaining silence almost indefinitely without any apparent discomfort.

In no time at all Lorraine folded. 'I met this boy on Easter weekend at Christian Camp,' she conceded. 'But he lives in Manchester.'

'That's a pity,' said Helen, thinking that even June could hardly disapprove of this connection.

'I wrote to him, but he never replied.' She shrugged. 'Don't say anything to Mum and Dad, will you?'

'Of course not, if you don't want me to.' Helen stood up, tugging at her skirt, which had ridden up over her slip as she lounged on the bed. 'I'd better be off now. I'll send you one of those mini sketchbooks to carry around with you. And, Lorraine, if you really mean it, I'll look up art courses at Croydon Tech. I'm sure it wouldn't be impossible to switch.'

Lorraine looked sceptical. 'Mum and Dad wouldn't allow it.'

'Of course they would. Even my parents allowed it. I'll talk to Clive.'

Helen wished her niece would show a bit more of the rebellious spirit that her generation was frequently accused of. She couldn't imagine those spiky teenagers in the record shop worrying what their parents would and wouldn't *allow*.

She leant over and gave her niece a kiss on the cheek, which was cool and smooth as chalk.

At the door, she turned back to say a final word of encouragement, but Lorraine had already rolled onto her side, facing away, with her radio pressed to her ear.

Chapter 8

The corset and the silk dressing gown were still caught in the tree outside the Tappings' house when Helen approached the iron gate. The more accessible items had disappeared from the shrubs and brambles along the front path, the work of tidy-minded neighbours rather than thieves, she decided. She stepped over the crumbled front wall and was regretting her open-toed sandals, when she was hailed by a woman peering through the foliage from the next-door garden. She had evidently been standing on a step or crate, as having secured Helen's attention, she said, 'Wait there,' dropped down out of sight and a moment later reappeared, panting, on the pavement side of the wall.

'If you're looking for the people who live there, they were taken off in an ambulance,' she said, out of breath but determined to bear witness. 'I just ran down from the top of the house when I saw you, in case you were wondering where they'd got to.'

'Yes, I'm aware,' said Helen, giving in to an irresistible impulse to meet self-importance with still greater self-importance. 'I was here at the time. I work at the hospital. Do you know the family well?'

The woman hesitated, as though torn between claiming special inside knowledge and distancing herself from any unpleasantness that might have been taking place under her nose.

'I can't say we knew them well. Or at all, really. I mean, look at the place. We used to see the old lady, Miss Tapping, going off to the shops with her basket. We only knew her name because the postman sometimes put her letters through our door by mistake. It was my husband who called the police. I wasn't here myself.' The note of regret in her voice was unmistakable.

'To report a disturbance, you mean?'

'Yes, shouting and banging and then clothes flying out of the windows. He thought it was vandals. We never knew there was a man in the house. My husband said he went off in the ambulance with hair right down to his slippers. It shook us up to think he was next door all that time and we never knew.'

'It's an unusual situation,' Helen agreed. 'Did they ever have any visitors?'

'Never. Not that we saw, and we've been here ten years. The winter before last, during the big freeze, my husband dug his way up to the front door to see if the old lady was all right. We gave her some milk and eggs and bread and she was ever so grateful, but we never went inside. There used to be another Miss Tapping, as well – the sister, I believe – but she died not long after we moved here.'

'That's interesting. Did you ever speak to her?'

'Just a hello if we met on the pavement. Very private, they were.' She glanced at the keys in Helen's hand. 'You going inside, then?'

'Just to pick up some of Miss Tapping's belongings. At her request.'

'I'll bet it's a terrible state in there.'

Helen smiled non-committally. She had a feeling that given the slightest encouragement, the neighbour would follow her indoors, still talking.

'Well, I'll let you get on,' the woman said with an air of defeat. 'If you need anything, I'm just next door.'

79

But she stayed put, watching from the pavement until Helen had let herself in and closed the heavy front door behind her.

Alone in the camphorated gloom, some of Helen's self-assurance deserted her and she stood for a moment, her breath not so much held as clutched, listening for any sounds from the abandoned house. She wondered whether the police had checked the place over after the departure of the ambulance, to see if any other horrors remained within. Now that the neighbour had mentioned a dead sister, Helen half expected to uncover her mummified remains. She was not here to snoop, she reminded herself. Miss Tapping had trusted her with the key in order to retrieve her tin box, if it existed. And yet if William was to be helped, some investigation into his circumstances and living arrangements would surely be useful.

The loose, broken floor tiles crackled underfoot as Helen made her way along the hall, opening doors as she passed to admit some light. The handles were sticky to the touch, their embossed faces reamed with dirt. She was now in a part of the house she had not explored on her previous visit.

The back room, facing south and possibly once a sunny parlour, was now cast into permanent dusk by the overgrowth of creepers, some tendrils of which had breached the window frame and snaked across the ceiling. Three lumpish armchairs hugged the grate, which was full of sooty rubble. A gateleg table stood against one wall, guarded by heavy wooden dining chairs. Pelts of dust lay along the picture rails and the topmost edges of family photographs and faded watercolours on the walls. A patterned rug, worn almost to threads, formed a corrugated surface on top of a larger, even sorrier carpet.

In the kitchen Helen discovered the ossified remains of the Tappings' last meal: half a cottage loaf and a dish of dripping with a piece of knotted string protruding from the congealed fat. Remembering the magpie, Helen opened the refrigerator with some trepidation, but it was empty apart from half a bottle of milk, a butter dish, a jar of fish paste, the leftover joint of beef and a speckling of mould on the back wall. The air within was pungent with decay and she shut the door again smartly.

The larder was a small room off the kitchen with two external walls, a green rust-freckled meat safe – now superseded by the mouldy fridge – and shelves containing dozens of tins, packets of dried food, porridge oats, cereals and jars of preserved fruit, all in the same shade of bruise and unidentifiable. A wooden trap in one corner held a piece of bacon rind and a severed mouse. Helen averted her eyes.

She located the enamel flour tin behind a hessian sack of earthy potatoes and dragged it into the light. As she rolled up her sleeve and prepared to probe its mealy depths, she could see the surface shifting, alive with weevils.

Barely six inches below the surface, her fingers made contact with a brick-sized box, wrapped in a muslin cloth and tied with multiple knots like a trussed joint. Although she would have been disappointed not to have found it, she was still surprised that Louisa Tapping's memory, in this regard, had been quite sound.

After brushing off the excess flour, she stowed it in her bag and went upstairs to investigate the upper floors. This was now quite beyond her remit, but having negotiated the neighbour and the mouse and the weevils, she felt she had earnt some latitude.

Leading off the middle landing were a bathroom and three large bedrooms, all more or less feminine in their décor and accoutrements. One, from which the articles of women's clothing had been flung, had a white rococo dressing table on which sat various cut-glass scent bottles, trinket dishes, a padded velvet jewellery box and an ivory-backed brush set, thick with trapped hair. The curtains and counterpane were a frothing cascade of ruffles, swags and pleats, sun-bleached at the edges and stiffened by dust. The wallpaper, scuffed and scratched in some places, bulging with damp in others, was patterned with fat pink roses and a trelliswork of twisted blue ribbons.

The wardrobe doors stood open and a flight of open drawers revealed a silky jumble of feminine undergarments. Helen had assumed this to be Louisa's room and the ejected belongings to be hers, but then in the bedroom next door, which was larger but with simpler furnishings, were more recent signs of occupancy: a glass of cloudy water and some denture cleaning tablets, a paper bag of barley sugars and a pile of library books by Jean Plaidy, due back the following week. This dressing table held fewer cosmetics and more family photographs: sepia men in British army uniform looking noble; an upholstered Victorian matriarch with two girls in white pinafores and a baby; a man in a stiff collar, with a huge walrus moustache, standing in front of a grocer's shop in an attitude of proud ownership.

The third room was the plainest of the three, almost monastic in its lack of comforts, with a dust-coloured carpet, brown curtains and a blanket of knitted squares over the bed. Even this showed evidence of past habitation – a wristwatch and a brass handbell on the bedside table, a pair of slippers parked under the bed, a plaid dressing gown hanging on the back of the door.

On the top landing, where Helen had waited while Gil questioned William, was an attic room, storage for all kinds of lumber, trunks, suitcases, a wooden cot, stained mattresses, broken picture frames and rolls of carpet. The other door led into William's room, which was small, with a sloping roof and dormer window. The floorboards had been more or less covered by a piece of carpet, amateurishly chopped, curling at the edges like dry bread and not quite reaching the skirting boards. There was a high single bed with a metal bedstead like a pair of gates at each end and a colourful crocheted blanket, neatly folded, on top of the eiderdown. A bookcase housed an encyclopaedia, a selection of children's classics, including *Kidnapped, Stalky & Co.* and *The Count of Monte Cristo*, and some books for boys with titles like *Hulton's Adventure Stories, Iron Men & Saints* and *Regimental Legends.*

There were no mirrors and instead of a dressing table was a small writing desk with a hard-backed chair. A silver tankard, yellow with tarnish, held several pencils and a fountain pen. All these details Helen took in with one sweeping glance, but it was the picture on the desk that held her gaze. It was an incomplete line drawing of a magpie, the head and one wing executed in the finest possible strokes, the rest a shadowy pencil outline waiting to be filled. The work was as delicate and detailed as an engraving by Dürer.

She opened the desk drawers to see if there were more, but one contained only a bottle of black ink, more pencils and rubbers, and the other was full of bundles of tea cards, sorted by category. There were sets of birds and wildflowers, freshwater fish and African wildlife, held together by elastic bands, and a drift of duplicates: coots and harebells and ring-tailed lemurs.

In the wardrobe she found what she was looking for. There were hardly any clothes: a few threadbare shirts, trousers and some terrible boots that might have come through the Somme. But in a leather-cornered suitcase were more than a hundred drawings of a similar style and standard to the magpie, of various subjects mostly taken from nature: badgers, foxes, cats, birds, plants, all signed with the initials WST. There were a few studies of hands and feet, the artist's own, perhaps, but no portraits. One sketch, which had been attempted over and over, was a cottage in a garden with deckchairs on the lawn and a hammock strung between trees. These were different from the rest, impressionistic and sketchy, with a skew-whiff perspective, but wistful and charming all the same.

83

At the discovery of this cache, Helen's pulse quickened and she felt a tingle of excitement. No one who had passed through the art therapy room during her residency had shown anything approaching this level of talent. Of all the professionals at Westbury Park, she was uniquely placed to help this hidden man emerge from his place of silence. Even Gil did not have her advantage.

Hesitating for only a moment to settle matters with her conscience, Helen selected a dozen of the drawings, including the cottage and the unfinished magpie, to take with her. William had kept them secure and might like to be reunited with them at some point. Knowing, too, how desperately she would miss her own materials, she pocketed the fountain pen from the silver tankard. Now that she examined it, she could see that the nib had been sharpened to a needlepoint.

It would soon be dusk and this was no place to linger after dark; she took a last look around, moving to the window that looked over the canopy of treetops, obscuring most of the garden as far as a tumbledown glasshouse with broken panes. From this high vantage point she could see away across the gardens and rooftops and chimney pots of South Croydon until her eye picked out another third-floor dormer window of another lonely attic bedroom, to which she herself would soon be returning.

Chapter 9

— *1960* —

There was something crawling in his beard. William opened his eyes to find Aunt Louisa standing over him with a pair of shears − the sharp one-handed pair that she used for cutting through the breastbone of a chicken, or severing the woody tendrils of ivy that grew through the air bricks and breached the window frames. It wasn't just the disturbance to his beard from her exploring fingers that had woken him. The room had grown darker as she approached the bed. William always knew what time it was just from the quality of the light falling on his closed eyelids and in this way he tracked the passage of the seasons from equinox to equinox and noted the changing times of sunrise.

He erupted from the sheets, throwing himself back against the iron bedstead. The shears flew from Aunt Louisa's hand and hit the wall, fetching out a chip of painted plaster and coming to rest on the floor by his desk.

'I told you I don't want my hair cut!' he protested, his hands springing to his neck as if to check that she hadn't already slit his throat.

Then he seized his thatch of beard and hair, bundled it down inside his pyjama jacket out of danger, and turned the collar up to his ears. He was, in truth, getting tired of his hair, which was so hot and itchy and brought the skin of his back out in a lumpy rash, but he was not going to submit to molestation by Aunt Louisa and her shaky hands, on principle.

'But it's too long,' she wailed.

'Too long for what?'

'Too long for a man.' She made no move to retrieve the shears but stood wringing her hands. 'You used to be such a lovely looking boy. What would Elsie say?'

This question made no sense as Elsie was dead and, though once opinionated on many matters, such as the proper way to hold cutlery, eat soup, lay a fire, boil eggs and deal with unwanted callers, had never, as far as he was aware, expressed any view about the appropriate length for hair or beards. He therefore made no attempt to answer.

'Let me cut it,' she wheedled. 'And I'll make you a nice bread pudding.'

He hesitated. It was some time since she had made one, because she would only use stale, leftover bread and William was too hungry to leave even the hard heel end of a loaf.

'It just grows again,' he replied. 'Anyway, how would you like it if I crept into your bedroom at night when you were fast asleep and chopped all your hair off?'

Aunt Louisa's eyes widened in horror. 'You wouldn't do such a wicked thing to your old aunty.' She clamped a hand over her mouth and a sob escaped between her scaly knuckles.

'Oh, don't be so soft. I was just saying.' William shook his head.

All the same, he thought, those shears have got to go. And the knives. She can't be trusted. He had to stop and consider for a minute whether he could be trusted and decided that he could and that he would hide a small paring knife in his room for sharpening pencils. Even at her most exasperating, he never wished her any harm. He still remembered the terrible week when she was missing and he thought her gone for ever. She had had some kind of seizure at Aunt Elsie's funeral and hit her head and been carted off to hospital, unable to get home or send word until she was well enough to discharge herself and hurry back to him.

As a concession, he started to plait his beard into three braids and tied his hair back loosely with a piece of string.

'It's still not normal,' Aunt Louisa grumbled, but she evidently felt that they were friends again as she made a bread pudding using bits of old loaves that she had been concealing under her bed for just this kind of emergency.

In the afternoon William read *Kidnapped*, as he did every six months or so, wishing that in the interval he would have forgotten some aspect of it that could be joyfully rediscovered. It was his favourite book and for the hero, David Balfour, he felt a kind of pure passionate love that he had never felt for any living person. In those moments of dissociation when he felt himself detaching from the world and beginning to doubt that he was real, it was a comfort to him to think that David Balfour existed in that same realm.

Aunt Louisa sat by the fire, which was unlit as it was only September, the empty grate hidden by a screen decorated with peacocks. She had finished sticking her Green Shield Stamps in their booklet and was now knitting a sock on four needles, using the wool from one of William's outgrown pullovers, unravelled, washed and rewound into skeins. It sometimes seemed to William that everything they owned had once been something else, diminishing in size and quality with each iteration. He could trace the lineage of every pincushion and needle case back via aprons and peg bags to their origin as garments, whole and sound.

As dusk fell there was a power cut, which sent Louisa into a panic in case the neighbours came to ask if they, too, had been affected or to borrow their stumps of candles. This fear was unfounded. Elsie had seen off overtures of friendship from the people next door as soon as they moved in and they had not called since.

William checked the fuse box in the cupboard under the stairs, dodging the cobwebs above and mousetraps below, but before he could find the candles and matches the electricity came back on again with a pop and a sudden flare of light. He fetched them out anyway, in case this brief loss of power was a warning of further longer-lasting deprivation.

He was pleased not to have to eat by candlelight, as dinner was fish pie, bristling with fine bones, a consequence of failing eyesight and erratic concentration on Aunt Louisa's part. For dessert there was another slab of bread pudding with Bird's custard, meanly sweetened as though sugar were still on ration.

They went to bed at nine, as normal, and William sat on his bed, fully clothed, until the sounds of protracted preparations for sleep – the creak of floorboards and the groan of ancient plumbing – were finally stilled and replaced by rumbling snores. Then he picked up his outdoor boots, dilapidated from age rather than overuse, and crept downstairs to the kitchen.

The squeal of the drawer as it slid open, metal on metal, and the jangle of the shifting cutlery tore through the sleeping house. William froze, waiting for Aunt Louisa to descend in full cry, but all was quiet above. Not without regret, he took the bread knife, carving knife, shears, bacon scissors and the boning knife with the tarnished steel blade deformed to rapier thinness by over-grinding and wrapped them in a piece of oilcloth. This he put in a canvas bag, one of several that hung on the back of the pantry door. There was a chance that Aunt Louisa would miss it, but it would be a minor loss against the absence of cutting implements, which would be of more distracting concern. It couldn't be helped.

The inside of his boots felt cold and sticky even through the thickness of coarse hand-knitted socks. They had once belonged to his grandfather, who existed to him only as a portrait above the fireplace, its brown varnish cracked like the surface of the leather.

He drew back the bolts of the back door, top and bottom, and stepped outside into the crumbling brickwork of the small terrace under cover of the tangled creepers. The air was cool and scented with the vegetable smell of damp foliage, moss, bark and fungi. Before long it would be winter and too cold for midnight excursions like this. High above him the moon appeared to bowl through the clouds. He stood for a while, allowing the blackness to reassemble itself into the shapes of tree trunks, shrubs, branches, sky. His night vision was good and it wasn't long before the details, too, were vividly before him. He never saw the garden from this angle in sunlight and would hardly have recognised it.

He made his way through the trees, across the uneven ground rippled with roots, past the ruined chicken coop to the listing glasshouse full of the dusty skeletons of pelargoniums in frost-shattered pots. After retrieving a trowel from just inside the door, he selected a patch of earth near the high wall that formed the boundary between the property and the side street that he judged to be free of roots. Under the canopy of branches he was quite hidden from view but remained alert to any noise or movement from the houses behind.

The wooden handle of the trowel was soft and rotten and pieces of it splintered off as he worked. After a few minutes he had managed to scoop out a shallow hole in which he buried the bag, marking its place with a miniature cairn of stones as a charm against forgetting. There was no chance of Aunt Louisa finding it. She hardly ever ventured into the back garden any more. Once, there had been a vegetable plot and a fruit cage and the hens, but that was long ago. Now, there were just things that took care of themselves: apples and maggoty plums and the cruel brambles.

Chapter 10

Helen found Gil in his office, frowning over the latest edition of the *Croydon Advertiser*. He spun it round so she could read it across the desk:

MYSTERY OF HIDDEN MAN
Police called to a disturbance at a house in Coombe Road on Sunday discovered a naked man with a five-foot beard living as a recluse with his elderly aunt. William Tapping, 37, who is mute, is not believed to have left the house in at least a decade. His existence was unknown to neighbours and authorities. Aunt and nephew were taken by ambulance to Westbury Park Hospital and are being cared for by doctors. Medical Superintendent Dr Morley Holt confirmed the pair were making good progress.

'I wonder how they got hold of this nonsense,' Gil said. 'The police, I suppose. He wasn't naked; he was wearing underpants and a blanket when we got to him. And his beard was two feet long at most.'

'*Making good progress,*' Helen snorted. 'Has William even spoken yet?'

'No,' said Gil, a trifle defensive. 'But I don't consider that a lack of progress.'

Since that glimpse of William in the hospital garden, restored by razor and scissors to an appearance of normality, she had seen him several times: in the day room, studying the large framed map of the Croydon area on the wall; sitting very close to the television, gazing at it in wonder; and outside, playing with Smokey the cat. Once, she had seen him standing at the open gates of the Park, staring down the driveway but making no attempt to cross this invisible boundary.

Gil had taken the unusual step of designating him a garden patient with freedom to roam in the grounds. This had caused some consternation on the part of Lionel Frant. His objections, aired at the next meeting, were twofold: 1) Ward patients usually had to earn that privilege through compliance with their treatment. 2) The system of rewards was a useful way of encouraging co-operative behaviour and needed to be applied consistently.

There had followed a lengthy discussion about whether mutism in itself could be considered non-compliance. Gil argued that since he had made a point of recommending no treatment other than observation and monitoring, William could not be accused of refusing to co-operate with something that didn't exist.

'This young man has been kept indoors for at least a decade, maybe two. I am not going to imprison him on the ward,' Gil had said, a hint of steel in his voice. 'I've seen no evidence that he is a danger to himself or others. And if we can't improve on his experience of life so far, then what are we actually for?'

The nursing staff were, in general, less exercised by William's promotion to garden patient, as this involved no extra work for them, than by his restlessness at night. Gil had caved in to their objections and prescribed sodium amytal to help him sleep or, as he put it to Helen, to help the late shift get through the night.

He had since had several sessions with William that he described as 'productive', though this did not necessarily encompass the patient breaking his silence.

'What do you do all the time if he doesn't say anything?' Helen wanted to know.

'Well, I don't bombard him with questions, if that's what you mean. I ask him if he feels like talking and if he doesn't, we maintain a companionable silence. We sometimes play chess.'

If there were some at Westbury Park who saw poverty of speech as a nut to be cracked by the application of pressure, Gil was not one of them.

'It must be frustrating for you.'

'Not at all. If you don't put a time limit on these things, there is no urgency.'

Helen nodded slowly. Sometimes, in the matter of their own relationship, for example, she wondered whether infinite patience was really such a virtue or just a way of avoiding uncomfortable decisions.

'Think of the father in the parable of the prodigal son,' he went on, 'eternally preparing a feast for the homecoming.'

'You see yourself as God?' Helen enquired with a raised eyebrow.

He had the grace to laugh at himself; even his vanity was somehow playful and endearing.

'At any rate, William appears to be adapting well to the new environment without antipsychotics,' Gil went on. 'That is what I would call progress. His poor aunt on the other hand . . .'

'Oh no! Tell me she is all right. I was just about to take her this.' From her shoulder bag she produced the tin box in its cloth wrapper. 'It was in the flour barrel, just as she said.'

A dusting of white powder landed on Gil's desk and he frowned. 'I'm afraid you're too late. She died in the night. William has just been told.'

Helen slumped. 'I didn't realise she was so sick. What did she die of?'

'Pneumonia. The usual.'

'How did William take the news?'

'Silently. The chaplain went to offer some words of comfort. Last I saw he was in the garden cuddling the cat. William, not the chaplain.'

'Poor William. Now he's got no one.'

'As far as we know. But the same is true of many of the people on the long-stay wards here.'

'I know. I should feel the same sympathy for all of them.'

She didn't, though. Her sympathy, if it was to translate into helpful action, was not inexhaustible and if it was spread too thinly, it would evaporate. William was its proper focus because she had been involved from the very beginning and was now even more so because she had discovered that he was an artist.

'Have you opened the box?' Gil asked.

'No, I was going to give it to Miss Tapping. I suppose it's William's property now.'

'Not necessarily. She may have disposed of her estate elsewhere. Shall we just see what's inside?'

Helen picked at the knots helplessly until Gil produced a penknife from his desk drawer and cut the string. The smallest of the three keys on the ribbon fitted the lock, though a paper clip would have done the job just as well. As a security measure, it was symbolic rather than practical.

Inside were five white twenty-pound notes held together in a clip.

'Christ,' said Gil. 'These have been out of circulation since the war. What a waste.'

Underneath was a bundle of three letters, stamped and postmarked but unopened, addressed to William Tapping. The handwriting on the envelopes was neat but immature and curiously squashed as though the writer had used a ruler to keep the lines straight. The postmarks were too smudged to be legible, but the stamps bore the head of George VI.

'These look pretty ancient, too,' said Gil, turning them over.

'Clive would know exactly how old they are,' said Helen. 'There's nothing he doesn't know about stamps.'

'He sounds fascinating,' said Gil. 'Of course, we'd know how old these letters are, too, if we just opened them.'

'But we're not going to, because they're addressed to William.'

'Yes, true,' said Gil, contrite.

'It's very odd though, isn't it? Keeping unopened letters like that. How would you know whether they contained anything important?'

'I suppose Aunt Louisa was trying to put a stop to a correspondence for some reason but drew the line at reading it.'

'Why not just burn them?'

'I don't know. Another uncrossable line, maybe.'

The last item in the box was a piece of folded newspaper dated June 1950. On one side was Births, Marriages and Deaths and on the other the obituary of a man called Douglas Samsbury. His name meant nothing to Gil and Helen, who scanned the entry to see if they could see any obvious connection to Louisa Tapping.

Douglas Samsbury had lived a colourful life – a painter and printmaker who claimed to have invented the individual exercise bouncer two years before George Nissen patented the first trampoline. During the war Samsbury had won a Distinguished Flying Medal for his part in capturing Pegasus Bridge in the first hour of D-Day 1944. He died in a gliding accident at an air show six years later.

'Perhaps we're looking at the wrong side,' said Helen, turning the page and glancing down the names to see if there were any Tappings among them. 'Well,' she said, defeated. 'Maybe it will make sense to William.'

'I think I'd hold off giving him the letters for a bit. The loss of his aunt will be a lot for him to process.'

'Of course,' said Helen. 'I did take something else from the house that I wanted to show you,' she admitted. From her bag she produced an envelope file and spread the sketches out on the desk between them. 'They were in William's wardrobe. There are plenty more.'

Gil took his time examining them. Finally, he looked up. 'Impressive. He's not been entirely idle during his years of incarceration.'

She gathered up the pages and returned them to the folder. 'I'm going to try and encourage him to visit the art studio. Maybe it's somewhere he'd feel comfortable.'

'By all means suggest it.'

'I just feel that he's someone I could actually help.'

Gil gave her a long sardonic look.

'I know, I know.'

There was a time when she had felt this about every patient, but experience had somewhat blunted that crusading sword. Most of the time she had to accept that her influence was limited and unknowable, not something that could be measured or proved.

She remembered a meeting shortly after her appointment in which Frant had tried to make the case for the statistical evaluation of her patients' artworks. Without this analysis, he claimed, the therapy had no more demonstrable validity than rug making or the assembly of ballpoint pens. Gil, in mischievous mood, had suggested that the paintings produced might be given scores for criteria such as 'colour', 'artistic merit', 'mood', 'symbolism' and so forth.

Oblivious to Gil's satirical tone, Lionel had agreed that with a few refinements, that might work. Morley Holt, who was not always present for these meetings, had jumped in to defend Helen. Babs, her one-time ally from occupational therapy, had started laughing, loudly. Dr Frant had withdrawn, wounded, and the issue had not been raised again. Still, Dr Frant's assumptions had rankled and, even now, Helen treated him with remote civility, determined to give him no opportunity to undermine her again.

William was sitting on his usual bench in the garden, facing the stand of fruit trees, cherry, plum and apple, now starting to drop their blossom on the tattered daffodils below. He still wore his dark glasses, whether against the unaccustomed glare of sunlight or the unwelcome glances of strangers, Helen wasn't sure. Smokey sat on his lap, enticed by a morsel of kipper saved from breakfast. William turned his face towards Helen as her shadow fell across the wooden slats of the seat but didn't smile or return her greeting.

She perched at the far end of the bench, angled slightly towards him. If he recognised her from their fleeting encounter on the landing at his house, he didn't betray it.

'My name is Miss Hansford. I'm the art therapist here. I'm very sorry to hear about your aunt.'

He gave the merest nod.

'If there's anything I can do, please let me know.'

There was silence.

'The other day your aunt asked me to fetch some of her belongings from your house and, while I was there, I picked up this. I thought you might like to have it.' She laid the chunky tortoiseshell pen between them on the seat. 'I know I wouldn't want to be without my own pen.'

The sudden movement disturbed the cat from its comfortable slumber and it repaid this injury by springing down from William's lap and stalking off. A little click of annoyance escaped him.

Helen pressed on, drawing out the cardboard folder from her bag.

'I also brought these. I hope you don't mind.'

His mouth gave the merest twitch as he recognised his drawings.

'You may not be aware that we have an art room here where you could come and paint or draw if you felt like it. I'd like to put one or two of your pictures on display in there – if that's OK?'

He turned his head towards her and she smiled into the impenetrable blacked-out lenses.

'Well . . .' She stood up, as if reluctantly bringing an interesting conversation to an end. 'I'll leave you to enjoy the sunshine.'

He nodded and his lips moved, fractionally, silently, to form the words *thank you*. Her face felt hot with pleasure and she wanted to say something, anything, to prolong the connection, but he had already turned away to look for the cat.

Chapter 11

On the Thursday following the appearance of the newspaper article, two unexpected things happened. The first, which was awkward and regrettable, led indirectly to the second, which was what Gil would call 'productive'.

During the afternoon session, one of Helen's patients, a young woman who suffered from periodic bouts of debilitating agoraphobia, had dropped red poster paint on the floor, which had then become transferred to the sole of her shoe and by degrees all over the floor. When the group had left, Helen washed the lino and returned the mop and bucket to the small side room, one of two that were used by patients who needed privacy to work. There was a mirror tile on the back wall above a washbasin and Helen stopped to check her appearance in case traces of paint had ended up on her cheeks or in her hair. A shadow moved in the glass and she spun round to find Lionel Frant standing behind her, a little closer than was quite polite.

'Goodness, you startled me,' she said, embarrassed to have been caught communing with her own reflection and wondering how long he had been there.

He took a step back but didn't apologise or smile.

'The art room door was open. It's advisable to keep it locked if you are in here alone.'

'I usually do,' she said, 'but I was clearing up a mess.'

This was not strictly true, but she was annoyed at this reproach. Gil seldom bothered with locking his door, or with any other rules that inconvenienced him, but no one ever made it their business to remind him of the protocols.

'I meant for your own safety,' Lionel added, softening his tone. His spectacles kept sliding down his nose and needing to be pushed back into place. The lenses were smudged with fingerprints.

Helen refrained from pointing out that the only person who had made her feel uneasy by following her uninvited into the studio was Lionel himself. She couldn't quite account for her antipathy towards him, unless it arose from her sense that he regarded art therapy as of unproven value.

He was not repulsive to look at, but rather someone you would pass on the street without noticing, and yet he did repulse her. There seemed to be a coldness and lack of sympathy in his manner that struck her as incompatible with his role. His interest in curing his patients, she felt, lay in proving that his method was the right one; for the people themselves he had no real affection.

Gil didn't like him, of course, considering him a reactionary, without ever quite admitting to anything as petty as professional rivalry. Helen had naturally absorbed some of his prejudices. It was hard not to – Gil's likes and dislikes were highly contagious.

'I didn't come here to criticise,' Lionel was saying, his Adam's apple jabbing above his collar like a beak. 'Quite the opposite.'

'Oh.'

This attempted shift in atmosphere did nothing to reassure Helen. In fact, she felt an awful sense of foreboding. He couldn't, could he, be intending to make a pass? She had never given him even the faintest signal that she was approachable. As far as she could recall, the temperature between them had never risen much above chilly and on her part at least it wasn't the kind of confected antagonism that masks sexual attraction.

She had been in this situation before with men and it never ended well. Without the solid reality of a wedding ring as a kind of guarantor of one's unavailability, there was always an expectation of gratitude at the very least, followed by dismay and sometimes disbelief at a refusal. If there was a form of words by which both parties could emerge from the situation without any loss of face, Helen had yet to discover it.

'I hope what I'm going to say won't be unwelcome,' Lionel said. 'In fact, I hope it will be welcome.'

He gave an awkward laugh, to which Helen responded with a frozen smile.

'I have bought two tickets to the RMPA summer dinner and dance and I wondered if you would come as my guest. It should be an enjoyable evening.'

At thirty-four, Helen thought she had grown out of blushing, but she now felt an unseemly heat sweeping up her neck.

'I'm sorry. That's kind of you, but I'm not free on that date. It's a long-standing arrangement, so . . .' The excuse sounded stiff and unnatural, even though it was quite true.

'I didn't think I'd mentioned the date,' Lionel corrected her, as though bent on mutual mortification.

'Well, I happen to know that it is on the fourteenth of May,' she replied, 'which is when I am already busy.'

She knew this because it was an event that Gil was planning to use as an alibi, while actually spending the evening with her, but this could hardly form part of her explanation.

'Ah. That's a pity.' He looked at his feet, then over her shoulder, anywhere but at her. 'If you can't make the four-teenth, perhaps I could take you to dinner on another day.'

Helen felt a tightening across her back and chest of muscles tensing in protest. This was the kind of unprovisional offer that required an altogether blunter refusal. To spare his feelings with a vague and friendly 'perhaps' would only postpone the problem to another day.

'I don't think so, Lionel.' She had never used his Christian name before and it felt uncomfortable in her mouth. 'I think it's probably best not to get involved with colleagues.'

She could hardly believe her own audacity in hitting on this of all things as an excuse.

'Oh.' He seemed more taken aback by the reproof to his professionalism than the rejection. 'Well, if you say so. I'm sorry to have put you in an awkward position.'

It took him a moment or two to reassemble himself, to assume again his superior status. He tried a smile, which presented as a ghastly baring of teeth, and then he departed as silently as he arrived, leaving Helen unsettled by the encounter and the clumsy way she had handled it. Belatedly taking his own advice, she went and locked the outer door against his possible return.

She lingered in the art room for ten minutes in the hope that he would be safely elsewhere by the time she ventured out. As she crossed the reception area on her way to the car park, she was hailed by Olive, the telephonist. One of the fearsome guardians of the switchboard, Olive always called Helen 'Miss', unless she was wearing her art overall, when she became 'Doctor'. She was a rich source of the kind of hospital lore that could only be acquired by listening in on phone calls.

'Miss, have you got a moment?' Olive riffled through the notepad on her desk and tore a thin strip from the bottom of a page. 'I've just had a call from a fella wanting to talk to someone about the fella who was brought in with the long hair. He said he knew him. I tried to pass his number on to Dr Rudden, but he was going early and he said to pass it to you. Could you ring him back or shall I give it to Dr Frant?'

'No, don't bother Dr Frant. I'll do it,' said Helen, taking the scrap of paper on which was written the name Alistair Duggan and a telephone number in Olive's neat round script.

'He said he read about him in the *Advertiser.*'

Thanking fate for her lucky timing, Helen put the note in her handbag and Olive swivelled back to the switchboard, which had started to blink and trill again.

Chapter 12

Helen sat at an empty table in the cafeteria at the Fairfield Halls, waiting for Alistair Duggan. She had come straight from work, leaving in fact a little early in order to make their appointment at 5 p.m. An afternoon performance had just ended and the foyer was crowded with concert-goers departing. The café, too, had filled up and people carrying trays of tea were wandering between the tables looking hopeful and then disappointed when she shook her head. She wished she had bought a drink before she sat down, but now she couldn't leave her place without losing it.

'How will I know you?' Alistair had asked.

'I'll be wearing a lilac-coloured coat,' Helen had replied, wondering even as she said it how helpful this was.

She had observed before now that men tended to have only the vaguest appreciation of the different shades of purple. She had considered adding, 'I have golden hair,' but realised this sounded affected.

'Right,' he had said, drawing out the single syllable to its full extent. 'I'm sure we'll find each other somehow.'

In the course of their telephone call, he had explained that he didn't live locally but went to see his widowed mother in Croydon once a week. It was during the previous visit that he had been browsing through the *Advertiser* while she put the kettle on and had come across the reference to William Tapping. It had been his suggestion to meet on his next trip and Helen found herself agreeing without quite knowing why.

Now, she could see a man of about the right age in a her-ringbone overcoat, gazing across the expanse of tables, his brow creased with concentration, in his quest to identify the colour lilac, perhaps. His gaze settled on her for a moment and she raised a tentative hand in greeting. He gave a smile of relief and threaded his way towards her, apologising to left and right as he squeezed between the chairs.

They shook hands across the table. He had red-veined cheeks and dark hair receding to leave a peak, which made him look old – even older than Gil, the standard against which Helen unconsciously measured all men and found them lacking.

'I managed to get a table but nothing to drink,' she apolo-gised. 'Shall I get us some tea?'

She made a move to stand but he put a hand on her shoulder.

'Let me,' he said, parking his briefcase beside the empty chair and joining the slow-moving queue for the counter.

She had told Gil about the meeting, to reassure herself that she was doing nothing unethical, and he had given her his amused look.

'What? You're not jealous that I'm meeting a strange man?'

'You know me better than that,' he had replied, leaning to kiss her, and she had admitted the truth of this with a slight narrowing of the eyes. Jealousy was an ugly emotion, unworthy of mature and trusting adults, but his nonchalant confidence that he had no romantic rivals hardly flattered her.

'Why are you giving me that superior smile?' she'd said. 'It's maddening.'

'Because your interest in William Tapping strikes me as singular.'

'You mean unprofessional?'

'No.' He'd considered for a moment. 'Extra-professional. Or do I mean supra-professional? Sentimental, anyway.'

Helen was roused from this uncomfortable reverie by the return of Alistair with a tray of tea and a couple of craggy rock cakes.

'Best I could do, I'm afraid,' he said, removing his overcoat and throwing it over the back of his chair, leaving Helen to deal with the refreshments.

The stainless-steel pot had an unruly spout that delivered scalding tea in more than one direction. When she had swabbed up the overflow and they were settled with their drinks, she said, 'It was good of you to get in contact. We're rather short of information.'

'Pleasure,' Alistair said through a mouthful of cake. 'As soon as I saw that piece in the *Advertiser*, I thought, good God, that's old Harry Tappers.'

'Why do you call him that?' Helen asked.

'Oh, we all had nicknames at school. There was one boy, Harry Travers. He was always getting into scrapes. For some reason one of the masters, Mr Swales – quite a decent chap, actually – took it into his head to call us all Harry and then the first syllable of our surname followed by "ers". So I was Harry Duggers, William was Harry Tappers, and so on. I mean, schoolboy stuff, but those names stick, you know.'

'I can imagine,' said Helen, who had never had a nickname, apart from the generic insults flung out by her mother – *Polly Longfrock, Sulky Sue* – which had no real grip. 'What do you remember of William? Was he in your form?'

'Yes, we started together September of '37. He was fairly quiet. But, I mean, we all were, if you knew what was good for you. You just kept your head down and tried to get through it.'

'That's not much of a recommendation for the place. What school was it?'

'Belwortham Hall. There were a lot of boys whose parents were in the military, posted abroad. It was pretty harsh. I think the powers that be felt that boys needed the Devil beaten out of them. A lot of the masters were quite vicious. But, you know, no worse than most.'

Helen broke off an outcrop of cake containing a burnt raisin. There was a pause in the conversation while she chewed effortfully.

'Did you meet William's family?' she asked. 'Did they have any connection to the military?'

'I didn't know him well enough for that. One didn't really meet chaps' parents – unless they took you out for a half holiday. I was only there for a year – until 1938, because luckily I got TB and spent the next year in a sanatorium.'

'Was it really so terrible?'

'I think if you come from a comfortable home with loving parents and at ten or eleven you are suddenly dropped into this alien environment with all sorts of rules and punishments and peculiar customs, it is very upsetting. I missed my little sister terribly.'

'Yes, I can see it must be. Were all the masters brutes?'

'Not all. But some of them had come through the first war and, looking back now, I think they were quite mad.'

'Would you describe William as a normal boy at that age – eleven? Not especially solitary?'

'He was just like the rest of us, trying to adapt and keep out of trouble. I wouldn't call him solitary. He was friends with a blond boy who was good at cricket. I can picture him. Harry Kenners.' He laughed. 'Can't remember his real name now.'

'I don't suppose you have any school photographs?'

Alistair looked thoughtful for a moment. 'I do remember a photographer visiting and all of us having to stand on a precarious arrangement of benches and Harry Travers passing out in the heat and nearly bringing down the entire row.' He smiled at the memory. 'I wonder what happened to him.'

'He's probably desperately respectable. Working for the Foreign Office and living in Esher.'

He laughed. 'Yes, like all of us. In our little boxes made of ticky-tacky.'

'Not quite all,' Helen said, thinking of William.

'No, indeed,' Alistair said, shaking his head. 'Poor fellow. How is he getting on?'

'It's hard to tell because he doesn't speak,' Helen said, looking at the crumbled remains of her cake without enthusiasm. 'I can't discuss the details of his case, of course, but you will have gathered that much from the *Advertiser*.'

In the busy cafeteria, the background murmur of conversation had risen now, driven ever higher by its competition with the scrape of chairs and clatter of crockery echoing off the linoleum floor and high ceilings.

'I wish I could think of old Harry Kenners' name,' Alistair was saying, tipping the teapot into Helen's cup and finding it empty. 'My brother might know, but he lives overseas and communication's a bit patchy.'

Helen raised her eyebrows. 'You had a brother at the school?'

'He was four years older and was there at Belwortham for a couple of years after I got TB. But older boys don't tend to notice the much younger ones. You look up, not down.'

Helen nodded. That was true of her schooldays, too. She could remember the glamorous head girl, Veronica Bartlett, with her silvery soprano voice, and every one of the fearsome sports captains and prefects, but of the people she had dazzled or terrified in her turn, nothing.

'My mother might have kept some old photographs. She's something of a hoarder.'

He had a way of maintaining eye contact and looking at her with deep and hopeful interest. If I gave him the slightest encouragement, Helen thought.

From one of the function rooms a stream of delegates emerged, talking in loud voices as they converged on the cafeteria.

'Well,' said Helen, not in the business of giving encouragement and conscious that they had annexed a table for long enough, 'that was very helpful.' Though it hadn't been, really.

Alistair took the hint and stood up, helping her into her lilac coat. They shook hands and rather than follow him out and prolong their farewells, Helen went to the ladies and reapplied the lipstick that had been lost to the teacup.

As she left the building and walked across the broad paved concourse the wind whipped at her legs, funnelled along the concrete gorge left by the excavations for the new underpass that would divide the east side of town from the west. Empty cigarette packets, sweet wrappers and whole sheets of newspaper went bowling past. Tiny eddies of dust and dead blossom whirled and spun, though there were no trees anywhere in sight.

Sitting on the edge of a raised stone flower bed was a student in a short plaid dress and crocheted beret. She was looking with great concentration at a bicycle leaning at a drunken angle against a bin and making sketches in a pad on her lap. It took Helen a moment to recognise the girl as Lorraine and it occurred to her how different she appeared – older, happier and freer – when away from home.

Chapter 13

—— *1956* ——

William could hear the faint tinkling of Aunt Elsie's bell from the room below, which meant she needed him. If it was Louisa she wanted, the ringing was more assertive to allow for her sister's deafness. It was two weeks since she had keeled over at the kitchen table while cleaning the silver, knocking over the Goddard's polish, which left a pink puddle on the tiles.

She had refused a doctor and taken to her bed, an event without precedent in William's lifetime. They had pushed the tarnished candlesticks, salvers, sugar dredger, cream jug, mustard pot and salt cellar to one side of the table to await her recovery and carried the paraffin heater up to her room to keep her warm. It was February and there was ice on the inside of the windows and the water in the lavatory bowl had frozen.

When Aunt Elsie summoned him, it was usually to read to her from *Little Dorrit* or to fetch down the ledgers from the top of the wardrobe, in which she recorded the domestic accounts. Expenditure: coal 6s 8d cwt; tea 1s 8½d; lard 1s 11d; matches 3d; aspirin 7d; Eno 2s 11d; Izal 1s 2d.

More urgent and intimate ministrations were performed by Louisa, who would answer the bell carrying towels, fresh laundry, rags, soap, bedpan or the bottle of kaolin and morphine.

She would sometimes be closeted with Aunt Elsie for an hour or more and emerge looking queasy and dishevelled.

William allowed himself to consider which of his aunts would make the better nurse. Louisa, though easily flustered by simple tasks and likely to fuss, was the more comforting presence. Aunt Elsie was brisk and efficient but had rough hands and little sympathy for the weak. After reflecting on their relative merits, he resolved not to fall ill.

Yesterday, Aunt Elsie had seemed a little better but had then done something so very out of character that he wondered if her brain was affected. Instead of asking for Dickens or her ledgers, she had beckoned him close and put a finger to her lips. This was curious in itself, because it meant that what she was about to say was not for Aunt Louisa's ears. William was used to secrets and silences and sideways glances – it was how they coped and kept him safe – but he had never yet been called on to form an alliance with Aunt Elsie.

'In my dressing table drawer,' she whispered. 'Nail scissors.'

He found them in a leather manicure set and gave them to her, but she shook her head.

'In the curtain hem. Cut it open.'

He picked up the weighted drapes and turned them over, looking enquiringly at his aunt, who gestured impatiently. Feeling along the folded material, he came to a section that felt thicker and was sewn up with different-coloured cotton thread from the rest.

'Shall I cut it?' he asked.

'Yes, yes.'

He pecked at the white stitches with the tiny scissors. Inside the hem was a brown envelope containing a sheaf of large white five-pound notes. For a second he was excited, then he remembered that money was no use to him.

'I'm giving this to you in case Louisa has trouble getting money out of the trust,' she said. 'If I give it to her, she'll put it somewhere and lose it.'

'Where will you be?'

She laughed and patted his hand.

Back in his bedroom, he counted the money: £60 – more than he had ever seen. Nowhere seemed secure enough to hide such a sum and he spent some while moving it from place to unsuitable place. Finally, he tucked the envelope inside the dust jacket of *Treasure Island*, which was a pleasing joke, and replaced it on the shelf, where it seemed to give off a luminous glow.

William found a few more of the missing edge pieces for the puzzle of Neuschwanstein Castle that he had begun that morning before making his way down to Aunt Elsie's room to answer her summons. If it was anything serious, she would have rung for Aunt Louisa, so there was no need to rush. *Little Dorrit* would hardly spoil.

He knocked twice and pushed open the door, releasing the sour smell of the sickroom, inadequately masked by squirts of Louisa's lavender cologne. The handbell lay on the carpet in the middle of the room, stirring slightly as though it had not quite come to rest. Aunt Elsie's arm was flung out, her head tipped back, mouth open and toothless, all life departed through those dry lips.

There was no need to approach the bed to confirm that she was indeed dead and William had no intention of doing so. He wondered whether he should open the window or close the curtains. He had no idea of the customs around death; it was grown-ups' business. He withdrew, shutting the door gently, and went to find Aunt Louisa, hoping she would not become emotional.

In the kitchen a pan of chicken soup bubbled on the stove, gritty froth gathering on the surface. Beside it stood a larger pan of handkerchiefs, boiling in their own soapy broth, and behind them was the glue pot of rendered bones, which was used for repairing broken china and wooden furniture. The windows ran with condensation from the steaming pots.

William cleared a spyhole in the glass. Aunt Louisa was outside on the paved area between the side door and the high boundary wall, running bed sheets through the mangle, cranking the handle with hands reddened by detergent.

He went out in his slippers to help her peg out the flattened sheets on the line that ran from the downpipe to a sturdy hook on the wall of the outside lavatory. She stopped and looked at him fearfully: he never normally helped.

'What is it?'

'Aunt Elsie's dead.'

Her eyes, already red-rimmed and wet from the chill wind, overflowed instantly and she clamped her lips shut to hold down a sob.

'I just found her in bed,' he explained, to reassure her that Elsie was still, in a sense, comfortable. 'What happens now?'

He would hardly have been surprised if Aunt Louisa had told him to wait until dark and then start digging, as had been the case with Boswell and Tiny, but instead she said, 'I'll have to call the doctor and the undertaker. Elsie left me a list, but I never looked at it. I said to her, "I'm not looking at that!"'

The doctor came out, so much more quickly to the dead, who were beyond help, than to the sick. Later, the undertakers arrived and conferred with Aunt Louisa in the front parlour, then Aunt Elsie was boxed and taken off in the back of a van. All the while William remained in his room with the door closed, working silently on Neuschwanstein and wondering if things would be different from now on.

Aunt Elsie paid the bills and performed rudimentary repairs to the property and went into Croydon now and then to deal with 'the trust'. This was always mentioned in reverent tones as though it were an oracle that had to be consulted and obeyed. Over the years he had heard it spoken of only by listening behind doors; it concerned money and could therefore never be discussed openly. 'We'll have to see what we can get out of the trust,' Aunt Elsie might say or, more rarely, 'Thank God for the trust.'

He had finished the edge now and began to sort the remaining pieces by colour: the grey roofs, the blue sky, the white castle walls, the yellow trees. He already knew which rooms would be his: the rectangular tower with its 360-degree viewing platform, from which he could watch the birds. He had read about Ludwig II of Bavaria in his encyclopaedia during the year when he had barely left his room and felt sorry for the reluctant king. In fact, he had read every single entry at least once, but some had impressed themselves on his memory more forcefully than others.

That was another thing that would be different without Aunt Elsie – the acquisition of knowledge would become more haphazard. She was the one who knew the answers to things, because she read books from the library about the lives of great men, inventors, scientists and generals. Whereas Aunt Louisa read only romances and never knew the answer to anything but had a kinder heart.

Another consequence of Aunt Elsie's death, which now occurred to him with guilty dismay, was that it would take longer to use up a box of Brooke Bond, which meant fewer tea cards for his collection. He already had nearly all of the British birds, apart from the puffin and the nightjar, and a dozen of the newer wildflowers.

Their first meal together, three having become two, was a strange and subdued affair. Aunt Louisa kept sniffing and saying 'Oh dear,' and casting glances at the empty chair, which was irrational in William's view, as the chair had been unoccupied all the while Aunt Elsie was in bed anyway.

'I should have made her go to hospital, but she was so stubborn,' she lamented, mopping her eyes with her napkin.

'I wonder where she is now,' William said.

Aunt Louisa looked at him in surprise. 'With Mother and Father, and Selwyn and Alma, and Rose. And God and Jesus and all the angels,' she added as an afterthought.

'If you believe in all that stuff, why don't you go to church?'

He hadn't meant it like that anyway. It was the body in that black box that concerned him. Was it in a room somewhere, stacked with others awaiting burial? He hated the thought of being shut in a box, even dead. He would rather be thrown on the compost heap and eaten by foxes, but when it came to his turn, he supposed, there would be no one left to do the throwing. This thought was alarming and he turned his mind from it.

'Because the pews are hard and it's full of busybodies,' Aunt Louisa replied.

Of all the classes of people to be feared, 'busybodies' were the foremost, closely followed by 'the authorities'. Death, unfortunately, seemed to necessitate a collision with both groups. This, compounded by grief, had robbed Aunt Louisa of all appetite; she cut off the untouched portion of her fish and pushed it towards William.

He flipped it onto his plate, feeling a little ashamed that Aunt Elsie's death had not diminished his hunger in any way. If anything, it had made him more aware of his body, the heart beating, the blood circulating, his breath coming and going, the whole machine in good order and needing only fuel. He wondered whether there would be more to eat now – three portions divided two ways – or whether Aunt Louisa would adjust the quantities downwards. He knew she had a sweet tooth, whereas Aunt Elsie disapproved of eating between meals and had the sort of lean, wiry frame that was powered by strong tea and self-denial.

He had his answer that night. At eight o'clock, the regular hour for hot milk and a biscuit, Aunt Louisa had passed him the tin of shortbread and said, with a guilty glance at the wing-backed armchair, its depressed cushions still bearing the imprint of Aunt Elsie's bony rump, 'Take two.'

She seemed to be working herself up to say something else; fidgeting in her chair and taking great sighing breaths. When he looked up at her, she gave him a smile that was anything but reassuring.

'You could come, you know.'

'Come where?'

'To the funeral with me.'

The ground seemed to tilt beneath him. 'You mean outside?'

'Yes. I think . . . I think it would be all right.'

This was such an astonishing claim in every way that for a moment he was speechless. He thought of the last few occasions when he had left the house, even briefly and with good reason, and broke out in a sudden drenching sweat.

'It's never been all right,' he said.

Aunt Louisa was fiddling with her necklace of glass beads.

'I know Elsie did what she thought was best. And she was so forceful, one didn't like to disagree with her. But since then, so much time has passed. How old are you now?'

'Twenty-nine.'

'Twenty-nine,' she repeated, almost in disbelief. 'I don't think it would hurt if you went to the funeral. If you felt like it.'

'But I don't feel like it.'

Aunt Louisa turned her face to one side, blinking. 'No, well, that's understandable.'

There was a clatter as the necklace, which she had been twisting and tugging, disintegrated in her hands, sending glass beads skimming across the floor.

On the morning of the funeral William found Aunt Louisa in the kitchen, sponging specks of mildew from the shoulders of her black wool coat. She had been younger and slimmer the last time she had worn it and it didn't quite meet across her middle. Her hair had been taken down from its scaffolding of pins, brushed out and then replaited and twisted into a low bun to accommodate a black feathered hat. Her face was powdered, her lips a ghastly clownish red. She didn't normally use make-up and wore it now with a kind of wincing discomfort, like new shoes. She had deliberated for some time over the undertaker's suggestion of a black car to follow the hearse. It seemed a waste of money for one person, when she could easily get the bus and meet them at the crematorium.

'But was it really the done thing?' she asked William, as if he would know.

If only Elsie had been around to ask – she would undoubtedly have had a view. There was a list, the folded sheet of paper, that Elsie had written a few days before her death. Louisa had opened it and on seeing the first three instructions – ring doctor, ring undertaker, register death (town hall) – had closed it up with a superstitious yelp and stuffed it in her apron pocket.

She retrieved it and spread it on her knee, squinting at it through half-closed eyes in case it contained truths too dazzling to be faced. Seated opposite her, reading upside down, William could hear Aunt Elsie's brisk tones in the list of instructions:

- Ring doctor
- Ring undertaker
- Register death (town hall)
- Choose cheapest coffin – <u>ask</u>!

- No black car – regular taxi
- No flowers – use dried arrangement on my chest of drawers
- Cremation – ashes in memorial garden with Mother and Father
- Solicitor for will and for the trust – Mr Eckerty, North End, Croydon

Poor Aunt Elsie, he thought, in her last days on Earth reduced to an administrator of her own funeral because he and Aunt Louisa could not be expected to know how things were done.

'I'll be back in two hours,' Aunt Louisa promised, forcing her puffy hands into tight black gloves. 'Perhaps at one o'clock you could bow your head and say a prayer for your aunty.'

She stood at the front door watching for the taxi so that the meter wouldn't 'gobble up all of our money', as she phrased it. There was a false start as she misidentified the rattle of the grocer's van, trotted down the path and had to retreat, but finally the car arrived and carried her off.

William put his head on one side and considered the vast, silent emptiness of the house. It was not the only time he had been left alone, but such occasions were rare enough to stand out in memory. He could think of no particular way of capitalising on this sovereignty. His hand strayed to the front of his trousers and then he remembered what day it was and felt ashamed.

Aunt Louisa had left him a ham and cheese sandwich for lunch with thick white bread cut from a split tin loaf. The unexpected largesse of the double filling, a treat to comfort him in his loneliness on a dark day, made his heart flip with excitement. They usually took their midday meal at twelve thirty and William could see no reason to deviate from this. He was too hungry to delay and if he ate early he would have a longer wait until dinner. He took his time over the sandwich, savouring the salty collision of flavours. It was gone too soon and, although no longer ravenous, he felt a kind of grief as he looked at the few breadcrumbs on the plate. He wondered if Aunt Louisa would let him have the same again tomorrow or whether it was an extravagance never to be repeated.

At one o'clock, as agreed, he closed his eyes and tried to conjure some happy memories of Aunt Elsie. She had never struck him; she had taught him chess and backgammon and procured interesting books from the library; she had protected him from 'the authorities'; she had rescued him from the thugs at the fairground and dressed his wounds; she had found him frozen half to death in the coal-hole when he had got shut out in the snow and warmed him back to life. But the things for which he could not forgive her – Boswell, Mrs Kenley – kept crowding into his mind, elbowing out the kind thoughts. It was always the way: his thoughts wouldn't be corralled or kept in line or banished elsewhere and the more he tried to evict the unwelcome ones, the more tenaciously they took up residence. *Don't think about it!* was surely the most useless advice ever spoken.

In the afternoon he took his sketch pad and pencil into Aunt Elsie's room, until her illness a place he had never had cause to enter. It had been somewhat tidied by Aunt Louisa: the bedclothes straightened, the bell replaced on the table, the curtains opened. They had moved the paraffin heater back to the front parlour, where it was needed on cold evenings. It moved him to see her slippers standing empty and her dressing gown hanging, round-shouldered, from a hook on the door.

From her window he could see a beautiful American oak, its bare branches sharply shadowed by the glancing afternoon sun and thinning out to a reddish frill like a diagram of a human lung. He sat and looked at it for ten minutes in the steady, attentive way he always did before beginning to draw anything so as to really see it, in all its particular living beauty. Then he worked as if in a trance, his right hand skimming over the page, covering it with a tracery of fine lines. It had to be done today; the light, changing all the time, would be quite different tomorrow. He couldn't work fast enough; the sun was dropping, the shadows stretching.

When he put down his pencil he was surprised to find that it was after three. Aunt Louisa was late. Now that he was conscious that her return was overdue, he couldn't help listening and watching for it. He wasn't missing her exactly, but her non-appearance was unsettling and his growing anxiety could only be allayed by the sound of her key in the lock.

By four o'clock it was dusk and he was confronted with a dilemma. Four was the hour appointed for tea and a biscuit (two biscuits since the death of Aunt Elsie). Was he to proceed without Aunt Louisa, only for her to arrive ten minutes later to a lukewarm pot? If she didn't return until dinner time, he would have missed out on tea altogether, for nothing. He carefully weighed the implications of each pathway before deciding to fill the kettle and set it on the stove, willing her to come back before it boiled. Its gathering whistle, normally a sound full of promise, was raucous and menacing in the stillness.

He drank his tea and ate two shortbread biscuits, but they gave him no pleasure. He couldn't think of any innocent reason why she would have failed to return. It occurred to him that he didn't even know where the crematorium was. There was no one to ask. Perhaps she had not had enough money to settle the funeral bill and had been detained by 'the authorities'. He wished now that he had handed over the £60 from Aunt Elsie, but Aunt Louisa had made no mention of being short of cash.

By six o'clock it was as dark as midnight and a mean sliver of moon glittered over the rooftops. A coach rumbled down the road, its brightly lit interior visible through the tree-filled garden, throwing sweeping shadows across the walls of the unlit parlour. William could not remember a single occasion since the war when Aunt Louisa had stayed out after dark and he felt himself on the verge of terrible panic. She had left no instructions regarding dinner. In the fridge was a wax paper packet of raw mince, oozing blood. In the vegetable rack were two onions and some frostbitten carrots. The sack of potatoes was in the larder. He wasn't sure how these elements combined to form cottage pie, one of their regular evening meals, cooking was so completely Aunt Louisa's business. Things were chopped and boiled or fried or put in the oven, that much he knew, but in what order and for how long was a mystery.

There was always the ham and cheese, of course, which even he knew how to deploy, so he built himself a replica of the lunchtime sandwich and ate it at the kitchen table, appreciating it as much as was possible while the worry over Aunt Louisa chewed at his guts.

The rest of the evening stretched ahead, to be filled somehow or just endured. He had never before relied on Aunt Louisa to entertain him and would happily pass hours in his room alone, but with her missing – the alarming word came to him for the first time now – his solitude couldn't be enjoyed.

At the back of his mind was the fear that there was something, besides waiting, that he ought to be doing and that he might be scolded for not having done when she returned. His confusion was total. However, it seemed important to honour the normal routines; to do otherwise would test fate, sending out a signal that Aunt Louisa was no longer needed. So at eight o'clock he made hot milk, for one.

He knew how to do this as he had seen it done. There was a particular saucepan for milk, just as there was one – white and scaley – for boiling eggs. Knowing this did not stop the milk from rising up and overflowing all down the side of the pan and into the gas jets, leaving only a scant half a mug to go with his two biscuits.

Bedtime presented another problem. The locking of doors back and front against intruders was a nightly ritual that was never neglected, but that was when they were all safely inside. He couldn't leave Aunt Louisa on the wrong side of a bolted door. After careful consideration of alternatives, William decided to lock up as normal but sit out the night in the front parlour so that he would hear the clang of the front gate and be ready to jump up and let her in at any hour.

He could picture it all so clearly that he was almost cheerful as he fetched blankets and pillow from his attic room and settled himself in the armchair with his legs extended across the tapestry footstool. He had *The Hobbit*, an old favourite, to read by the friendly glow of a table lamp. But as the grandmother clock scraped and chimed its way around the hours, he lost confidence again, unable to explain to himself why and how she might come home in the middle of the night. Sometime after twelve, the book slipped from his hand and he dozed.

He was woken by the sound of the council dustcart in the side road, the shouts of the dustmen and the clash of metal bin lids. In his anxiety he had forgotten they were due. Dragging the old zinc bin from behind the side gate into the front garden was another thing Aunt Elsie did that had fallen to Aunt Louisa. Now, their rubbish would go uncollected for another week. His blankets had shuffled down to his feet and he was cold and stiff-necked from the unfamiliar contours of the armchair.

She was not coming back. He would have to manage, like Robinson Crusoe, he thought, only better off because far from being cast adrift, he was safe indoors, with everything he needed for living. Invoking one of his fictional heroes gave him courage and he resolved to be similarly industrious and resourceful so that if Aunt Louisa did return, he could show her all the things he had accomplished on his own.

The first job after dressing was to relight the kitchen boiler in order to heat the water, warm the kitchen and prevent the pipes from freezing. He used fresh coal from the scuttle, shovelling the cold dead ash and clinker into a bucket. After dark, he would empty it in the garden and refill the scuttle from the bunker.

Breakfast was the next hurdle. The milk was on the doorstep and would need bringing in, because there would be no porridge without it and it was part of Aunt Elsie's lore that uncollected milk bottles were the sort of things to attract the attention of busybodies.

It was daylight now, a bright winter morning with a crust of hard frost glittering on the path. He hovered behind the front door in a state of uncertainty for some minutes. Opening it no more than an inch, he checked that all was quiet and no pedestrians or vehicles were passing. His heart clubbing wildly, he stepped outside and was immediately dazzled by the daylight. The gate, the path, the garden of brambles blurred and swam.

After snatching up the two milk bottles, he retreated inside and shouldered the door shut, leaning against it for a moment to recuperate. Apart from the whooshing of blood in his ears, all was quiet. He risked a glimpse through the rippled glass in the central panel. Nothing.

William thought he knew the principles of porridge making, but he misjudged the quantities and the resulting gloop grew thicker and thicker, requiring more and more milk to bring it to order, until he had a whole panful, enough to last a week, bubbling and popping on the stove. Well, he thought, it would get eaten one way or another.

It surprised him how much time was taken up with the business of living; half the morning gone already and he hadn't picked up a book or a pencil. He experienced a belated appreciation for the many invisible offices performed without thanks by Aunt Elsie and Aunt Louisa. The jobs women did weren't difficult, but they certainly ate up the hours.

In the garden two squirrels were playing chase, flowing up and down the trunk of the hornbeam, jumping from branch to slender branch. He stood and watched them for a long time, transported, as he always was, by the freedom of animals. Sometimes they stopped and appeared to be watching him, or rather checking that he was watching them, before bounding off again.

There was a grey film on the windowpane. He rubbed at it with the cuff of his jumper, clearing a fist-sized hole. Plucking the tea towel from its rubber grip, he finished the job begun by his sleeve. The glass was suddenly, shockingly, clear; every pine needle, leaf and filament of frost leapt into the sharpest focus. The tea towel was now filthy. He set about washing it out, an enterprise only partly successful, which left a tidemark of scum around the sink. Dirt is never destroyed, only transferred, he thought, dispirited by this experience of housework.

Now, it was lunchtime. There was enough bread, stale but not mouldy, for another ham and cheese sandwich. The crust he tore into pieces and flung out of the kitchen door for the birds.

In the afternoon he went back to his drawing of the oak tree, but the clouds had rolled in now and it looked quite different today, the branches somehow flatter, without any definition, so instead he read *The Hobbit* until it was time for tea and two biscuits. He stayed in the kitchen, where it was warm from the boiler, rather than moving to the front parlour and it occurred to him that Louisa had only been away just over twenty-four hours and already he was doing things differently.

He would have to tackle the mince eventually, but not tonight. There was still ham and cheese to be finished, so he ate the remains of each with a spoonful of what he thought was chutney but turned out to be mincemeat and not so very different. He reassured himself that if Aunt Louisa turned up tomorrow, she would have nothing to reproach him with. He found it perfectly possible to hold two contradictory thoughts in his mind at once and believed with equal conviction that she would be back at any moment and that he would never see her again.

At night-time he locked and bolted the doors and went upstairs to his attic room, and although he was just as restless and wakeful as before, he was at least comfortable in his own bed.

On the fifth day of William's solitude, the fresh food ran out. There were, of course, jars of preserved fruit and tins of spam, beans, rice pudding, pink salmon, pilchards, peas, carrots and chicken soup by the dozen in the larder. But these, he had always been given to understand, were for emergencies – another war, perhaps – and he wasn't entirely sure whether his situation qualified as an emergency, so he didn't touch them.

He had reheated the porridge each day to an ever more glutinous consistency and used up all the eggs, scrambling them to rubber. The mince he had put in a saucepan with a little water and stirred over a high heat until it turned grey. He tipped it into the enamel dish Aunt Louisa always used for cottage pie and directed his attention to the potatoes. The peeler was a drum that stood in the corner of the kitchen, with a rotating base and sides lined with coarse metallic grit like crushed diamonds. By attaching the pink rubber hose to the cold tap and cranking the handle at speed, he could flay a pound of potatoes in under a minute.

Even at a rolling boil, they took a long time to turn to mash, the outsides collapsing first, while the inner core remained stubbornly solid. Eventually, the whole lot was reduced to a watery slurry, flecked with the last few scraps of peel. This he flopped on top of the mince, which was now cold and congealed, and then put the dish in the oven, hoping that some miraculous alchemy would take place within to transform these unpromising beginnings into Aunt Louisa's cottage pie. The result was disappointing; only hunger and an ingrained aversion to waste made it edible.

Sometimes he stood in front of the shelf of tins and surveyed the colourful labels with longing, calculating how long this bounty might last. Even if he used only one a day – an ungenerous allowance if the tin in question contained something like peaches – they would be gone within three months. And then what? There was always milk, on the doorstep every morning. He marvelled at the human ingenuity, the organisation, the chain of individual skills responsible for this daily blessing. If there had only been an equivalent system for the delivery of bread and butter, cheese and ham, he would have asked for nothing more.

A week after Louisa's departure, William was raking out the boiler early in the morning when the doorbell rang. The sound sent a jolt through him and he froze, crouched on his heels. He waited a moment and then crept out into the hallway and scurried upstairs to his usual vantage point for reconnaissance work behind the curtain in Aunt Rose's room.

He was just in time to see the milk float pulling away from the kerb. On the doorstep, along with the usual pint bottles was a note requesting payment of eight shillings and ninepence. This was a problem. If he didn't settle the bill, the milkman would keep returning and ringing the bell, and might even stop delivering altogether.

There was the envelope of cash inside *Treasure Island*. He could put a five-pound note out with the empties, but this was far too large a sum to leave on the doorstep and likely to cause complications if the milkman didn't have enough change. He might feel inclined to ring the doorbell again. The ramifications were disturbing. As far as William was aware, there was no other money in the house.

He sat for a while at the kitchen table and applied himself to the matter. He could see what he needed to do and it would solve both of his problems: the lack of change and the shortage of fresh food. It was a bold plan and something he would not have chosen, but Aunt Louisa had said it would be all right and these were unparalleled times.

He found a piece of notepaper in the bureau and, in his neat, childish script, wrote:

I have gone to the shops to get some food as we have run out.
I will not talk to anyone. I will come straight back.
    William.

Over his usual ensemble of shirt, pullover and trousers, he put on his wool coat bought for him by Aunt Elsie from Kennards after the time when he nearly froze to death in the snow. He had hardly had occasion to wear it since, but he hadn't done any more growing and it still fitted as well as it ever had, which was not all that well. Slippers wouldn't do for February, so he wore his old leather boots.

In the hall wardrobe, among the mangy furs and shabby mackintoshes, was a homburg belonging to his grandfather, Ernest Julius Tapping, founder in 1904 of the chain of grocery stores bearing his name, who looked out from his portrait over the fireplace as though with a faint air of disappointment at the remnants of his dynasty.

The hat, he felt, would afford him protection from the bright sunlight and the stares of strangers. He had taken one of the five-pound notes from its hiding place and put it in his inside pocket, pressed against his pounding heart. Deploying the same precautions for taking in the milk, he checked that no one was passing before stepping out and pulling the door shut behind him.

His hand tightly gripped the keys to reassure himself that he was not locked out, but even so, the feeling of being on the other side of the closed door was extraordinary and terrifying, and it took him a moment or two to gather himself before he could turn and face the street and the world beyond it. He walked down the path and through the iron gate, blinking against the sun.

A little way ahead of him on the pavement, a man and woman were walking arm in arm. At the sound of the gate, they turned to look at him and he met their careless glance with an expression of pure panic. The woman made a whispered remark to her companion, who turned again. A car swished past; he could feel the eyes of the driver on him as little points of heat on the back of his neck. A coach thundered down the hill, swaying perilously close to the kerb and buffeting him so that he clutched at his hat. The passengers turned as one, staring at him, their faces furious with accusation. At the corner a man on a solid black bicycle with a trailer full of packages squealed to a halt at the junction. He rang his bell and shouted something at William as he pedalled away, his actual words lost in a gust of wind.

In the distance a group of schoolboys approached on the way to the park, kitted out for football, their studs clattering on the pavement. They had already noticed him and soon they would surround him on the narrow path. Beneath his feet, the ground heaved and swelled; above, the sky was enormous, the clouds hectic.

And then, suddenly, at a command from their schoolmaster at the back, the crowd of boys stopped their jostling and shoving and parted, falling neatly into two columns. Between them, advancing unsteadily but with great dignity and purpose, in a black coat and with her feathered hat balanced on top of her bandaged head, was Aunt Louisa.

For a moment it seemed they might throw their arms around each other, there in the street, but the feeling passed.

'I thought you were never coming home,' William said, realising only now that she was back how sorely he had missed her. 'Where have you been?'

'Worrying about you, that's where,' his aunt replied, which was no kind of answer. 'I've had such a time of it. How long have I been away?'

'A week,' he said, wondering what could have happened to make her unable to count the days.

'A week!' Her eyes were round with disbelief, but seconds later she was distracted by his appearance. 'Your grandfather had a hat just like that,' she chuckled.

He steered her back towards the house, relief mixed with disquiet. There had been too much change lately; all he wanted was for life to go back to normal.

Chapter 14

On the evening of the Royal Medico-Psychological Association summer dinner, for which Lionel Frant had tickets but no partner, Helen and Gil went out to a Chinese restaurant in Soho, chosen because it was far enough from his family and hers to be quite safe. It was a newish establishment and had yet to attract a regular clientele; the dining room was chilly and almost empty.

Gil was in a gloomy mood because he had learnt earlier that day of Morley Holt's intention to retire at the end of August. The news had been announced at an afternoon staff meeting and it had thrown a considerable shadow over their evening, for reasons Helen couldn't quite understand. The opportunities for a night out did not arise so often that they could be careless with them and it was taking all of her patience to keep this one on track.

'Will you apply for the job?' she asked as the waiter brought tiny blue-and-white porcelain bowls of clear, glutinous soup, in which threads of chicken and yellow beads of sweetcorn were suspended.

'I suppose I'll have to,' Gil sighed.

'Why, if you don't want it?'

Helen shivered in her thin cardigan, envying Gil his corduroy jacket. The tablecloth was cold, almost damp to the touch, while the white wine was warm.

'Because Lionel certainly will and if he gets it, I shall have to resign.'

'You wouldn't!'

He stared at her in surprise. 'You underestimate me.'

This mention of Lionel made her uncomfortable. She had not told him about Lionel's invitation and her refusal, knowing that Gil would take an unseemly pleasure in the idea of his colleague's humiliation. It was the first secret she had kept from him and even she could see that it was an odd one to choose. She felt no allegiance to Lionel and if the incident flattered anyone, it was her. 'Look at me,' she might have said. 'Quite the prize, aren't I?' But she didn't say it, or even think it overmuch. And then, today, as she passed Gil in the corridor at speed on her way to the refectory, he had reached across and tucked the label into the back of her collar just as Lionel was coming around the corner. It was not the gesture of a colleague and Helen felt sure Lionel must have noted it.

'What about your patients?' Helen said, laying down her flat-bottomed porcelain spoon. 'You wouldn't just abandon them?'

'If Lionel becomes superintendent, there soon won't be any patients,' Gil retorted.

There was only one other couple in the restaurant, eating in an unbroken silence, suggestive of a decades-long marriage, and Helen was aware of their own voices carrying.

'What do you mean?' she whispered, having a sudden vision of Lionel stalking the corridors of Westbury Park with a giant syringe of paraldehyde, dispatching the inmates left and right.

'They want to close these big places down and turf everyone back out into society,' Gil replied, pushing his bowl away to indicate that he was finished.

This was a gesture that Helen had only just noticed and begun to find irksome. A hovering waiter immediately pounced to clear their plates.

'And Lionel certainly won't put up a fight. He'd do anything to curry favour with that shit, Powell.'

The waiter's face remained politely impassive in the face of this attack on the former Health Minister.

'Why would Lionel want to close down his own hospital?' Helen asked. 'Put himself and everyone else out of a job. It makes no sense.'

'He probably fancies a career in politics.'

He produced a pack of Players from his jacket pocket and shook out a cigarette. In her company, he only smoked between courses and after sex. Very early in their relationship he had lit up when they were together in his car and she had opened the window an inch to stop the smell from getting in her hair. He had stubbed out the cigarette straight away and said, humbly, 'I'll give up if you want me to.'

She had thought, He will give up for me, but not for his asthmatic daughter. Naturally, she had not asked it of him and he had continued to smoke, in those limited contexts when together and with greater dedication when apart.

The waiters, gliding silently on the soft carpet, brought a multitude of dishes all at once – spring rolls, fried rice, sweet and sour pork, beef chop suey and chicken chow mein – and conversation was suspended while they dealt with the food. For Helen, eating out was still a thrill and a treat, especially when it marked no special anniversary or occasion. She saw it as a sign of how far she had shaken off her background.

Her parents detested foreign food, without ever having tasted it, and never went to restaurants in case they encountered an unfamiliar flavour or were exposed to ridicule in some way. Even Mrs Gordon had been a more adventurous cook than her mother, though her experiments had not always been welcome. Clive had inherited some of their parents' prejudices, against garlic and mushrooms, and rice except as a pudding, but June had at least managed to introduce spaghetti into the family menu.

Once the waiters had departed, and she and Gil had achieved a certain rhythm with their chopsticks, Helen returned to the subject of the changes at Westbury Park.

'I think you'd make a very good superintendent. You could run the place just as you like – appoint people who share your ideas.'

'My ideas are too radical. The nursing staff would all leave. Can you imagine if I told them we are no longer prescribing Largactil and sodium amytal. There'd be a riot – and not just the patients.' He gave a chesty laugh.

'Perhaps that's because the nurses can see for themselves that the patients benefit.'

'But do they?' Gil said, plucking a single dried shrimp from the rice. 'They may sleep more, and be calmer and more manageable, which is certainly a benefit for the people looking after them.'

'Why not just ask the patients themselves if they feel better for it?'

He slapped the table and the crockery jumped.

'There you have it! If we just listened more and treated less.'

'I thought you partly agreed with the idea of closing these places down, anyway. If you don't believe half the people in there are ill, surely getting them back out is the goal?'

'I don't say they're not suffering in some way. I just begin to despair of the revolving-door effect. There must be a better way.'

'You sound so defeated, Gil,' Helen said, chasing a slippery water chestnut around the bowl with her chopsticks. 'As if we're doing no good at all.'

Gil had abandoned his chopsticks now and was using a spoon. Helen struggled on. It was a matter of courtesy, she felt.

'Of course I'd be very much in favour of patients and thera-pists living together in smaller communities, without these rigid hierarchies,' he went on. 'But I don't imagine for a moment that will happen.'

'And how do you propose to break down the doctor–patient hierarchy? It will take more than just removing your white coat. Or swapping seats.'

She had walked in on one of his consultations recently to find him lying at full stretch on the couch in an attitude of deep relaxation, while his patient, a young man called Martin, sat in Gil's swivel chair with his feet up on the desk.

'That would be a start. Symbolically.'

'You'd still be the doctor. Whatever you wear and wherever you sit,' she said, and he laughed.

He never minded her mockery or disagreement because his confidence in his rightness was already impregnable. Even if he couldn't defend it in words, it existed at some deeper, untouchable level.

'The truth of the matter is that for a lot of our patients the best we can do is care, not cure.'

'Would you put William in that category?' Helen asked.

'I certainly can't imagine him living independently.' He watched her labours with the chopsticks with amusement. 'They use spoons in Southeast Asia, you know,' he said.

'It seems rude not to make an effort, though,' Helen replied, deftly capturing a single wizened pea from the fried rice.

Gil made a show of peering around the room in search of this phantom audience. 'Do you think the waiter cares about your choice of cutlery or has even noticed? He is probably worrying about whether he can pay his rent this month, or wondering if his wife's lack of interest in sex is permanent, or whether his son will pass the eleven-plus.'

'Then we'd better tip generously to help allay at least one of his worries.'

Gil leant across the table to kiss her, extinguishing the candle with the sudden movement.

'You want even waiters to love you,' he said.

It wasn't that, she thought. All of her minuscule acts of kindness, charity, unselfishness were like grains of sand dropped into the scale to try to balance the great boulder of Wrong that she perpetrated every day against Kath and The Children.

'And you want even patients to love you,' she replied.

'Only as much as I love them.' He threw back the last mouthful of wine. 'Which isn't much.'

Their conversation, Helen realised, had hardly strayed beyond the precincts of Westbury Park, as though this were the only thing that united them. They had told all of their history, many times, and Gil was not one to dwell on the past or romanticise his youth. Talking of the future, though, raised uncomfortable reminders of how far off was any prospect of their situation changing.

'Did I tell you I've started drawing again?' she said, remembering something recent that she could tell him. She had taken a sketch pad with her on a walk after work, just as she had advised Lorraine to do, and done a series of quick studies.

'No. I don't think I knew that you had stopped.'

'It struck me that I'd barely picked up a pencil since I left college. Not surprisingly, I was a bit rusty.'

The waiter materialised at their table to relight the wick.

'So it's more like playing a piano than riding a bicycle?' Gil said when they were alone again.

'Yes. And I haven't been practising my scales. But I'm going to get back into the habit.'

'I like the idea of you swishing through the long grass with your easel.'

'Well, it wasn't really like that,' Helen admitted. 'I just sat on a bench by the allotments.'

The silent couple in the corner had finished their meal and paid their bill and were now being helped into their coats. The waiter hurried ahead of them to open the door; a blast of cool London air, smelling of drains, rushed in as they departed.

'Promise me we'll never reach that stage,' said Gil, shaking his head.

Helen didn't reply, because she was watching the woman tuck her hand into the crook of her husband's arm and lay her cheek for the briefest moment on his shoulder as they waited at the kerb for a taxi. Far from despising them, she had been thinking how pleasant it must be to have such a careless abundance of time together that whole evenings could be comfortably squandered without a word spoken.

Chapter 15

Helen was in the art room watching one of the long-stay patients apply sweeping strokes of poster paint to the back of a roll of wallpaper with the finesse of someone creosoting a fence. Smashing Mathilda, as she was known to the orderlies when they were out of earshot of senior staff, chattered and chuckled to herself as she worked and took such obvious pleasure in her task that Helen could not bring herself to suggest any refinements to this technique. Mathilda had earnt her nickname from a tendency to seize and destroy any china crockery that she came across, even if presently in use by someone else – a much less alarming proposition in the art room than in the refectory.

At one of the other tables, a middle-aged woman called Cynthia, who preferred to work on a smaller scale, was attempting a self-portrait in chalks. She had been admitted several times during Helen's tenure, suffering from a form of nervous collapse, and seemed to view Westbury Park as a haven from the chaos of life outside. After a few weeks of medication and recuperation, she would be discharged back into the care of her demanding husband and selfish in-laws, who would treat her with marginally more consideration for a few months and then the cycle would begin again.

'There is nothing wrong with her,' Gil insisted to Helen. 'It's her circumstances that are intolerable. What she really needs is someone to tell her husband not to be a shit.'

She was not the only patient with this kind of presentation. Helen felt particularly protective of the various Cynthias at the Park, seeing in them something of her own mother. Of course there was no possibility that Mrs Hansford would ever admit herself to what she called a mental hospital or consider one a place of refuge. Her breakdowns, when they occurred, took place in the home, behind net curtains and clenched teeth and hands pressed against ears.

It was a warm day and the upper windows were open, admitting air scented with detergent. From the laundry block came the rumble of the huge machines, the clang of metal cages being shunted back and forth and the brisk, barked calls of the workers.

Mathilda had covered all the exposed paper and a fair amount of the table with her brushstrokes and, with Helen's assistance, was now unrolling a fresh expanse to conquer, dragging the painted section onto the floor, where it gathered in loose, wet folds.

A faint sound of scratching on wood made Helen look up and she saw William peering through the glass panel. At her approach, he retreated and she found him loitering in the corridor some way off. His cheeks and neck were still ravaged by nicks and the raised spots of a shaving rash, but he had removed his sunglasses.

It was the first time she had seen his face so exposed and she found it disconcerting to be able to look into his eyes, which were dark brown with a bluish cast at the edge of the iris. He had a way of looking both at and through her, focusing on a point beyond the back of her head and interrupting contact with a series of rapid blinks.

No one has really looked at him for years, she thought, and so she lowered her gaze and said, 'Come in. We're only a small group today, but if you want to be by yourself, there's a side room you can use.'

He followed her into the studio and stood just inside the doorway, as though deciding whether to bolt before committing himself. Then he walked over to the print of Dürer's *Melencolia I* on the wall behind her desk and stared at it for some minutes.

'What's he doing here?' Mathilda said in a whisper that carried to all four corners of the room.

Helen saw William's shoulders stiffen and replied, 'He's come to draw and paint, same as you.'

This satisfied Mathilda, who returned to her wallpaper, chuntering under her breath.

At last, William turned and spotted his own sketches of fox, badger, cat and magpie displayed on the wall between prints of Van Gogh's boots and Wright's experiment on a bird in the air pump, and a swift blush spread over his face to the roots of his wiry hair.

Helen had assumed he would opt for the privacy of the storeroom, but instead he sat at a table in the corner, appearing somewhat dazed by the profusion of materials at his disposal. After examining the sharpened pencils of different grades, the boxes of coloured pastels and chalks, the crayons, charcoal and watercolour palettes, and making some experimental marks on his paper to test for thickness of line and colour, he chose a cobalt blue pastel and pushed the rest aside.

Helen watched him turn it over and over in his fingers, twirling it like a baton, while his gaze roved around the room, flicking this way and that, as though he were somehow memorising the shapes and angles. This went on for some time until she wondered if this was as much as he could manage for one day. Then, smoothing out the A3 page in front of him, he put his head down and, without looking up again, began to sketch very fast, with his arm moving loosely from the shoulder, the sharp edge of the pastel skating over the paper.

After fifteen minutes he stopped and sat up, looking critically from the drawing to the room and back again. Helen moved closer, not stealthily but keeping a considerate distance, as you might with an apparently tame creature who might be startled. She had made the mistake before with patients of showing too quick and keen an interest in their work before they were ready, prompting them to screw up the page or deface it before her eyes.

Even at this safe distance, and seeing it upside down, she could see it was a remarkable drawing, the scale and perspective of the room perfectly captured, faithful to the details of the shapes and forms but with a flowing freedom of line. There was Mathilda, hunched over her table, and Cynthia in the background, and Helen herself, standing by her desk, alert and watchful. There had been people at college – but not many – who had this gift to translate solid forms effortlessly into lines and spaces. You couldn't teach it and she knew that she herself didn't have it.

The most striking thing, to Helen's mind, was how different in style this sketch was from his fine, minutely detailed ink drawings of birds and animals. From the sheer number of these that she had uncovered, she had imagined this ultra-realistic draughtsmanship to be his only skill, perfected over many years of his incarceration.

Mathilda, having run out of poster paint and looking to replenish her stock, sidled over. 'Oh, that's good,' she said, her ability to appreciate talent in others only sharpened by her own struggles. 'That's proper art. Look at this, Cynthia,' she called. 'We're even in it. Look at my fat back!' she cackled.

William defended himself from this sudden searchlight of female attention with a sustained attack of blinking. Helen led Mathilda back to her table and mixed up a fresh pot of poster paint. She had always tried to discourage patients from passing comment on each other's work, but at the same time she felt a teacher's natural joy in a student's talent and the fierce desire to nurture it.

Over the following days William returned to the art room daily unless it was especially busy and the tables and side rooms already occupied. Sometimes he made no effort to produce any work but occupied himself washing brushes, sharpening pencils or tidying the coloured pastels, arranging them in their boxes according to colour or length as the mood directed. He was not the only patient who enjoyed this kind of task and sometimes Helen found herself having to disarrange trays of neatly regimented materials before morning classes so that there would be enough disorder to go around. It made her think back to the unpicking of rugs that had so incensed her on her arrival at Westbury Park. It's not the same, she told herself. It's not the same at all.

Chapter 16

On Saturday afternoon Helen was tackling her overdue house-work, scouring the bath with Ajax powder, when there was a knock at the door of her flat. As she had not heard the bell ring downstairs, she assumed it must be one of the residents, most likely Mr Rafferty. Since her offering of the leftover boeuf bourguignon, he had returned the Pyrex dish along with a gift of potted hyacinths.

Touched by his gratitude and his evident loneliness, she had got into the habit on Sundays of cooking a double helping of something hearty like a casserole or fish pie and taking a portion down to him. During the week she generally ate lunch at work and made do in the evening with a simple omelette or ham salad, but she enjoyed cooking and, with an appreciative recipient for her creations, began to look forward to this small act of neighbourly service.

Persuaded that it must be Mr Rafferty, it took Helen a second or two to recognise the caller, in spring coat and headscarf, as June, so unexpected was her presence on the doorstep. June had never visited the flat before, was not a believer in dropping in, and was a reluctant and nervous driver.

Clive had bought her a little Ford Anglia to give her some independence and keep her away from his Rover, but a fear of turning right was proving a serious obstacle. Avoiding this manoeuvre would frequently involve June in multiple diversions, taking her further and further from her destination. On occasions she had been known to abandon the car halfway and complete the journey on foot rather than cross a busy main road.

For a moment Helen was assailed by the alarming idea that Clive had walked out on her, pushed to the brink by her neurotic tidying, perhaps, and she was unable to keep a note of panic from her voice.

'June. Whatever is it? Is everything all right?' she babbled, ushering her over the threshold. 'I didn't hear the bell.'

'Some old man with a dog was just coming out as I came in. I'm sorry to barge in on you like this,' said June, pressing the back of her hand to her forehead to demonstrate nerves tested to destruction. 'I didn't know who else to talk to.'

Disconcerted by this partial compliment, Helen led June into her sitting room, casting a wary eye around for any of Gil's belongings. He stayed too seldom to need to keep any of his possessions here, but he was forgetful and occasionally left behind his reading glasses or house keys and once his copy of *The British Journal of Psychiatry*. Although there was no danger of June recognising any of his things, evidence of male occupancy might lead to curiosity, which would need to be deflected.

'This is a quaint little room,' June said, temporarily distracted from her sorrows by the need to evaluate Helen's quarters and decide whether they implied some covert criticism of her own taste in furnishings. 'Very arty.'

'Oh, well, hardly any of it is mine,' she said, quick to disown the ugly furniture and balding carpet. In truth, all the touches that could be deemed 'arty' − the rag rug, the lacquer screen, the patchwork cushions, the hand-painted lampshades − were hers alone.

Having installed her visitor in the least lumpy armchair, Helen made a pot of tea and while it was stewing on the plywood coffee table between them, she prompted June to share her troubles.

'It's Lorraine,' said June, squeezing her eyes shut to hold back a tear. 'She's getting so peculiar, I can't tell you.'

'Peculiar how?' Helen asked, perturbed in spite of herself.

It was less than a week since she had caught sight of her niece outside the Fairfield Halls, absorbed in her sketching.

'Well, for one thing she spends all of her time drawing little pictures in a sketchbook. Even at the dinner table.'

Helen almost laughed but caught herself just in time. 'Oh, that's my fault,' she admitted. 'I told her to keep practising her drawing. She's quite good at art and I thought she needed a bit of encouragement. Sketching is a harmless pursuit, surely?'

She poured the tea into two dainty china cups that she seldom had an opportunity to use, as Gil was so opposed to anything he considered 'refined'.

'Not when it's taken to extremes,' June replied. 'Certainly not at mealtimes. That's not the worst of it. Sometimes when I talk to her, she just ignores me and goes completely rigid, as if she's having a fit.'

Helen frowned. 'Do you mean like a kind of seizure? Did you call the doctor?'

'It doesn't last long enough to call the doctor. One minute she's standing there stiff as a board and staring, and the next she's back to normal again. Anyway, I don't want to get the doctor involved. He might think she's loopy.'

'Does she remember these episodes afterwards?'

'I don't know. I didn't think to ask if she remembered them. I just say to her, "Lorraine, snap out of it. You're going to do yourself some damage."'

'And does that work?' Helen asked sceptically.

'Sometimes. And then she goes and lies down on her bed and I can hear her laughing hysterically.'

'What does Clive say when this is going on?'

'He's never there. I tell him about it and he says, "Well, she looks all right to me," but that's because it doesn't happen when he's around.'

Helen couldn't help feeling that this might be significant.

'It must be very worrying for you, June. Have you asked Lorraine if she can tell if one of these attacks is coming on before it happens?'

'I don't know how to talk to her, Helen. She's not herself any more. She's . . .' There was a pause as June applied a white hankie to her cheeks, which were now tracked with inky tears. 'Got a nasty streak.'

'Oh, June. I can't believe Lorraine's got a nasty bone in her body. She's a lovely girl.'

Helen reached out and squeezed June's free hand with its neatly painted pearly nails. It was the most intimate physical contact that they had ever had and it felt strange and uncomfortable. She wondered how soon she could let go.

'Maybe she's unhappy with the idea of secretarial college,' she suggested. 'And this is a way of forcing you to pay attention to what she wants.'

'I thought she'd enjoy it. She seemed to like the idea of typing and shorthand. I thought she'd found her niche.'

She pronounced it *nitch* and Helen had to busy herself for a moment with the tea tray to hide a smile.

'Would it be such a problem if it turned out not to be her . . . thing?' she asked. 'Lorraine's so young. She might have changed her mind. It's not so long ago that all she wanted to do was hairdressing.'

'Oh, it was just that Wendy giving her that idea,' said June, making a gesture of dismissal with her hankie. 'She's a bad influence. Lorraine *wants* to be a secretary. In fact, Clive has said he might be able to get her a job in his place when she gets her City & Guilds, which would be ideal.'

'I'm not sure I'd call it that,' said Helen, who thought working with one of her parents was just about the last thing Lorraine needed. 'Surely a little independence would be good for her.'

'But that's just it, Helen,' June insisted. 'She doesn't want to do anything under her own steam. I have to practically force her out of the house. She lies on her bed listening to music and won't come down and talk to us any more.'

'I don't think Lorraine is any more obsessed with music than most girls her age. I was dotty about Bing Crosby.'

'At least Bing Crosby looked like he had a bath and combed his hair. These singers now are so scruffy and dirty. And they can't even sing in tune.'

'I'd offer to have her to stay with me,' said Helen. 'If she'd come. But I've only got one bedroom. Even the couch isn't big enough to sleep on. It's hardly suitable.'

'You'd think she'd be desperate to get away as she seems to hate us so much,' said June, who appeared not to have heard this empty offer.

Her bottom lip jutted miserably and she looked momentarily a worn and weary version of her teenage daughter.

'Oh, June, she doesn't hate you. That's nonsense. She's just a confused adolescent. I'm sure we were the same at that age.'

But even as Helen said this, she knew it wasn't true, of her at least. There had been no room for rebellious energy in her youth. It all had to be conserved for predicting and forestalling her father's rages.

June didn't seem to be listening; she was rooting in her raffia shopping bag, from which she presently produced a crimson leather book with 1964 embossed on the front in gold leaf. As she flicked through pages closely covered with neat handwriting in blue ballpoint, illustrated with doodles of hearts, daisies, lips and eyes, Helen gave a belated yelp of disapproval.

'June, that's not Lorraine's diary! You wouldn't!'

June turned pink at the rebuke. 'I didn't intend to read it. I was in there dusting and I knocked it on the floor and some postcards fell out, so I went to put them back and' – she continued her search – 'here it is. *I hate Mum. I hate her stupid voice.* She doesn't say anything about Clive. Only me.'

'Don't tell me,' Helen squeaked, appalled at being implicated in this act of betrayal. 'You *can't* read her private diary. And you especially can't read it to me.'

'How else am I supposed to find out what she's thinking if she won't talk to me?' June said, but she closed the book and put it back in her bag. 'Anyway, if it's so private, why does she leave it lying around?'

'Because she trusts you not to snoop. It's a compliment.' Which you do not deserve, Helen's inner voice added. 'It's even worse than eavesdropping. Nothing good can come of it.'

She hadn't been a regular diarist herself, but during moments of high emotion as a schoolgirl she had occasionally committed her thoughts to paper and knew that it would have destroyed her if anyone had read them.

'How can I face her, knowing what she really thinks of me?' said June in a watery voice. She was on the verge of a proper weeping fit. Helen sensed that even the mildest gesture of kindness would set it off. She had never seen June vulnerable before and it made her skin prickle with discomfort.

'That's not what she *really* thinks of you,' Helen insisted. 'It's what she thought, angrily, for one minute and has probably forgotten. Just like you probably think unkind thoughts about Clive now and then. To yourself. And that's why you must forget it and never read it again.'

'It's easy to criticise, Helen,' June said with a long sniff. 'Being a mother is not easy and if you haven't done it yourself, you can't really appreciate how hard it is.'

Helen stood up and began clearing the cups with unnecessary briskness and carried the tray into the tiny kitchen. You hardly need to have been blessed with children to know that reading someone's diary is wrong, she wanted to snap, but their relationship wasn't nearly strong enough to withstand an exchange of home truths. Instead, she threw the taps on and let the water thunder into the sink and banged a couple of cupboard doors for relief.

When she returned to the sitting room, June was on her feet buttoning her coat. From the pocket she drew out a ribbon of chiffon, which she shook out into a scarf and fastened around her lacquered hair.

'You're probably right,' she conceded without making eye contact. 'I'll put the diary back and won't mention anything to Lorraine. You won't say anything to anyone?'

'Of course not,' said Helen, now uncomfortably squeezed as the confidante of both mother and daughter. She began to feel that if the list of things she could not say grew any longer she would soon end up as mute as William.

Chapter 17

— 1953 —

Something interesting was happening in the park opposite. It began with the arrival overnight of a few large caravans, which had gouged muddy furrows in the grass of the big field. These were joined by more over the following days, along with trucks carrying monstrous structures of painted metal, bales of folded canvas, wooden planking and miles of cable.

'Something to do with the coronation, no doubt,' Aunt Louisa declared, though that was still more than a month away.

'I expect they're the Mitcham Funfair people,' said Aunt Elsie, drawing her lips into a thin seam of distaste. 'An advance party of them stopping off on the way. What a nuisance.'

'It hardly seems worth all that effort if they're to take it down and move on so soon.'

'Well, that's what travelling fairs *do*,' said Aunt Elsie with her usual impatience. 'They travel.'

William, who was listening to this conversation, wondered how the presence of a fairground might possibly inconvenience someone who never set foot in the park.

During the afternoon he stationed himself at Aunt Rose's window, from which the view was partially shielded by net curtains and the branches of the alder. From here he watched wiry young men, stripped to the waist and slick with sweat, assembling wooden platforms, flights of stairs, canvas booths with scaffolding skeletons and a monstrous metal roundabout from which hung swags of shivering chains. It was a pleasure to listen to the hammering and clanging and the hollow knock of mallet on wood, and see this instant village of tents and rides spring up on the same field where once, long ago, he had flown his kite. The men were so nimble and strong, balancing six planks of wood on one shoulder or tossing fat coils of rope to each other as though they weighed no more than a ball of wool.

There was one in particular who caught his eye; he couldn't have said why. Perhaps because his hair was roughly cut and untidy like William's own. Aunt Louisa did her best with the scissors from her sewing bag, but barbering was not one of her skills and she didn't dare take the blades close enough to his scalp and neck to copy the way all 'normal' men wore their hair now. He didn't complain; to do so might result in Aunt Elsie taking over and she would think a nicked ear nothing to fuss about. The man had broad, powerful shoulders, biceps the size of grapefruit and a carved torso, ridged with muscle, like the 'Discobolus of Myron', one of William's favourite illustrations in the Antiquities section of his *British Encyclopaedia*. Although William had no skill at estimating people's ages, and tended to think everybody much older than himself, he decided that this man, like him, was twenty-six.

Forgetting himself momentarily, he drew aside the net curtain to get a better look. The man lowered himself easily from the top of an A frame of swing boats, hanging briefly from the crossbar to perform a few pull-ups before dropping to the grass. As he straightened up, wiping his hands on the seat of his trousers, he seemed to stop and stare directly at William from right across the park.

It was impossible at such a distance to be sure what he was looking at, but there was nothing else, apart from the blank

149

faces of Edwardian houses, to draw the eye. Then – all day the memory of it made William's heart gallop with panic and guilty pleasure – the man raised his hand and waved. William sprang back from the window as though shot in the chest and flattened himself against the wall. He heard the man's laughter but knew that he couldn't have done from so far away over the confused racket of machinery and hammering; it was just in his head.

After five minutes in the shadows, he regathered his courage to peer through a torn flap of net. The man had disappeared, absorbed back into the crowd of workers. He saw me, though, William thought, and he waved at me, as though he wanted to be my friend.

'We'll have to lock up carefully tonight,' said Elsie, as if they didn't always. She was unclogging holes in the salt cellar with a darning needle while she waited for dinner.

'Oh yes,' agreed Louisa, pounding boiled swede to mush and flopping it onto three plates alongside braised pig's liver and spring greens.

'Why?' asked William, who was always anxious about security. He was already seated at the table with his yellowing linen napkin tucked into his collar and fanning out across his chest.

'Because those fairground types are notorious thieves,' said Aunt Elsie.

'They look a rough bunch,' said Aunt Louisa, who had also spent some time at the window.

'Mr Eckerty had his pocket picked at Battersea Pleasure Gardens during the festival,' Aunt Elsie remembered. 'They jostled him in the queue for the Sky Wheel.'

'They work in gangs,' Aunt Louisa confirmed. 'Like Fagin,' she added for William's benefit. Examples from literature made more sense to him.

'Do pickpockets break into houses, then?' he asked, not liking the sound of so much lawlessness on his doorstep.

'I don't know about that,' Aunt Elsie conceded, 'but we don't want to give them any opportunity. Funfairs are a magnet for undesirable elements. I'll be glad when they've moved on.'

'Amen,' said Aunt Louisa.

Their curious version of grace concluded, they began to eat.

William, remembering the man's wave, grew hot and cold with confusion. He hadn't looked like an undesirable element – quite the contrary – and the thought of being *jostled* by him was almost overwhelming. It pained him to think that someone he thought of as a friend might be a thief or worse. Perhaps his aunts were wrong in this instance.

This was not an especially comfortable idea, for if they were wrong about this, then what else? To face this possibility was dizzying and he retreated from it as though from a crumbling cliff edge.

For a while there was only the sound of cutlery on china and the chewing of soft, wet food. It wasn't his favourite dinner; every mouthful, whether meat or vegetables, tasted of a different kind of metal. For pudding there was tinned rice pudding with bottled plums, which was at least sweet and filling.

Once dusk fell, he crept back into Aunt Rose's room and, standing well back, watched the figures in the park still congregating, the tips of their cigarettes glowing like fireflies in the twilight. There were paraffin lamps in the windows of some of the caravans and, already, some pale moonlit laundry pegged out on lines. Somewhere a wireless was playing.

The evidence of a community, settling down for the night in the usually empty park, made William feel both lonely and comforted, and at eight o'clock he went downstairs for his hot milk and a game of backgammon with Aunt Louisa.

The following day more rides arrived on a convoy of huge trailers, which blocked the road in both directions while they tried to make the sharp turn onto the field. William watched from the window again as men leapt from the high cabs to act as marshals, waving the lorries through.

There was no sign of his friend among the criminal elements, as he supposed he must now think of them, though it would be hard to recognise him again if he was wearing a shirt and cap, as many of them were. He felt guilty at the hours he had wasted in idle gazing and resolved instead to abandon his post and return to his room to work on his house of cards, which was up to its fifth storey. He had been adding to it over the course of some weeks with increasing caution as it grew higher and there was more to lose.

Extreme delicacy had to be deployed when entering his bedroom to avoid causing a draught and he had been unable to risk opening the window. For the same reason, his aunts were temporarily denied all access, which caused them no great disappointment, as without ventilation, the place had started to acquire a musty, masculine smell.

Although fully committed to leaving his watching post and resuming work on this project, William had in fact not moved from behind the curtain. He would grant himself one more quick glance and then go. Stooping to peer through the triangular rend in the net, he gave a start and retreated. Sauntering up the path, as though coming to pay a visit, was a young man in a flat cap, shirtsleeves and grey trousers. One of those from the fair, certainly – perhaps *the* one – though it was impossible to tell from this angle. William froze, waiting for the strangulated snarl of the doorbell and wondering what manner of conversation would take place if Aunt Elsie got there first and what manner of trouble he would be in if it was discovered that he had been exchanging signals with undesirables. He felt the old, sick dread of being scolded, but all he could hear was the flap of the letter box and the whisper of paper dropping to the mat. He scurried down the stairs and snatched up the folded page. The house was undisturbed: in the kitchen, Aunt Louisa was de-veining kidneys for a pudding. The suet dough had been rolled and pressed into the basin. Outside, Aunt Elsie was mending the roof of the fruit cage with a piece of wire netting borrowed from the derelict henhouse.

William crept back up to the top landing, his hand closed damply around the piece of paper. He didn't trust himself to enter his room; his tremors of confusion would act like an earthquake on his card palace. Instead, he sat on the top step and read the message:

Come Along to the Coronation Fair!
Thursday to Saturday in Lloyd Park
Fireworks by Brocks of Crystal Palace
Dodgems, Lightning Swirl, Octopus
Ghost Train, Chairoplanes, Boxing
And a host of stalls and sideshows!

He looked at it for some minutes in wonderment. It was his first invitation since Francis had asked him to Sussex for the summer holiday – a golden time from another life. Of course he couldn't go. His friend would be disappointed, might even be out looking for him, but his aunts would never allow it. After all their precautions to keep him safe over the years, not to mention the horrors of those rare occasions when he had left the sanctuary of the house, it was impossible.

The last time, when he had been looking for poor Boswell in the snow, Aunt Elsie had found him nearly frozen to death in the coal-hole, and they had almost had to give in and call out a doctor. He knew he must have been dangerously ill, because she didn't scold him, even when he was well again. Going out was unthinkable.

Nevertheless, he did think about it, for the rest of the day and as he lay in bed preparing for sleep. He imagined himself slipping out across the road, moving anonymously among the crowds. In his dreams he was always brave and free and next to invisible, attracting no attention.

By the following morning, William's fantasies had grown more detailed and convincing, his delusions of competence now impregnable. Of course he must go. He got up at daybreak, drawn to the window to watch the garden waking. Outside, the trees were washed in milky sunlight, the birdsong orchestral in its intensity. He luxuriated in the music until it fell silent and then he went back to bed and dozed again.

On waking for the second time, he promised himself he would attend to his routines and not watch the fair at all until dusk. It was his bargain with the universe; if he kept his part, all would be well.

He did his crossword and his chess and his reading and added another wing to his card palace with a touch as delicate as settling snowflakes. Aunt Elsie was in the glasshouse potting up tomato seedlings and planting lettuces in trays on the wooden shelving. Through the green filter of algae on the panes, he could see her moving as though underwater.

Aunt Louisa was washing the kitchen floor with a string mop, flopping grey water into the corners, smearing the dirt around without ever quite banishing it. She would finish the job on her hands and knees with a rag and then Aunt Elsie would come stamping in from the garden in her outdoor shoes, shedding chunks of mud from cleated soles.

William could feel his attention being tugged towards the front of the house and the fair field opposite and had to keep strict command of himself. Over the years he had grown skilled at this kind of challenge, setting himself a complex or repetitive task that would devour the slow-moving hours of an afternoon.

It was a while since he had attempted the Brock Cottage memory game, which was regrettable since there was a chance that while new details might surface, old ones recalled on an earlier occasion might be forgotten. The exercise took the form of an imaginary tour, starting at the front door, down the hallway and then room by room through the house, furnishing it from memory as he went. One room, of course, he had only glimpsed through a half-open door but never entered – Mr and Mrs Kenley's bedroom – so this he passed over.

There was the sitting room where they played card games in the evening after dinner on some nights and even burnt logs in the grate, though it was summer and quite warm enough without, just because he and Francis liked to see the flames leaping. With eyes closed, he travelled up the narrow creaking stairs, counting off the prints of wildfowl on the wall, to the landing with its sagging floor and tasselled rugs.

Through the low window, deep-set into the roughly plastered walls, he saw the garden, the hammock, the stream, fields and woods and the pond with the shy dace. On the right was his and Francis' room, with its twin beds with matching blue-and-white counterpanes, the chest of drawers with the ship in the bottle on top and the wardrobe where they had hidden the bucket of water containing the trophy perch that they couldn't bring themselves to throw back. On the wall between the beds was a brass barometer, stuck on Fair, and an iron horseshoe. A pair of binoculars, for watching the foxes and badgers, hung from the end of Francis' bed by a bald leather strap.

Now at a distance of fifteen years, he couldn't be sure whether he had it all quite right. The colour of the bathroom walls, for example, he always saw during this reimagining as duck-egg blue. Now and then, though, when remembering a specific incident, like the time Mrs Kenley walked in on him and found him crying, he seemed to see the walls as the colour of brick dust. He was also unclear about what he did with his clothes. Were they kept in his old brown suitcase under the bed or in the wardrobe with the fish?

When he had finished with the cottage, and the garden with its broad lawn where they played cricket, all four of them, and Mrs Kenley – a woman! – hit the ball for six right over the roof, he tried a different challenge. The aim was to stitch together a whole day of memories, starting with the moment of waking in the morning to the smell of bacon frying in the kitchen below, and ending with his cheek on the cool pillow, and Francis, turned to stone in the bluish light of the moon through the curtains, sleeping in the bed beside his. It was an impossible feat.

With two whole weeks – as much as 200 waking hours of memories to be mined – he could not reclaim enough material for one full day. Of course, several hours could be accounted for by Mr Kenley reading a chapter of *Moonfleet* each night, performing the voices of John Trenchard and Elzevir Block. No one had read aloud to him since he had mastered reading to himself at the age of five under the tutelage of Aunt Rose and he found the experience uncomfortable at first. Gradually, however, the story began to consume him and he looked forward to it as one of the best parts of the day.

There had been countless hours, too, spent in perfect idleness by the stream, lying on his stomach watching the speckled trout. But still, so much time unaccounted for, it pained him to think that it was lost to him for ever.

The wheezing hurdy-gurdy music from the fair field inter-rupted his reminiscences, fetching him back to the present and his impending project in all its recklessness. For courage he reread the paper invitation, rolling it up and placing it inside the napkin ring for safe-keeping and luck.

At dinner time, Aunt Elsie was peevish.

'The noise!' she complained, pressing her hands to her ears. She never wore gloves in the garden and there was dirt under every nail and ground into the creased skin of her knuckles.

Each ride and stall seemed to produce its own source of music; it came together as a storm of tuneless metallic thumping. Out in the kitchen the cacophony was somewhat muffled, but still hard to overlook altogether.

'Do you think they mean to go on all night?' Aunt Louisa asked, dumping a spoonful of lamb stew on Elsie's plate with a clatter. Much of the meat had fallen off and shrunk to nothing, leaving mostly bones and gravy.

'That's a mean helping,' Elsie said, poking at the fleshless chop with her fork.

'Have some of mine,' said Louisa, performing a hasty redistribution, which left her nothing but fat and onions. William noticed this manoeuvre with sympathetic approval. It was better to be hungry than scolded. There were always biscuits later.

The scanty serving didn't trouble him. He was too sick with anticipation to have any kind of appetite, but for appearances' sake, he cleared his plate.

'They hadn't better. If it goes on after ten o'clock, I shall go over there myself and give them a piece of my mind.'

This declaration made William uneasy, but it was hard to tell if Aunt Elsie was serious. She was so fiercely opposed to any outside interference in their own affairs, it seemed unlikely that she would set out to involve herself in the affairs of others – especially 'criminal elements'. But she might well consider excessive noise as a form of intrusion and it wasn't impossible to imagine her donning coat, hat and gloves and striding over the road at one minute after ten in a mood of righteous fury.

He half wished he could do the washing-up, as it would have passed the time until they went to bed, but he was never permitted to help with housework or anything unmanly. The manly tasks, like digging the vegetable patch or unblocking the gutters, were also off limits, as they involved going outdoors in daylight.

His contribution to the running of the household was limited to fetching things down from high shelves and moving heavy furniture so that one of the aunts might sweep underneath. He had ruled himself out of the emptying of mousetraps. If he had his way, the mice would come and share the crumbs from his plate and nest in his dressing-gown pocket.

After dinner, they sat in the cold back parlour with the wireless on, not at a volume to be listened to, but so that its murmurings should mask the distant rumble of the fairground. Aunt Elsie looked through her ledger, making notes on recent outgoings and shaking her head over any increases in expenditure. After this kind of accounting exercise there tended to be a period of belt-tightening, which would last until the next successful petition to the trust, when things like coffee and golden syrup might reappear in the larder.

Aunt Louisa sat at the card table with her tatting, moving the slender wooden bobbins, like so many fishing floats, from one side to another, over and under, pinning as she went and making barely visible progress with the fine lace panel. William wouldn't have minded learning how to do this himself, perhaps because of the association with fishing, and because the process required such patience and care, but he was deterred because the items produced – collars, doilies, handkerchief trims – were so useless and unexciting.

William was pleased to see that after their hot milk, neither of his aunts was much disposed to stay up and by nine thirty, the house was quiet. His courage almost failed him as he fetched his outdoor shoes and stood by the front door. He had caught a glimpse of himself in the glass on the landing and there was something not quite reassuring in his appearance. His trousers were a little too short, his jacket a little too snug. He looked different from the men who worked the fairground, but he couldn't quite say why. They all in some way resembled each other; he did not.

Money was the other thing. There was the black tin box in which he used to save the shillings and sixpences slipped to him occasionally by Aunt Rose when he still had use for them. He took a palmful of change, untouched in years, and remembering pickpockets, slipped it inside his left sock, where it slithered down beneath the soft arch of his foot. It would take some getting at now, he thought with satisfaction. The front door keys were too large and irregular-shaped to fit in his sock, so he took the lace from his right shoe and wore them around his neck, tucked inside his shirt. Their cold, solid presence against his breastbone was reassuring.

For a second he stood in the open doorway, just inside the house, and listened to the mechanical gasp of the organ music and the squeals of the girls on the rides. The whole dizzying kaleidoscope of light and movement made his head pound, but it was too late to fail now. Drawing the door closed without a sound, he checked to left and right and, limping from the deficiencies in his footwear, made his way down the path and through the iron gate.

It was wonderful and terrifying to be at a fairground among hordes of people and yet quite alone. He observed the way the crowds shifted and parted without communicating or colliding, like shoals of fish. He noticed, too, how every ride and booth played its own music, and the way the sounds separated and merged as he left one and approached another. The overlapping pools of noise made his ears fizz, but it was somehow bracing, like the application of a rough towel to itchy skin.

He stood watching the dodgem cars for some while, trying to fathom the rules of the game. There seemed to be an element of race and pursuit involved, with some drivers using their steering skills to avoid collisions, while others were determined to nudge and bump and cause chaos. Occasionally, three or more cars would become wedged together at the side of the rink, with more piling into the pack, until the man in charge of the ride would wade into the fray and spin them round by their poles, and push them off with one foot, back into the flowing traffic. There were no winners or losers to this game as far as he could see.

After a few minutes of frenetic noise and motion, the music faded and the cars slid to a halt. The drivers and their passengers climbed out, straightening their clothes, and straggled away. William was not tempted by the dodgems. The rules were too uncertain and it was hard to tell whether the shouts and screams were entirely friendly. The Lightning Swirl and the Switchback were also out of bounds, as there was a chance that he might have to share a compartment with a stranger.

For a while he wandered between the rides and sideshows in the hope of recognising the man who had waved to him and perhaps thanking him for his invitation. This would require immense boldness, but he felt sure the man was friendly and could hardly be counted as either a busybody or 'the authorities'.

By night, however, the fairground workers were dressed in shabby jackets and flat caps or greasy overalls and William began to lose all confidence that he would recognise the bare-chested man with the powerful muscles in such attire. Besides, it was difficult to peer closely into a stranger's face without being scrutinised in turn; the man taking bets in the boxing booth had given him quite a threatening look, causing William to reel away in confusion.

A tempting smell of cooking reached him, briefly displacing the less pleasant odours of trampled mud, diesel, cigarette smoke and the oily animal scent of so many woollen jackets. He traced the source to a man selling sausages cooked over a brazier. William squatted down to liberate some change from his sock, finally handing over a warm, damp sixpence, which the stallholder accepted with some muttering. The sausage was hot as coal and no less charred, and William's fingers and face were soon black with sooty smudges. By the time he had disposed of the whole sausage, he was as grimy as a chimney sweep.

Emboldened by this successful transaction, he made his way to the Chairoplane and joined the queue. The individual seats, shivering on their metal chains, were sufficiently far apart to reassure him that he would not be forced into close proximity with anyone peculiar. Even though there was quite a press of customers, William noticed that they kept at a respectful distance, as though understanding his anxieties. Some even went so far as to cover the lower part of their faces to protect him from their germs. People are very good, he thought.

There was another hold-up as he had to winkle a threepenny bit from his sock and a few comments from the queue, but soon he was installed in his swaying chair, held in by the slackest of chains. It seemed hardly sufficient as a safety precaution and William was having second thoughts, when the whole structure gave a lurch and began to revolve and it was too late. The wooden seat was flat and slippery and tipped him forwards. He clutched at the vertical chains from which it was suspended, so that his nails dug into his palms. The machine gathered speed and at the same time the chairs rose up above the heads of the crowd, fanning out so that he was almost horizontal.

A woman in front of him screamed as her headscarf was whipped away into the darkness. As it flew past him, he felt his unlaced shoe work lose and, within seconds, the wind had sucked it from his foot and cast it down into the crowd. His eyes streamed and the chains creaked and strained and dug into the side of his leg as he slid to the edge of the seat. He was not enjoying himself and wished he was back in his bed at the top of the house, safe and quiet and with his full complement of shoes.

It had been a terrible mistake. The motion was making him dizzy and sick; his mouth filled with regurgitated sausage and burning bile. He felt it scour his throat as he forced it back down. At last it was over and the machine slowed and stopped, though the trees and sky continued to whirl around him as his fingers fumbled with the safety chain and he staggered onto the wooden boards.

'Oi, watch it,' said a short, weaselly youth with a greased quiff, a cigarette wagging in his mouth, as William accidentally brushed against him before regaining his balance. There was a tension in the way he held himself of tightly coiled anger. 'Fuck are you doing?'

'I'm looking for my shoe,' William replied.

He could feel the cold mud seeping through his sock and it was not pleasant, but it was the impossibility of explaining its absence to his aunt that was the more pressing emergency.

'He's looking for his shoe,' the youth announced to his two companions in a mincing voice and they burst into rowdy laughter.

William stepped back uncertainly. He had not thought there was anything objectionable in his voice. His aunts had never said so.

As he turned away to resume the hunt for his shoe, there was an explosion and the sky lit up in a shower of sparks. His arms flew up to protect his head; sudden loud noises could still induce panic. A succession of piercing whistles ripped through the sudden hush, followed by four deafening reports. Overhead, glittering flowers of green and red bloomed in the darkness.

Keeping his hands clamped to his ears, William threaded his way between the press of bodies, fixing his gaze on the beaten grass now illuminated in the magnesium glow of the fireworks. The screech and thump of rockets continued with hardly a pause, obliterating the appreciative sighs of the spectators. The music continued to pump from its separate islands, louder than ever before.

Limping with one foot wet and muddy and the other hobbled by a sock full of coins, William completed a circuit of the fair without success. As he faced south across the field, he glanced at the shadowy outline of his house in the distance, half hidden by the trees, and then froze as he saw a glow of light between the curtains of an upstairs window. Aunt Elsie's room. If she had been woken by the noise and was even now coming down to give someone a piece of her mind, she would find the door unbolted and the key missing. The horror of this eventuality stopped the breath in his chest.

Abandoning all thoughts of his shoe, he stumbled back past the sausage seller and the boxing tent and the dodgems, tripping over guy ropes, treading on bottle tops and cigarette butts with his unshod foot. Sheets of paper were blowing about his ankles from an overturned bin. There were hundreds of them ground underfoot, mashed into the mud. A gust of wind pinned a torn scrap to the front of his jacket and he peeled it away and read:

Ghost Train, Chairoplanes, Boxing
And a host of stalls and sideshows!

'Oi, nancy boy!'

The three youths were leaning against the counter of the rifle range, smoking and watching the women's skirts blowing back as they came down the helter-skelter. With one movement, they pushed themselves upright.

William looked around to see who they were addressing, but he didn't stop or slow down, because getting back home was now the priority. It had been a mad, foolish plan. There was no invitation, no friend, and now there would be a scolding to be faced for nothing.

The downstairs light was on now, describing Aunt Elsie's progress through the house. He stumbled forwards, but his path was blocked. The three young men who just seconds ago had been behind him were somehow in front of him. Their posture was not friendly.

'Got any money, nancy boy?' the weasel-faced one said.

William didn't intend to look at or even think of his feet, but he must have done, because before he could change direction, they were on him and his face was in the mud. Someone was tugging at his remaining shoe, tearing it off as though intending to bring the whole foot with it, and then they were kicking him with heavy boots and stamping and explosions of pain in his back and sides flowered like fireworks behind his eyes. There was dirt in his mouth and the taste of sick and he was the mouse in the schoolyard with the boys' laughter ringing in his ears. The pain was exquisite; it took away all fear of death. He felt himself floating and free. Then, through a commotion of voices and running feet, he was gripped under the arms by strong hands, pulled up and thrown like a sack of coal over the back of his unknown saviour and carried home with Aunt Elsie, once again his rescuer, running alongside.

Chapter 18

Helen had not expected to hear any more from Alistair Duggan, but in late May, three weeks after their meeting at Fairfield Halls, she received an A4 envelope containing a copy of a school magazine, *The Belworthian*, dated 1938. The front cover showed a selection of black-and-white photographs: the chapel; a group of mud-covered boys playing rugby; the Great Hall with a visiting dignitary presenting prizes; a boy in cricket whites standing at the crease poised to receive a delivery. An accompanying note read:

Dear Helen (if I may),

My mother has come up with the goods. She has every issue from '32 to '38. On a brief flick through this I can find no mention of William Tapping – or me, for that matter – but I never distinguished myself at any sport, so it's not surprising. But on the front cover, standing at the crease, is our man Harry Kenners. I don't suppose it will be an easy job to find him, given the passage of time. No need to return this, by the way.

Best wishes to you – and Harry Tappers, should he remember me.

Alistair Duggan

Helen turned to the inside cover and read the captions. Cover photographs by J. Swales. Clockwise from top left: Founders' Day service at the Old Chapel; The Rugby 1st XV take on St Saviour's for the cup; His Honour Judge Nigel Walton congratulates the winners at prize-giving; Francis Kenley scores a half-century against Sutton Valence.

She looked again at the picture of the boy in cricket whites. Even if he could be found, it seemed unlikely that he would know or remember anything helpful about William's early life. But Alistair had said they were friends; it was not inconceivable that William might be happy to be reconnected with someone who had known him as a boy, now that he had no living relatives.

'How would you go about finding someone, with just their name and approximate age?' she asked Gil the next time they met in his office for a hasty assignation between appointments. She showed him the magazine and reminded him of her meeting with Alistair Duggan. 'Not an especially uncommon name, either.'

Gil peeled through the pages of *The Belworthian*, smirking at its tone of self-congratulation.

'Ambrose Whystan-Pettigrew was a convincingly tormented Othello to Edmund Garnett's winsome Desdemona,' he read, and then paused over a team photograph of the victorious Rugby 1st XV in flannels and blazers, holding the county cup. 'Nineteen thirty-eight. They had no idea what was coming. I wonder where they are now.'

'That's very much my question,' Helen said. 'How would I find someone?'

'I suppose you could call the school, but I can't imagine they'd know the current whereabouts of some old boy from before the war. You could phone every Kenley in the London directory and hope he's related to one of them. Or put an advertisement in *The Times*. But that wouldn't reach everyone.'

'Perhaps it's all a wild goose chase,' said Helen, daunted by the poor odds of success. 'What will it achieve, anyway?'

'I don't think it's a bad idea at all,' said Gil. 'If he could be found, he might provide William with a gateway back into the world.'

'It must be an awful thought, to have no family or friends, or even acquaintances to call on.'

'He hasn't yet shown any sign of wanting to build new relationships,' said Gil. 'He seems to prefer animals to humans, as children often do. I see him sitting with Smokey on his lap sometimes and he looks almost contented.'

'Most of his drawings were of animals. But I thought that was just because they were the things he could see from his window. Foxes and birds and so on.'

'He also has an attachment to certain possessions, like a child with a favourite toy. That silver band, for instance.'

'It's a napkin ring,' said Helen. 'With an engraving of a badger. Such an odd thing to hang on to.'

'It's a talisman of some kind. A charm against . . . what?'

'Using the wrong napkin?' Helen hazarded and they both laughed. 'We're talking about him as if he's a 37-year-old child.'

Gil thought about this for a moment. 'It's hard to come to any conclusions about him when communication is so limited. But I do feel that, apart from his aunts, he has probably had no exposure to other people since puberty. There's something very childlike and innocent in his demeanour.'

'Yes, I feel that, too,' said Helen.

'He behaves around adults the way my Colin used to when he was about eight. Fearful. Deferential. He has no sense of personal status. That's why it would be so interesting to see the way he interacts with a friend from schooldays. Would he relate to him as a fellow adult or a fellow child?'

'Yes, you're right. He always adopts the subservient position in any relationship. He never claims the advantage of being male, or senior, even with a younger female.'

'It might just be general detachment. Just a standard way of coping with life in an institution.' Gil flicked the front cover of *The Belworthian* with his forefinger. 'If he went to boarding school, he'll already be an old hand. You put on the uniform, abandon all hope of privacy or autonomy and try to be as invisible as possible.'

At the end of the day, Gil left Helen the key to his office so that she could use his telephone to call all the Kenleys in the London phone book. She had borrowed the E–K directory from Olive in reception and was dispirited at the scale of the task. As a general rule she disliked the telephone – in her experience, usually the bringer of disappointing news or a peremptory request to do something she would rather not. Pleasant things – gifts, cards, love letters, invitations – tended to come by post.

Even though she would not be paying the bill, she dutifully waited to begin calling until after 6 p.m. for the cheap rate. The many F. Kenleys who were not called Francis were swiftly dispatched, but the several promising Francis Kenleys, who on questioning turned out to be retired colonels or elderly justices of the peace, took longer to process. By seven o'clock she was beginning to weary of the apologetic sound of her repeated enquiry and long for her simple supper and a hot bath. Later, she would swear to Gil that she had firmly decided that this call to M. Kenley of Tranmore Mansions, Chiswick, would be the very last – evidence, he retorted, of her tendency to lapse into superstition when tired.

'Marion Kenley,' said a warm, confident female voice.

'Is Francis there?' Helen asked, a formula that experience had proved the most effective in achieving her end in the fewest possible words.

'Francis? No, he hasn't lived here for years,' came the puzzled reply. 'Did he give you this number?'

'No. I just tried the phone book. I'm trying to track down a Francis Kenley who was a school friend of William Tapping in the 1930s.'

Down the wires came the silence of held breath and Helen felt her pulse quicken with the excitement of success. She had found him and she had known she would from the moment she heard the woman's voice.

'Goodness, that's a long time ago. Francis is my son,' the voice explained. 'Is William all right?'

'Ye-es,' Helen replied, stretching out the word over two syllables by way of qualification. 'I mean, physically he's quite well. He is currently a patient in a psychiatric hospital. I am one of his . . . therapists. We are trying to piece together some of the facts of his early life.'

'Has he lost his memory that he can't tell you himself?'

'We don't know. He is mute.'

'Oh dear. Poor William.' Mrs Kenley sounded quite shaken. Then, in a slightly sharper tone, she said, 'How did you come across Francis' name?'

Helen's explanation of the intervention of Alistair Duggan seemed to reassure her.

'I can give you Francis' number, but I don't know that he'll be much help. They were certainly friends. William came to stay at our house in Sussex during the holidays once, but that was a lifetime ago – before the war.'

'You must have got to know him quite well, then?' Helen said.

'For that fortnight, but not otherwise. Francis is an only child, so we let him invite a pal to come and stay during the summer. They used to go fishing and build camps in the spinney and have campfires. All those things boys get up to. We hardly saw them. But he was a very nice boy. I liked him very much and I'm sorry to hear that he's . . . not . . .' Her voice wavered.

'Did you meet his family? He was living with an elderly aunt until recently.'

'I recall there were aunts but no parents, but I only met one of them, briefly. My husband, Basil, may have spoken to the others, but I can't ask him as he's no longer with us.'

'I'm sorry,' said Helen inadequately.

'Oh, well,' said Mrs Kenley, smoothing away the awkwardness of a stranger's condolences. 'It was some years ago now. Let me give you Francis' number.' She rattled it off.

They are close, Helen thought. She calls him often. From the sound of her voice – soft, intelligent, sympathetic – Helen pictured a tall, slender, grey-haired woman in a pleated skirt and camel-coloured twinset, standing by the upstairs window of a mansion flat looking out onto the plane trees of a quiet street. One of those capable women who worked for the BBC or drove ambulances during the war, who in their retirement looked out for their elderly neighbours and sat on committees and let their spare rooms to foreign students and wrote letters to people in prison – and were always busy but never tired. She is probably none of these things, Helen told herself, and all I have done is imagine someone as different as possible from my own mother, who has no interest in other people and is never busy but always tired.

As usual, thoughts of her mother prompted a wave of guilt, swiftly followed by a cancelling backwash of resentment. A visit was long overdue. It was weeks since she had failed to attend the get-together at Lorraine's birthday party and weeks earlier than that when she had last been to see them at home.

She should ring her tonight to apologise and arrange a time but knew that she wouldn't. After spending so long on the telephone, it was the very last thing she felt like doing.

Francis Kenley's number was engaged. Helen felt sure it must be his mother, calling ahead, but could think of no reason why such forewarning was necessary. The news of William's illness would hardly land like a hammer blow if they had been estranged for over twenty years. Some people, of course, just enjoyed passing on news of mutual acquaintances, particularly if it was tinged with misery.

When Helen finally got through, the phone was picked up immediately and Francis made no secret of the fact that he had been told to expect her call.

'I understand you want to ask me about William Tapping,' he said. He spoke quietly in the clipped, educated accent of his class. 'I'm not going to be much help. It was so long ago.'

'You were friends at school?'

'Yes, but not for long. My parents took me out of school when I was twelve, so I was only there for about a year.'

'Oh. Did you have TB, too?'

'No. Why do you ask?'

'I was speaking to another boy from your year – former boy, I should say – Alistair Duggan. He left after a year because he had TB.'

'Duggan,' said Francis with a kind of wonderment. 'I'd forgotten him. I'm glad he recovered. No, not TB in my case.'

'Ah. And you didn't keep in touch with William once you left?'

'No. There wasn't really any means. I wrote once or twice, but he didn't reply and that was that.'

'When you knew him, did he have a normal home life?'

'I don't know about *normal*,' he replied. 'I'm not sure I knew that there was any other kind. I thought all families were alike at that age.'

'Were you aware that he was being brought up by his aunts?'

'Yes, I knew that his parents were dead. But no one took much interest in your background, who your people were at school. The only thing that mattered was being a decent chap, a good sport. Tapping was one of the decent chaps.'

'I wonder,' Helen said, 'whether you'd be prepared to come and visit him, provided he is willing, of course. He has had almost no contact with the outside world for at least ten years, but we suspect many more. It's hard to know because he won't speak.'

There was a longish pause and when Francis spoke, his voice was tight with reluctance. 'I-I don't know what good it would do. He probably hasn't given me a thought for twenty-five years, if he remembers me at all.'

'When we discovered him in a house in Croydon, he was in a neglected state, living as a complete recluse with his aunt, who has since died. As far as we know, he has no other friends or relatives.'

'God. Poor fellow,' Francis said. 'It's a wretched story, but . . .'

Helen sighed. She knew what was contained in that barely audible 'but': a refusal to get involved in the untidy life of a mere acquaintance from long ago. It was understandable. A lapsed childhood friendship didn't confer any obligation; she had expected too much.

'I'm sorry for putting you in this position,' she said. 'I thought maybe seeing someone from the past, who knew him when he was well, might encourage him to speak again. But I see now it was too much to ask.'

'It's all right,' said Francis in a chastened tone. 'No apology needed. It's just that I don't think we'd have anything to say to each other after all this time. I can hardly remember myself at eleven, never mind anyone else.' He gave an awkward laugh.

He is uncomfortable, thought Helen, recognising someone who, like her, hated to disappoint and having said no tended to feel wretched rather than relieved.

'Thank you for your time, anyway.'

'Don't mention it. And thank you for everything you are doing for William. I'm full of admiration for people like you.'

'Oh, I'm not at all admirable, I promise you,' Helen laughed, but she was touched by the compliment and turned it over in her mind – another grain to be added to the balance in the final weighing.

They said goodbye and she replaced the receiver, her shoulders sagging with weariness at her wasted evening. It was nearly eight o'clock and all she had to look forward to was an egg salad if she could be bothered, a bath and a bleak novella by Yukio Mishima that Gil had pressed on her when she would much rather read Dorothy L. Sayers.

Chapter 19

A visit to her parents could not be postponed any longer and so the following Saturday, Helen returned to her childhood home in Lewisham. As always, when entering the house as an adult, she had the feeling that the place had shrunk – the rooms had become smaller, the ceilings lower, the passage narrower. The garden, which had once seemed a world almost too vast to be explored, was a modest rectangle of lawn between two narrow flower beds. At the furthest end, beside the wall that gave onto a back alley, was the shed used by her father as a workshop or refuge, depending on his mood. The whole area was not much wider than the house and less than thirty yards long.

Her mother opened the front door, her face flushed from the heat of the kitchen, where she had been basting the roast. The Hansfords ate their main meal in the middle of the day and held their routines sacred.

'Hello, stranger,' she said. There was something reproachful in that greeting and in the way she held Helen's shoulders and gazed at her as though to reckon up the changes that had taken place since the last visit.

'Hello, how are you? How's Dad?' Helen replied, noting these inferences and choosing to ignore them, for now.

'Oh, you know. Go and see him. He's in there.' She twitched in the direction of the front room.

There were only two places that he could be found: the shed or his armchair in front of the television. Even though the set was switched off, he sat before it in an attitude of expectation, not comfortably slumped but leaning forwards, on the edge of his seat with the heels of his hands on his knees. A cigarette was pinched between finger and thumb and a ripple of smoke rose from the inch of ash at its tip to join the haze filling the upper half of the room.

At the sight of Helen, he lurched to his feet and stumped towards her on legs ravaged by arthritis. Having once towered over her, he was now just the shorter of the two. He had never been the most physically affectionate of fathers and they collided rather than embraced, encumbered by his burning cigarette and the bottle of whisky that she had brought as a wedding anniversary gift. There was no evidence that they celebrated this festival themselves, but she still dutifully marked the occasion.

It was the war that had caused the estrangement between father and daughter, that and his ill temper. He had left when she was a child of nine and returned when she was a girl of fourteen and unknowable. He was not a violent man in the conventional sense; he had never struck her or her mother, but he hardly needed to. His sudden rages, prompted by some trivial domestic inconvenience – a mislaid cigarette lighter, sour milk in his tea – kept them all in a state of quivering obedience. Foreseeing and heading off the sort of event that might trigger an explosion required a level of vigilance that made complete relaxation impossible. The fact that his ire was aimed not at them but at some nearby object that confounded him didn't make it any easier to ignore; for quiet people, raised voices are experienced as a kind of aggression even when directed elsewhere. There was nothing to be done but escape at the earliest opportunity, which she and Clive had done, leaving their mother to weather it as best she could.

Hearing the clang of the saucepan lids and the rattle of the cutlery drawer, Helen left her father to his cigarette and the blank TV screen and went to offer her help in the kitchen. Her mother was at the stove, pounding the lumps of flour from a pan of gravy with a wooden spoon. She looked round without smiling. Bitter disappointment had carved deep lines in her face, turned down the corners of her mouth and rounded her back.

'Can I do anything?' Helen asked in the bright voice she used with patients.

'No, it's all done. Ask your father to cut the meat.'

A shrunken joint of beef, no bigger than a man's fist, sat on the carving dish. To accompany it were roast potatoes, cabbage and carrots – the second vegetable a tribute to Helen's presence.

They ate at the kitchen table – the house was too small to accommodate a dining room – Helen and her mother on one side, her father on the other, their knees and feet contesting the limited space beneath. Helen began by asking about Lorraine's birthday meal, which she had thought a safe topic and one that might generate some cheering memories.

'Well, we had to go to *them*, of course. They won't come here.'

Visits to Clive and June were one of her mother's few pleasures and her only form of social outing, yet even so, she couldn't stop herself from sniping about them.

'Have you tried inviting them?'

'Oh, I don't mean to make a big to-do of it. But they could call round now and then.'

'I suppose they are busy with work.'

'June only works part-time. She could pop in. Clive bought her that fancy car and I don't think she ever uses it.'

'She's a nervous driver. And there are a lot of right turns between here and Shirley.'

Helen laid down her knife and fork to prevent herself from clearing her plate before her parents had taken their first mouthful. She was ravenous and the portions were modest. Her mother was still deploying salt, pepper and horseradish, each operation performed as if in slow motion.

'I see Clive's got himself a cine camera,' Helen prompted.

'Oh yes, he kept waving that in our faces. More money than sense. But it was a nice evening,' she conceded. 'June makes very good pastry.'

'She nags that girl half to death,' was Helen's father's summary of proceedings. He was an unlikely advocate for Lorraine, she thought, but one that might come in useful.

'I don't think she's accepted that Lorraine's growing up.'

Her mother had still made almost no headway with the meal. She cut up a piece of carrot and a morsel of beef and arranged them on the end of her fork, raised it halfway to her lips and then laid it down untasted. 'I'll tell you who we *did* have a visit from the other week. Out of the blue.' She was looking at Helen expectantly as if waiting for her to guess.

Helen blinked. 'Well, who, then?'

'Our Kathleen. Cousin Mary's daughter. She just turned up on the doorstep – no warning.'

'How nice,' said Helen uneasily.

Navigating a conversation about Kath Rudden without revealing that she knew anything she wasn't supposed to know was a test of her fluency at deception that she took no pleasure in passing.

'She was on her way to visit a friend in Lewisham hospital and thought she'd call in for a cup of tea. Luckily, we had some biscuits.'

The gravy had a skin on it now. Helen tried to think of an innocent question that any normal person might naturally ask about a visit from a distant cousin, but everything that came to mind sounded strange and false. 'Did she stay long?' she managed.

'Yes, we had a lovely chat. She looks just like her mother.'

'She said she was going to come and see you – when I went round there for dinner about three years ago. I wonder what took her so long.'

'Oh well, people always say these things.'

'I suppose you caught up with all the news from that side of the family?'

Helen's father had finished eating and pushed his chair back from the table to enjoy a cigarette between courses. He had already heard all this once and his eyes had that cloudy expression of one who was no longer emotionally present.

'Mary's got diabetes,' her mother said with a hint of relish.

There was still evidently a trace of rivalry between the various branches of the family and rude health was the one area in which she could triumph. As she gathered up the plates and placed them beside the sink, she went on to enumerate the afflictions of other long-forgotten relatives. The names meant nothing to Helen, but the litany of illness and infirmity had a depressing effect even so: arthritis, dropsy, gallstones, gout, shingles. There seemed to be scarcely one member of the extended tribe who was not bedridden.

'Good heavens,' she interrupted at last as her mother was momentarily distracted by the task of serving pudding. The string handle of the basin was proving hard to unpick and the pan of custard needed pouring into a jug. 'Was there no good news?'

At last the knots were untangled and the suet sponge was inverted onto a plate with a sucking sound and a billow of steam. Molten strawberry jam flowed down its slopes and pooled at the base.

'Oh yes – if you can call it good at her age. Kathleen's in the family way again.'

This news, so casually delivered, set off a series of small explosions in Helen's brain. From far away she heard a voice – her own – say with perfect composure, 'They've got two older children already, haven't they?' while her face burnt with the sudden shock and the effort of suppressing it, but no one was looking at her. The pudding, domed and streaked with red, was suddenly obscene and nauseating.

Her mother scooped a portion into a bowl and a blob of boiling jam flew off the spoon onto Helen's wrist. She gave a yelp and seized the opportunity to escape to the sink, where she was able to turn her back on the table and hide her confusion and dismay. *Pregnant.* Don't think about it now, she told herself as she let the cold water pour over her arm. Later. Be normal. *Another child. Eighteen more years.*

'. . . I noticed it straight away, but I hardly knew whether to congratulate her. I mean, she's in her forties. Very dicey . . .'

Her mother's voice flowed on. Helen dried her hand and returned to the table, her discomposure now safely ascribed to the jam burn, which had left behind a pink mark the size of a sixpence.

'In what way, dicey?' that other, responsive Helen asked.

'I think with older mothers there's a risk of the baby being abnormal. I remember a neighbour of ours when I was a child had a baby when she was forty-nine and he was born with no ears.'

'God alive!' muttered her husband. 'Do we have to have this while we're eating?'

Her lips clamped shut and for a moment they proceeded to eat in silence. Helen attempted a morsel of suet, moving it around her dry mouth and swallowing effortfully. It took all of her willpower not to gag.

Opposite, her father had spilt a drip of custard on the front of his pullover. It was just the sort of lapse that would once have riled him to fury, and no one would want to be the one to point it out. It seemed to glow, a pustulant, sickly yellow, and Helen felt her stomach squeeze in protest.

In her current state of mind, her usual precautions and appeasements seemed suddenly ludicrous and she said, 'Dad,' with unaccustomed sharpness and pointed at his chest.

To her surprise, he picked up his napkin and cleaned himself up without a murmur.

Why didn't he mention it? the inner voice continued to clamour. He must have known for ages. This evasion on the part of Gil was almost the worst of it, for if she wasn't his confidante, the keeper of all the secrets of his heart, what was she?

Her mother was looking at her strangely.

'I'm sorry,' Helen said, laying down her spoon and resting a hand on her stomach to indicate repletion. 'I can't manage another mouthful.'

'Oh well.' Her mother shrugged carelessly, but she was no good at disguising when she was offended. 'It used to be your favourite.'

Having already apologised once, Helen gave no more than a flickering smile and began to clear away. While she and her mother washed the dishes, her father disappeared to his shed to work on some piece of wood carving that was his current pretext for recusing himself from the company of his wife.

Once they were alone, her mother said, 'I hope I didn't upset you just then, with that talk about babies. I didn't think it was something that bothered you, with your career and so on. But then, I wondered . . .' She flapped her tea towel helplessly. 'I don't know.'

'It's all right, really,' said Helen, touched by this rare spasm of empathy. 'I don't think about it most of the time. I'm not in any position to, so . . .'

'I wish you could have met someone nice,' her mother burst out. 'It's a shame. You'd make a lovely mother, but how are you ever to meet anyone in your line of work? A girls' school and then a mental hospital, I ask you.'

Helen felt quite choked to see herself through her mother's eyes as perpetually lonely and unloved and she longed to correct her. This was impossible, of course. But the idea that the few crumbs of commitment that Gil could spare her from his laden table were all that stood between her and the accuracy of this image filled her with desolation. Without the assurance of his love, she had nothing.

'Well, actually, a man at work did ask me out to dinner a few weeks ago,' she said, to correct the pitiable impression her mother had formed of her chances. 'But I turned him down.'

She watched the transit of emotions, from hope to disappointment, cross her mother's face.

'Oh, why ever did you do that?'

'Because I don't like him. And' – it occurred to her for the first time – 'I don't think he really likes me.'

Her mother was nonplussed by this reasoning.

'Your generation has a queer way of carrying on,' was her verdict.

Helen left as soon as was decent after lunch, promising to come again before long. She was desperate to get back to the sanctuary of her flat and brood in solitude and be by the telephone if Gil should call. It was out of the question for her to ring him at home; she could only wait and hope. There was no good reason to imagine he would, just because she wanted him to. They had spoken in his office only two days ago, when he had asked her to take a day's leave on the following Tuesday so that they could go into the countryside together.

As she let herself into the hallway and checked the telephone pad to see if there was a message, Mr Rafferty was just coming out of his flat with the whippet on a lead. His face brightened at the sight of her and Helen could tell that he was eager to talk, but she had no stomach for neighbourly chit-chat and cut off his greeting with a brisk 'Good afternoon,' without breaking her stride. She sensed rather than saw him shrink back into himself as she ran up the stairs and was pierced with shame.

The flat was as she had left it: quiet, uncluttered and comforting. She dropped her bag, stepped out of her shoes and lay on the couch. The relief at giving way to self-pity and no longer having to pretend that all was well was immeasurable. Her teeth ached from the strain of clenching her jaw in a ghastly false smile. Even though she was now alone, she couldn't cry. Without an audience, there was no point to tears.

She had not been naïve enough to imagine that Gil and his wife no longer had sex. He had never claimed as much and she had chosen not to ask and not to mind. Now that she found herself confronting the unimpeachable reality of a pregnant Kath, however, she found that she did mind. A new baby changed everything – poisoning her feelings for Gil, postponing almost indefinitely any hope of a future together, and exposing the shaky structure of their relationship and the rottenness of its foundations. It made the daily contortions of conscience impossible to bear. She could hear Gil disputing with her. *What difference does it make? Deception is deception whether there is one child or seven.*

For a full five minutes she contemplated the end of their affair: her cool resolution; Gil's desperate pleading; her determination. It almost persuaded her that it could be survived. Her imagination, though, took her no further than that first sorrowful parting, with all its potential for passionate reconciliation. An eternity of tomorrows without him, without love of any kind, perhaps, was much harder to face.

She ran herself a bath, a reliable consolation in times of trouble, and threw in a handful of rose-scented bath salts – more spoils from June's job at Allders. She lay for a long time on the gritty enamel, trying to empty her mind of all troubling thoughts, focusing on the slow, hypnotic drip-drip of the tap, but there was no comfort to be had. The water in the tub was cooling rapidly. Twice she topped it up with hot, but the moment was fast approaching when she would have to get out and face the even cooler air of the tiled bathroom on her wet skin.

Her face in the mirror looked pink and mottled and suddenly old. Beside the washbasin sat the little dial pack of pink contraceptive pills that she had been taking so conscientiously for the past three years without any slip-ups. She took one now, choking it back with a kind of fury, along with two sleeping tablets. But even medication was no match for the restless churning of her thoughts, which kept her wretchedly awake until just before daylight.

Chapter 20

1947

The white cat had been appearing at the kitchen door for several days before William dared to leave it a saucer of watered-down milk. He knew Aunt Elsie would be livid if she found out he was wasting their rations on a stray or, worse, some family pet that was already being fed elsewhere. He had his arguments prepared: he was ready to take his tea black and forgo the splash of milk on his porridge. No sacrifice was required on her part.

The cat did not look well fed enough to belong to a family, but then neither did William, who had been more or less hungry since 1940. If it was a stray, he would adopt it; if not, he was happy to share.

The predicted confrontation was not long delayed. Stepping outside one morning with a basket of wet sheets for the mangle, Aunt Elsie had trodden in the saucer, tipping milk over her slipper. Her curses brought Louisa hurrying out of the front parlour, where she had been sweeping the grate and laying a modest fire for later, when the temperature was forecast to dip into the forties.

'I suppose you knew about this,' Elsie said, wringing out the toe of her felt slipper into the sink with an expression of disgust. 'That boy will be feeding our bread to the sparrows next.'

William, listening to this from the stairs, decided he should make an appearance to deflect the blame from the innocent Aunt Louisa.

'She didn't know. I only used the milk from my breakfast. I don't mind going without.'

'And you'll be wanting to feed it your fish supper, too, no doubt.'

William was half inclined to agree. He was not fond of fish, the way they experienced it – more skin and bone than flesh, rather like Aunt Elsie herself.

'Cats can take care of themselves,' she persisted without waiting for a denial. 'It can hunt birds and mice if it's hungry.'

'I won't give it any of our food. Just my milk,' he promised.

'It's not coming in the house,' Aunt Elsie added. 'It'll foul the carpets. And what if the real owner comes looking for it, knocking on doors and causing a fuss?'

'That's hard on him,' Louisa said timidly. 'When he can't go out in the garden in the normal way. It would be company for him.'

Aunt Elsie, who was no tyrant, conceded defeat with a long out-blow of breath. 'It can come in the kitchen. But it's not to be shut in the house overnight.'

She laid the rinsed slipper on top of the boiler, forced her feet into the mud-crusted shoes that she wore for gardening and went back outside to continue her labours at the mangle.

This negotiated outcome suited William, who was used to creeping into the garden on clear nights, even in winter, to watch for foxes or badgers and breathe in the scent of the dying year and map the stars. He thought they already knew this. He would be able to keep an eye out for the cat, too.

'I'm going to call her Boswell,' he confided in Aunt Louisa.

'That's a queer name,' she said, washing her sooty hands at the sink. 'Wherever did you get that from?'

'Francis had a dog called Boswell.'

'Oh,' said Louisa. 'I should have thought Snowdrop was a better name for a cat.'

For a moment she was wrong-footed. The Kenleys were never referred to even indirectly and now it seemed the memory of their wretched dog would ambush them every time the cat came mewing to the back door.

'Or Fluffy,' she suggested with desperation.

'She's short-haired,' said William, shaking his head. 'Not a bit fluffy.'

Undaunted, she continued to refer to the cat as Snowdrop, hoping that usage would win out in the end. Boswell had an unlikely ally, however, in the shape of Aunt Elsie, who was an admirer of the great biographer and had therefore no reason to question the provenance of the name or to connect it with the unmentionable Kenleys.

'Why are you calling Boswell "Snowdrop", for heaven's sake? Are you losing your wits?' she demanded of her sister one morning, and the non-literary pseudonym was promptly abandoned.

For a few months Boswell lived among them as a part-time guest, admitted each day just after breakfast and turfed out again at night. Elsie paid it no special attention, but Louisa was soon, like William, making secret sacrifices of morsels of her own rations. One day he caught her in the act of hiding a fish head, destined for soup, in her apron pocket until Aunt Elsie had left the room and it could be flung out of the back door to the waiting Boswell, but they never openly acknowledged the conspiracy.

William himself spent hours each day playing games with the cat, teasing her with the tassel of his dressing-gown cord or a jiggling cotton reel, delighted by her patient focus and sudden lethal pounce. Sometimes when she settled drowsily in a warm patch of sunlight on the kitchen floor, he would take his sharp-nibbed fountain pen and draw her with tiny feathered strokes. The best moments, though, were when she came to him and sprang onto his lap and lay curled there for hours, submitting to be stroked and petted, and he knew he was loved.

If there was one thing about Boswell he could not quite find it in his heart to approve, it was her habit of catching birds and leaving them, maimed and twitching, on the back doorstep. On one occasion there was even a gruesome headless squirrel, the raw flesh of its neck exposed, its lush tail still stirring in the breeze. He knew it was the cat's nature to hunt and he wouldn't have been so repelled if she had at least eaten her prey, but this was just killing for sport, and he needed no reminders of the world's savagery.

At the end of January came the first of the blizzards. As people who already lived as though permanently under siege, the Tapping sisters took a certain grim pleasure in circumstances that condemned others to similar privations. It was in this way that they had accommodated themselves to the war, until 1944 at any rate, when even shared misery was no comfort.

Apart from anxiety about Boswell, confinement on account of drifting snow made little difference to William. The garden was transformed into an unfamiliar landscape of pillowy shapes and glittering statues. A wheelbarrow, a birdbath, a spade left in the ground were all made soft and strange. Opposite, the park's allotments became one smooth meadow, traversed by snaking trails. Up on the rise, children dragged toboggans and trays and threw snowballs at the men with shovels who came to clear the paths.

The Co-op boy was not delivering on his bicycle, so Aunt Elsie took two string bags and stamped off to the grocer's in a long fur coat that had belonged to her mother in the days of their prosperity. It was now a flattened and mangy hide, reeking of camphor. She returned with a week's provisions and scarlet cheeks nipped by cold.

According to the *Croydon Times*, a baby had been found in a pram parked outside a public house under an inch of snow. Aunt Louisa read out the item in a tone of outrage and disbelief at the human wickedness on their doorstep. The ill-treatment of children always made her tearful.

'Was it frozen solid?' William wanted to know. He was worried about Boswell, who had not come to the back door as usual that morning.

'No, thank God. The two men who found the pram wheeled it to the police station just in time.'

'That will have given the parents a proper jolt when they came out of the pub,' said Aunt Elsie with satisfaction.

The weather continued to toy with them. Blizzards, then a thaw, then falling temperatures and slushy pavements frozen to crags of ice, then more blizzards and drifting snow banked against the front door. In the bluish moonlight, William went out and dug a path to the coal bunker but found it was nearly empty. Charringtons would not deliver – fresh supplies of fuel could not get through from the north of England, which was even harder hit, and local factories were threatened with closure. Aunt Elsie went out again to get paraffin instead, but she had left it too late; there was none to be had. She bought candles in case the power was cut off altogether, but they already had plenty and candlelight would not keep them warm. They continued to keep the kitchen boiler just alight, to keep the pipes from freezing, feeding it the smallest possible helping of coal to eke out their dwindling store. The rest of the house chilled rapidly around them and became almost uninhabitable. They congregated in the kitchen, clad in outdoor clothes. William, who had had no overcoat since he was a schoolboy, wore his dressing gown belted over his warmest jumpers, double socks and balaclava. Excursions into the arctic reaches of the house were undertaken in the spirit of reckless self-sacrifice.

Occasionally, Boswell presented herself at the back door at breakfast time, to the annoyance of Aunt Elsie. She begrudged letting it inside, with the accompanying inrush of icy air, in case it should somehow soak up a share of their boiler's meagre warmth, but knew she was outnumbered. At bedtime, though, she was immoveable and the cat was put out, mewing piteously.

One night in February when the snow was falling heavily again and the cat had not been seen for two days, William delayed his ascent to the upper storeys until his aunts had filled their hot-water bottles and taken themselves to their chilly beds. Judging that he was quite safe from their interference, as once in bed there was almost nothing that would induce a sane person to leave it, he began his act of desperate rebellion.

Boswell must be found and brought in overnight, to share his bed if necessary. He opened the door no more than four inches and waited for the cat to extrude itself through the gap. When she failed to appear, he peered out into the moonlit garden through the fall of blurry flakes. There was no sign of movement, but from somewhere beyond the trees came a distant yowl. He could feel the heat of the kitchen flowing out into the snowy night. Shutting the door again, he took off his outer pair of socks in order to crush his feet into the outgrown pair of shoes that served him for his occasional forays into the garden. Then he retied his dressing-gown cord and went outside, closing the back door gently behind him.

The change in temperature was sudden and brutal, but he did not intend to linger in the garden for more than a minute. Boswell usually needed no encouragement to come inside. He stood on the short, curved path he had dug to the coal cellar. It had already started to fill in, soft powder on top of ice. Even beneath the trees the snow was deep; above him, the branches of the fir tree sagged and trembled under their white pelts. He waded off the path towards the distant greenhouse, following tracks of disturbed snow, the cold plucking at his ankles. Dry flakes clung to the front of his dressing gown and blew into his face, sticking to his eyelashes without melting.

'Boswell,' he whispered into the darkness.

His cheeks were rubbery and numb. If she couldn't be found in the next five minutes, he would have to go back indoors and put on warmer clothing – gloves and scarf and Grandpa's boots. He began to hope that Boswell did indeed belong to a family up the road, as Aunt Elsie maintained, and was even now warm and comfortable in an airing cupboard on a pile of towels. He heard the yowl again, from several gardens away, clearly identifiable now as a fox.

He had reached the greenhouse, transformed into a fairy-tale cottage with snowy thatch, and peered through the freckled glass. Its dry cobwebbed interior would have provided Boswell with shelter from the blizzard but was firmly shut and William's frozen fingers could get no purchase on the slippery handle. A gust of wind whipped at his face and behind him an avalanche of snow slumped to the ground from the Scots pine. Where did the birds go to roost in this weather? he wondered.

His feet were too sore to continue any further, the toes like loose pebbles digging painfully into his flesh. Ahead lay the ruined henhouse, abandoned now these three years since the fox took Tiny, having slaughtered the rest of the hens. The wire netting had collapsed, parts of it since repurposed by Aunt Elsie as a fruit cage to protect the raspberry canes from birds. The wooden coop, tilted to one side on broken feet, seemed to ride the drifts like an ark. The hatch, warped and broken, hung from one hinge. He wondered if there was still any straw or sawdust within, which might have served Boswell as a warm bed.

He put his hand through the hole and withdrew it sharply as it encountered something hard and cold. Fearfully, already half prepared for what he would find, he leant forwards and looked inside. Boswell was curled up as though asleep, eyes closed, fur stiff with ice.

William's chest heaved in protest and a sob escaped him. He would have carried the body back to the house with him rather than leave her out here alone, but, to his horror, he found the corpse frozen to the floor and immoveable. It was only now that he realised, almost too late, that he was numb with cold and that if he delayed any longer, he would lie down and expire himself, here in the garden.

He shuffled back towards the house, blinded by the whirling flakes. Soon, thank God, he would be inside and warm, under the covers with a hot-water bottle between his knees. He fumbled with the door handle, his fingers burning, confusion turning to panic as it wouldn't open. Sometimes the wood swelled in the rain and caught on the stone step, but there was no movement at all now. It was bolted top and bottom.

He pressed his forehead against the glass to see if there was any gleam of light from within. It was Aunt Louisa, he was sure, who had come back downstairs and, finding the door unlocked, slid the bolts home. She was, of the two sisters, the most fanatical about security. Aunt Elsie had a sharper, more suspicious mind and would have realised immediately what he was up to and made a point of catching him out.

He was almost too confused and defeated to think what he needed to do. If he could wake Aunt Louisa, she might be prevailed upon not to mention anything and he would avoid a scolding. But her room faced the street, and the high side gate was padlocked shut and the key on a hook indoors.

He felt a kind of rage against them both for locking him out without a thought, for banishing Boswell, his only real friend. He was so cold and tired, his hair wet and crusted with ice, and his bladder was bursting. Perhaps he would die out here just inches from safety and they would find him in the morning and be sorry.

There was a sudden release, a rush of urine, warm and wonderful at first and then instantly cold, stinking and disgusting.

'Aunt Elsie,' he whispered up at her curtained window. 'Help me.'

With stiff fingers, he packed a small snowball and threw it at the glass. It hit the brickwork and fell away as dust.

'Aunt Elsie,' he called, a little louder.

This time the snowball hit the window with a low *thunk*.

A light flared in the house next door and he cringed, flattening himself against the wall. This was the unforgivable sin above all others, which would bring calamity down on them all. Better to crawl into a snowdrift and fall asleep like brave Captain Oates.

To his right was the entrance to the coal cellar. His dead fingers scrabbled uselessly at the wooden hatch, but after a few kicks it shuddered open. The steps descended into a terrible darkness, dirty and reeking of anthracite dust, but at least dry and sheltered from the biting blizzard. The opening was so small that William had to bend almost double to fit under the lintel. As he unfolded himself, his shoe slipped on the slimy top step and he jerked upright, knocking his head on the rough brick ceiling and pitching forwards into space.

Chapter 21

It was only as Helen drove into the car park the following Monday and saw Gil's usual space empty that she remembered he was away at a conference in Bristol. This meant that their conversation – Helen tried not to think of it as a showdown – would have to be postponed until their day off. She didn't have long to ruminate on her frustration, as she had hardly proceeded more than a few paces inside the building before Olive signalled that she had two visitors – a Mr and Mrs Kenley.

This designation confused Helen into expecting a married couple, but as she turned to where the pair were sitting, she realised she was looking at mother and son.

Marion Kenley wore her silver hair in a neat chignon like a Frenchwoman or Princess Margaret. Even though she was plainly dressed in a navy wool suit and flat shoes, there was something almost regal in her appearance. Serenity, perhaps, or just self-assurance, Helen thought. Francis Kenley, though bearing a family resemblance – blue eyes and a long straight nose – looked much less relaxed, shifting uneasily on his vinyl chair and tapping its wooden arms. He sprang up as Helen approached, either from politeness or impatience; it was hard to tell. He was smaller than Gil and had a far less commanding masculine presence. He met her gaze not with a sparkle of flirtation like Alistair Duggan had done, but with the careful courtesy of a clergyman greeting a parishioner.

Helen looked from one to the other with curiosity and introduced herself. It seemed that Francis was to be the spokesperson.

'I'm sorry to turn up unannounced,' he began, lowering his voice as a group of nurses burst through the double doors beside them. 'But after we spoke the other day, I talked to my mother' – he looked over at her with a smile – 'and she persuaded me that I'd perhaps been somewhat hasty, and that coming to see William was the right thing to do. If he'll see us.'

Helen felt somewhat ambushed by their unheralded appearance. She had not yet broached the subject with William and had intended that any such meeting would be planned in advance and mediated through Gil. But Gil was not here, she thought vengefully, and there were no rules that she was aware of that prevented William from receiving visitors if he consented to do so.

'I haven't actually mentioned it as a possibility to William yet,' she admitted. 'I imagined arranging an appointment some time in advance and then preparing him.'

'I'm sorry. It's my fault,' Marion Kenley said, rising to her feet. 'We were going to visit an old friend of my husband in Limpsfield today and I saw on the map that this was hardly out of our way. But you're quite right. You can't spring it on him.'

'No, of course. Absolutely not. We shouldn't have come,' said Francis, seizing the opportunity for postponement with rather too much alacrity.

'Perhaps we could come back another day, if you're not too busy, Francis?' his mother offered.

Helen hesitated. Now that she had them here in her grasp, she was reluctant to let them go. Other commitments and second thoughts might yet arise to prevent a future visit. The fact that Gil was not available to supervise was no fault of hers.

'No, don't let's waste this opportunity,' she said, glancing at her watch. Her first class was not due for an hour. If the meeting went well, a future visit could be arranged; if badly, she would be there to step in and bring it to a close early. An hour was plenty. 'I'll go and find William now and see if he is amenable.'

Breakfast was over and William was on his favourite bench overlooking the lawns with Smokey curled up on his lap. Other garden patients were already outside, taking their daily exercise or enjoying the fresh air away from the wards. A group of men was doing callisthenics, led by a lean and muscled instructor in shorts and a singlet. He strutted among the prone bodies, barking commands and counting down from twenty as they performed effortful press-ups with arched backs and sagging stomachs.

'Morning, William,' Helen called as she came within range.

He inched over to make room for her on the bench without disturbing the cat or taking his eyes off the exercise class.

'I have some news that might interest you,' she said. It was important to prepare him carefully for the unexpected arrival of long-lost acquaintances, but time was limited. 'I wonder if you remember an old school friend you stayed with one summer.'

He didn't move, but through the wooden struts of the seat she could feel a tremor of tension.

'Francis Kenley,' she went on, and watched the colour rise into his pale cheeks. 'I wonder how you would feel about a visit from Francis and his mother. They are both keen to see you, if you're happy to meet them. Of course, you don't have to.'

He turned towards her for a second and his face displayed a flickering confusion of emotions – disbelief, pleasure, panic.

She took a deep breath. 'The thing is, William, that they are actually here, right now, if you want to see them. But if you would rather wait for another day, that's fine. I'll ask them to come back. And if you don't want to see them at all, that's fine, too. But I need you to let me know which it's to be.'

All this time he had remained staring straight ahead, chewing his bottom lip. Without turning towards her, he gave a slow nod and stood up, pouring the cat gently onto the grass. His jacket was a little short in the sleeve and wouldn't have met in the middle even if there had been a button still attached, and his trousers gathered in pleats over his gym shoes. Helen's heart gave a lurch.

'William,' she said. 'You have porridge on your chin. May I wipe it off?'

But before she could offer him her hankie, he had used his cuff.

Helen had briefly considered bringing the Kenleys outside to meet William in the garden, but it was a public space and there was nothing to stop other patients from wandering over and interrupting. Gil's office, though available and perennially unlocked, was too much a psychiatrist's consulting room, with quite the wrong atmosphere. She settled on the art studio as being both spacious and private, and moreover a place where William felt at home. Telling him to present himself there in five minutes, she returned to reception to fetch the Kenleys and prepare them, as far as she could.

'As I mentioned on the phone, he doesn't speak, so it's probably best not to ask him direct questions. And his social skills – eye contact and fidgeting and so on – are a bit rudimentary.'

'Oh, I'm sure we'll manage,' said Marion cheerfully. 'Francis and I can chatter away to fill any silences. We won't stay long if things get sticky.'

Francis looked considerably less comfortable than his mother at the idea of 'chattering away'.

Helen was pointing out William's pen-and-ink drawings on the gallery wall, when he knocked at the door. She had

196

intended to monitor William's reactions to this potentially difficult reunion, but it was Francis she found herself watching as the former friends caught sight of each other for the first time. He had done his best to conceal his shock, but his smile of welcome was a brittle mask. Poor man, she thought, he doesn't know what to say or where to look.

Fortunately, Marion took command of the situation and approached William with a beaming smile and open arms.

'Ah, William, how lovely to see you after all these years,' she said, stopping just in front of him so that he could meet her in a hug or not as he chose.

William hesitated and then lunged forwards and allowed himself to be gathered into her arms. Towering over her, he held his arms out, uncertain what to do with them, finally giving her a few thumps on the back as though to relieve a choking fit.

Mrs Kenley gently disengaged herself, taking hold of William's hands and looking him up and down.

'You're looking wonderfully well,' she declared. 'Isn't he looking wonderfully well, Francis?'

At last the two men faced each other.

'Yes, very well,' said Francis with desperate joviality.

Helen felt for him in his awkwardness. He had known how it would be and hadn't wanted to get involved, but his mother had persuaded him and now he was suffering. As she turned her attention to William, she could see that he was, if anything, the more disconcerted. He was blinking rapidly, not in his usual nervous way, but because his eyes were brimming with tears that he was trying to contain.

'Francis,' he said in a voice that was high and hoarse, and full of sorrow and wonder. 'Why do you look so old?'

Chapter 22

'I'm sorry,' Marion Kenley said, dabbing at the corner of her eyes with a large, folded handkerchief. 'That was harder than I expected.'

William had departed for his Monday morning shift at the library, where he made himself useful reshelving books. Helen and the Kenleys remained in the art room for a brief post-mortem of the reunion before her first class of the day.

'I've never heard him speak before,' Helen said.

Although hoping for just this outcome, she had been unprepared for the curious treble of his voice, so completely at odds with his coarsely masculine appearance. Francis seemed the most taken aback.

'You were very natural with him, Mother,' he said. 'I'm afraid I was worse than useless. I knew I would be.'

'Oh no,' said Helen. 'It was you he wanted to see. That came across loud and clear.'

'I know,' said Francis unhappily.

'He looked so different and yet sounded just the same as when he was eleven,' said Marion. 'It was quite unsettling.'

If his visitors had been taken aback, William himself was no less shaken by the depredations of the passing years.

'You've gone grey!' he had said to Marion by way of greeting.

And she had laughed and said, 'I know. Quite some time ago and almost overnight.'

'If you see someone every day, you don't notice them getting old,' William explained. 'Like Aunt Louisa.'

The visitors nodded. Helen had urged them all to sit, drawing her own chair back so that it was just outside the group. She was finding William's voice so distracting, so strange and hoarse, that it took all of her concentration to focus on what he was saying.

'I suppose you are probably married by now,' William said to Francis after a pause.

'I was,' Francis replied. 'My wife died six and a half years ago.'

I bet he knows to the very day how long ago it was, thought Helen. Now that she knew this about Francis, she felt warmer towards him; it explained the sadness she was now convinced she had heard in his voice on the telephone.

'Was she pretty?' William asked.

From his wallet Francis produced a photograph of a young woman on her wedding day, smiling not at the photographer, but at someone else, away to the side, her face radiating joy.

'That's Evelyn,' he said.

William took it, nodded and passed it back.

'She was beautiful,' said Marion, laying a hand briefly on her son's knee.

'Inside and out,' Francis said quietly, and Helen was appalled to find tears spring to her eyes.

Don't you dare, she commanded herself. This isn't your tragedy.

'How is Boswell?' William asked suddenly. 'Is he still a good boy?'

Mother and son exchanged glances.

'Sadly, he's no longer with us,' said Marion. 'He lived to a ripe old age, though.'

'I had a cat called Boswell. Named after your Boswell,' William said. 'She died, too. In the snow.'

'That's sad,' said Marion. 'Animals are a great joy, but you do miss them dreadfully when they're gone.'

'William is one of our most talented artists,' Helen put in, thinking that perhaps they had talked enough about death. 'And he's particularly good at animals.'

'And birds,' said William.

'Yes, birds, too,' Helen agreed. 'I've shown you the ones on the wall, but there are more.' She went to the chest of wide, shallow drawers where she kept patients' work and produced the few sketches that she had retrieved from the house in Coombe Road. 'Do you mind if I show them?' she asked William.

He gave an embarrassed wriggle but made no objection. Francis studied each one without hurrying, making the occasional murmur of appreciation before passing it across to his mother.

'Oh, these are exquisite; you are talented, William,' she said, holding up the half-finished drawing of the refrigerated magpie. 'Look at the intricate shading on those tail feathers.'

Her praise was so enthusiastic, with just the right amount of detail, that Helen wondered if she had once been a teacher. Something about her reminded Helen of a popular mistress at her junior school, Miss Calvert. When she had left to get married, the whole class, boys and girls alike, had cried piteously.

'And do you draw from life or from illustrations?'

'From looking at the real thing and remembering it in my head,' said William. 'You can't get a bird to sit still.'

'This is Brock Cottage,' said Francis, who had come across the sketch of the house and garden. 'I'd forgotten that hammock.'

Marion leant across. 'Oh yes, and there's the old sumac tree that came down in the storm. You've captured it all just as it used to be.'

'It's not very good, really,' William insisted. 'There are gaps.'

'You must have the most extraordinary memory,' Marion said.

As if prompted, William started patting his pockets with increasing agitation, eventually finding what he was looking for inside the lining of his jacket. He produced the silver napkin ring and passed it to Marion with an air of apology.

'I expect you've been looking for this,' he said.

She accepted it with some surprise. 'Oh. The badger. Good heavens – I haven't used these for years. And you've had it all this time?'

William nodded. 'On the first night when we had dinner, you said, "This one with the badger on is yours" and I thought you meant it was mine to keep. So I took it home with me. But when Aunt Rose saw it, she said that's not what you meant at all. So I was going to bring it the next time I came to stay and put it back in the drawer with the other napkin rings. But then I never did come to stay.'

'Well, I'm not surprised you thought that and you are very welcome to it,' said Marion, handing it back to William. 'You have obviously taken good care of it.'

'It's my most precious thing,' said William. 'And badgers are my favourite animal.' He went to replace it in his jacket pocket and then, perhaps remembering the torn lining, changed his mind and kept hold of it.

'Yes, we used to see them at the bottom of the garden in Brock Cottage.'

For a while Helen listened as they reminisced about the holiday William had spent with the Kenleys in Sussex in 1938. It was clear that his hosts' recall of the details was nothing like as sharp as William's.

'We had a log fire every night.'

'Did we? In summer? Good heavens, how decadent.'

'Boswell got stuck down a rabbit hole and we had to dig him out.'

'That I can believe. Daft dog.'

'We caught a perch and kept it in a bucket in the wardrobe overnight and it died.'

'I do remember fishing,' Francis admitted. 'But not keeping anything.'

'Your father read *Moonfleet* to us at bedtime.' William stopped as if suddenly struck for the first time by that man's absence from the gathering and the conversation. 'Where is Mr Kenley?'

'He died ten years ago,' Francis said. 'He had lung cancer.'

'Aunt Louisa died last month,' William replied. 'I've got no aunts left now.'

Now that the conversation had swung back to death again and time was moving on, Helen decided to bring the meeting to a close. She had noticed Francis' discreet glance at his watch and was aware that her ten o'clock group would soon arrive. As if reading these signals, Marion reached over and gave William's hand a squeeze and said that they ought to think about making a move, and they all rose.

As they stood in a semicircle, saying their stilted goodbyes, with promises to come again soon from Marion, William risked a quick glance at Francis and then looked down at his feet again and mumbled, 'You never wrote.'

'The thing is,' Francis said, 'I'm sure I did write.' He seemed to have relaxed a little now that the ordeal was over. 'The way I remember it, *I* wrote but *he* didn't reply. But it's all so long ago I can't be sure – and it hardly matters now.'

Hearing this, Helen jumped up and hurried to the desk drawer where she had locked Louisa Tapping's tin box while she and Gil pondered what to do with it. She produced the thin bundle of unopened letters and passed them to Francis.

'Is this your writing?'

He turned them over and stared at her in surprise. 'Yes, it is. Where on earth did you get these?'

He passed them across to his mother while Helen explained their provenance.

'My God. I must have written them back in about 1938.' He screwed his eyes up to examine the smudged postmark.

'And his aunts kept them from him?' said Marion. 'What an extraordinarily unkind thing to do.'

'We've been wondering what to do with them,' said Helen. 'Dr Rudden has, I mean. We weren't sure what they might contain and it seemed too soon after Aunt Louisa's death to risk upsetting him.'

'Well, I doubt they say anything very alarming,' said Francis, glancing at his mother. 'Some old drivel about the dog or my latest Meccano model, I should imagine.'

'It's the fact of their being confiscated that is the upsetting thing,' said Marion. 'He must have thought we'd just abandoned him.'

'There was another thing in the box, along with some out-of-date banknotes. I don't know if it means anything to you.'

Helen showed Marion the obituary of Douglas Samsbury torn from *The Times*. The Kenleys looked it over but shook their heads, unenlightened.

'Well, anyway, I must let you go,' said Helen as her ten o'clock class arrived at the door. 'But I think we can count today a great success. It's the first time he's spoken. Thanks to you.'

She had to subdue a flutter of satisfaction that it was she who had discovered and recruited the Kenleys and not Gil, with his decades of learning and expertise, who had achieved this breakthrough. There was of course no guarantee that, having once spoken, William would not lapse into silence again, but

Helen remained hopeful that the Kenleys had gently opened a door and shown him that he had nothing to fear.

'Yes, that extraordinary voice,' said Marion, her own sounding far from steady. 'Poor William. He was such a lovely boy, so full of promise. I feel so guilty. I should have done more.'

'Oh, nonsense,' said Francis, sounding almost stern. 'You couldn't have known how things would turn out.'

'We've no evidence that he was mistreated by his aunts,' Helen reminded them. 'He seemed very fond of his Aunt Louisa, right to the end. And he wasn't a prisoner – in any conventional sense.'

'But surely it's the unconventional kinds of imprisonment that are the hardest to escape,' said Marion.

Chapter 23

'It must have been quite a moment. I wish I'd been there,' said Gil, stopping on the footpath and pulling Helen towards him for another kiss. There was no real envy in his tone, just pleasure in her success and an eagerness to see where it might lead.

'It was. I told them he was mute and might not respond and then he just . . . spoke, in this very high, child's voice.'

'There's a condition called puberphonia, where the male voice doesn't break. It hadn't occurred to me that might be why he refused to speak.'

They had arranged to meet at the car park of the White Bear in Fickleshole and take a long walk through the countryside with a picnic. It was a route they had done before, a favourite of Gil's as it offered a secluded spot away from the path where they could make love in the open. The gentle shushing of the wind through the leaves and the sprinkled sunlight on their bare skin made him quite lyrical. He was never so romantic indoors. On all of their walks they had not so far encountered anyone on the track, which was overgrown in places with cow parsley and nettles, which had to be gallantly kicked aside or trampled down by Gil.

He had still not mentioned Kath's pregnancy and having already been incubating her grievance for forty-eight hours,

Helen was reluctant to bring the matter up immediately and poison the rest of the day. She had wanted to tell him her news about William while he was still in a sunny mood and part of her also wanted to see whether he would take the opportunity to broach the subject without being challenged.

'Do you think that's really a reason to stay silent for months?' Helen asked. 'His voice was just . . . unusual. I mean, we know he was in the habit of talking to his aunt. She told us as much.'

'But she would have been used to it. And perhaps the Kenleys had only ever heard him speak that way, so he didn't see them as a threat.' He was holding her hand, kneading the fingers gently as they walked along.

'I was there too, though.'

'Yes. Clever old you.' He stopped again to kiss her.

'Why was I no longer a threat?'

'Perhaps because reconnecting with the Kenleys trumped everything.'

'I wonder. I'm not sure this will prove to be the big breakthrough I hoped. Without them, he'll probably just lapse into silence again.'

'It's possible.'

They were crossing a large field of broad beans just coming into flower. The soil was chalky and dry and there were thistles growing between the neat drills and across the path. Apart from their voices, the only sounds were the rustle of insects and the distant sputtering of a biplane, away towards Biggin Hill.

'Do you think they might be persuaded to come again?' Gil asked.

'Mrs Kenley, yes,' said Helen. 'Francis, I'm not so sure. He seemed deeply uncomfortable. But some people can't deal with anyone who's a bit different.' She thought of her mother, who rather would jump off a bus than share a seat with someone like William.

'You think Mrs Kenley was all right, though.'

'Yes, she was extraordinary. I can't really explain it, but she seemed to give off a sort of aura of calm.'

Gil raised his eyebrows.

'I mean, most of the time we're surrounded by patients who are emitting distress signals more or less continuously. She was the exact opposite; she seemed to absorb all the tension in the room.'

'You sound quite smitten.'

'I just found her incredibly soothing. Maybe I was comparing her favourably with my own mother.'

This mention of her mother was a mistake. Now, Gil would ask how her recent visit had gone and this would provide the obvious gateway to the awkward conversation that remained to be faced. But she didn't want to open the gate yet, so she quickly asked, 'How was Bristol?'

'Well, it's always bracing to realise how much opposition there is in the profession to new ideas.' He gave a short laugh.

They had reached the edge of the field now and crossed a road between high hedges into the wood. The bluebells were nearly over; just a scattering of bruised blue petals remained in a sea of green foliage. Next year, thought Helen, we must remember to come earlier, even if the weather is too cool for a picnic, and then remembered that by next year everything would be different and she might be alone.

Gil was carrying all the provisions – cheese, bread, pâté, red wine and two glasses wrapped in napkins – and the blanket in a green canvas rucksack, a relic of his solo walking tour to Scotland in 1938. He often talked of this episode as one of the peak experiences of his life. He had recently left school and set off to the Highlands for six weeks with just *Ulysses* and the complete Wordsworth for company. Apart from the occasional shopkeeper or crofter, he had barely spoken to another soul for six weeks but had never once felt lonely. Then had come his medical degree, interrupted by the war, and then marriage, and his youth was over. He had been back to Scotland since with Kath and the children, but it hadn't been the same; just scenery and small domestic crises, with none of the soaring epiphanies that had been an almost daily occurrence at eighteen. He still felt a deep attachment to *Ulysses*, Wordsworth and the rucksack, though. Helen liked his stories of this trip and often indulged him in their retelling. That they would go there one day together, she now realised, was another delusion.

From the bluebell wood they joined the rough track that led between uncultivated fields and paddocks to their favourite picnicking spot, through a gap in the tangled hedgerow, beyond a fallen tree and a thicket of brambles that provided a screen and a deterrent to any intrusion by fellow walkers. However, as they approached, they could see that the hawthorns had been hacked back and the blackberry bushes slashed, so that their usual corner was visible from the path. They exchanged a look of outrage and disbelief at this desecration of their holy place.

'Why on earth would anyone start clearing this area?' Gil said, his grip tightening on Helen's hand as though she might be about to give up the whole idea and turn back. 'It's not used for anything.'

'It's all completely exposed,' Helen lamented.

Nevertheless, they made their way towards their regular spot and stood there surveying the crushed and wilting vegetation and the uninterrupted view of the footpath.

'Perhaps if we move closer to the fallen tree . . .' Gil suggested. 'And lying down, of course, we won't be so conspicuous.'

'I don't know,' said Helen, who suspected that for Gil, lack of privacy wasn't the barrier to disinhibition that it was for her.

'It's not as if we have ever passed a single person on the path. I think we're the only people who use it,' Gil said, crouching behind the bole of exposed tree roots to see how much cover it provided.

'And yet someone has clearly been here,' Helen pointed out. 'Perhaps we should just eat the picnic and then go back to mine.'

The words had hardly left her lips, when there was a crashing sound of breaking twigs, which made them both start, and a large dog came bursting out of the undergrowth in the corner of the field and bounded towards them. It was an English setter with a silky, fringed coat and freckled face, and presented no kind of menace, capering around them and taking off through the trees, from which direction came the reproachful whistles of the owner. Helen laughed; Gil remained stony-faced.

Without acknowledging her suggestion, he shrugged off the rucksack and began to unpack the contents, unrolling the blanket and laying out the food. Helen felt the faintest vibration of discord between them, aggravated by her grievance about Kath, of which he was serenely unaware.

She sat down, kicking off her tennis shoes and allowing her sticky feet to cool in the breeze. Gil reached over and undid the top button of her sundress, a familiar gesture of ownership that today annoyed her. Perhaps if he had offered her a glass of wine instead, the day would have unfolded quite differently, but it is by these small acts that relationships are made and unmade.

'What would you say if I told you I was pregnant?' Helen said, surprising herself with the question. It was not at all what she had planned to say, but she took a vandal's delight in the chaos it would cause.

If Gil experienced a moment of raw fear at this outburst, he did well to master it and his face was expressionless. For a moment he looked into her eyes as though trying to read her motives, and then said, 'Well, that would rather depend on how *you* felt about it.'

Fine words, thought Helen, but she had no desire to torture him any further, on this particular rack at least, so she said, 'Good answer. I'm not, by the way.'

Having done a decent job of concealing his dismay, Gil was less successful at hiding his relief. 'Is this your way of telling me you would like to be?' he asked, ready to indulge her now that the immediate danger had passed.

Helen stretched out her legs and lay back on her elbow, watching him unwrap the food. 'No, I don't think so,' she said. 'The circumstances are not exactly ideal.'

'I agree,' he said cautiously, setting out the wine glasses and snapping open the corkscrew.

Helen waited. She could hardly have provided him with a more natural way in to a confession about Kath's pregnancy, and yet he still didn't use it. She would have to be the one to take a scythe to the day. A weary sigh escaped her and he looked up.

'Are you all right?'

'Yes, yes, I'm all right,' she replied, trying to keep her voice neutral. It was permitted to be sorrowful, but not hectoring or shrill. 'I'm just wondering when you were planning to tell me about Kath and the baby. When it's born?'

Gil's hand gripped the throat of the wine bottle. A lesser man might have blurted out 'How did you know?' as if that were the most important matter at issue, but Gil was better than that. He closed his eyes briefly against the bright light of accusation.

'I'm sorry. I should have told you. I've been waiting for the right moment, but there never is a good moment for this sort of thing. You can imagine that neither of us is overjoyed at the prospect of being parents again.'

'But how did you imagine that not telling me was going to work?' Helen insisted, ignoring this call for sympathy.

'I suppose, at first, part of me didn't expect the pregnancy to come to anything, given Kath's age and . . . history. I suppose I thought I might not need to tell you at all.'

'You mean you were hoping your wife might have a miscarriage?' Helen's voice was cool, analytical.

'No, not *hoping*, not like that. Just waiting to see.'

Helen shook her head. There was nothing he could say that wouldn't condemn him, one way or another.

'How did you find out?' he asked finally.

'Kath called on my parents out of the blue. They passed it on when I saw them at the weekend, as a bit of "family news".'

Gil had carried on uncorking the wine, as if this was not something that needed to derail their picnic, or their relationship, and handed Helen a full glass.

'Well. Cheers,' she said with a bitter laugh and then looked away, her eyes suddenly stinging.

He reached for her free hand. 'Darling, don't. This doesn't have to make a difference to us.'

'Of course it does. It changes everything.'

'Must it?'

He looked so defeated that she was almost persuaded. Then she thought of another eighteen years of secrecy and concealment, plans made and cancelled, and playing not just second but fifth fiddle, and knew that she couldn't and mustn't do it.

'I can't see a solution. I can't ask you to abandon Kath while she's pregnant or with a baby. If you did, I'd lose all respect for you. And if we go on the way we are, I'll lose all respect for myself. I already have.'

For some reason she couldn't fathom, it was Marion Kenley's kind, wise face that came to mind as she said this. They had barely met and Helen knew nothing about her, and yet she felt convinced of her goodness and shrank from the idea of her disapproval.

'I understand,' said Gil, summoning every atom of his therapist's skill to manage this catastrophe. 'But you don't have to do anything or decide anything this minute. We love each other. We're not monsters.'

She gave him a weak smile. He had chosen his words well. She wanted desperately to believe in the image of herself as an essentially good person put in an impossible situation, but she was not comforted for long.

'No, we're not monsters, but we are behaving monstrously.' *I want to look at myself in the mirror without guilt*, she thought but didn't say. *I want to be beautiful inside and out.*

Gil took the wine glass from her and set both on the uneven ground, where they promptly toppled over, staining the grass purple. They had lost all interest in food and drink now. He lay back on the blanket and pulled her gently towards him.

'Come here. We don't have to do anything. I just want to hold you.'

She allowed herself to be drawn down beside him and they lay tucked together, staring at the sky and the gauzy veils of cloud drifting overhead.

'I know you are going to leave me,' he said. 'I can feel you pulling away. And I don't blame you, but I'm just asking you not to act on impulse. Think it over for a couple of weeks – I'll leave you completely alone if you like; I won't even come near you – and see if life apart really is better. That's all.'

He had one arm around her shoulders. His other hand fluttered at the open neck of her dress and slipped inside to settle on her left breast.

'I don't know,' she said, shifting slightly. 'Of course it will be awful at first. Being apart. Maybe for a long time. But, eventually, perhaps it will be bearable.'

She was talking about the end of their affair while he continued to caress her, to draw her closer to him, to undo another button and then another. This is no way to leave someone, she thought, playing at parting while giving in to desire. He tugged at his belt and guided her hand to the front of his trousers.

'Fuck!' Gil said suddenly, sitting up and clawing at the back of his shirt. 'Christ, that hurts!'

He sprang to his feet and a wasp dropped onto Helen's bare leg. She gave a yelp and flicked it away, noticing as she did so that there were now three or four more circling around Gil's head, and another two on the blanket beside her.

'Where have they all come from?' he raged, twitching and ducking and batting them off, with the jerking movement of a string puppet.

She jumped up, flapping her skirt and backing away, taking care where to put her feet. To an onlooker, their capering would have looked only comical, but neither of them were laughing. The collapse of this solemn and precarious moment into farce was too humiliating to be funny. Now, she could see the entrance to the nest – a neat hole in the side of the hollow tree trunk beside them, from which more wasps were emerging, attracted by the sticky pool of spilt wine.

'Vicious bastards,' he fumed, craning to inspect the damage to his own back. 'There's not even a mark!'

They retreated to a safe distance and stood looking at the ruins of the picnic while regathering their dignity, but the interruption was fatal and the moment of intimacy lost.

'Let's go,' Gil said. 'This wasn't meant to be.'

Helen rebuttoned her dress and stuffed her feet back into her tennis shoes while Gil gallantly re-entered the fray to drag the blanket away from the nest and bundle the uneaten food back into the rucksack.

If they could have laughed at themselves and dealt with that prankster, fate, like any other bully, it would have been better, Helen thought as they hurried away, still swatting and tossing their heads like fly-maddened horses. Instead, they seemed to have accepted its estimation of them as fools and victims. Gil had taken her hand, but there was a chasm between them of unshared thoughts running on parallel paths.

She didn't repeat her invitation to come back to her flat and they parted in an atmosphere of melancholy, with nothing settled.

'I love you. Think about what I said,' were Gil's last words as he got into the car and they went their separate ways.

There was a heaviness in her tread as Helen walked up the path to the wide front door with its cracked paint and stained-glass fanlight. Listlessly, she flipped through the uncollected post in the basket on the hall table. There was nothing for her, but by the telephone someone had taken a message in heavy ballpoint, which had engraved the notepad to a depth of several pages: FLAT 3. JUNE RANG. PLEASE CALL HER BACK.

She had no spare emotional capacity for a conversation with June – the mere thought of it made her want to weep with weariness – but there was something about those imperious capitals that tweaked at her conscience. So, she rang the number and, getting no reply, tried again in the late afternoon and then in the evening, when she finally got through and learnt from Clive that Lorraine had suffered some kind of mental collapse and been admitted to Westbury Park.

Chapter 24

— *1944* —

The piano had not been tuned for five years, which made no difference to Aunt Elsie or Aunt Louisa, who couldn't play it and had no ear to judge the corrupted sounds it now produced. Aunt Rose was the musical one and still took pride in her skill at the keyboard, even though her only audience was indifferent. The sound of the piano reminded them of the convivial gatherings of their youth, happier times now over, and even jaunty tunes made them sad.

The instrument had belonged to their mother and was invested with memorial power. The house was full of such heirlooms, tended like gravestones in honour of the dead. It was as custodian of her mother's relics rather than as a music lover that Aunt Elsie had arranged for a piano tuner to visit between Christmas and New Year.

Mr Mortimer duly arrived on the twenty-ninth of December in his Morris Ten with a leather case of tools and a jar of honey from his hives in Sussex. He was thin, as all decent people were after four years on rations, and long-sighted, with eyes blown up to cartoonish proportions behind powerful glasses.

From his attic room, William could hear the babble of voices below and the creaks and knocks of the piano lid being removed. He had always kept out of sight when a stranger was in the house, of course, but at seventeen was going through what Aunt Rose called a 'dreamy phase' and spent most of his time upstairs, content in his own company. All three aunts had stayed to watch the proceedings, to begin with at least; Elsie in case Mr Mortimer was light-fingered with the ornaments; Louisa because it was something different to watch; and Rose because she was the pianist, and because male visitors, even of this elderly and unglamorous kind, were a rarity.

After a while the voices stopped, replaced by the plunk of individual notes over and over. William was arranging his lead soldiers, boxes of them accumulated since he was small. He laid them out not according to the patterns of military campaigns, which held no interest for him, but so that they formed intricate pictures when viewed from above – an owl, a tiger's head, a skull.

Up the stairs came the light, tripping steps of Aunt Rose, as distinctive as her voice or her perfume. A moment later there was a tap on the door.

'Billy?'

She was the only one who called him that and the only one who bothered to knock. In she came and flopped down on his bed, in the posture of the drowned Ophelia but on her chest a pack of Rothmans and a lighter, instead of scattered wildflowers.

She was wearing one of her smart dresses, bottle green with pink stitching. Unlike Aunt Louisa and Aunt Elsie, who favoured sturdy woollen skirts and hand-knitted cardigans that didn't show the dirt because they were already dirt-coloured, Aunt Rose refused to bow to dreary practicality. 'What's the point of saving things for best when the best is all over?' she sighed. During all those nights of bombardment, she had taken to sleeping in her finest clothes out of sheer defiance.

Now, they slept in their own beds. The cellar, which had been their regular shelter during the Blitz, would be no protection against the new rockets, which arrived with no warning and pounded a house to dust. There was no effective precaution against this fresh terror, so responsibility for one's survival lay with fate. For protection, Aunt Rose wore a lucky rabbit's foot; she had offered it to William but he had refused, revolted at the idea of hanging a dead animal's remains around his neck.

From her reclined position on his bed, she gave a blustery sigh. She had made up her face for the piano man but he had been a disappointment – old and unable to flirt because he needed to listen to the notes. He had practically ejected her from the room, she said, for talking.

'But,' she added, 'he didn't come empty-handed, so there will be bread and honey for tea.'

'I wish we had bees,' said William.

'And a fish pond, and dancing shoes, and a dog and a tennis court and a silver fox tie and someone to dance with,' she laughed. They used to play this game of 'I wish I had' when he was little, each one adding another item to the list until memory failed. It wasn't so much fun now, when there was so little prospect of having any of the things they wanted, however modest. She lit a cigarette and lay blowing smoke at the ceiling.

'Let's play cards,' she said when it was smoked down to the stub and pinched out.

Of his aunts, she was the one who could always be talked out of her sewing or darning or diary writing for a game of backgammon or Chinese chequers or rummy. It was a terrible thing to have a favourite – the word made him shudder – and yet, in his silent, stifled heart, she was his. At thirty-four, she was much the youngest of the sisters and was still treated by her elders as the baby, for whom exceptions must be made, but who also needed keeping in line. He saw less of her now that she had a job during the day. None of the Tapping sisters had ever worked, until rumours of the government's plans to draft single women into factories and farming and other masculine occupations reached even the sequestered residents of the corner house. It was Mr Eckerty, the administrator of the trust, who had hinted that Rose might be vulnerable to this policy and suggested that he use his many contacts to find her a clerical job before she was conscripted into something less congenial. It was agreed by all that she would never make a nurse; she was too squeamish, feather-brained and impractical to be of any use.

Instead, thanks to her pleasant voice and attractive appearance, she had been taken on by The Gas Company as a receptionist. She would set off in the morning in her neat wool suit and velour hat, gas mask swinging, with almost a skip of relief at escaping the gloomy house. Most of her colleagues were men too old or unfit to be called up and their names came up in conversation at dinner. Mr Havers, Mr Belper, Mr Cotton. Of Mr Harrison, there was no mention any more. There was also a secretary, Morag, whose Glaswegian accent Rose took off and whom she referred to as her friend. Naturally, none of these faceless characters ever came near the house.

As well as snippets of conversation, Aunt Rose also brought back the sorts of rumours and gossip that didn't find their way into the papers. When the scent factory had been destroyed by a bombing raid, the *Croydon Times* reported that there had been no fatalities. The figure carried back by Aunt Rose was forty-six. This seemed too precise to be disputed, but Aunt Elsie said she was more inclined to believe the printed word than office gossip.

'Oh, they won't put the real numbers in the paper,' Aunt Rose had said with the air of someone repeating a piece of managerial wisdom. 'They don't want to put it about that we've had lots of casualties. That would just make the Germans cock-a-hoop.'

'Well, in that case, you shouldn't go telling all and sundry that there were forty-six dead,' Aunt Elsie retorted. 'You're doing the Germans' work for them.'

'You're hardly all and sundry,' Rose objected. 'Anyway, I think it's better to know the truth than be told a tissue of lies.'

Aunt Elsie shot her a look. 'Untruths are unfortunately necessary sometimes.' There was something pointed, sharpened almost, in the remark.

'Especially when it comes to keeping people safe,' Louisa agreed.

Truth or safety, William thought. Must it always be one or the other?

He hated a lie, because it could never be undone. Even if you confessed, how could anyone believe the confession of a liar? Every future statement, however innocent, would have to be viewed with scepticism, tested and verified, rather than assumed to be true. It was better to be silent, he thought.

He had experienced a short episode of mutism six years earlier, which had been paralysing and frightening and quite beyond his control, and since then he had deployed it in a voluntary capacity on more than one occasion. It was regarded by his aunts as a minor malady and just another sign of his difference.

He selected the blue deck of cards from the box and entertained Aunt Rose with his shuffling tricks, honed over countless hours of idleness. He could cut the pack over and over one-handed, and flex and flick them in a neat arc from one hand to the other, or spread and flip them over in a smooth wave. He had all the skills of a croupier, without ever having seen one or known such a job existed. Aunt Rose could hardly have been more impressed if he had taught himself Greek. Everything about him was a wonder to her.

They played a hand of regimental rummy, William sitting on the wooden chair, Aunt Rose on the bed, with the little desk between them, and then a fierce and high-speed game of racing demon, with much slamming and accidental bending of cards. Aunt Rose insisted on playing for money – hers, so William couldn't lose. She was always finding excuses to slip him a few shillings, even though he had no opportunity to spend it. Still, he liked to thumb the coins into his black tin box with the slot in the lid and hear his fortune grow.

After these games she was bored again and restless.

'Billy,' she said, prowling the room, looking at his shelf of books and the few familiar ornaments as if something new and fascinating might have materialised since her last visit. 'Wouldn't it be wonderful to get away? Just get up and go.'

Her trailing hand rested on the framed photo of him as a baby in the arms of his parents. It was the only one taken of the three of them together. She picked it up and looked at it through narrowed eyes.

'I took that picture, you know. And then before the film was even developed . . .' She replaced it gently.

'Go where?' he said, choosing to follow up the first of her comments rather than the second.

'Oh, I don't know. Somewhere far away from Croydon.'

'Like Scotland?' The land of David Balfour. It was the furthest place he could think of that was reachable in current circumstances and one that held a certain appeal.

'I don't know. I was thinking of somewhere warmer. The French Riviera. When the war's over, I mean.'

'I don't think it will ever be over,' William said without emotion. In truth, it made little difference to him. The anxiety he felt for his own safety and freedom had somehow been shared out across the whole country and this provided a queer sort of comfort.

From the front parlour, the striking of individual notes had given way to chords and arpeggios rippling up and down the scale, a sign that the job was nearly done. Aunt Rose sprang up.

'I'd better go and test it. They'll be expecting a tune. And I was going to give him some eggs for the honey.'

She swept out, leaving behind a trace of her rose-petal perfume, her dreams of flight apparently forgotten.

William put the cards back in their box and straightened the furniture. From his high window, criss-crossed with tape, now peeling at the edges, he saw her trotting down to the henhouse, coatless, clutching her arms across her body against the cold. She was the one who looked after the hens: Myrtle, Philly, Ada, Goldie and Tiny. They were her babies and he wondered how she could have thought of running off to France without them. It was just another spasm of regret for her lost chance and wasn't to be taken seriously, he decided.

For tea there was bread and honey and stewed apples with honey and coffee and the luxurious sweetness made the four of them quite cheerful. Aunt Rose played 'The Clouds Will Soon Roll By' and 'Someone to Watch Over Me' and then some Debussy, almost swooning with pleasure over the piano's new brightness of tone.

The collective fit of good temper seemed to have set in for the evening, so William fetched down his Chinese mah-jongg set – a Christmas present from Aunt Rose, purchased at Kennards at no small expense. He knew no more about it than that it required four players and the occasions when all three aunts were amenable to games were rare.

The card table was unfolded and the wooden box opened with due ceremony, the tiles tipped out onto the baize. The booklet of rules ran to many pages and William grew self-conscious and dismayed under his aunts' gaze as he tried to make sense of them.

'It's very like rummy,' he began, 'but with three suits instead of four. Characters, sticks and circles. Oh, and then there are winds and dragons.'

The three women started to pick over the pieces, exclaiming at the intricate designs as he turned the pages. The scoring was incomprehensible and William was wondering whether it could be dispensed with altogether and replaced with some simpler system using pennies for a win, but he could already sense Aunt Louisa growing restless. There was a drama serial on the Home Service that she was following and if she missed an episode, she would be at sea. He turned back to the beginning and began to read aloud:

'Each player's hand always consists of thirteen pieces, and in his turn he draws a fourteenth piece and discards a piece, thereby maintaining his hand at the correct number. The object of the game is to get a complete hand of fourteen pieces, which with certain exceptions must consist of four sets of three pieces, each set being either three identical pieces or a sequence of three consecutive numbers in the same suit and a pair of identical pieces known as The Head.'

'Oh, Billy, this won't work,' said Aunt Rose at last. Her hands fluttered over the patterned tiles as though selecting chocolates from a box. 'It's too complicated for our feeble brains. We'll never get the hang of it like this.'

There was a mutinous rustling and fidgeting around the table. The convivial atmosphere of earlier had evaporated.

'Perhaps,' Aunt Louisa ventured, with a glance at the clock on the mantelpiece, 'it would be better if you took it away and read all the rules and *digested* them, and then tomorrow you can teach us how to play. Hmm?' She tipped her head to stare at him over her glasses.

'Oh, all right,' he replied, dragging the tiles towards him and shovelling them back into the box. It would be another one of those games for which he would have to devise a new set of one-player rules. 'We won't, though, will we?'

'Yes we will,' the sisters chorused, their faces eager, guilty.

He took the box upstairs and stowed it on top of the wardrobe with other items that would never be used: fossil hammer, tennis racket, a bucket and spade bought by the Kenleys in the summer of '38, his kite. If they wanted to play mah-jongg, they would have to come to him; he wouldn't mention it again.

Extinguishing the light, he drew back the blackout curtain. Through the window he could see a hard, bright moon, not quite full, drenching the garden with bluish light. He would creep out later and watch the stars. As far as he was concerned, the blackout, though depressing as to its cause and duration, was a blessing in its effect. On clear nights the galaxy was opened up for him to explore, fathomless and somehow comforting. Set against its cold infinity, human troubles seemed to lose a little of their power.

Aunt Louisa, contrite after catching most of her serial on the wireless, opened the door, his hot-water bottle in her outstretched hand.

'We're off to bed,' she said. 'Sleep well, dear.'

'Thank you,' he replied, accepting the bottle in its knitted jacket, and the apology that was included.

As soon as she had gone, he would take the cover off; it seemed to gather all the heat to itself. Her mania for knitting and crocheting extended far beyond a rational desire to insulate. She had moved on from teapots, boiled eggs and saucepan handles, and had turned out woollen covers for the piano stool, the bread bin and the door knocker.

William took the spare blanket off the bed and wrapped it around his shoulders. He had outgrown his last winter coat years ago and no one had noticed or thought to buy him another. It was understandable and he knew that if he pointed out this omission, a coat would immediately be forthcoming. No one would say, which was true, 'You hardly have any use for an outdoor coat,' and so he had never asked for one, but he said it to himself.

As he crept downstairs, he could hear the muffled plunks of Aunt Rose practising the piano with her foot on the mute pedal. He waited to see if he could recognise the piece from the strange dead percussion; not impossible, as her repertoire was confined to a dozen or so favourite pieces. *La fille aux cheveux de lin*, he decided, but a horribly suffocated version.

The music stopped but Aunt Rose did not appear. When he put his head around the door, he saw her standing on the hearthrug gazing up at the portrait of Grandfather Ernest as though in a trance. He could interrupt her and see if she wanted company, but instead he chose the stars. The talk of women was tiring sometimes and so he turned away from the front parlour and crept out of the kitchen door.

In the few minutes since he had looked out of the window, the moon had risen and shrunk, but its light was still fierce. Beyond the trees, just in front of the henhouse and nowhere else, was a curious scattering of snow. He had not thought it cold enough and then he realised with a jolt of panic that it was not snow but feathers.

The door to the coop swung open. Inside was a scene of slaughter: blood, down, viscera. There seemed to be no survivors. Myrtle, Philly, Ada, Goldie – all slain in a reckless feast of killing. He stood, winded by horror at what he was seeing, the air squeezed from his lungs. From the roosting box came a rustling sound and a sleek fox, eyes blazing, faced him with Tiny in his clamped jaws. She was still alive, her wings twitching. And then it was gone, streaking across the garden, onto the upturned wheelbarrow, the greenhouse roof and over the wall.

Without a second's reflection, William took off in furious pursuit, hauling himself over the wall, skinning his hands and losing the blanket as he went. He dropped down onto the pavement side, beyond the boundary of the house for the first time in six years, just in time to see the fox loping away up the hill away from the park.

It was not moving fast and was somewhat impeded by Tiny's limp form flapping between its front legs. William could easily have outrun it, but there were front gardens on both sides with picket gates and spindly hedges under which it could easily slip and vanish. There was no light apart from the moon gleaming on the white feathers. William had good night vision – it was sunlight that blinded him – and even in the velvety darkness he could make out the pale blurred shape of Tiny as the fox emerged from one of the gardens and cantered along the middle of the road to the brow of the hill.

He had not run like this since rugby training at school and there was no strength in his legs for acceleration. His lungs burnt with every breath as he laboured up the slope, but he kept on, his panting grunts the only sound in the hushed street. There was no sign of life from the blank-faced houses on either side.

At the corner he stalled, bent double, astonished at his own weakness. He felt suddenly a long way from the safety of home and yet he had come hardly any distance. There was the fox, fifty yards away, fixing him with that remorseless stare. He couldn't hate it; all carnivores had to hunt and he could perhaps have forgiven the snatching of one hen if the others had been spared. It was the recreational killing that sickened him.

The fox seemed almost to shrug and turned away into the front garden of a large house set back from the road. The blackout curtains had not been properly closed and lamplight leaked from a triangular gap at an upstairs window. In the absence of any other artificial light, it was dazzling.

There was a choice of routes into the back garden where William could not trespass. It was too late anyway. The bird was dead, its head hanging down from the fox's jaws. As if it had all been a game, the fox dropped – in fact, almost spat – the hen onto the path and then turned and vanished into the shadows at the side of the house.

William gathered the mortal remains of Tiny; its snowy plumage was curiously undamaged. Someone would have to tell Aunt Rose her babies were all dead, and even without being told it was her doing, she would remember not properly closing the door in her haste to fetch Mr Mortimer some eggs.

William was nearly home when he heard the double explosion: one bang, a screaming whistle and then another bang. His route had followed an almost perfect rectangle and he couldn't have said where the sound came from, just that it was nothing, *nothing* like the bombardment of the Blitz, even when the bombs had landed in the park opposite. It was not something that could be experienced as noise at all. It was too vast and terrible; it threw him off his feet and made the ground quake.

When he opened his eyes minutes or perhaps hours later, he expected to be blown in half and the world around him obliterated – trees uprooted, houses pulverised – but there was nothing to see at all. The park, the road, were still the same. On the doorstep he met Aunt Elsie, who pulled him inside, gibbering. Her mouth was opening and shutting, naked and cavernous without its dentures, but making no sound.

He held up the corpse of Tiny to explain about the fox, but she looked at him blankly. She pushed past him and ran into the street, turning one way and then the other and almost dancing from foot to foot in confusion about which way to run. He hadn't noticed Aunt Louisa in the gloom of the hallway, almost unrecognisable with her hair uncoiled and hanging to her waist in a young girl's braid. She seemed to fall on him, not scolding but hugging him with relief. Now that he was indoors and safe, though, she, too, stepped past him and went to look for that other, who had followed him out into the darkness to fetch him back and had not come home.

Chapter 25

Lorraine was sitting on the edge of her bed in the ward in her brushed cotton dressing gown, picking at her nail varnish. Without make-up and with her hair pulled back in an Alice band, she looked about twelve. Her expression was foggy and she gave a faint smile, more of apology than welcome, as she registered the arrival of a visitor.

Helen sat beside her on the bed and put an arm round her slumped shoulders. 'Hey. Did you think you would come to keep me company at work?'

Lorraine blew a puff of air through her nose by way of a laugh and said, 'Yeah.'

'Your mum said you had a bit of a turn yesterday.'

She had had the whole story from Clive and June the night before. Lorraine had been halfway through her maths exam at school, when she had started to feel unwell. The pages of numbers and symbols had suddenly seemed overwhelming, frightening, and she had fled from the exam room in tears.

June had been called and had to come and collect her, driving in a state of high panic, attacking right turns and hill starts and the crowded car park until she was almost as overwrought as Lorraine. Helen could hardly imagine a less comforting presence in a crisis.

Clive had met them back at the house and both parents had sprayed Lorraine with anxious questions about her symptoms, which she had been unable to answer. She had said she couldn't hear them over all the quacking noises in her head and couldn't understand anything they were saying, and she had sat in the corner of her room curled into a ball with her hands over her ears to block out the voices until they had called the doctor. She had been admitted, voluntarily, to Westbury Park by Lionel Frant and was being treated as his patient.

This was the aspect of the situation that caused Helen the most unease and regret. If only she and Gil hadn't been off on their disastrous tryst the day before, Gil would have been the one to admit Lorraine and be responsible for her care – a much more reassuring prospect.

'How are you feeling today?'

Lorraine shrugged. 'I don't know. I don't know how I'm meant to feel.'

'Oh, Lorraine.' It wrung her heart to hear the flatness in the girl's voice.

'I don't feel ill, but I suppose I must be.'

'Why must you be?'

'Because everyone says I am,' came the doleful reply.

'Who says so?'

'Mum and Dad and the doctors – the GP and that man yesterday.'

'What do they say?'

'Mum and Dad say I must be ill or I wouldn't be behaving like this.'

'What about Dr Frant?' Helen tried to keep her voice light and free of any undertone of disapproval. Without full confidence in the person treating her, Lorraine could hardly be expected to make progress, but all the same, Helen wished it had been anyone else.

'He just asked a load of questions and said "mmm" a lot and said he'd see me again tomorrow and then the nurse gave me some pills to take. I can't remember the name. They had z in. Or an x.'

'They all do,' Helen smiled. 'The important thing to remember is that you will feel better soon. Come to the art room. If you feel up to it.'

'Maybe,' said Lorraine. Her eyes filled with tears. 'I don't really feel like anything.'

It was lunchtime before Helen had an opportunity to find Gil and regale him with news of Lorraine. He had been doing ward rounds, then seeing patients in his room and then had an urgent call-out to a house in Limpsfield, but she finally ran him to ground outside Morley Holt's office, where he had been to discuss his intention to apply for the vacancy.

'I need to talk to you,' she said.

He seemed surprised and pleased to see her so soon after their ambiguous parting the previous day and Helen realised she was now in the uncomfortable position of asking a favour while refusing to grant one. She had not changed her mind overnight about the necessity of parting, but this was not at all what she wanted to talk about.

Gil nodded and they reconvened at the art room a few minutes later, having come there by different routes. As soon as the door was closed, he took a step towards her, but she stopped him with a shake of the head.

'Something's happened. My niece, Lorraine, was admitted yesterday. Voluntarily, thank God. By *Lionel*. We've got to get her transferred to you.'

He looked nonplussed, both by this development and by her reaction to it, and Helen remembered now that she had never bothered to tell him about Lionel's clumsy invitation and her even clumsier rebuff.

'On what grounds?'

'Well, because he's Lionel! You've said yourself he overprescribes. He'll have given her a diagnosis of schizophrenia the minute she mentioned hearing voices and pumped her full of chlorpromazine and God knows what else. If he hasn't already.'

'Whoa!' said Gil, holding up his hands. 'I know Lionel and I disagree on ideology, but I don't think he's guilty of malpractice. He believes he's doing the best for his patients. Anyway, pretty much everyone disagrees with me on ideology, if Bristol was anything to go by. They all think chlorpromazine is a wonder drug.'

'But she's not schizophrenic. She's just a normal young woman who's struggling with all these family tensions.'

Gil raised his eyebrows, as he always did at the word 'normal'. 'I can't go barrelling in and demand to take over another doctor's patient. It's unheard of.'

'You said you'd resign rather than work under him!' Helen reminded him. Her voice had risen at least an octave and she knew it was working against her. 'Is that supposed to fill me with confidence?'

'Oh well, that's just because I wouldn't want to take orders from him,' said Gil. 'He'd be insufferable.'

'I don't want somebody insufferable treating my niece! I don't trust him. He doesn't like me and he'll be deliberately punitive.'

'First, how will he even know you are related?'

'We've got the same name, Gil! And it's bound to have come up. June will have said something.'

'And, secondly, why would he feel punitive towards you of all people?' He spoke slowly and calmly, as if to one of his patients.

They were interrupted by a loud and sudden grinding noise from outside as two of the laundry staff struggled to wheel a huge metal cage of bed sheets past the window. It had a buckled wheel and they were laughing and swearing at its hectic progress. Helen waited until they had turned the corner before replying. 'He collared me in here and asked me out to dinner and I turned him down in a rather blunt way. I mean, he left me no choice, but it was very awkward.'

At last, she had wrong-footed him.

'You never mentioned it,' he said with the merest flicker of a frown.

Helen blushed. It was only yesterday that she had berated him for withholding information from her. This was trivial in comparison, but still.

'I felt sorry for him. I didn't want you to gloat.'

Gil shrugged to imply that he was above all this.

'But it gets worse. A few weeks later, you passed me in the corridor and tucked my label in — it was an intimate sort of gesture — and he saw.'

'Well, if he did, he hasn't done anything about it. And, realistically, what could he do? There's nothing preventing relationships between colleagues.'

'He can't *do* anything. But it's grounds for resentment. And now he's got some measure of power over Lorraine. I don't like it.'

Gil ran a weary hand through his hair. 'I think you attribute more conventional human emotion to the man than he actually possesses. I doubt he's capable of treating Lorraine according to any principle other than his usual unimaginative, by-the-book, describe-and-prescribe method.'

'That's the very last thing she needs. I wish you could just talk to her. You'll see what I mean.'

'By all means I'll have a friendly, unofficial chat to her, as her grandmother's cousin's son-in-law eight times removed, or whatever I am. Happy?'

She gave a grudging nod, aware that he didn't take her objections entirely seriously and was only humouring her. Rather than give up at the first sign of resistance, she would go higher.

Morley Holt was dusting the succulents on his windowsill when Helen knocked. He seemed unembarrassed to be caught in this somewhat frivolous activity and showed no inclination to abandon it.

'Miss Hansford,' he said, waving her to a seat while he continued to wipe the leaves of his sempervivum with a damp handkerchief.

He had a gift for remembering names and always acknowledged her when he passed her in the corridor. He had visited the art room on several occasions unannounced, staying just long enough to make her worry that it was some kind of formal appraisal, but it never was. He gave the impression that his staff were every bit as important to him as his patients and that he would refuse no unreasonable request. Helen had not so far put this to the test, but she had not forgotten that when Lionel Frant had raised the idea of quantifying the value of art as a therapy, Dr Holt had been one of the first to come to her defence.

'How are you, Hellin?' he said with his curious way of pronouncing her name. 'I'm sorry I haven't been in to see you for a while, but I'm afraid meetings tend to get in the way of my walkabouts.' He applied the tip of a paintbrush to one of the hard-to-reach crevices of an aloe.

'Very well, thank you. I've come to ask for your help with a . . . family matter.'

He gave her his full attention now, laying aside his cleaning materials and taking a seat at his desk.

'A family matter,' he repeated with a trace of unease.

Perhaps he thinks I'm pregnant, thought Helen, and began to explain her concerns about Lorraine, a little hurriedly to allay any such fears. 'My niece has just been admitted as a patient of Dr Frant.'

'Oh dear, I'm so sorry.'

'Yes, well. I rather hoped she might be under Dr Rudden, as − I can't remember if you're aware of this − he is also a distant relative by marriage. And I think . . . that is . . . her parents and I would obviously feel more comfortable if she was in the care of Dr Rudden . . . as part of the extended family.' This was a stretch, as she had as yet heard no such thing from Clive and June.

Dr Holt looked momentarily bewildered. 'I'm sorry. Are you saying you want Dr Rudden to treat this young woman *because he is related to her*?'

'Well. I mean, not only that. I think Dr Rudden is an excellent psychiatrist and would give her the best possible care.'

'Dr Frant is also an excellent psychiatrist,' Dr Holt replied. 'You don't have any specific objections to him that I ought to be aware of?'

'No, no, nothing like that.'

'I'm glad to hear it.'

He waited, smiling. Like Gil, he had the habit of allowing silences to expand until his petitioner stepped, floundering, into the void.

'I would just prefer it if Dr Rudden were responsible for Lorraine's treatment,' Helen said lamely.

Dr Holt peered at her over his half-moon spectacles. 'My dear Hellin, this is most irregular.'

'I suppose a situation like this doesn't arise all that often.'

She was uncomfortably aware that she had not made her case well, that perhaps she had no case at all, beyond a prejudice against Lionel and a thoroughly unprofessional partiality to Gil.

'In the normal way of things, one might well have ethical concerns about a patient being treated by a family member, certainly. But hardly the other way about.'

'Oh well, Dr Rudden is a very *distant* relative. By marriage. They have never even met. His wife's mother and Lorraine's grandmother are first cousins.'

The superintendent's brow furrowed with the effort of processing this lineage.

'Have you already spoken to Dr Rudden about this?'

'Yes, briefly.'

'And what does he have to say about it? I should have thought he would be very uneasy about poaching a patient from a colleague. It would set a very odd precedent.'

'Yes, he obviously wouldn't feel comfortable doing that. But if the request came from you . . .'

Dr Holt drew in a thin, whistling breath and glanced at the clock on the mantelpiece. 'I'm not persuaded that this scheme is necessary or desirable. But I don't want to be hasty in making a decision, since you have taken the trouble to bring it before me and it is clearly important to you. I have a meeting with the hospital board in five minutes, but I'll give it some thought and let you know by the end of the day.' He stood up.

'Thank you,' said Helen, convinced now that her errand had been useless – worse than useless, in fact, as he would now regard her as someone with questionable judgement.

'You won't mention anything to Dr Frant?'

'If I decide there is any merit in your request, it will be essential to do more than merely "mention" to Dr Frant why the young woman is no longer to be his patient.'

She was making it worse now. He would think her an idiot. 'I'm sorry, I shouldn't have asked. I wouldn't want him to think I have gone behind his back or that I don't have confidence in him as a doctor. Thank you for listening anyway.'

'It's always a great pleasure to see you, my dear.'

As she left the office, Dr Holt turned back to his succulents, rotating the pots through 180 degrees to stop them from leaning towards the light.

At the end of the day, when Helen was putting some clay models in the kiln for firing overnight, the superintendent's secretary brought her a letter, marked confidential, and left it on the desk. Without bothering to wash her hands of the film of clay that was now drying at the edges and beginning to crack, Helen tore open the envelope. She knew it would contain a refusal; if it had been good news, he would have told her in person to enjoy the benefit of her gratitude:

3 June 1964

Dear Helen,

I have as promised deliberated at some length over your request and find myself unable to agree to it, for several reasons.

First, and perhaps least importantly, precedent. It is not and never has been our practice to allow patients or their families to choose which doctor is allocated to their case. This seems to me a principle worth upholding.

Secondly, Dr Rudden's position as a relative of the young woman, albeit a distant one, should in fact preclude him from treating her as his patient to avoid accusations of preferential treatment, conflict of interest and other ethical considerations.

(You may be asking yourself if your own relationship to the patient ought therefore to prevent her from attending art therapy sessions. To this I would say that the two cases are not equivalent, as you are in a supervisory rather than a clinical role and not providing any 'treatment' as such. Thus, the prohibition does not apply.)

*Finally, I took it upon myself to speak to the young woman
and happened to encounter her mother, who was visiting.
During an informal conversation, and unprompted, she declared
herself quite satisfied with the treatment her daughter was
receiving and singled out Dr Frant for particular gratitude. This
ought to reassure you that the immediate family is happy with
the current arrangements.*

    Yours sincerely,
      Morley Holt MRCP
      Medical Superintendent

Helen dropped the folded paper on the desk in frustration and
scrubbed her hands at the sink with Palmolive soap and a nail
brush until her skin smarted. She accepted the justice of Dr
Holt's points, but his last paragraph made her uneasy. A conversation with June would almost certainly have revealed that
it was not 'the family' pressing for Dr Frant's removal. It was
mortifying to have been caught out in this pointless untruth.
She was also worried that Dr Holt might have discussed the
issue with Lionel himself; he had certainly made no assurances
not to. Altogether, she felt that her well-meant interference
had done Lorraine and herself no favours at all.

Chapter 26

Gil sat in his usual ultra-relaxed pose, legs extended and crossed at the ankle, one arm over the chair back, while William sketched his portrait and Helen washed brushes and palettes at the sink. It had been Gil's idea to observe William in the art room, reasoning that having already broken his silence in that setting, he might be persuaded to do so again. If he was absorbed in an activity that required some concentration, the conversation could proceed in the background, without being the focus of the meeting. Helen had refrained from reminding Gil that he had agreed to stay away from her for a couple of weeks; William's presence at least guaranteed that their inter-action would remain purely professional.

As ever, Gil's approach was leisurely, patient. He had accepted the role of artist's model without a murmur, barely flinching when William muttered 'Keep still.' Helen had to turn her head away and chew the inside of her mouth to stop herself from laughing.

Every so often William looked up, squinting at his subject for a few moments, and then lowered his head and scribbled furiously. Never having used an easel, he could not be per-suaded to now, preferring to work hunched over a table as he had at home, with his paper flat in front of him.

At last, Gil stirred himself to begin a conversation. 'I gather you had visitors on Monday. Would you like to tell me about that?'

There was no reply. He's not going to do it, thought Helen with something like perverse pride in her protégé. She did not really want him to retreat into silence; it was self-evident that communication was essential to his rehabilitation, and yet she couldn't help feeling a flutter of satisfaction that she had so far succeeded where Gil had not.

'I was just wondering what moved you to speak on that occasion.'

William sighed. Without looking up, he said, 'Because Francis is my friend. I wanted to talk to him.'

If she had closed her eyes, Helen would have believed she was listening to a boy rather than a middle-aged man.

Gil marked this significant moment with no more than a quick, flicked glance at Helen.

'How did it feel, seeing him again?'

'I knew this would happen.' William's voice was a whisper of disappointment.

'What would happen?'

'If I started speaking, you would keep asking me more and more questions.'

'So, is it questions you don't like, rather than the act of speaking itself?'

'That's a question.'

At the sink, Helen smiled to herself. William was no fool, she thought, wondering who would prevail in this gentlemanly battle of wills.

'All right. I won't ask questions. In fact, you can ask me questions instead. Go on – anything you like.'

Gil was also no fool and there was no word or phrase yet invented that had the power to embarrass or shock him. He had fully anticipated turning the tables, she decided, and had assumed an almost horizontal posture as a gesture of subservience. Perhaps in this he had gone too far; he had begun to make fractional adjustments to his position and she recognised the familiar grimace that indicated that his back was tweaking.

'Am I mad?' said William.

He had still not made eye contact with Gil but kept his head bent over his sketch.

'No, I don't think you're mad.'

'Some people here are mad, though.'

'Some people here are certainly suffering, but I don't think the word "mad" is really accurate or helpful.'

'Mathilda is definitely mad,' William said.

Someone had left the staffroom door open and a tray of coffee mugs clearly visible on the draining board. She had had quite a spree before one of the nurses had intercepted her.

'The way I see it,' said Gil, 'society is prepared to tolerate a range of behaviour, which it deems "normal". Outside that range is behaviour that might be deemed eccentric but harmless – growing a very long beard, for example. And then beyond that again there is behaviour that prevents people from functioning in society and causes them and others anguish. Smashing crockery, for example.

'It is our job to alleviate anguish and help them to function. Of course, different societies draw these boundaries in different places. So, if there is no absolute agreement about what is "normal", there can hardly be agreement about who is "abnormal" or "mad".'

Helen had heard this speech, or a version of it, more than once and it struck her now, as then, as persuasive and true and yet also somehow missing something important. 'Society' – with its iron rules and arbitrary labels – was not some powerful, unified group. It was everyone – the eccentrics and the anguished and the doctors and the patients included – so it could hardly speak with a single voice.

'Taking your clothes off in the day room and smashing all the crockery is mad, though,' William insisted.

'It is certainly very inconvenient if you are wanting to make a cup of coffee,' said Gil.

It took William a few seconds to recognise this remark as a joke and his usually guarded expression brightened, and he gave a surprised bark of laughter. The sound made Helen look up – she realised it was the first time he had displayed a sense of humour. If the session achieved nothing else, this was surely progress.

The sketching continued in silence for a minute or so until, without waiting for a prompt this time, William asked, 'Will I stay here for ever?'

'That rather depends. If you were well enough to go home and find some way of supporting yourself, I don't see why you shouldn't in due course. This isn't a prison – the gates are always open.'

'But who would look after me?'

'That is one of the things to consider.'

'I don't *mind* it here,' William said hastily.

'That's good to hear,' said Gil, in the smooth tone of the desk manager at a country hotel.

There was a pause as William stopped to sharpen his pencil, an operation he performed with great concentration, and then he said, 'When will I see Francis again?'

Forgetting his duties as a model, Gil turned towards Helen. 'That would be up to Francis. Sorry,' he added, reverting to his previous position as William made a murmur of irritation.

'People are my least favourite thing to draw,' he sighed.

'I can get in touch with the Kenleys and see if we can organise another visit,' Helen volunteered without much confidence. Privately, she suspected that Francis felt his duty was now done and he would make excuses to avoid another meeting. It would be down to her to translate these apologies to William in a way that would not hurt.

'There. Miss Hansford will arrange it,' said Gil, ignoring her reproachful signals. She had made no such promise. 'Ask me another. Anything you like.'

'What is the worst thing you ever did?'

Gil paused. 'I married a woman I didn't love,' he said at last.

Helen realised she had been holding her breath. She should have known he wouldn't demean himself by lying to William unnecessarily. It was as if there was only so much duplicity in him and it had to be conserved for his wife and mistress.

William seemed unimpressed.

'I've told you my secret, William,' said Gil casually. 'Now tell me something about you. Your earliest memory.'

William had his head down, pecking at the page with the tip of his pencil. There was a long wait before he spoke.

'My parents died in a car crash. It wasn't my fault. I was a baby.'

'And then what?'

'I don't want to talk any more,' said William. 'It hurts my throat.' He made a choking sound. 'I've finished. Can I go now?'

He was almost at the door before Gil was on his feet inspecting the portrait. It was quite different in style from his minutely detailed animal drawings and was made up of fine fluid lines that gave no more than an impression of Gil's languid posture and dishevelled hair. All the detail had been reserved for the armchair, which had been vividly rendered in thousands of tiny points of lead.

'It's very good. May I keep it?' Gil called, to which William replied with no more than a nod as he left the room.

Helen, looking over his shoulder, felt that William had captured an aspect of Gil without perhaps even realising it. A refusal to be caught.

'Should I be insulted?' Gil asked. 'I seem to be less interesting than a chair.'

Helen laughed. Without the inhibiting presence of William, there was a danger Gil might steer the conversation towards their own predicament, so before this could happen, she said, 'That went well, don't you think?'

'Very.'

'Do you think speech therapy could help with his voice?'

'To make him sound more "normal", you mean,' said Gil, giving her a sardonic look.

'Yes!' said Helen, her own voice emerging as an indignant squeak. 'What is wrong with that?'

'I think it's possible that exercises could lower his voice by a semitone or two, but I'm not sure he sees it as something that needs fixing. When you first mentioned it, I thought it might be the reason for his reluctance to speak. But that clearly isn't the case, or at least not the whole case.'

'But it's such a distraction from what he's actually saying. It's the only thing you notice about him.'

'It may make other people feel uncomfortable, but surely that's their problem, not his?'

'Gil, you are such a fanatic!' Helen protested. 'Not all conformity is bad.'

He smiled at her without conceding.

'I spoke to Lorraine, by the way,' he remembered, pressing his hands into his lower back and wincing.

'Oh, good,' said Helen, who hadn't expected him to co-operate quite this quickly. 'And how did you find her?'

'Quite delightful, of course. How could she not be?' he said with heavy gallantry.

'I meant clinically speaking,' she said, refusing to accept the flattery.

'It's a little early to say,' he replied. 'I'll go and see her again tomorrow.'

Chapter 27

They had refused an Anderson shelter because there was no one to do the heavy work of digging it in and covering it with earth. William could easily have done it and would have jumped at the chance of a project like this, but it was unthinkable for him to be seen in the garden by nosey neighbours, even in wartime. Especially in wartime. Anyway, they had a cellar that would do just as well, accessible both from the kitchen and from a hatch outside for the delivery of coal.

He and Aunt Louisa had rigged up a sheet on a piece of dowel to form a partition to hide the unsightly coal heap and swept and scrubbed the half that was to form their shelter. It was furnished with one mattress, shared by Rose and Louisa, a metal camp bed upholstered in stiff green canvas for William and an upright kitchen chair for Aunt Elsie, who never slept during a raid or attempted to. The camp bed had to be treated with extreme caution, as the slightest movement caused it to tip over or crumple. There were blankets and pillows, a bucket of water, and a chamber pot hidden behind the sheet curtain. It was made clear that this was only for situations of the direst need and that resorting to it was selfish and unpatriotic.

In a brick alcove was an old biscuit tin containing 'emergency supplies', sealed shut against damp, mice and incursions by

Aunt Rose. No one else would have dared. It would never be opened, for there might always be another, greater emergency to come. Night lights and matches lived in a pair of terracotta flowerpots, but even though the room was windowless, these muffled flames were kindled only with great trepidation, as much for fear of bringing down the wrath of the authorities as of drawing German fire.

William preferred his solitary attic room to the damp cellar full of aunts, but he was no rebel and certainly didn't think as some imaginative souls did that bad things only happened to other people. Experience had taught him otherwise and he accepted the need for unpleasant precautions in this as in so much else.

Aunt Rose was the one most likely to forget instructions and tire of the rules. She had already wondered aloud whether in the event of a direct hit they would be buried alive in the cellar. For this she had received such a fierce rebuke from Aunt Elsie 'for scaring the boy' that she had been brought to tears. The thought had already occurred to William, but he would have preferred it to have stayed in her mind, unvoiced.

Once it was apparent that the threat was real and that the nightly air raids were causing destruction not just in London, but also in Croydon, and not just to the factories and airfield, but also to the park opposite and the adjoining streets, Aunt Rose had taken to sleeping in her best clothes and using her mother's fur coat as a blanket.

'If I die, at least I'll die well dressed,' she said. 'And if the whole house goes up in flames and I survive, at least I'll have one decent outfit.'

William's favourite part of the day was when she came in from her job at The Gas Company, bringing what she called 'news from the shires'. Her speciality was 'the near miss', a story related by one of her colleagues about a friend of a friend, or a cousin of a neighbour – someone at any rate unimpeachable but just too far removed for verification – who had survived by the narrowest of margins or in some comical manner.

'Mr Belper said his sister's mother-in-law was sitting in the bath upstairs when a blast took the whole side off the house. She couldn't get out because there was no floor to step onto – only the bit the bath was standing on.'

'Morag's landlady said that her brother in West Croydon was caught by the hospital bomb. The explosion blew a manhole cover through their front window and it took off his leg – no, don't pull a face, Louisa, it was an *artificial* leg! He'd already lost the real one in the last war.'

Aunt Rose's three-pounds-a-week wage was mostly swallowed up by the expenses of the hungry house – coal, paraffin, the electric light bill – but it was understood by her sisters that she needed her little treats or she became melancholy, and so the appearance of a pair of kid gloves, Lux soap, a copy of *Housewife* magazine would pass unremarked. Sometimes, too, she came back from the office with hard-to-find items – sweets, chocolate, her favourite Rothmans cigarettes – gifts from her colleague, Mr Harrison. At first this was regarded by Aunt Elsie and Aunt Louisa as a great coup and a cause of celebration, then suddenly it wasn't any more and Aunt Rose stopped mentioning him, though the treats kept coming. This development was puzzling but suited William; instead of being divided four ways, the offending Maltesers and caramels were smuggled up to his bedroom by Aunt Rose and shared in secret.

While Aunt Rose was out at work, Aunt Louisa occupied herself with cooking, cleaning and laundry. Aunt Elsie took responsibility for the garden, chiefly the large vegetable patch beyond the trees. She was always looking to expand this allotment; the ground near the house was strangled with tree roots and hopeless for cultivation, but the trees were important for privacy.

For a while she had had her sights on a sunny but modest flower bed by the wall, which Aunt Rose had planted with hollyhocks, lavender, delphiniums, allium and a pink rose tree. It had taken years to bring this patch to maturity so that everything was perfectly positioned for height and spread and produced a display of pinks and purples from early to late summer. William was aware that in the many quarrels over this piece of disputed terrain he was somehow a pawn.

'I know you love your flowers. We all love flowers, but we need every scrap of earth for vegetables,' Aunt Elsie whispered when she thought he was asleep during a night in the shelter.

He wasn't pretending to sleep, merely lying very still to prevent the camp bed from pitching him out.

'It's not easy making three lots of rations go four ways,' Elsie continued.

'Well, you might have thought of that on Registration Day,' Rose hissed back.

Beside her on the mattress, Louisa was purring evenly.

'I did it to keep him safe. As you well know,' came the reply.

He never heard how that conversation ended, because the all-clear sounded and Aunt Louisa sat up suddenly and said, 'Are you there, Selwyn?' and there was an awkward silence because the tragedy of his parents, Selwyn and Alma, seldom broke the surface and no one knew quite what to do with it when it did.

'What did you mean about making three lots of rations go four ways?' William asked Aunt Rose the next time they were alone. 'Don't children get coupons?'

'Oh, Billy, you can't worry about things you overhear. It was just me and Elsie being grumpy.'

'I couldn't help overhearing. You were talking right across me.'

'I'm sorry. Have a Malteser. Mr Harrison gave them to me.'

They took one each and there was a moment of quiet communion as they let them slowly dissolve on the tongue.

She pushed the box towards him. 'You keep them up here. You've got more willpower than me.'

'What did you mean about Registration Day?' he persisted.

'Oh. Well. Look.' She was right about having no willpower. 'We had to fill in a form, ages ago, at the beginning of the war, to say who was resident at this address. So your Aunt Elsie thought it would be a good idea to leave you off the form so that no one would know you were here.'

'But if I'm not here, where am I?' William asked.

'Nowhere officially. Which is good. So no one will want to know why you're not at school. But it means you don't get a ration book. Which is not so good.'

'Does that mean we won't have enough food?' His voice rose even higher. The idea of this state of hunger lasting or getting worse was almost more dreadful than the bombs. Apart from a fleeting sensation of not-quite-fullness after meals, he was always ravenous. They already gave him far more than his share; twice what they allowed themselves, so he could never object. He remembered when he was small how meals used to be no more than a nuisance, an interruption to the real business of his life, which was playing in the park, and how bitterly he resented coming in for tea. He wished he had banked every missed crumpet and slice of cake, every offer of second helpings refused.

'Of course there will be enough, Billy,' Aunt Rose promised, turning a watery gaze upon him.

A few days later, the flower bed was gone, the shrubs and bulbs dug up and the ground raked over and scored with neat drills. Only the pink rose bush in the corner of the plot had been spared. In response, it erupted almost overnight in an extravagant display of frothy blooms, as if making the case for its survival. Aunt Rose cut some of the nearly blown flowers and brought them indoors to give up their last gasps of scent in the back parlour. Fallen petals she gathered in a bowl for her bedroom.

247

Up close, their perfume was sweet and soapy and somehow clean. William would have liked some for his own room, which had a sour, musty smell of old books and even older furniture, but he knew that it was unmanly to care for flowers, so he didn't ask.

'What's that smell?' Aunt Elsie said in her usual blunt way, coming into the kitchen in search of a ball of twine while Aunt Rose was refreshing the water in the vase.

'It's the "Comte de Chambord",' she replied, a name that sounded to William like a Dumas villain, rather than something to be found in a garden in Croydon. 'You know – the one that you spared.'

'Ah,' said Aunt Elsie, mindful that she had had the best of the compromise. 'Yes. Very nice, too.'

There were more roses the next day, not the French aristocrat this time but a dozen white, long-stemmed, wrapped in tissue paper and brought in under Aunt Rose's summer coat. William, sitting on the landing in a trance of boredom watching a spider spin its web between the banisters, saw her come in and move stealthily towards the stairs, when she was intercepted by Aunt Louisa.

'Oh, what's that?' she asked, tweaking at the wrapping paper and adding in a lower voice, 'Another gift from Mr Harrison?'

'Yes.'

Aunt Rose's laugh was like the tinkling of the crystal chandelier in the hallway when Aunt Elsie took it down and wrapped it in muslin to save it from the bombs. She leant in and whispered something in her sister's ear and Aunt Louisa let out a strangled gasp.

Dinner was late that night. Dinner was never late. William had been reading on his bed, but no one had come for him or called him, so he had to leave Edmond Dantès in the Château d'If and investigate.

There were no cooking smells coming from the kitchen, which meant a cold collation at best, though there was nothing, as far as William could remember, from earlier meals left over to collate. Instead came voices, not raised exactly but tense and mutinous. He stopped on the bottom step, not concealing himself in any way that would be deceitful but waiting and listening.

'A good opportunity for you, you mean.' This was Aunt Elsie.

'For William, too. Carshalton's a nice area. Nobody knows us. We could have a normal life again.'

'Marry this Mr Harrison if you must, but you're not taking William. You must be mad even to think of it. Think of the questions.'

A jolt ran through William and his heart began to flutter and thrash like a bird in a chimney. He had heard the name Harrison before; until today, it had belonged to one of Aunt Rose's colleagues at The Gas Company, a source of chocolate and treats, but now it was uniquely menacing. Would this stranger be coming to live with them here, or worse, taking Aunt Rose away with him? The thought of such monumental change was shattering.

'But this could be my last chance!'

'What have you told him about William?'

'Nothing. I've never said a word.' There was the metallic snap of a cigarette lighter and a moment later a needy inbreath.

'You can't just foist a fourteen-year-old boy on someone. He may not want to take on responsibility for a child.'

'I think he would. I think he'd do anything I asked,' Aunt Rose said.

'And how on earth do you propose to explain why he's not at school or on the register? We'd have the authorities involved before you can say knife.' Aunt Elsie's voice, sharp and jabbing, was not unlike a knife itself.

'You just want to keep me a prisoner here for ever.'

'Nonsense. You come and go as you please, and you always have done.'

'We just want to protect William.' This was Aunt Louisa's first, tentative contribution.

'You don't. You just want to punish him. And me.'

'Oh, Rose, that's not true!' Aunt Louisa's voice was a wail.

'Take no notice of her,' Aunt Elsie said. 'She's being silly and selfish. It's the flower bed all over again.'

'We're not stopping you from getting married, dear. But William must stay here.'

'But how would I be able to visit him if I'm not even allowed to tell James he exists?'

'Well, you'll have to make your choice,' said Aunt Elsie.

There was a pain in William's chest of breath held to bursting point. He exhaled and sat down dizzily on the stairs. The bump and creak seemed to fall in a momentary lull in the conversation.

'Shh, he's coming,' whispered Louisa, and then the three women all began to talk at once in artificially high, cheerful voices.

Nothing much was made of the lateness or the meagreness of dinner — a can of celery soup bulked out with a few early potatoes from the garden, and bread and margarine — or the fact that Aunt Rose was not eating with them but had gone to bed with a headache.

Afterwards, he took the box of Maltesers down from their safe place in his room and knocked at her door. He was desperate for something sweet but wouldn't help himself without her. There was no reply, even when he said, 'It's me, William,' and when he let himself in, the room was empty, the satin counterpane undisturbed. Puzzled, he made his way downstairs again, but she was not in the front parlour with Aunt Louisa, who was listening to Lord Peter Wimsey and darning lisle stockings over a wooden mushroom, or in the kitchen with Aunt Elsie, melting candle stubs for new night lights.

'Where's Aunt Rose?' he asked. 'She's not in her room.'

'Probably seeing to the hens,' Aunt Elsie replied without turning.

William backed out of the room, holding the Maltesers behind him. The best view of the garden was from the bathroom on the first landing and from here he looked down on the figure of Aunt Rose in her cotton overall and leather gloves, slamming the spade into the roots of the 'Comte de Chambord'. It had been hacked down to the ground until all that remained was an empty socket of earth. The severed branches formed a neat pyre and drifts of bruised petals were strewn across the path like confetti.

Chapter 28

Before Helen had the chance to contact Marion Kenley to pass on William's request for a second meeting, she received the following letter:

Dear Miss Hansford,

I hope you will forgive my writing to you in this way. Since our visit the other day I have been reflecting on William's situation and wondering how I can help him. It weighs on my conscience that years ago I did not properly follow up concerns that I had about his welfare and that this failure on my part may have contributed to his suffering since and his current unhappy circumstances.

I'm afraid I cannot give details about the background to this without betraying the confidence of more than one person, something I am not prepared to do. I can only say in my defence that, at the time I am speaking of, my own family was going through a period of difficulty and I allowed this to become my focus.

I should add that I was most impressed with the care that William has been receiving from you and with your encouragement of his artistic gifts. If there is any way that I can support him, either financially or as an advocate or

guardian if such a thing is appropriate, I would be happy to
hear from you.

    Yours sincerely,

    Marion Kenley

Helen needed no further prompting to telephone Marion and invite her to visit Westbury Park again at the earliest opportunity. The letter, with its intriguing suggestion of secrets and regrets, was exactly the kind to arouse her curiosity and demand immediate action. The prospect of seeing Marion was, in any case, a pleasant one.

If she had hoped that an announcement that there are things that cannot be told was merely a tantalising preamble to telling them, she was soon disabused. Marion's integrity was non-negotiable.

'Your letter was very enigmatic,' Helen hinted when they spoke on the telephone.

'I'm sorry for being so mysterious, but that's the way it has to be, I'm afraid,' Marion replied, dismissing all further enquiry for ever.

'It's very generous of you to offer help,' said Helen, accepting the rebuff as her due. 'I'm not sure what William's financial situation is, but he doesn't have any immediate need of funds while he is here. He certainly needs a friend, though – especially someone who remembers him as he was when he was well. He has already asked when he might see Francis again.'

'Ah,' said Marion. 'I thought he might. I can't, unfortunately, volunteer Francis for further visits. Only myself.'

'No, of course not. It was good of him to come at all. It must have been very uncomfortable for him.'

'I think it was and I certainly can't put pressure on him to do anything he doesn't want to do. I'm aware that William was very attached to him as a boy. Very attached. Whereas Francis had other friends, William only had Francis. And I can't help feeling that while Francis is now a grown man whose childhood is firmly in the past where it belongs, William is still somehow stuck there.'

'I know what you mean. Perhaps it's his voice that gives that impression.'

'Maybe,' said Marion. 'In any case, unless there is a sudden change of heart, it will just be me, which may be a disappointment to him.'

'I'll prepare him,' Helen promised. 'I'm sure he'll be delighted to see you.'

'Where's Francis?' William asked Marion by way of greeting.

'I'm afraid he's at work. He sends his good wishes, though.'

'What does he do?' Helen asked, remembering her first impression that he was a clergyman.

'He's a solicitor,' said Marion.

'Same as Mr Eckerty,' William said, as if this connection would be apparent to all.

'Mr Eckerty?' Helen asked casually, trying not to pounce. It was the first time he had ever volunteered the name of anyone outside his immediate family.

'He's a solicitor . . . the trust,' William said without much conviction.

It was clear to Helen that this was the beginning and end of his intelligence on the subject and that probing further would do no more than silence him. Eckerty was a helpfully uncommon surname, however, and Helen resolved to make enquiries.

The three of them were sitting on the arrangement of benches overlooking the lawns and fruit trees. Gil had intended to be present, if only to get the measure of Marion, but had been called away to deal with some emergency.

There had been no rain for over a fortnight and the grass was starting to show parched patches. The soil in the flower beds was baked dry, but the roses had bloomed in blowsy profusion. She had thought the garden an ideal setting for this second meeting and suggested that William take Marion for a stroll around the grounds to point out the areas of interest. If conversation did not flow, there would be plenty to look at.

Although in the evenings he spent as much time as possible in front of the television, transfixed by the mysterious worlds of *Coronation Street* and *Compact*, during the day he was often to be seen in the grounds. Once, she had observed him in the rose garden, moving among the shrubs, smelling the flowers, and furtively snapping the head off a fat pink rose and carrying it off in his breast pocket.

In Marion's presence, Helen had handed over to William the undelivered letters from Francis, with a brief explanation, and watched his face crumple with confusion. He didn't open them straight away but sat looking at them for a long time, frowning and then, finally, smiling.

'I thought he never wrote,' he said in wonderment.

He seemed to have no bitterness for the forces that had kept this knowledge from him for twenty-five years.

'He did write,' Marion affirmed.

William put them in his pocket for later, like someone who has trained himself not to gorge on treats but to make them last for the longest possible time, in case that is all there will ever be.

Helen watched them head off together – William tall, unkempt, awkward; Marion petite, elegant, serene – and wondered at the curious bond between them.

Chapter 29

—— December 1938 ——

Dear Francis,

I am not allowed to go outside or talk to anyone or let anyone know I am here or I'll go to borstal, Aunt Elsie says, so I stay in my room mostly. I don't mind. It's better than school. I think I can learn things just as well from books. I have a set of the British Encyclopaedia and I read a different entry every day. There are twelve volumes with about 400 pages in each volume. Most entries are a page – some are longer if it is a big topic like Napoleon or aviation.

I have calculated that it will take me thirteen years and two months to read them all at this rate. I started with Volume 1, but then I thought that was a bad idea, because I would only know about things beginning with A, so now I read the first entry from each volume in turn, and then the second. If it is something boring, I skip to the next, but it feels like cheating, so even if the next entry is boring, too, I have to read it.

Sometimes after dark I go out into the garden and watch for badgers, but I've never seen one. Foxes sometimes and even a rat. I wonder if you are at Brock Cottage. I wish I was. How is Boswell? Give him a tummy rub from me. From Aunt Rose's window I can see right across the park and people walking their dogs. I don't think I would ever be lonely if I had a dog.

Dear Francis,

    I wonder where you are. I am in my house all the time, except when I go out in the garden at night so no one can see me. If anyone rings the doorbell I stay in my room until they've gone, but no one ever does come, really. I have made a fort out of matches. It is quite good, if I say so myself.

Dear Francis,

    For Christmas, Aunt Elsie gave me this fountain pen, Aunt Rose gave me a crystal radio set and Aunt Louisa gave me a pullover. We had roast chicken and played pontoon. I won 3s 9d, but there is nowhere to spend it, so I am keeping it in my tin until it is all right for me to come out. I don't know when that will be.

Dear Francis,

    I'm sorry I haven't been able to post any of these letters, but I don't know your address. I know Brock Cottage isn't your main house and I can't even remember the name of the nearest village. I remember we went down to the coast one day and that place was called West Wittering, but it was a long drive, so I don't think that would be much use to a postman.

Dear Francis,

    I wish you would write to me.

William put the letters back in his wooden box where he kept important things and put the box at the back of his wardrobe. He wouldn't write any more. It had been fun to begin with, thinking to himself that Francis would surely soon write to him, since his parents must have his address as they had dropped him back home on two occasions. When he did, William could reply with all the one-sided correspondence he had amassed.

No letter had come, though, and so none could be returned. A painful truth drilled into his mind like a bird jabbing into the lawn with its sharp beak in search of a worm. Francis had been his best, his only friend, but the equivalent was not true of Francis, who was popular and did not think of him in the same way. They were bound together now, of course, by the things that mustn't be talked of, but perhaps Francis wanted to forget William along with everything else. The idea was too painful to be faced.

The prospect of staying at home and never going back to school, any school, had been the substance of his daydreams for so long that the accompanying loss of freedom hadn't troubled him at first. It had taken him by surprise, too, how little he had been punished. All that was required of him was not to go outside and not to mention anything about it. He had received more of a scolding the time he had put a cup of hot milk on the little cherrywood table in the front parlour and left a scorched mark on the polished surface.

A few nights earlier he had overheard his aunts arguing about him.

'I don't see why he can't go out and play,' Aunt Rose was saying.

'Someone might wonder why he's not at school.' This was Elsie. 'And get the authorities involved. And what if the Kenley people decide to start talking about it? That woman was *very* indiscreet. You weren't there.'

'Why couldn't he go to a day school round here? No one need know why he left that other place.'

'Are you quite mad?' Elsie retorted. 'What if something like it happens again? What if it's in his blood?'

'What do you mean by that?' Aunt Rose reared up at this.

'You know what I mean.'

'If you're talking about bad blood, you might remember that it was Mother who was cuckoo.'

'Oh, Rose, how can you say such a wicked thing!' This was Aunt Louisa's first intervention. Like William, she avoided conflict as far as possible and did as she was told. 'And do keep your voices down. He might be awake.'

They had gone quiet then and William had been left to puzzle over notions of bad blood and cuckoos, which made no sense to him.

A warm scent of baking drifted up from the kitchen, distracting him from these gloomy thoughts. Aunt Louisa had said she was making drop scones today to go with the last of the plum jam. If he timed his entry well, there might be spares or drips of burnt batter to sample. As he emerged from his room in the eaves, the doorbell rang and he froze, alert and ready to retreat into his hiding place, as he always did when there were callers.

He caught Aunt Elsie's impatient, 'Oh, who's that now?' as she shrugged off her housecoat and flung it out of sight.

The heavy front door opened with a sucking sound and then there came the murmur of female voices, one hard, one soft, their words unintelligible, apart from his own name, which fell cleanly on his ear in a tone he half recognised.

He crept down to the first-floor landing as the door clapped shut. Aunt Elsie looked up at him, startled, guilty, as he peered over the banisters.

'Who was that?' he asked, his heart kicking.

Aunt Elsie gave a sort of wave of dismissal. 'Oh, no one. Those people.'

He tore into Aunt Rose's bedroom and looked out to see Marion Kenley climb into the passenger seat of their grey Bentley motor car. If he had stood there a moment longer instead of bounding down the stairs, she would have seen his stricken face at the window when she glanced back, unconvinced, at the house.

'What are you doing?' Aunt Elsie cried as he wrenched the front door open.

Mrs Kenley had left the iron gate ajar and he burst through it onto the pavement, in time to see the ghostly trail of exhaust from the Bentley as it rounded the bend in the road.

'Come back!' Aunt Elsie hissed from the doorstep.

He tried to call after them, opening his mouth in a roar of despair, but no sound emerged. There was just a tightness in his chest and the useless clicking of his tongue. Mr and Mrs Kenley had come for him, as he knew they would, and been sent away. He turned on Aunt Elsie, raving silently, his jaw working up and down. She caught his trailing cuff and pulled him inside.

'Do you want to end up in borstal?' she gibbered. 'Where they send all the bad boys? Do you?'

'What's going on?'

Aunt Rose came out of the kitchen, where she had been applying the hot tongs to the front of her hair. A clump of corkscrew curls trembled as she moved. William was sprawled on the bottom step with his hands over his face.

'That woman came to the door,' said Aunt Elsie with a little less assurance now. 'They were passing and she wanted to check that William was all right. I thought that was a cheek. And I don't believe they were just passing at all.'

'You could have asked her in,' Rose protested. 'They were very good to Billy last summer.'

William unshielded his eyes and looked up at her gratefully. She was the only one who had any inkling of what it was like for him.

'I thought it was best to say that he was away at school so they don't keep coming back. We don't need any interference from them.'

On the stair, William writhed in his mute fury. I summoned them, he wanted to explain. I summoned them just now with

260

my thoughts and you sent them away and I'll never see Francis again now. His chest burnt. He had read in his encyclopaedia of torture by pressing and could feel the weighted slab crushing the voice out of him.

'I'm only trying to keep him safe,' Aunt Elsie remonstrated. 'Isn't everything I do for William?'

Chapter 30

Lorraine was not only recovering from her nervous collapse at school, but she was also, in Helen's estimation at least, better than she had ever been. Whether it was the medication prescribed by Dr Frant, the unofficial interviews with Gil, the therapeutic benefits of art or the temporary respite from home that had effected this change, Helen couldn't say. The only thing that seemed to threaten this state of equilibrium was a suggestion that she might soon be well enough to leave.

'No, I'm not,' she said, shaking her head in furious denial at Helen's casual query. 'I'm not better enough.'

'I just thought you seemed to be making such good progress,' said Helen, taken aback by Lorraine's vehemence.

'That's because I'm here,' she insisted. 'If they send me away, I'll just get worse again.'

In Helen's experience, Lorraine wasn't the only patient to become quickly attached to whatever sanctuary Westbury Park offered, but it was rare for someone young and only mildly unwell to want to prolong their stay.

'Wouldn't it be nice to see your friends again?'

Lorraine gave a shrug of supreme indifference.

'Are you looking forward to being back in your old room at home?'

'No,' came the firm reply.

Lorraine had already forbidden her parents from visiting – a prohibition that was causing them some considerable dismay.

'It seems very harsh,' June complained to Helen in one of her frequent telephone calls to gather any crumbs of intelligence about Lorraine. 'In a normal hospital, you can go in every day at visiting time. I don't see why this should be any different. I can't believe it's that Dr Frant who's put her up to it. He seemed so nice.'

'I really don't know,' said Helen. 'I don't think he would discuss her treatment with me on principle.' *On several principles*, she thought. 'But surely it's best to accept what she says and let the treatment run its course.'

'I just want my old Lorraine back.'

'Well,' said Helen, unable to collude in this impossible dream, 'from what I see of her, she is certainly improving.'

'I'm glad you're there to keep an eye on her. At times like this, family is everything.'

No great effort was required on Helen's part to perform this act of surveillance, as Lorraine was a regular visitor to the art room. If it was busy, she sometimes chose to work in one of the small side rooms, but otherwise sat at one of the corner tables and practised her sketching, making multiple studies of the same subject in different materials.

She had already made her presence felt in other ways, pleading to be allowed to change the radio station from the Third Programme to Radio Caroline. Helen, who was rather attached to a background of soft classical music and believed it to have a calming effect on her classes, had hesitated before allowing this brash new sound in the art room. She gave in because she didn't want to be thought a dry old stick and an opponent of modernity, on the understanding that if there were complaints from the other patients, they would revert to the previous arrangement. To her surprise, nobody made any sustained objections to exchanging Vivaldi and Ralph Vaughan Williams for The Dave Clark Five or The Rolling Stones, and if Helen herself began by feeling less than glad all over at being regularly exhorted to shake it, or twist again, or not to throw her love away, she concealed it well.

One unforeseen consequence of Lorraine's visits to the art room was the development of a curious friendship with William. Helen would never have imagined her niece to have the confidence or maturity to feel easy in the company of a man more than twice her age, especially one with such strange habits and history. This was a girl who was too nervous to take the 166 bus after dark, who, according to June, could not be persuaded to leave her room to go and meet her friends. She wondered whether it was William's very oddness, his childlike nature and undeveloped masculinity that made him unthreatening to a girl on the cusp of adulthood.

Lorraine's first appearance at the art room happened to coincide with one of William's sessions. He was already there, in his usual seat, working on a pen-and-ink drawing of a cane chair with a pair of overalls thrown over the back. It was executed in his old engraver's style, detailed and exact. Lorraine, shy in the face of talent, but otherwise unintimidated, stood watching him work at a distance for some minutes. He was aware that he was being examined and a hot blush crept up from his buttoned collar and swept over his cheeks. He bent his head closer to the paper and clamped his tongue between his teeth, the better to concentrate.

Helen, supervising work on a mural and mediating in a territorial dispute between Mathilda and Cynthia, now watched Lorraine watching William. For a while it seemed as though this silent stand-off might never end. Presently, Lorraine sat down at the table opposite him and laid out her paper and pencils.

'I wish I could draw like you,' she said quietly. 'Will you teach me?'

William looked over his shoulder and, realising that the remark was directed to him, blushed an even fiercer shade of crimson. 'I'm not a teacher,' he muttered.

'But you could be,' said Lorraine.

'I just draw what I see. That's all. I look at it and then I draw it.'

'I try to do that, too. But it never comes out quite right.'

For a moment he returned to his work and neither of them spoke. Lorraine made a few tentative marks on her paper and then tutted and rubbed them out. This pattern of drawing and then erasing was repeated a few more times.

'You should get rid of that thing,' William advised without looking up. 'Throw it away.'

'I can't. I make too many mistakes,' said Lorraine.

'They're not mistakes. They're all part of the picture. I had a rubber once, but it wore out, and then I didn't have one any more and that's when I started to draw properly.'

'Maybe you're neater than me.'

He shook his head. 'Drawing isn't meant to be neat.'

Helen, listening in to all this, felt her pulse quicken with excitement.

There was something new, alert and mischievous in Lorraine's expression as she jumped up and threw the rubber through the open window, to land in the flower bed. 'There!' she said.

Mathilda gaped in astonishment and hurried to the window as though she had just seen a man go overboard.

'Well, William,' Helen said. 'It looks like you just taught your first lesson.'

At the next class, Lorraine had reciprocated by attempting to teach William to dance. Chubby Checker had come on the radio and she had sprung up and taken his hands to show him how to do the twist. He had stood there, as unresponsive as a maypole, while she tugged his arms and shimmied about, but his resistance had been one of bafflement rather than hostility.

Eventually, Mathilda had joined in and before the song was over, half the class were up on their feet gyrating. There had been a moment when Helen felt the mood might tip over into a kind of frenzy and she might not be able to restore order, but it hadn't happened and later she admitted to herself that it had been one of her better classes.

Chapter 31

Within minutes of letting themselves out through the changing rooms and running the long way round, past the tennis courts, William was wishing he had his overcoat. There hadn't been any time for planning. Everyone would be filing in to tea now and it would not be long until they were missed.

It was a foggy evening; the air was thick and sulphurous in the sallow light from the windows of the Great Hall. It seemed to have taken on the sour, cupric flavour of the mashed swede that had been served up at lunchtime – an age ago now, swallowed up by history and irretrievable. The trees at the perimeter of the field were blurred to smudges.

William's stomach churned. He would have to stop, but Francis was getting too far ahead and they would lose each other. He ploughed straight across the long jump pit and then in a sudden panic ran back and kicked the sand across his footprints.

'Come on,' Francis urged, his voice hoarse from the cold air.

The gates were open; it was a prison made of rules not walls and they felt almost cheated at how easy it was to escape. Out on the country lanes they were vulnerable, though, to inquisitive passers-by and they ducked into the wooded common and stumbled between the trees over ropey roots and the wet mulch of dead leaves. A car approached so cautiously in the fog that its distant rumbling and milky headlights gave the boys plenty of opportunity to retreat deeper into the woods.

Now, William had grit from the sandpit in his shoe, digging into the ball of his foot. He banged his heel against the ground to knock it under the arch where it wouldn't be felt. Francis, with his long, springing stride, was way ahead. The railway station was two miles away; William knew this because he had often rehearsed a flit of this kind, though in less terrifying circumstances, and only as a fantasy.

'I've got to stop,' he called. His guts were clenching and unclenching and he only just dragged his trousers down in time. He was grateful for the curtain of fog now, concealing his shame. Everything was disgusting. He wiped himself on handfuls of frosted oak leaves, flinching from the shock of ice against his burning skin. To clean himself up, his handkerchief would have to be sacrificed. Even at this extremity, there was still enough guilt left over to regret its loss as he scuffed it into the undergrowth.

'We'll get the train to my house. My parents will know what to do,' Francis had said.

'But what will you tell them?' William had asked, because he hardly had the words to describe it all and couldn't think of any fate worse than trying, especially to a woman – to *Mrs Kenley*!

'I'll just say what happened. I'll explain that it was an accident.'

His confidence in the infinite power of his parents to make all problems vanish had almost been enough to persuade William that it was true. He had no such faith in his aunts. Now, though, Francis was not so reassuring, was in fact starting to get impatient.

'Hurry up! Where are you?' His words were muffled by the fog.

The only points of brightness in the dark were the occasional street lamp and the amber glow from the window of an isolated cottage. William had blundered off the path and hungry brambles snatched at the cloth of his trousers. His eyes burnt with tears. The only way he could tell that Francis was still ahead of him was the rustle of his footsteps and the sudden whip of branches springing back into his face.

At last, the lights of the village began to bleed through the fog and the church spire loomed above the mist as though half drowned. Francis had stopped for breath by the gate but took off again as soon as William caught up, so he had no chance to rest himself and was quickly left behind again.

A train had just come in as they reached the railway bridge and they could hear the slamming of doors and a shrill whistle, friendly sounds of ordinary life continuing.

In the tiny ticket hall they stood dazzled for a moment by the light, aware of the curious glances from a few fellow travellers. Their faces were red and streaked with tears; they were shivering and coatless, their shoes caked in mud. Francis stood in front of the printed information board in a state of bafflement.

'It's not here,' he said.

'What isn't?'

'Amersham. That's where we need to go. There are hardly any names on here. I thought you could get a train from anywhere to anywhere. I don't understand it.'

'We'll have to ask the man,' said William, pointing at the ticket booth, before which a woman in a fawn coat and hat stood rooting in her purse.

Finally, she counted out the right change and received her ticket, then stepped aside, apologising. Something in her costume or demeanour – the fur collar and hat, or the lipstick, perhaps – put William in mind of Aunt Rose, although there was no real resemblance, and the thought of his aunts and home and the terrible trouble that would have to be faced brought a sob to his throat.

Francis was talking through the hatch to the booking clerk as William turned away to subdue the heaving in his chest. 'Oh,' he kept saying. 'Oh . . . I see.' William felt for his handkerchief to wipe his eyes and then remembered he had discarded it in the woods. His right hand still felt soiled. He didn't dare look at it but kept it in his pocket.

Francis turned back to him, shoulders slumped. 'We can't get a train to Amersham from here. This is just a branch line. We'll have to go to Paddock Wood and then into London and then somewhere else. I didn't realise that's how it worked.'

William, too, if he had ever thought about it, would have imagined that railways were spread like a grid across the country, connecting every town directly to every other town. Of course, on reflection he could see why this wouldn't work. They looked at each other helplessly.

'We can't stay here,' William whispered. 'They might already be looking for us.'

'We'll go to Paddock Wood and then I'll ring my parents and my father will come and collect us.'

Francis' confidence in his father's ability and willingness to rescue them and solve all problems was immense and enviable. There had been no comparable figure in William's life and any hopes of recruiting one such at school had led to utter ruin. His teeth chattered and he thought with regret of the thick scarf that Aunt Louisa had knitted him in an approximation of the school colours, which he had never dared to wear because it was not quite uniform. It languished in the chest of drawers beside his bed. His torch and poker dice and gyroscope were in there, too, and he wondered if he would ever see them again.

Francis had taken one shoe off and was peeling back the inner sole. In the hollow sat half a crown. This was so unexpected, so much more like the sort of thing Aunt Elsie would have thought of as a way to foil thieves, that William could only stare.

'For emergencies,' Francis explained. 'And this is one.'

He bought two ninepenny tickets while William went to the gents' lavatories to wash his hands. The water was cold but felt scalding to William's raw fingers. There was only the dry, cracked remains of a bar of coal tar soap on the basin and it produced no more lather than a stone. As he raked his nails across it, a man came in and stood behind him, urinating noisily. Still exposed and buttoning himself up in a leisurely way, he walked past William and made a little clicking sound as though urging on a horse. When William turned at the odd sound, the man gave him a slow wink and left without washing his hands.

Francis was waiting by the gate with the tickets, fidgeting with cold and agitation, when William scuttled out. William didn't mention the man and the wink. It was just another thing he didn't like or understand.

The two boys stood at the unlit end of the platform wreathed in fog. The poor visibility amplified every sudden noise – a cough, the rasp of a match, the slam of the waiting room door – making William flinch. He heard them all as a prelude to running feet, policemen with whistles or, worse, the head-master, tapping his vengeful way towards them, firing sparks from his Blakey's heel protectors.

The wind had picked up and the fog was starting to disperse, but even so, they heard the approaching train long before they saw it. There was something majestic and terrifying in its massive silhouette and the crushing power of those wheels.

The boys waited until the few other passengers on the plat-form had boarded before darting out of the shadows and into an empty carriage. On any other occasion it would have been an adventure to catch a train with Francis after dark to some mysterious destination, but not tonight. In any case, Francis had moved to the opposite corner, as far away as possible, and could hardly look at him.

He hates me, William thought, and for a brief unclouded moment he thought he knew why, but then the train gave a lurch and Francis looked up and gave him a quick smile of relief and encouragement, and he didn't know what to think. For a moment he allowed himself the luxury of imagining that everything would be all right.

Mr Kenley, who had taught him how to play croquet and float on his back and had read *Moonfleet* to them, would hear it all from Francis and then, somehow, explain it to the aunts without William needing to say a word. Perhaps he would stay at Francis' house for a while, or even go to Brock Cottage, but this part of the daydream wouldn't quite come into focus. He realised he had no idea what the next hours and days would bring.

The train stopped at Goudhurst and the two boys exchanged anguished glances as an elderly gentleman opened the door of the carriage. Seeing it already occupied, and by schoolboys, he seemed to have second thoughts but boarded anyway and, as soon as he was settled, snapped open his newspaper in front of his face. Now, Francis slid along the banquette to William's end to give the newcomer more room, and apart from the swish of the turning pages, the rest of the short journey passed in silence.

At Paddock Wood the train emptied and they followed the trickle of passengers at a distance to the ticket hall and squeezed into a telephone box. The interior had a sour, unclean smell of exhaled breath and tobacco smoke. William pressed his nose against the soap-scented back of his hand and breathed sparingly through his mouth.

Having broken into the half-crown piece for the fare from Cranbrook, Francis now had change for the crucial call. It didn't matter, though, he explained to William, because you could just ring the operator and tell her the number you wanted to call and ask to reverse the charges and the person at the other end would have to pay. His mother had taught him this in case he was ever stuck without any money. William, whose aunts had not bothered to impart this useful lore, wondered how Aunt Elsie would react to receiving a call on such terms and decided she would probably quarrel with the operator over the cost and slam the phone down.

Francis thumbed two pennies into the slot and began dragging the dial around with one finger. At first it seemed there was only silence and then a click and a crackly voice and Francis hastily jabbed at button A.

'Hello, Father. It's Francis . . . Something's happened. Can you come and get us?' After that initial display of self-assurance, at the sound of his father's voice, Francis' own had become choked. William couldn't hear the responses, only a metallic chirping. 'Me and Tapping . . . Paddock Wood Station . . . We've run away. We can't go back. There's been an accident and we don't know what to do.' And then came the four words – so few! – that made it real to William at last. 'Tapping's killed Mr Swales.'

Chapter 32

The offices of Eckerty & Lamb Solicitors (Wills, Trusts, Probate) were situated above a cobbler's shop in the old part of Croydon near the alms houses and the street market. The cries of the stallholders and the heady fumes of glue and boot polish followed Helen up the narrow stairs to the upper storey. It had taken her no great effort to find them once she had a name.

'There are hardly any of us left,' Mr Eckerty agreed when Helen commented on its rarity and seemed almost proud of his clan's imminent extinction.

He was about forty – younger than she had expected, having imagined someone who had known Louisa Tapping in her prime. That, he explained, was his father, on whose retirement he had taken over the administration of the trust. They sat in his wood-panelled office, talking across a desk a foot deep in files, ledgers, contracts and correspondence. The windowsill, filing cabinet and armchair were similarly buried.

A few minutes after Helen's arrival, a secretary in a brown tweed suit brought in a tray of tea but, finding no flat surface to put it down, was forced to back out again, defeated. Helen couldn't help comparing these surroundings with the empty wastes of Gil's consulting room but stopped short of drawing any conclusions about the relative industry or efficiency of the two men. The psychiatrist's realm was the invisible mind, whereas the law was built from paper, perhaps.

Mr Eckerty explained that he had written several letters to Louisa Tapping that had gone unanswered, as had telephone calls. He had even taken the trouble of calling at the house but could see the place was deserted.

'There were some items of women's clothing in the branches of the tree,' he said with a shiver of disapproval. Most of his father's dealings had been with Elsie Tapping – not the eldest of the sisters but the one with the firmest grip on administrative matters, as he put it. 'She was much more abstemious than was strictly necessary,' he added. 'The trust was not short of funds, but she seldom made any applications. There were school fees for a nephew, but that stopped abruptly in 1938.'

'My patient, William,' said Helen. 'So he stopped attending school at the age of eleven or twelve?'

'I can only say that no further requests for the payment of school fees were made, but it doesn't necessarily follow that his education ended then.'

'No, I suppose not. It seems to be at that point that he disappeared from public view.'

'And he's not capable of giving an account of those years?'

'He speaks very little and won't answer questions. When he was first admitted, he was completely mute, but he does at least talk now – in a limited way.'

'It's a sad state of affairs,' Mr Eckerty agreed. 'I met Miss Louisa Tapping a few times and remember thinking her quite eccentric, but I had no inkling that anything untoward had been going on.'

'I suppose every home has its secrets. But perhaps theirs had more than most.'

'My father met Elsie Tapping on many occasions over the years. He used to say she was very odd. She once brought a bucket of horse manure to the office as a gift for him to put on his roses. She'd shovelled it off the road outside their house and brought it on the bus because they didn't grow flowers or vegetables any more and she didn't want it to go to waste. Of course, his own garden was miles away in Haywards Heath and he took the train to work, so I don't know how she imagined he would get the stuff back home. He had to carry it into the town hall gardens and dispose of it discreetly under a bush.' He shook his head at the memory.

'I was wondering, if William is the last surviving member of the family, does that mean the trust passes to him?'

'That would depend on the terms under which it was set up. I can't share the details with you, you understand.'

'Of course,' Helen said humbly.

'I will certainly look into it. If William doesn't have capacity, the courts will need to appoint a guardian.'

'I think he certainly does have capacity and I'm sure his doctor would agree. But could he nominate a guardian to act on his behalf anyway, if he has no aptitude for money and paperwork? There's a family friend who is very level-headed.'

'Perhaps we could arrange an appointment with all the parties concerned.' Mr Eckerty took out a slim diary from which he withdrew a white-topped pencil the size of a toothpick.

'William is free more or less all the time, but Mrs Kenley, the friend, is rather busier.' As she said this, Helen felt sure that Marion would make herself available however inconvenient it might be.

'I'm very glad we've re-established contact with William,' Mr Eckerty said as they set a provisional date the following week. 'We've been holding a letter for him since 1937.'

Helen looked at him in astonishment. 'But why wasn't it delivered?'

'Our instruction was just that he was not to receive it until the last of his aunts had passed away. And as you have helpfully furnished me with that information, all I need is a copy of the death certificate and it's his.'

After leaving the solicitor's office, Helen went to Allders to buy some nylons and a new white slip in the shorter length that wouldn't show below her skirt hems. She looked for June in the perfume department, with the idea of using her staff discount, but it was her half-day, so Helen somewhat grudgingly paid full price.

She had stopped at the bakery in the arcade, tempted by a display of chocolate jap cakes, when she became aware of someone standing a little closer to her than was polite. She turned sharply, to find herself glaring into the cheerful pink face of Alistair Duggan.

'I thought I recognised you,' he said. 'Even without the lilac coat.'

Her frown relaxed. 'Oh, hello.' She remembered that he was not local. 'Are you here to visit your mother?'

'Yes, that's right.' He held up a cake box, tied with blue ribbon. 'Just stopped to pick up some treats for her tea.'

'Same here,' said Helen, though, of course, there was all the difference in the world between buying a single cake for oneself and a box of 'treats' for sharing. She would not enjoy it so much now.

'I've been meaning to get in touch, actually,' he went on, 'to ask about how old Tapping is getting on.'

'Ah. Not bad, thank you. He's acclimatising quite well to life on the outside. Although it's not really the outside – just a different kind of inside,' Helen conceded. 'I managed to track down Francis Kenley, thanks to you.'

They had moved away from the queue now and were walking towards George Street, without any agreement as to their eventual destinations.

'I spoke to my brother after our meeting, to see if he had any recollection,' Alistair was saying as they emerged into the open air. He lowered his voice as they navigated a knot of pedestrians blocking the narrow pavement. 'I must say, it opened quite the can of worms.'

'Oh dear, I'm sorry to hear that,' said Helen, and then felt that perhaps an apology was not quite right. After all, wasn't her job – and everyone else's at Westbury Park – dependent on the belief that such cans were better open than closed? 'In what way?'

'It's not your fault, good heavens.' He took her elbow as they crossed the road. 'I mean, I knew he'd been unhappy at school. We all were. You sort of expected it – and I escaped early because of the TB, of course. We'd never really discussed school – you didn't in the holidays; it was the last thing you wanted to think about. Anyway, I mentioned Tapping and the piece in the *Advertiser* and then I started talking about the old place. I said Mother still had some of the magazines from the 1930s with photos of the sports teams and what have you. And it all came out.'

They parted for a moment and he stepped off the kerb to allow a young woman pushing a broad pram to pass between them.

'Sorry. Go on,' said Helen when they were side by side once more.

'Well, he started talking about how awful it had all been. He'd never said a word about it before, but one of the masters had taken a bit of a fancy to him and used to invite him up to his room and interfere with him.'

'How disgusting,' said Helen, her face reddening with outrage. There were such men in the world, of course; she had read of their crimes with incredulity in the newspapers. But a schoolmaster, of all people, an educated man, charged with the special care of children . . . It was sickening.

'Forty-one years old, Jack, and he broke down in tears telling me about it. I don't think I'd ever known him to cry before – not even at our father's funeral.'

'And he'd never mentioned it to anyone until now?'

'Not a word. In fact, even now he made me promise I wouldn't say anything to Mother. Not that I would, of course.'

'I suppose at the time he would hardly have had the words to describe what was happening.'

'That's just it exactly,' said Alistair. 'We were kept in absolute ignorance. And anything to do with bodily functions was regarded as filthy and unmentionable.'

'Did this go on all the time he was at school?'

'No. He said the teacher moved on to younger boys each year. There was always a new favourite. Apparently, he liked the blond, sporty types. I was safe on both counts.'

They had emerged from the narrow street of shops onto the broad, windy plain that was the site of excavations for the new underpass – a vast canyon of concrete posts and steel rebars, diggers, cranes and mountains of displaced earth. It was such a desolate public space for this intimate, painful revelation. We should be somewhere private, closeted, Helen thought, but she couldn't interrupt him now.

'Jack said he still feels guilty for doing nothing about those other boys. But he was just so relieved it wasn't happening to him any more.'

'What could he have done? Would anyone have believed him?'

'Not a chance. When he told me the master's name, I could hardly believe it myself. He was one of the decent ones – the one who gave us the nicknames Harry Duggers and so on – we all liked him enormously. Mr Swales, his name was. I could have believed it more easily of one of those other sadists, but not him.'

'I wonder if anyone ever spoke out or reported him.'

'Well, here's the curious thing. According to Jack, he was there one day and gone the next. This was the term after I'd gone down with TB, so I never heard about it. Apparently, he fell off a ladder and struck his head and never recovered. But they didn't make much of it, for such a popular teacher. There was a memorial service in the chapel and that was that; he was never mentioned again.'

'Not mentioning things seems to be the school's motto.'

'Yes. *Noli dicere,* or some such. I never was a Latin scholar.'

'I hope your brother hasn't suffered too much from being reminded of all this. But I suppose the pain is there whether it is acknowledged or not. I know my colleagues at Westbury Park would say that it is better not to repress painful memories. I mean, it's one of the core principles, really.'

'I think it helps somewhat that the fellow who did it is safely dead. I do wonder how much it has affected Jack over the years. He hasn't had what you'd call a conventional life. He went into the colonial service after the war, lived in Aden and then moved from post to post. Malaya, East Africa and now Hong Kong. He's never married and never settled anywhere for long.'

'You can't really know. We're built of so many experiences, don't you think?'

'I'm not sure why I told you all this.' Alistair shook his head. 'I don't suppose it has anything to do with Tapping's predicament.'

'No, maybe not,' said Helen, though she couldn't help feeling that it had. It was not William she was thinking of but a blond boy with a cricket bat who scored half a century against Sutton Valence and left school suddenly after just one year.

Chapter 33

Although it was now after six o'clock and well past the end of her working day, Helen determined to return to Westbury Park and pick up the copy of *The Belworthian* magazine from her desk drawer to see if it confirmed her suspicions.

As she drove in, she saw Gil's Zephyr parked slantwise in its usual space. He was not in the habit of working late and she remembered that today was the day of his interview with the hospital board for the superintendent's job. In observing their temporary state of estrangement, she had forgotten to wish him luck and hurried to his office to make good this omission by asking him how it had gone. There was also much to discuss of what she had learnt from Mr Eckerty and Alistair Duggan. On account of the late hour, and propelled by a sense of urgency, she did not bother to knock before walking in.

Gil and Lorraine were sitting side by side on his couch, their heads very close together. There was nothing especially untoward about this; his methods were unorthodox and he was not above lying stretched out on the floor alongside a patient if it made communication more likely. At the interruption, however, both of them started – guiltily, it seemed to Helen – and straightened up. This was the unsettling thing – not the sitting close together but the breaking apart. For a moment, as she looked from one to the other, she felt a frisson of dark energy in the room, like the crackle of electricity before a thunderstorm. Gil was of course the first to recover.

'Hello,' he said, standing up, not hastily like a man with something to conceal but with his usual assurance. 'Lorraine and I were just having one of our chats.'

'Good,' said Helen with a brittle smile, unable to quite match his equanimity. Of the three of them, he was the only one in full possession of the facts and Helen felt her disadvantage keenly. 'I came to tell you about my meeting with the Tappings' solicitor.'

She half expected that Lorraine would take the hint and excuse herself, for this conversation was clearly a confidential matter, but her niece showed no sign of moving. She had, if anything, settled back onto her elbows in a more relaxed posture. Helen noticed that her feet were bare, her scuffed leather pumps parked under the couch.

Of course, she berated herself, *of course* Lorraine would fall in love with Gil. It could hardly be otherwise. No man would ever have talked to her so intelligently or listened to her with such attention. Never mind that he was as old as her father; his maturity would be part of his appeal. The worst of it was that Helen had already been half aware of a change in Lorraine, without suspecting its cause. Her reluctance to be discharged, her transformation from despondency and inertia to lightness of heart now made a disagreeable kind of sense: symptoms of dawning infatuation, nothing more.

'I'll catch you another time if you're busy, Gil,' she said, trying to add an edge to her voice that was audible only to him.

He seemed to receive the unspoken message and said, 'No, do stay. Lorraine and I had finished.'

Thus dismissed, Lorraine stood up abruptly and forced her toes into her abandoned shoes, flattening the backs under her heels. Gil held the door open in such a way that Helen was unable to see any exchange of glances between them as Lorraine departed and she wondered with a surge of paranoia whether this was deliberate.

At last they were alone and he turned to her.

'So, what news from the solicitor?' he said in a businesslike tone, no doubt designed to realign the conversation in a direction of his liking.

Helen refused to play along.

'Gil, what are you up to?' she said with an impatient gesture.

He had moved behind his desk, but refrained from taking a seat before she did.

'What do you mean?' He looked innocent, injured.

Helen wasn't sure exactly what she did mean. Chiefly that she regretted her original well-meant impulse to bring them together.

'She is clearly in love with you. Are you saying you hadn't noticed?'

'Oh, that.' He gave up waiting and threw himself back in his chair. 'All of my patients are in love with me. It's part of the process.'

'But Lorraine isn't one of your patients,' she reminded him.

'Well, not officially, no.' He reached for his cigarettes and lit one hungrily, his exhalation of smoke forming a temporary veil between them.

'You were just going to have a friendly conversation with her. But it seems to have become quite a regular thing.'

'I thought that was what you wanted. Didn't you go and badger Morley Holt with just that in mind?'

'Yes, and he refused. Very wisely, I now see.'

'What's made you change your mind? You're not accusing me of anything, are you?' There was a crackle of hostility in his voice.

'No, no, I'm not *accusing* you. Though you looked very furtive when I came in just now. And I can see trouble ahead if you let Lorraine get too attached to you. She already doesn't want to leave. Now I know why.'

'I was not *furtive*,' Gil protested. 'I was just startled. People usually knock.'

Helen's face was a mask of composure, behind which her emotions boiled. Having forfeited the right to consider herself special in his eyes, she was just 'people' now. She felt herself shrivel.

'I'm sorry I barged in,' she said as steadily as she could. 'I'd just found out something interesting that I wanted to tell you. And I didn't expect you to have someone with you after hours.'

'I have to see Lorraine "after hours" since she is not my patient – as you just pointed out.'

For a long moment they looked at each other with matching expressions of mistrust. Gil was the first to relent: he couldn't bear anyone to think ill of him, even fleetingly. He crushed out his cigarette and raked a hand through his hair.

'What are we arguing about, exactly?'

'I certainly didn't come here looking for an argument,' said Helen.

It went against her nature to withhold feminine comfort when it was sought, but she was not ready to capitulate quite yet. Although she did not for a moment suspect him of having any serious designs on Lorraine, she couldn't shake the suspicion that he was enjoying his influence over her and that he was more flattered than he should be by her infatuation. Nauseating though this idea was, she could not afford to alienate Gil as she had a feeling that a weakening of any one bond in this awkward triangle of alliances would necessarily strengthen the others. The most important relationship, she now saw, was between herself and Lorraine, and it was here that the work must be done.

'I actually came to say sorry for not wishing you luck with the interview. And to ask how it went.'

This apology, though it was for a quite different matter, with no bearing on the scene that had just played out, brought about a temporary end to the conflict, on the surface at least.

'It went as well as I could have hoped,' Gil said, his spirits instantly restored. 'The board seemed very receptive to my ideas, although I suppose I didn't bring up any that were likely to alarm them. They're a very conservative bunch.'

'When do you find out?'

'They've still to interview Lionel and one more candidate, who isn't available until next month, so it'll be a while yet. The thing to consider is whether I really want it.'

'Surely you want it?'

'I'll be pleased to get the job, but that's not quite the same as doing it.' He laced his fingers together and flexed them with a popping sound. 'There are some things in its favour.'

The extra mouth to feed, for one, thought Helen.

'Anyway,' he went on, 'tell me what you've been up to. Not seeing you makes me grouchy.'

She gave a stiff smile. His charm was not having its usual effect and the tired old treads of their relationship had never seemed less appealing. Once, she would have delighted in telling him every detail of her news. It had been one of the great pleasures of being together, as important as sex.

'I ran the Tappings' solicitor to ground. He – and his father, mainly – have been administering a trust for the family since before the war. I suggested appointing Marion Kenley as a guardian if William doesn't want to get involved in financial matters. There's also the issue of the estate – that house in Coombe Road and the trust. The solicitor has Louisa Tapping's will, though he wouldn't tell me what's in it, obviously. It's possible William could be quite well off.'

'Good work,' said Gil. 'Though I can't really see him living independently, however well off he is.'

'There was another thing that happened today – quite unexpected. I ran into Alistair Duggan in Croydon.'

Gil looked blank.

'That chap who was at school with William briefly. He told me that his older brother had been molested by one of the teachers – that wasn't the word he used. It just made me wonder. According to Alistair, he'd never spoken about it until now. And he wasn't the only one.'

Gil pulled a face. 'You're thinking of William?'

'Not necessarily. This man apparently had a thing for athletic blond boys. I was thinking of Francis Kenley. Do you think it's something I can just ask him? I mean, it might be something he's deliberately tried to forget.'

'If it happened, he won't have forgotten it, I promise you,' said Gil. 'And the alternative to difficult conversations is silence, which I naturally think is worse. You don't have to go in like a bull at a gate. It will be apparent quite quickly if he doesn't want to talk about his schooldays and you'll have to respect that.'

'And if he'd rather talk to someone like you, I could give him your number?'

'Of course. You can call him from here if you like.'

'It's all right.' For some reason she couldn't quite articulate, she did not want him there listening while she spoke to Francis.

'And . . . Helen, have you had time to think about that other thing?'

It was so unlike him to speak indirectly, as if he was afraid to name the other thing in case the terms offended her.

'Er . . . no . . . yes.' She shook her head. 'My feelings haven't changed – I still can't see a future for us.'

He held up his hands. 'It's all right. I don't want to rush you if it means making the wrong decision.'

Only he could have the massive self-assurance to imagine that their near falling-out over Lorraine was a promising route back to favour, Helen thought. She may have allowed smooth words and good manners to prevail, but underneath she was anything but calm.

'I know I can't leave things hanging like this. There's the flat, for one thing. I can't go on accepting your money.'

'Oh, to hell with the money,' Gil exclaimed. He seemed more offended by these bourgeois considerations than he had been by her suspicions about Lorraine. 'I miss talking to you,' he said. 'Among other things.'

'I've been distracted by work – William and so on.'

He gave her a sardonic look that she could not quite read.

'What?' she asked, frowning.

'Some might say I'm not the only one who gets over-involved in a patient's affairs,' he said. 'That's all.'

'Is this a convenient time to talk?'

Helen was using Olive's telephone in the empty office in reception; her free hand fiddled with the dial of a heavy brass calendar, scrolling back through the months. She was still smarting from Gil's remark but had been unable to formulate the arguments necessary to defeat him. He had apologised, assuring her that he did not doubt her professionalism and hoped that she had the same trust in him, and they had parted in an atmosphere of uneasy truce.

Alistair Duggan's copy of *The Belworthian* was on the desk in front of her, open at the first page. *Francis Kenley scores half a century against Sutton Valence. Cover photographs by J. Swales.* This was him, the beast, behind the camera. She had felt the name tweak a thread somewhere in her memory and here it was.

'Yes, of course. How can I help?' Francis' voice was polite, reserved.

'I'm sorry if what I am about to say is difficult.'

'Has something happened to William?'

'Oh no, nothing like that. This is about the past, not the present.'

'Go on,' he replied, warily, it seemed to Helen.

'It's to do with your old school. I bumped into Alistair Duggan again today, quite by chance. He was the one who put me on to you in the first place.'

'Yes, I remember. He had tuberculosis, you said.'

'Yes, well, he told me that he had mentioned William to his brother, who was also a pupil at the school. He lives overseas now and they weren't in regular contact.' She paused for breath, but Francis said nothing. 'Are you still there?'

'Yes. I'm listening.'

'Alistair's brother told him that one of the masters there had molested him over a period of months. He'd never said a word about it to anyone. The man's name was Swales.'

Again, Francis gave back nothing but silence.

'I wondered whether you or William had come across this man or knew about his behaviour.'

This was not quite honest on her part. She knew very well that Francis must have come across him – she was looking at a photograph that proved it.

'He taught history,' Francis said in a flat voice. 'Everybody liked him.'

'What I've told you doesn't come as a surprise?'

'No. I just wasn't aware there were others.'

'I'm so sorry if this is difficult. You know that the man is long dead?'

'Oh yes. I knew that. Look, do you mind if I call you back later? I can't really talk about this until I've made a phone call. There are other people to consider.'

Chapter 34

'Do you want to stay for this bit, William?' Marion asked.

They were sitting side by side on the couch in Gil's consulting room. Helen was in the swivel chair and Gil was perched on the windowsill. Outside, heavy rain was falling, battering the roses and turning the bruised petals in the flower beds to mush.

William looked at his watch and shook his head. 'It's lunch in seven minutes. And then library.'

His days were carefully mapped into segments of scheduled activity, mealtimes and scheduled inactivity, and he observed these daily offices as faithfully as any novice. This meeting was an anomaly, disrupting a period of quiet reading in the day room, which he was keen to resume.

Marion and William had spent half an hour in private conference and they had then been joined by Mr Eckerty to assess William's capacity and inclination to manage his financial affairs or to appoint Marion as his proxy. He had no interest in money or property and its provenance or disposal. His aunts had always done all that, he said, and apart from a little cash to spend at the shop on chocolate and soap and toothpaste, he had no use for it.

Papers duly signed and witnessed by Helen and Gil, Mr Eckerty departed, promising to send the details of what

William could expect as a beneficiary of the trust and Louisa Tapping's will.

As soon as William had left, Helen looked at Marion expectantly. She was, it seemed, the keeper of all secrets and confidences, appointed by both Francis and William to be their spokesperson.

'You know already, I think, that Francis was molested at school by one of the teachers,' Marion said.

Helen nodded.

'It started in his second year there, in the autumn term after William's summer holiday at Brock Cottage. What you won't know, and what his aunts had been concealing for years in their – let's be charitable and call it *misguided* – way, was that William, in coming to Francis' defence, had struck the teacher and accidentally killed him.'

There was no word or phrase yet invented that could shock Gil and his face gave nothing away, but Helen was not so skilled at hiding her feelings, which were plainly inscribed on her face.

'We discovered the abuse and the death at the same moment. The boys had run away from school and telephoned my husband for help. They were only missed after tea when they failed to turn up for prep. Obviously our priority was the boys, but as soon as we had got them back to our house and reassured them as best we could, there was a difficult call to be made to the school and an even more difficult one to William's aunts. You can imagine.'

'You must have been distraught,' said Helen. 'Those poor boys.'

'My husband, Basil, was magnificent. We agreed that I would speak to William's aunts and he would deal with the headmaster. We both had a very strong feeling that no one would benefit from the police being involved. The man responsible was beyond help or justice and his family, if he had any, would hardly welcome the revelations about his character. We were very clear that Francis and William should not be questioned and should be kept out of things as far as possible.'

'No doubt the school was only too happy to bury the scandal,' said Gil.

'Indeed,' said Marion. 'I should make it clear that if the teacher had survived the fall, then we would *certainly* have reported his behaviour to the police, for the safety of the other children at the school. But our first concern now was Francis and William.'

'How did William's aunts react to the news?' Gil asked, offering Marion a cigarette, which she refused, and lighting one of his own.

'I spoke to Louisa Tapping first, because she was the one who answered the telephone, but she quickly became almost incoherent with panic and her sister Elsie took over the call. I remember trying to explain what had happened in plain terms and finding it impossible to get them to acknowledge reality or to accept that I was acting in William's interest. I don't think paranoia is too strong a word for it.'

'This was – what? – 1938 and they had lived a sheltered life, perhaps,' said Helen.

'Well, yes,' Marion conceded. 'They were spinsters, a little older than I was, ten years maybe, but the same generation and absolutely unable to face or even think about any "unpleasantness".'

'How did you deal with the "unpleasantness" yourself, as regards Francis, if I may ask?'

'I was not a professional like you, Dr Rudden, and I had never come across a pederast before and would hardly have believed such people existed if I hadn't read occasional reports in the newspaper. But what I was quite clear about was that

Francis should not be made to feel that any disgust or shame attached to *him* and that he must not feel that there was *anything* he could not tell us in plain English.'

'That was very wise of you.'

'It didn't feel like wisdom, I can tell you. It was an overpowering instinct that we had to be able to talk about it without any squeamishness, in exactly the same way that we would if a burglar had broken into the house and hit him over the head. I don't imply that the two events are equivalent, by the way.'

'Of course not,' said Gil.

'Just that in both cases the child has been the victim and shouldn't be ashamed.'

'And how did Francis respond to this approach?' Gil asked, drawing hard on the cigarette so that the orange tip crackled and an inch of ash dropped to the carpet before he could save it.

'I've made it all sound very straightforward,' said Marion, extracting a white handkerchief from her sleeve and passing it from hand to hand without actually applying it to her eyes, which were starting to fill. 'It wasn't, though. I don't know if Francis himself thinks we handled it well, now that he's more or less the age we were at the time. Perhaps I'll ask him. We just wanted him to accept it as something horrible that had happened to him that would never happen again. And that he would recover. And I believe he did.'

'What about William?' asked Helen. 'What sort of state was he in?' She had found it hard to think of anything except the terror he must have felt at eleven years old. To have killed a man, even accidentally, and even a man who deserved no sympathy, and to believe that punishment was always and for ever around the corner was beyond her imagining.

'He was cold and hungry, and very scared. He cried a lot and clung on to me. We wrapped them in blankets in front of the fire and gave them tea and toast and told them that everything

292

would be taken care of. We weren't at all sure at that stage *how* they would be taken care of.'

'Did he speak to you at this point or was he mute?'

'I think it was Francis who did the talking. He told us exactly what had happened. It was clearly an accident. I mean, the shove was deliberate, but the fall was just unlucky. This man had an attic room where he used to summon Francis on some pretext. There was a trapdoor in the floor with a ladder leading to a storeroom below. If they heard anyone coming up the stairs, Francis was supposed to climb down there and hide.

'You might think it was no more than the man deserved, falling down there and breaking his neck. But this wasn't some-one they hated – of all the masters, he was the one they had liked the most. I don't know if that makes it worse. I suppose degrees of awfulness don't really come into it.'

'I'm interested to know how the school responded to the news. It's hard to imagine.'

'Basil telephoned the headmaster, Mr Grey, to report the abuse and the death of the master, whose disappearance hadn't even been noticed at this point. Mr Grey wasn't a terribly worldly man. He was almost more horrified at the idea of the scandal than at the events themselves.

'Perhaps I'm being unfair. Anyway, he very much agreed with the importance of presenting the man's death as an unfor-tunate accident that didn't involve any other party. This was one point on which the school's interests and ours aligned.'

'The police would have had to get involved at some level, surely?' said Helen.

'Oh yes, and there was an inquest, many months later, which recorded the death as accidental, though of course we didn't go.

'The headmaster invited us, and Elsie Tapping, into his office a few days after Basil's phone call. In my innocence, I thought he was going to apologise to us for having a child molester on his staff. It was the most extraordinary meeting. I think Basil and I were the only two sane people in the room.'

'It's interesting that you say that,' said Gil. 'In what way did you see William's aunt as not sane.'

For a moment Helen feared that he was going to treat Marion to his regular lecture on the limitations of labels.

'Well, for one thing, she had tried to dress up, but it was a very shabby best – a long dress and an awful fur coat that reeked of camphor. Of course, her clothes are neither here nor there; it was more that she was almost paralysed with deference to this gibbering old fool. And as soon as Basil began to describe what had been done to Francis, she actually covered her ears.'

'My God,' said Helen. 'Because it was just too painful to hear?'

'Perhaps,' said Marion. 'But I think it was more that it was *unseemly.*'

Even Gil, who never interposed his own feelings into a professional conversation, allowed himself a shake of the head at this. He levered himself from the windowsill and pressed his hands into the small of his back. 'Sorry,' he said. 'Do go on.'

'At first we were talking at cross purposes. When Mr Grey said a terrible wrong had been committed under this roof, or some such phrase, we naturally assumed he meant the assaults on Francis. The discussion became quite tangled as we realised that was not what he meant.

'It took all of Basil's advocacy skills to force him to face the fact that the school had harboured a criminal. I'm afraid Miss Tapping was not much use as an ally. She just kept repeating that her brother had once been a pupil at the school, as if that had any bearing on anything.'

'The brother who died in the car crash – William's father,' said Gil.

'Perhaps it was her way of reminding him that William was an orphan,' Marion conceded. 'Anyway, Basil managed to press home that unless Francis and William were kept out of any investigation, we would take out a full-page advertisement in the local paper advising the parents that their sons were not safe at the school.

'He absolutely crumbled at this threat. I challenged him to reassure us that there weren't other such deviants at the school. He called in the matron and made her stand there while he asked if any boy had ever complained to her of being "touched in a filthy way" by one of the masters. It almost killed him to say the words.

'She went scarlet in the face but said, "No, never," and he made her promise to ask any boy who came to see her for whatever reason if it had ever happened to them. We knew he couldn't possibly prove that there weren't any others, but we wanted him to know that we would always be watching.

'He then seemed to turn on Miss Tapping, as though he needed to assert himself over someone, having failed with us. He said that of course William would not be able to return to the school, and that the taking of a life was a terrible thing and that it would be in all our interests if the incident was never spoken of again.

'We were outraged on her behalf, but she was completely cowed by him and blethered a kind of apology – as if William was the criminal. There was definitely an air of threat in the way he spoke to her that was completely absent in his dealings with Basil. And then before we could recover, he suddenly stood up and announced that he was going to say grace, and he declaimed it over our heads and then ushered us out of the building.'

'And from that point did you have any further contact with William or his aunts?' asked Gil.

'None. No, that's not quite right. We encouraged Francis to write to William to invite him down to the cottage for the Easter holiday and to reassure ourselves that he was all right.' She cleared her throat; the handkerchief had had quite a mauling by now and was twisted around one finger like a fat bandage. 'We never got a reply – now, I know that he never received the letters.

'After a couple of months of silence, I made Basil drive me down there in the hope of seeing him, but it was Elsie who came to the door and told me he was away at school. She didn't enquire about Francis or ask us inside. I didn't entirely believe her, but I didn't pursue it. I feel terribly guilty about that now. If I'd known how he was living and continued to live . . .' She stopped, her throat suddenly tight.

'You could hardly have imagined how things would turn out,' Helen said.

'No.' Marion recovered her composure with a few long breaths. 'But the thing is, I didn't follow it up, because just like William's aunts, we, too, didn't want to be reminded of what had happened. If Francis had ever pressed us to try to contact William again, we would have done, but he didn't. He wanted to forget, and that meant forgetting William, too.'

'It was a very natural response,' said Gil.

'Any parent would have done the same,' Helen agreed.

'But when a family turns inwards like that, innocent people suffer.' As she said this, Marion shook her head.

'It's worth remembering that William doesn't know the life he missed, only the life he had,' Gil said. 'And he has never criticised his aunts or accused them of unkindness. They loved each other in their way. I'm not defending their behaviour. I just ask myself what is best for William now. Would he be happier and better able to face the future if he was made to believe that his aunts were monsters?'

'When you talk about the future for William, what is it that you see? Will he be here for ever?' Marion asked him.

Gil gave a theatrical shrug. 'There is no for ever with institutions like Westbury Park. We've been living on borrowed time since 1957. It's a matter of when, rather than if, it's closed down. Fortunately, the wheels of government move slowly and not always in the same direction.'

'I agree with you that it would be cruel and unnecessary to persuade William to see his aunts as evil, but surely he needs to be relieved of the anxiety that the authorities may still be interested in pursuing him for an accident that happened when he was a child. Apart from ourselves, there can hardly be anyone still living who knows the facts.'

'That process has already begun,' Gil said. 'You're part of it. The fact that he talks to you and walks in the grounds in daylight shows he is no longer bound by the rules of his old home.'

'So, his silence was fear of being found out rather than shame about his voice?' said Helen.

Her mind was still turning over the impossible idea that William had been in hiding for all these years because of his aunts' delusional fear of retribution. If he had only been blessed with parents like the Kenleys instead, how differently his future might have unfolded.

'In my view,' said Gil, 'I think it's unlikely he will ever be a great talker. He's not used to it and it tires him. But he can communicate when he wants to and that's what matters.'

'Well,' said Marion, standing up and hooking her bag over one arm, 'it has been a weight off my mind – and heart – talking to you today. Perhaps I should have tried psychoanalysis earlier, but I always thought it wasn't terribly British.'

'It has some reputational difficulties,' Gil agreed. 'Though of course some might argue that it is those terribly British qualities – shame, silence, avoidance of unpleasantness, for instance – that make it necessary.'

Chapter 35

Francis was off again, rehearsing for the public speaking competition. It was organised by the Bible Society with a prize of one guinea for the best orator, ten shillings for the runner-up. Mr Swales, who was responsible for coaching all the candidates, had selected Francis to represent his house. Often, in that golden hour between the end of school and tea, or the end of prep and bedtime, Francis was nowhere to be found and when he did show up, it was always 'public speaking' that was to blame. He seemed to derive no enjoyment from this great privilege and grew impatient when questioned about it.

'I just have to practise reading this psalm, really, really slowly in a stupid voice like the chaplain's,' he snapped, so William learnt not to ask.

William himself was a little envious of his friend's promotion. He wouldn't have minded being singled out for special treatment by Mr Swales, or trying to win a guinea, and couldn't detect anything in Francis' speaking voice that would have recommended him, above all others in the house, for the role. His jealousy ran in two directions, as he also resented Mr Swales for monopolising Francis' free time, leaving him so often alone during rec. He wondered what they talked about during all those hours of rehearsal. Not just psalms, surely?

Everyone said that school would get better once William went up a year – everyone being Mr and Mrs Kenley and his aunts, who were his only sources of information.

'Selwyn was miserable at first,' Aunt Louisa assured him. She always called him Selwyn, never 'your father'. 'He used to try to make himself sick at the end of the holidays by eating soap. But once he settled in, he had a splendid time and went on to be head prefect and captain of rugby. You'll be just the same.' And she put her hand out to ruffle his hair and then thought better of it.

William, standing in the bathroom holding the tablet of Aunt Rose's Bronnley lavender soap up to his nose, wondered how much he would have to eat to make himself sick without actually dying. Its perfume at this proximity was already making his eyes sting. He extended his tongue, tentatively, just making contact with its waxy surface, and then retracted it as the chemical flavour filled his mouth and his stomach contracted in violent refusal. He had gargled and spat and held his tongue under the running tap, but the taste stayed in his mouth and the smell in his nose all evening.

He prayed that, since the holiday at Brock Cottage, things at school would improve. Francis and he would be allies now with that summer to bind them. He would never tire of reminiscing about the secret pond; the midnight walks; sleeping out; the sand fort at West Wittering; Boswell; the souvenir perch in the wardrobe – there were enough memories there to last all year. And, at Easter, Mrs Kenley had said they could go back there again. He held on to this shiny half-promise, which had become conflated in his mind with the precious silver napkin ring; sometimes he would take it from its hiding place and turn it over and over, stroking the engraving of the badger, feeling its power and knowing that he would soon return.

Francis himself never mentioned the Easter holiday or seemed to look forward to it in the same way. Brock Cottage was nothing special to him, or if it was, he could enjoy its specialness with the careless confidence of ownership. William's invitation, so informal and vaguely expressed, and subject to countless fragile contingencies, could be forgotten or withdrawn at any moment.

Every time he caught sight of Francis talking to another boy with any expression of pleasure, William felt a tremor of fear. Those lessons – French, Latin – where Francis was in a different, higher class, seemed interminable. He could hardly concentrate on his own work for imagining the alliances that might be forming in his absence.

Francis himself was oblivious to these anxieties and unaware of the power he wielded. He didn't show any signs of transferring his loyalties from William elsewhere. If anything, he had a tendency to withdraw from all of his classmates equally and spend more time hiding in the library or the chapel, or the san, with a variety of those ill-defined symptoms – headaches, stomach ache, earache – whose authenticity could never be proved.

Nevertheless, William couldn't feel quite secure in this friendship, or confident that his attachment to Francis was reciprocated in equal measure. There had been one terrible moment when he had forgotten himself and called him 'Francis' instead of 'Kenley' in front of their classmates. It had been a momentary lapse from that state of perpetual alertness that was necessary to avoid the thousand possible infringements of the iron code by which they all lived now. The other boys had pounced on this, jeering, 'Francis, Francis.' It made it so much worse that it was a girl's name. Francis, innocently implicated in this mockery, was coldly furious.

'Don't ever call me that here,' he muttered when they were alone.

'I didn't mean to,' William said, mortified.

Even after a year, he couldn't get used to the surrender of his name. It had been stripped from him on his first day at Belwortham.

'What's your name, boy?' one of the masters had asked, not unkindly, as he stood, utterly at sea in the emptying courtyard as the crowd of other boys drifted away, apparently secure of their destination.

William was looking at the timetable written in the back of his prep diary and trying to make sense of its runic mysteries.

'William, sir.'

'Well, Williams, why are you standing there gawping instead of going to class?'

'It's not Williams, sir, it's William. William Tapping.'

The master frowned at him as though he'd said something rude.

'Well, Tapping, you can forget all about William while you're within these walls. Leave it at home with Mummy, eh?'

This remark perplexed him. It seemed to be asking him to do the impossible.

'I haven't got a mummy, sir. She's dead,' he said in a puzzled tone.

The master's look of discomfiture had turned rapidly to irritation that he was being made to feel uncomfortable by a pupil.

'I'm sorry to hear that, Tapping,' he said briskly. 'But it was just a figure of speech. And, Tapping,' he added, 'don't answer back.'

William nodded, rendered dumb by this command. What, he wondered, was the difference between answering and answering back?

So, at a stroke, he became Tapping, a name that was also a sound – of a blind man feeling his way with a white stick or a prisoner trying to communicate through a solid wall. It was a relief when old Swales hit on those nicknames and for a while they all called each other Harry, going into convulsions of laughter. 'Hey, Harry, where's Harry?' 'He's with Harry.'

Swales' lessons were the only ones that were tolerable, because he was funny and made history seem like a series of adventure stories for boys, full of death and drama. Because he was popular, he never needed to keep order by meting out punishments; he merely hinted at a withdrawal of approval and they fell back into line.

The days were ruled by bells; nothing happened without them – from waking, washing and breakfast to lights out, the hours and minutes were all accounted for. Punishments were various, creative and at the whim of the individual master. There was no system of avoidance or method of appeal that William could divine. There were casual humiliations, like standing nose and toes to the wall, and a more uncomfortable version involving outstretched arms; lines; cancellation of Saturday afternoon exeat; beatings with ruler, cane or slipper, its leather sole highly polished from decades of use.

In his first week, William had been pounced on by the games master for idly picking grass while he sat on the pitch listening to a lecture on the rules of rugby. He had been made to run around the perimeter of the field for the rest of the period, under the eyes of the whole school, it seemed to him. It was not a terrible punishment, compared to others, but it added to his sense of mystification. He had not realised it was forbidden to pick grass and it worried him what else he didn't know.

It wasn't just the masters who were harsh. The boys were savage in their own way. The first time an older pupil, a complete stranger to William, passing him in an otherwise deserted corridor, had barged at him, knocking him to the ground, it had shaken him to the core. He had done nothing to provoke his assailant, who seemed to take no great satisfaction from it, as though it were a kind of tiresome duty. Growing up in a house of women, William had experienced nothing like it.

The timetable was inexorable; every Monday was identical to every other Monday. It was only by the unpredictable acts of aggression that the weeks could be differentiated. They stood out with all the more clarity against this unchanging background. Even a good memory – the moment he and Francis became friends – was tainted by association with an event so sickening that they never talked of it.

It was a summer afternoon and William was coming back from the cricket nets, when he noticed a crowd of boys gathered in a corner of the schoolyard, pointing at something on the ground. Congregations of this kind often signalled a fight and were therefore to be avoided, but the spectators were unusually quiet, so he sidled up to see what had excited their interest.

A mouse, barely the size of his thumb, with a pink thread for a tail, was running along the ground, keeping tight to the bottom of the wall. It was so tiny and so fast that William realised that what he had formerly taken to be mice, living in the compost heap at the bottom of the garden at home, or stiff and dead on the end of Aunt Elsie's shovel, must have been rats.

One of the boys at the front of the group took a sudden step forwards and the mouse froze and scuttled back into the corner. There was a ripple of laughter. William didn't join in. The mood, which until now had been one of mere curiosity, seemed to sour. Another boy stamped his foot down and the mouse scurried back the way it had come, always hugging the angle between the wall and the floor.

A game of tormenting the mouse, sending it running back and forth, now developed among the boys in the front row, egged on by those behind. William, watching reluctantly, knew better than to try to intervene but felt that his presence would somehow protect the mouse from harm. *You'll never catch him,* he thought. *He's too quick for you.*

'What's going on?' demanded a second-former called Tanner, pushing his way to the front.

He had come from the nets and had his bat slung over one shoulder. There was a swaggering confidence about him that made William shrink.

'Whack it,' said a voice, a suggestion met by a few murmurs of dissent.

'No, leave it alone,' said Francis, who had just joined the group in time to catch this last remark.

It went against all the rules of survival for a first-former to tell a second-former what they might or might not do and Tanner threw Francis a look of pure contempt before lunging forwards and trapping the end of the mouse's tail with his foot. The creature skittered on the spot in panic for a second and then Tanner brought the bat down, not once but twice, three times until it was smashed to a pink paste. There was a moment of shocked silence and then some laughter and jeers of approval.

William reeled away, nauseated by the cruelty and bravado of his classmates, and bumped into a white-faced Francis. He recoiled, apologising, and then saw in Francis' eyes a matching expression of outrage and disgust.

'I hate them,' said Francis in a choked voice.

'I wish the mouse was alive and he was dead,' William replied.

All of his carefully subdued unhappiness, the feelings of loneliness and self-pity rose up now and overwhelmed him. Hot tears, girlish and shameful, spilt down his cheeks. He knew it was as much himself as the mouse that he was crying for and that made him feel even worse.

'Come on,' said Francis, and without any further discussion, they hurried away from the group and then broke into a run, past the fives courts and the changing rooms towards the old library.

As they rounded the corner, Francis, who was just ahead, collided with one of the masters coming the other way, almost knocking him off his feet.

'Whoa!' said Mr Swales, clutching Francis' shoulder for support. 'What's the hurry?'

The two boys almost collapsed with relief. If it had been anyone else, they would have been in unimaginable trouble.

'Sorry, sir,' Francis mumbled.

'Well, well, if it isn't Harry Kenners and Harry Tappers,' Swales said and then stopped, taking in William's brimming eyes and tragic expression. 'Are you all right?'

William quickly wiped his face on his sleeve, leaving slimy trails on the felt of his blazer.

'Yes, sir. It was nothing. Just a mouse,' Francis volunteered.

'Just a mouse. Very important creatures in mythology, mice, of course,' he added.

It was the sort of thing Mr Kenley would say, William thought, with his way of knowing something about everything.

Mr Swales turned around so they were now heading in the same direction and laid reassuring arms around their shoulders, gathering them up and steering them away from the schoolyard to the quiet of the cloisters. William could smell the oily lanolin of his wool jacket and the leather buttons on his cuff now resting close to his ear.

'Come this way and you can tell me all about it.'

Swales was always good to them after that. He wasn't prone to fits of inexplicable rage like some of the masters, who seemed to William to be quite mad. When he passed them in the corridor, it was with a nod and a smile and once even a wink. William didn't quite understand the language of winking. He thought it was something only common people did. He remembered Aunt Rose once saying that the coalman had winked at her and Aunt Louisa saying 'Saucy!' and giggling. This didn't quite square with Mr Swales and it only happened once, so he soon forgot it.

From that summer term, he and Francis were friends, and though they didn't sit together in class, deskmates having already been assigned at the beginning of the year, they sought each other out at break and lunchtimes, and found plenty more common ground than just a tendency to prefer animals to human beings.

They were both without brothers and sisters and had grown up taking adult company and conversation for granted. Sometimes when Francis spoke it was with the vocabulary and opinions of a middle-aged man, in phrases borrowed from his father. William's aunts' sayings and beliefs translated less well to the purlieus of a boys' boarding school and there were occasions when he found himself losing confidence halfway into a sentence. He once told Francis that he wouldn't be having a bath because it was 'the wrong time of the month', something he had overheard Aunt Rose saying and thought a proverbial excuse for avoiding anything unpleasant. Francis had looked at him strangely.

The difference between having one friend and none was colossal and transformative. School was no less awful, but its awfulness was a burden more easily carried by two. The existence of another person who felt the same and didn't despise him was a source of both comfort and power. There were rare moments of freedom, too, when he and Francis were briefly beyond the attentions of bullies or masters or the tedium of lessons and prep, which were pure pleasure.

One Saturday afternoon, not many weeks after the mouse incident, William had his exeat cancelled for some infraction that he never quite understood, by the same games master who had objected so furiously to the picking of grass. Instead of walking into the village to buy sweets, as was usual, he was tasked with tidying out the gym cupboard.

As far as William was concerned, this was no great sacrifice. On the path through the woods there was always the risk of ambush by older boys, who would relieve smaller fry of their pocket money or their sweets and, in the event of any resistance, their trousers. The gym cupboard, by contrast, was a place of sanctuary and, as it turned out, a treasure house of curiosities never deployed in games lessons. Francis, on hearing of the 'punishment', had quickly volunteered to stay behind and help. At the end of morning school, almost sick with excitement, the two boys hurried to the store, shut themselves in and surveyed their kingdom.

'Look at all this stuff,' Francis breathed.

'How come we never use it?'

As well as the familiar things like cricket pads and tennis racquets in wooden presses, there were masks, foils and rapiers for fencing; medicine balls; dumb-bells and croquet mallets. Francis picked up one of the rapiers and gave it an experimental swish.

'En garde!' he said, striking a pose like Errol Flynn.

William had clambered onto the pommel horse and was sitting astride it, rocking gently as though riding the range. Presently, he threw himself off onto a pile of canvas mats and lay there, dazed. They weren't nearly as soft as they looked.

Francis had discovered the springboard and was bouncing experimentally. They took it in turns to practise a somewhat foreshortened vault over the wooden box and would have kept it up much longer if they hadn't been concerned that the noise they were making might attract attention. Like visitors shut in a museum after hours, they prowled the aisles, turning over the exhibits with the delight of illicit possession.

'Do you think we ought to clear up?' William asked at last in a doubtful voice. To his mind, it did not look especially untidy, compared with home, but he did not want to incur an additional, less agreeable punishment.

'In a minute,' said Francis. He had found a box of quoits and was trying to hook them over a set of spring-loaded cricket stumps.

Next, they devised a game called pirates, which involved circumnavigating the room without putting a foot to the ground. They scrambled over the equipment and leapt from box to mats to horse until William missed his footing and brought down a precarious tower of benches with a terrific crash. This prompted them, finally, to do a hurried clear-up, returning all the balls, gloves, mallets and beanbags to their proper place in the cupboard, straightening mats and bats and racquets and stumps.

Afterwards, as Francis lay on top of the vault, recuperating and tossing a cricket ball from hand to hand, he said, 'My parents have got a cottage down in Sussex. We go there every summer. You could come if you want.'

This invitation, offered so casually, seemed to William to crack the universe open so that light from another world streamed in.

Now, Francis had vanished again. The public speaking competition was over and the Bible Society's guinea had gone to a chap called Acland in the fourth form, whose every syllable was fully enunciated in a voice that throbbed with emotion and made his classmates writhe with embarrassment. But Francis was still missing. He had been in maths, the last period of the afternoon, and it was nearly tea and he had still not put in an appearance in the common room where they usually met to play draughts or chess. With only a few minutes of rec left,

William decided to hunt in the less obvious places. The san could be ruled out: no one was ever taken ill *after* lessons and *before* tea. He tried the dormitories with no success. The double row of identical beds, neatly made and untouched since morning, offered no hiding place. As he crept out again, he saw a flicker of movement at the end of the long corridor; Francis, surely, flitting to the staircase, but where from?

At the end of the landing there was only a locked door to the upper floor that housed the masters' accommodation, lumber rooms and who knew what else, and was strictly out of bounds. PRIVATE – NO ENTRY TO PUPILS, an engraved sign on the door declared in three-inch capitals. Travers had tried the handle once, of course, but it didn't budge.

'Kenley?' William called, but there was no reply and the distant slap of footsteps on the stone stairs didn't falter.

He ran to the last room on the landing, the first-form dorm, also out of bounds but not locked, burst in and ran to the window. Below, emerging from the doorway and crossing the cloister to join the queue for the dinner hall, was Francis.

'Where have you been?' he whispered when they were sitting at the long wooden table with their plates of stewed mince and mash. Conversation had to be conducted in low voices. If they rose above a murmur, one of the patrolling masters would slam a flat length of wood on the tabletop and it would mean silence for the rest of the meal. Francis was combing the lumps out of his potato with a fork, making no serious effort to eat. William had helped himself to four slices of bread, provision of which was unlimited, and was working his way through them as a precaution against later hunger pangs.

'Nowhere,' Francis replied without much conviction.

'You must have been somewhere,' William said, his mouth full. 'It's not possible to be nowhere.'

Francis made no reply to this but frowned darkly into his plate.

'Anyway, I saw you going down the old stairs. Where did you come from?'

'Nowhere. It wasn't me,' Francis insisted.

He had abandoned the potato, raked into furrows, and was probing the grey meat. Presently, he hooked a piece of tubing with his fork and held it up for inspection. Some argument ensued about whether it was a rubber band or a piece of intestine and as neither of these options appealed, Francis made a retching sound and laid down his cutlery.

'I can't eat this.'

It was rare for anyone to leave an entire meal, however unwholesome, and the boys within range were soon contesting his mauled leftovers.

'It definitely was you, though,' William persisted.

It would have been easier to bear if Francis had simply said, 'Shut up, I'm not telling you.' It would have stung, certainly, but would have been easier to take than this obvious lie.

For this remark he was rewarded with a cold, blank stare. It struck him then that the Francis of Brock Cottage had changed utterly, while he, William, was still the same. It was as if his friend was now on the other side of a fast-flowing stream, too far away to communicate clearly, and there was nothing William could do either to join him or to fetch him back.

The next day things had returned to normal and Francis was himself again, as long as he wasn't contradicted or challenged. William perceived the terms of this truce only dimly, with instinct rather than reason. Always in his mind was the mirage of that half-promised visit to Brock Cottage at Easter. If he misspoke or stumbled in ways he couldn't even understand, it might dissolve before his eyes and the future would hold nothing for him.

Sometimes he wondered if Francis might really be ill. There had been those visits to matron, which he had assumed were just ruses to get out of lessons. But it was only a matter of weeks ago that Harry Duggers had gone to the san with a cough and then suddenly his parents had taken him away and the other boys were saying he had TB and would probably die. The thought of Francis being carried off in similar circumstances and leaving him behind was too terrible to contemplate.

It was the day the pigeon flew into the nave during chapel that William found out what Francis did during those periods of absence. The bird had begun swooping low over the boys' heads as they knelt at prayer, causing outbreaks of sniggering and unrest, and had resisted all efforts to wave it towards the open door. Eventually, after it had left a spatter of droppings across the chancel and worship had been thoroughly disrupted, the boys had been ushered out and the groundsman had dispatched it with his shotgun, leaving a bloodied feather stuck to the vaulted ceiling.

In the afternoon it was cross-country, the route restricted to circuits of the playing fields because of thickening fog. William had no hope of keeping up with Francis and there was no expectation that they would run together. By the time he returned to the showers, tired, muddy and cold, Francis had disappeared again.

Going through a door marked PRIVATE – NO ENTRY TO PUPILS was as alien to William as killing a mouse with a cricket bat and yet, somehow, he found himself on the other side of it, looking at a curved flight of wooden stairs. If he was caught by one of the masters or domestic staff here, he would have nothing to say for himself; he had prepared no excuse and could think of none and so he moved quickly.

The wooden treads let out creaks of protest as he climbed, emerging finally on a long, narrow corridor with a low ceiling and a worn red runner on the floor. There were closed doors to left and right, whether bedrooms, studies or storerooms,

William had no idea. Something drew him to the far end of this hallway, where another even narrower staircase rose steeply to a room under the eaves. He could hear the murmur of a voice – Francis' voice. The words were inaudible, but the rise and fall and the pitch of it was as familiar as his own.

In another second he was standing in an attic room lit by the sulphurous foggy twilight from two dormer windows and the orange bars of an electric fire, a necessary luxury as the two people inside were unclothed.

Francis was facing him, frozen. Mr Swales wheeled round, his face a mask of panic. William had never seen or imagined anything like the tableau before him. It was incomprehensible and his brain rejected it. The man was a lunatic; nothing and nowhere was safe any more. He thought of the mouse and Tanner's cricket bat slamming down over and over on something already dead. Everything was disgusting.

Mr Swales reached for a shirt hanging on the back of a chair and covered himself up. Francis was shivering. He looked at William with desperation. 'Help me,' he seemed to be saying, but the words that emerged were, 'Go away!'

'No, no, Tapping, come here.' Swales' voice had lost none of its friendliness.

William did not move. 'I just came to find Kenley,' he stuttered. 'He'll be late for tea.'

Mr Swales smiled. 'Right, well, you run along to tea, Kenley. And you and I will have a little talk.' He made a beckoning gesture with a flat hand.

Francis was gathering his things.

William took a step back. A shimmering black wave rose up from his feet and over his head. He sensed but didn't see Swales coming for him. All he could hear was the beating of wings and the sound of the gun echoing off the chapel walls, the crash of the cricket bat.

'I'm not going to hurt you.' Swales gave a grunt and stumbled, reaching out for William to steady himself.

The touch of his hand on William's arm jolted him from his paralysis and he wrenched himself free and shoved Swales back, driving forwards with his whole weight, just as the boy in the corridor had once done to him. When the blackness cleared, Swales had vanished and Francis was staring at him, round-eyed. There was a popping sound and a fullness in his ears and his shoulder rang with pain.

Just to the side of where Francis stood was an open trapdoor in the floor, a dark void from which no sound issued.

'What have you done?' Francis whispered.

Chapter 36

Lorraine was not in any of the usual places and had not visited the art room since their encounter in Gil's office, which made Helen suspect she did not want to be found. This alone was a compelling reason to seek her out.

It was the end of the working day, but Helen had nowhere pressing to be and an empty summer evening alone in her flat held little appeal. Soon, she knew, she would have to face up to life as an unattached woman, to fill her time, take up new hobbies, affect an interest in people and activities that she didn't truly feel and be both self-reliant and sociable. Not yet, though: all that would call for levels of energy and resolution that she couldn't quite muster.

In the day room, a dispute was in progress among a group of female patients about the proper way to do a jigsaw. The pieces had been tipped out onto the table and several hands were stirring them. As Helen put her head around the door, one of the women appealed to her to mediate.

'Nurse, nurse,' she called, beckoning with a nicotine-stained finger. Stray pieces of the puzzle were caught in the woollen cuffs of her cardigan. 'Tell them you have to do the edges first, then the sky.'

The others turned on her, drowning her words with suggestions of their own.

'I think the edges would be a sensible place to start,' Helen said, looking around to check that Lorraine was not present. 'But there are no rules about these things.'

She withdrew, swiftly, cries of 'Nurse!' following her down the corridor.

In the TV room, William was sitting in his regular seat a few feet from the set watching *Animal Magic*.

'Have you seen Lorraine?' Helen asked, positioning herself in his field of vision.

He frowned and shook his head without taking his eyes from the screen. Nothing short of the dinner bell had the power to distract him from the miracle of television. His posture, leaning in, hands on knees, and his rapt expression put Helen in mind of her father. He, too, had no special preferences as to programmes – it was the phenomenon itself that held him enthralled. She left him absorbed in the commentary of a sardonic giraffe and went outside to continue her search.

There were extensive grounds beyond the main gardens that Helen seldom had reason to visit and it was here on a bench outside the chapel that she at last found her niece, smoking a cigarette and reading a fat novel. Helen, who was not aware that she smoked, was momentarily surprised and then suddenly not.

It was pointless to pretend she had come upon her by chance and she didn't try. Lorraine looked up with a wary smile and squeezed her book closed between her knees, saving the page with one finger as though prepared for no more than the briefest interruption. Her hair was held back off her forehead in a wide Alice band. Her complexion, once flawless, was now speckled with raised spots and pustules, a side effect of her medication.

'I haven't seen you in the art room lately,' Helen said.

'I haven't felt much like drawing. I've been busy with other things.' She blushed through the lie. Even the fullest programme of activities at Westbury still involved aeons of empty time.

'That's a pity,' said Helen. 'I was going to suggest taking your portfolio along to Croydon Tech. They might have some Fine Art courses for you to consider, instead of secretarial college.'

There was a brief flicker of interest in Lorraine's expression before it reverted to neutral.

'What are you reading?' Helen asked by way of deferring the more difficult conversation.

Lorraine reluctantly revealed the fat paperback to be *The Tin Drum*. Helen almost laughed. She must be smitten indeed. There was only one person who could have recommended such a book to a sixteen-year-old girl, whose usual taste in reading matter ran to *Fabulous* magazine and Laura Ingalls Wilder.

'Goodness, that's very highbrow. How are you finding it?'

'It's a bit long,' Lorraine conceded.

'You don't have to read it just because Dr Rudden told you to.'

If she was taken aback by Helen's acuity, she concealed it well.

'I can see that it's probably amazing. If I could just concentrate a bit better. I think it's the pills making me stupid. Anyway,' she added with a flash of defiance, 'Gil's not my doctor.'

'No, indeed. He certainly seems to spend a lot more time with you than he does with his actual patients.'

'I just like talking to him. He's interesting and funny. What's wrong with that?' Lorraine blew out smoke with a jerk of her head.

'Well, nothing, if that's all it is. I'm just worried that you might be getting . . . over-attached to him, because, as you say, he is interesting and funny, and no doubt very sympathetic and kind. And people often fall in love with their therapist, almost without realising it. Even when he is not strictly their therapist.'

'I'm sixteen,' said Lorraine quietly. 'I'm not a child.'

Helen's heart quailed at this non-answer.

'Anyway, I don't understand what you mean by *over-attached*. We can't help our feelings.'

Helen let the alarming ambiguity of 'we' pass unchallenged.

'But you do realise that Dr Rudden – Gil – is very much married. To our cousin. Who is expecting their third child as we speak.' Her mouth was dry as she delivered this homily. She was, she knew, the very last person on Earth entitled to preach on the sanctity of the Rudden marriage, the claims of cousinhood or sexual ethics. And yet she felt the rightness of her objections somehow transcended her own unfitness to be their messenger. 'So, if you find yourself attracted to Gil, the best thing you can do is to avoid being alone with him. Stop seeing him altogether, in fact, and then you won't be tempted to make your feelings obvious and put him in the awkward position of rejecting you.'

Lorraine wouldn't look at her.

Lighting a fresh cigarette from the embers of the last and puffing furiously, she said, 'It's too late for that. I've already told him. And he didn't "reject" me.'

The brakes seemed to have failed and the discussion was now hurtling towards a cliff edge.

'Oh, Lorraine. I don't know what to say.'

It gave Helen no satisfaction that the deep unease with which she had approached this interview had proved well founded. She herself had been the architect of this – she now saw, entirely predictable – disaster; had gone out of her way to bring Gil and Lorraine together against the advice of Morley Holt, who had wisely acted to prevent it.

'I don't know why you sound so apologetic,' said Lorraine, looking baffled. 'I'm not sorry. I'm glad. He understands everything I'm thinking before I even say it. And he feels the same.'

'He said that?' asked Helen, in as steady a voice as she could manage.

317

'I know you think I'm too young to understand these things and know my own mind. The older generation always does.'

Helen flinched from this as though she'd been slapped. It was, after all, more or less what she herself used to think about Clive and June. She had not expected to find herself put on the shelf with them, labelled 'old people who don't get it'.

'Gil is of course very much the older generation himself,' Helen said with a certain acidity. 'The same age as your dad, in fact.'

'He doesn't act old,' Lorraine replied. 'He's not stuck in the past.'

This barb was meant for Clive, Helen reassured herself, but even so, she suddenly felt ancient, as remote from those young women who drank brown ale in Battersea on Friday nights and had sex with some lad behind the bins after closing time as she was from the Edwardians.

'Maybe not,' she said. 'But he is certainly stuck in his marriage.'

'There is such a thing as divorce,' Lorraine said as casually as if she was discussing options for dinner.

It took all of Helen's self-control to respond calmly to this fantastic announcement. Divorce had been mentioned no more than two or three times during her three-year relationship with Gil and always in the context of an unimaginably distant future.

'Lorraine,' she said with a dry mouth. 'You're not having sex with him, are you? I have to ask.'

Lorraine's look of outrage was beautiful to Helen.

'No,' she said in a tone of disgust that her aunt should even be familiar with such terms.

'But he has talked about getting a divorce?'

There was a pause.

'No,' Lorraine admitted. 'I was just saying. People talk about marriage as if everyone stays married for ever, like they did in the old days, when that's obviously not true any more.'

By degrees, Helen's heart rate returned to normal. They were in the realm of delusion now, she told herself. Nevertheless, Gil had some explaining to do.

In the distance, the bell in the tower rang a mournful peal summoning the residents to dinner. Lorraine extended her bare legs, which had been tucked under the bench, and stood up in one languid movement as though operated from above by strings. On her feet was a new pair of elegant dove-grey pumps, from Anello & Davide of Oxford Street.

Chapter 37

The ornamental gardens at Coombe Wood were busy on a Saturday morning in summer and Helen, waiting by the old stables because the tea rooms were full, wondered whether this really was the best meeting place she could have suggested. She had put on the yellow shift that Gil used to like and then, fearing that it looked too dressy for the occasion, had covered it up with a grey cardigan. This had a moth hole on the front, which had to be hidden by a pearl brooch – an eighteenth birthday gift from her parents – which was transferred from garment to garment exclusively for this purpose.

She had the advantage of catching sight of Francis before he saw her and watched him walk up the slope from the gate with his otherworldly air of an off-duty vicar. Mothers with prams and small children on tricycles flowed around him unheeded.

Francis had rung her at work to ask if they might meet somewhere convenient to her as he wanted her advice on a sensitive matter and she had been so thrown by the call that she had been temporarily unable to remember a single suitable venue. Her flat was out of the question, a pub was too boozy and intimate, and there was something of the mothers' coffee morning about the department-store cafes in Croydon that would have done for a female friend, if she had such a thing.

She had met Gil here once in the very early days of their affair when she was still living with Mrs Gordon. They had been walking along holding hands, exulting in the mere fact of each other's existence, when he had suddenly dragged her off the path into the rhododendrons. For a moment she had thought he was overcome with lust, but he had just spotted his daughter Susan's piano teacher heading in their direction. The memory, long submerged, rose to the surface like a bubble of unpleasant gas. It had been a tawdry business from the very start, but she had chosen not to notice.

Francis looked up at last and brightened as she gave him a wave.

'I'm afraid every table in the tea room is taken,' she said as he came within range. 'But if we walk, we might find a bench.'

'This is rather nice,' he replied with a gesture that took in the pond, the parade of white hydrangeas, the tall trees and the wide blue sky. 'Let's just walk.'

'It is nice, and yet I hardly ever come here,' Helen admitted as they made their way at a leisurely pace through a gap in the yew hedge to an area of neat lawns and flower beds bright with echinacea and red campion.

'I suppose there's the feeling that the things on our doorstep will always be there, so we don't need to pay them much attention. I live in Wimbledon, but I've never been to the tennis.'

'I've never even been to a concert at Fairfield Halls,' said Helen. 'Though everyone says it's just as good as the Festival Hall. Perhaps we all feel that anything under our noses can't really be up to much.'

'Well, this is all very philosophical for a Saturday morning,' Francis said as they wound their way between high rhododendrons with stiff glossy leaves.

Helen wondered when he was going to come to the point. 'I was puzzled that you think I could advise you about anything,' she hinted.

'It's my mother. She's got a bee in her bonnet about William and I don't want her to do anything rash.'

'I can't imagine your mother doing anything you'd disapprove of. But go on.'

'She has this idea that she wants to offer him a home with her in Brock Cottage.'

Of all the possible futures that Helen had tried to imagine for William, this had never occurred to her. It seemed an act of heroic generosity. 'Goodness, your mother is a remarkable woman.'

'She is,' Francis agreed. 'And I don't often disagree with her.'

'I wasn't aware that she was living there.'

The path gave way to a shady area of tall Scots pines, their scribbled foliage dark against the summer sky.

'She doesn't. She kept the cottage for holidays and for sentimental reasons – and thinking that she might have grandchildren one day, I suppose. If she goes ahead with this plan, she'd have to give up her flat in Chiswick and her little job playing the piano at the ballet school, and her neighbours, and move there permanently. Become his full-time carer, effectively.'

Another aunt, thought Helen. But a better one.

'Presumably she has thought of all this?'

'Yes, so she says.'

At the top of a flight of sloping steps the trees thinned out and there was a bench hewn from a fallen tree trunk. In the misty distance was the vast new skyscraper, St George's House, dwarfing the old Victorian clock tower. Without any discussion, they made for the bench and Francis brushed off the dirt and spread out his jacket for Helen to sit on. She noticed an ink stain the size of a sixpence on the silk lining where a pen must have leaked and, for some reason, this endeared him to her.

'You're not happy with that arrangement?'

'It's not just about my happiness, Helen.'

He had never called her that before and it made the name sound suddenly unfamiliar, with its dead second syllable.

'I just think it's a reckless thing to do, because there's no possibility of changing her mind if she finds that *she* isn't happy. What if they don't get on? What if he becomes unpredictable and difficult? It's a lifetime commitment.'

'What does she say when you put this to her?'

'Like a lot of good-hearted people – I'm not one, in case you can't tell – she is hugely optimistic about human nature, her own and other people's. She thinks of it as a favour that will go both ways. He'll keep her company and help her do the garden and walk the dogs. And she'll encourage him to be more independent. She doesn't see it as the act of charity that it surely is.'

'They might both stand to benefit from the arrangement, though,' Helen said. 'It might be rather comforting to have someone around who can do practical stuff.'

'But is there any evidence he can do practical stuff – or wants to? He seems to me more like an overgrown child, without any adult skills, apart from draughtsmanship.'

'It's possible that, over time and with encouragement, William might gain a measure of independence. Dr Rudden thought it unlikely, though.'

'This is my worry.'

A young couple, about Lorraine's age, as far as Helen could judge, wandered into the clearing, their arms around each other's waists, heads pressed together either side of a small transistor radio from which the jangle of a pop song was just audible. In her free hand the girl was carrying her shoes.

Francis watched their departing backs with a kind of wonderment. 'I was never young like that. What is it they hear in that music that I don't?'

'Well, *I* hear The Hollies,' said Helen with a certain

323

self-satisfaction at recognising the track from Lorraine's birthday gift.

Francis looked at her, impressed. 'There is a side to you that I hadn't imagined. How do you know these things?'

She smiled, pleased to have surprised him. 'I'm teasing you, really. It's pure coincidence. I only know about three pop songs and that's one of them. My niece is a fan. I'm more of a Madam Butterfly person myself.'

He nodded. 'I'd admit to being more of a Frank Sinatra person. Even perhaps a Connie Francis person.'

'Oh, me too!' said Helen, delighted. She had never learnt to dislike them, in spite of Gil. 'I know they're sentimental mush, really.'

Francis gave her a sideways glance. 'But isn't that sometimes exactly what's required?'

There was a pause.

'I'm sorry, by the way,' Helen said.

'Whatever for?'

'Because I brought William back into your life to try to help him, without thinking whether it would help you. And it hasn't and I'm sorry for that.'

'You don't have anything to apologise for.'

'For dredging up all those painful memories.'

He looked away beyond the trees.

'No, you're quite wrong there. The past is always with me, but it's also the past. It didn't ruin me. It didn't.'

'I can see that. You aren't remotely ruined, but a lot of people would have been.'

It was easier to talk sitting side by side like this than facing each other across a table in a crowded tea room.

'That's because I had the most incredible parents. Both of them. Just exceptional people.'

'Yes, and it's precisely because your mother is so exceptional that she wants to do this thing for William, who wasn't so fortunate.'

'I know, I know. But it's also because she feels guilty that we dropped contact with him after he had come to my rescue. And that she somehow owes him the sacrifice of the rest of her life. And I maintain that she doesn't.'

Helen felt the sincerity of his objections, but at the same time she couldn't help rejoicing in the brilliance of Marion's scheme. It offered William the best chance of a meaningful life outside the walls of Westbury Park.

'What would you have me do that you can't do yourself? Your mother will hardly listen to me more than to you.'

'I think she would. She admires you very much for what you've done for William. You're quite alike.'

'Are we?' said Helen, nonplussed by this comparison. 'I don't see it at all.'

'You're both good people who put yourselves out to help others.'

Helen put up a hand to ward off the compliment. 'I'm not like that at all. It's my job to help the patients at Westbury Park and half the time I make a thorough hash of it.' She was thinking now of Lorraine and her own woeful intervention. 'In my private life I'm not exactly a beacon of good behaviour.'

Her face was pink from the discomfort of this veiled confession. To go into details with a mere acquaintance like Francis would be too much. She wished she had just accepted the undeserved praise and changed the subject.

'It takes a good person to admit their faults so readily,' said Francis. 'But I didn't mean to embarrass you, so I'll shut up.'

Helen laughed. 'To go back to our earlier discussion, I'd be happy to talk to your mother about her plans to see if she's really considered all the implications. For example, in the event of her death—'

'Exactly!' said Francis with some energy. 'She's sixty-two. William's only thirty-seven. She is in good health, but if anything happened to her, then what? He would presumably become my responsibility. There's no one else.'

Helen nodded slowly. 'Yes, all that would have to be carefully weighed and arrangements put in place.'

'I don't mean the cottage,' Francis insisted. 'He's welcome to it. I've got a house of my own. I don't need the money. It's William himself. I can't imagine ever feeling really comfortable with him.'

'Because you've changed or he's changed or . . .?'

'Because what I feel for him is mainly pity and that's not a good basis for friendship. There would always be this . . . imbalance between us.'

'I don't see that you should feel you'd have to take him on full-time. There might be paid companions who could do that sort of thing. I think if you put all this to your mother and told her that it would make you unhappy if she went ahead, I really don't think she would. It seems to me your happiness has always been her priority.'

Francis shook his head. 'But I don't want to blackmail her like that.'

'So, you want me to be your advocate and get her to come to the same endpoint by another route?'

'Yes. No. Put that way, I sound like a selfish monster. Perhaps I am.'

He looked suddenly tired.

'I don't think you are. And I do see your dilemma. But it's my job to be William's advocate.'

'Yes, you're quite right.'

'And to my mind, this seems like the best possible outcome for him. He adores your mother.'

'He always did. I think the cottage cast a kind of spell on him and he's spent his whole life trying to get back there.'

'Is it all still the same?'

'Yes and no. The house itself has hardly changed. Even some of the furniture is still there. The garden has been redone over the years. And there's now a modern housing estate where there used to be fields and a little close of bungalows up the lane.'

Helen grimaced at the idea of this desecration.

'We were lucky to have it at its best before the war, when it was surrounded by farmland and open country. But people have to be housed and you have to accept that not all of the new building will be conveniently far away. It's still very pretty. You should come down and visit next time Mother's in residence. She'd like that.'

'Oh, well . . .' said Helen, feeling that an invitation issued on behalf of someone else could hardly be accepted.

'Anyway, I've taken up enough of your time already,' said Francis, looking at his watch.

Taking his cue, Helen stood up, noticing as she straightened her dress that the yellow fabric was smothered with hundreds of tiny flies. Francis didn't appear to be similarly besieged. She exclaimed irritably and began to swipe them away.

'Hold on,' Francis said. 'You'll smear them against your dress. It's the colour yellow that attracts them. They think you're a flower.'

Leaning towards her, he began to blow the flies gently away. The unexpected intimacy of this gesture left Helen feeling pleasantly confused.

'There,' he said, having dislodged the majority without any damage to her dress. 'Now you need to keep moving.'

As they walked at a brisk pace down the hill to the entrance, a thought occurred to Helen. 'You know, William might be able to contribute financially to his own keep. He stands to inherit from the trust, doesn't he? And there's the house in Coombe Road.'

Francis stopped and turned to her. 'I knew there was something else I meant to tell you. Something relevant to what we've been discussing.'

His eyes were the same intense blue as his shirt, Helen noticed, and the resemblance to Marion, which she had once thought so striking, seemed to have grown less so over the course of the morning. His wasn't an especially handsome face, but there was something attractive and open about it that improved with closer acquaintance. Distracted by this thought, she realised she had missed what he was saying and had to catch up. It was something to do with the papers from Mr Eckerty.

'Apparently, William won't inherit a penny,' Francis was saying. 'The trust passed to the four children of Ernest Tapping and any of their legitimate offspring. But it seems William was not legitimate.'

'I thought his parents were the older brother and his wife who died in a car crash. That was what William told us.'

'Well, his birth certificate tells a different story. Unfortunately.'

'So who gets the proceeds of the trust if not him?'

'Here's the queer thing. In the event that there are no legitimate heirs, it all goes to Westbury Park.'

Chapter 38

On Friday, Helen was tidying the art room after the last class of the week, when Gil put his head around the door. Seeing that she was alone, he came in and sat on the corner of the desk watching as she gathered up the assortment of clay ashtrays, coil pots, deformed figurines and unidentifiable lumps ready for the kiln.

The strains of *Tannhäuser* on the Third Programme and water thundering into the sink had masked the sound of his entrance and it was a moment before Helen was aware of his arrival. It was the first time they had met since their uncomfortable encounter in his office, and her conversation with Lorraine since had done nothing to allay her suspicions – quite the reverse. She knew that a row of some kind was now inevitable and probably irreversible.

'Hello,' she said, turning off the tap, though not the radio. 'I've been meaning to come and talk to you.'

'And I've saved you the journey,' Gil replied with a smile.

She had assumed that Lorraine would have ignored her warnings and by now would have relayed to him all the details of their discussion, but his easy, unwary manner suggested this wasn't so. The idea that Lorraine might have heeded her advice to some degree gave her courage.

Today was the first time that Lorraine had come back to an art class and Helen had taken it as a sign of reconciliation, though they had not had a chance to speak privately. Lorraine had chosen to work alone in the storeroom on her painting while the rest of the group made clay models. She had given Helen no more than the flicker of a smile as she left.

'I know I was supposed to keep away,' Gil was saying. 'But it's killing me.'

There was a time, quite recently, when these words from Gil would have conquered her entirely, but now they glanced off her like paper darts. The shock of finding she felt nothing left her momentarily speechless.

'Say something,' he said, sounding less assured.

'Why did you buy her a pair of shoes?'

Of all the aspects of his behaviour that she might have questioned, this was hardly the most reprehensible, and yet it was only as she said it that she realised how much it had hurt her.

She saw his face sag for a second and then he gathered himself and straightened up so that he was no longer lounging against the desk.

'Because it was her birthday,' he replied gently.

'Yes, three months ago.'

'And the shoes she had were falling apart. I wanted to cheer her up.'

'Is that the way you usually go about cheering up your patients?' Helen asked, pinning him with her gaze.

'I didn't buy them for her "as a patient". I bought them for her as my young relative. Haven't we already had this conversation?'

'Yes. And since then, Lorraine tells me that she is in love with you and that you feel the same.'

Gil started. 'I never said that.' His voice was indignant, affronted.

'So, what did you say?'

'I can't remember exactly. But certainly not that.'

'I wonder where she got the idea, then?'

Helen continued to stare at him, stony-faced. For a long moment he didn't answer, but she held the silence as he had taught her.

'I may have told her she was beautiful,' he conceded. 'Yes, I think I did.'

Helen rolled her eyes.

'But that was only because she was self-conscious about her skin – the drugs have given her acne, as I could have predicted. I was trying to reassure her.'

'You don't think she might have interpreted the compliment, the shoes, the flattering recommendation of difficult novels, as signs of romantic interest? Because I certainly did when you used the exact same tactics on me.'

'That wasn't *tactics*, Helen,' said Gil in a wounded tone.

'Then or now?'

'Look, I was just trying to be encouraging, to make her feel noticed. I never said anything about love. It's you I love. That hasn't changed, by the way.'

The sobbing of violins from the radio that accompanied this declaration was positively scornful.

'You've no reason to feel suspicious or jealous,' Gil pressed on, glaring at the source of the noise.

Helen had managed up to now to be the calmer, more rational of the two, but that reference to jealousy brought the heat to both her face and her voice. Although she had no interest in reviving her relationship with Gil, and her concern now was all for Lorraine, it had still been poison to feel herself to be so soon and so cynically replaceable.

'This is nothing to do with jealousy. All I care about is the effect of your behaviour on Lorraine. I can't believe it can do her anything but harm to believe you have feelings for her.'

'Oh, to hell with Lorraine!' Gil burst out. 'I only spoke to her as a favour to you. It's us I care about.'

'There is no us any more. There's just you and Kath.'

'Can we turn this bloody thing off?' Gil demanded, striding to the radio and silencing it with a twist. 'I can't take on you and Wagner at the same time.'

In the sudden hush that followed there came the merest click of sound. It was barely there at all, but both Helen and Gil froze in acknowledgement of this other presence in the room.

One of the side doors swung open and Lorraine stood there, pale with shock. She seemed almost to shimmer with pain.

'Oh, fuck,' said Gil, tipping his head back as if calling on heaven to come and help him out.

The three of them faced each other with matching expressions of anguish, an unholy triangle of utter mortification.

'Lorraine, I'm so sorry if you overheard that,' Helen began, trying to remember exactly what incriminating or hurtful things had been said. 'I didn't realise anyone was still here.'

'I just came back to get my cardigan,' Lorraine said. 'I heard every word.'

'Lorraine,' Gil pleaded.

She ignored them both, unstrapped her shoes and dropped them on the workbench beside her. 'I'll just go to hell, shall I?' she said in a choked voice.

'Don't say that,' Gil appealed to her. 'Sit down and let's talk this out.'

'I hate you.'

She made a bolt for the door, but he intercepted her and at this attempt to block her exit, she lashed out furiously, hitting him in the face and kicking out, though without much force now that she had surrendered her shoes.

'Get off me!' she screamed as he seized her wrists. 'Let me go!'

'I'm not hurting you. As soon as you calm down, I'll let you go. Don't fight me.'

He had hold of her firmly now, pinning her arms to her sides to restrain her, and was talking soothingly, but she wouldn't be soothed.

'For God's sake, Gil, let her go,' Helen cried, watching the girl's anguished writhing. Her short dress had ridden up, exposing her knickers, heaping humiliation on humiliation. 'You're hurting her!'

A shadow moved in the doorway and, suddenly, William was in the room, halted in his uncertain, splay-footed stance and rigid with confusion at the scene of violence in front of him.

'Help me!' Lorraine screamed, crying real tears now.

If Gil had just taken this interruption as the signal to release his grip and allow Lorraine to escape and nurse her wounded pride in private, Helen thought later, the whole calamity might have ended very differently. For Gil, however, it was a matter of professional principle that he alone could quell unruly outbursts and Lorraine's struggles showed no sign of subsiding. The tussle continued, taking no account of this new audience.

What happened next unfolded with both a slow inevitability and also so fast that before Helen could take a step, William had launched himself at Gil and dragged him away from Lorraine by the neck. At the first slackening of his hold, Lorraine tore herself free and fled from the room. Gil put up no resistance to his manhandling by William – though it would hardly have made a difference if he had – but staggered back, knocking a tray of clay models off the shelf and striking his head on the sharp corner of the kiln as he fell.

Helen and William stared at each other in horror and then she dropped to her knees beside Gil's motionless figure. He was slumped against the side of the kiln and a trickle of blood was beginning to stain the back of his collar.

In the distance came a commotion of running feet. William put his face in his hands.

'I'll tell them it was an accident,' Helen said.

But these words, far from reassuring him, seemed to bring before him an intolerable reality, and he crashed through the fire-escape door and took off at a graceless gallop across the lawn without looking back.

Chapter 39

News of the altercation travelled around the precincts of Westbury Park with various embellishments and inaccuracies almost before Gil had been carried off in an ambulance. Helen was never quite sure what role she had been ascribed in the drama, as for some time afterwards she noticed that conversation stopped abruptly when she walked into the staffroom unannounced.

For a moment she had considered accompanying Gil to hospital, then remembered that it was not her but Kath who belonged at his side in this crisis. Helen had sat with him on the art room floor while one of the nursing staff had cleaned and bandaged his head wound and staunched the blood, and he had refused to let go of her hand. He had only lost consciousness for a matter of seconds, but it took him a little longer than that to remember where he was and what had happened.

It was the first time Helen had ever seen him vulnerable and meek; the abrupt transition from doctor to patient had stripped him of all of his usual power.

'Sorry,' he kept murmuring to the nurse, and 'Thank you so much.'

'Tell William I'm fine and he's not to worry,' was his last remark to Helen before he was stretchered away.

She telephoned Kath immediately from Gil's office, sitting at his desk, the sleeve of her art overall still wet with his blood. They had not had any contact since their meeting at the Ruddens' house three years earlier and it seemed to Helen as though these two encounters formed the bookends of her and Gil's affair.

Kath apologised for being out of breath; she had just been upstairs making beds.

'You mustn't worry, Gil's all right,' Helen began, mindful of Kath's condition and knowing there was no way to begin this kind of phone call without causing alarm.

'What's happened?' Kath came back, unreassured.

'He was trying to restrain a patient who was getting agitated when one of the other patients tried to intervene and in the scuffle, Gil fell and hit his head. He's all right – awake and talking – but they've taken him off to Croydon for an X-ray and so forth.'

'Oh, God, is he really all right?'

'Yes, I spoke to him before he went. He wanted me to tell you, obviously.'

'I knew this would happen sooner or later,' Kath said. 'There's no proper protection for staff at that place. And Gil will always put himself in the thick of things.'

That last remark was certainly true, Helen thought, though perhaps not quite in the way Kath imagined.

'Will you be able to get to the hospital?' she asked, remembering that Gil's car was still outside in its usual space.

'I'm sure my neighbour will give me a lift. He's very good.'

'If you need someone to look after the children . . .' Helen said, a half-offer that she felt bound to make but hoped would be refused.

'Oh no, Susan's perfectly sensible. She can mind Colin for a while.'

'And Mother tells me you've another on the way.'

'Yes. At my age,' said Kath, and Helen could hear the weariness in her voice. 'I don't know what we were thinking.'

'Ah, but a new baby is always a blessing,' said Helen, wondering whether 'thinking' had had much to do with it.

'That's what Gil says. He was the one who always wanted a third child. So, he's thrilled to bits, of course.'

Of course, thought Helen. *Of course he is.*

She had not expected this fresh betrayal, but now saw that in the graceless, stumbling descent that was the only way out of a dying affair, there was always a little further to fall.

'That's all as it should be,' she replied, summoning every last shred of her tattered dignity.

She would inspect her injuries later: now, she had work to do.

By seven o'clock she had searched the gardens and visited all the common rooms and areas to which patients had access, but the grounds were extensive and the buildings labyrinthine and it would have been impossible for her to find someone who was determined to stay hidden. With a heavy heart she made her way back to the main office. Clive and June would have to be told that Lorraine was missing and in what circumstances.

In spite of the heat from the still warm sun pouring through the high windows, Helen's skin rose in goosebumps as she dialled her brother's number. It was for once Clive who answered and Helen felt weak with relief that it was not June to whom this news would have to be broken.

'Hi, Clive, it's me,' she said in a voice of doom.

'Oh, hello, Helen.' He sounded unusually buoyant and it cost her a moment of real regret that she would soon have to puncture his mood. 'Good of you to ring.'

'Er, well, it's about Lorraine.'

'Do you want to speak to her?'

'What? Is she there?'

'Yes, curled up on the sofa watching *Ready Steady Go!* Just turned up on the doorstep saying she was homesick.'

Clive's cheerful tone gave Helen hope that Lorraine had not, so far at least, gone into detail about the real reason for her return.

'Did she say anything else?'

'No. Just that she missed us and wanted to come home. I must say, it's lovely to have her back.'

In the background, Helen could hear the lively chatter of the TV set.

'Oh, OK. That's good news. She left quite abruptly and I just wanted to check that she was all right.'

Gratitude and relief for this undeserved deliverance made her voice crack.

'Shall I put her on?'

'No, no, don't disturb her,' Helen said quickly. There was a difficult conversation to be had with Lorraine, but apologies were best delivered in person and so it must wait. 'I'll let them know that all is well and check what's going on with her medication.'

Clive lowered his voice. 'I always said there was nothing wrong with her. She's no more schizophrenic than I am. If that place has done anything, at least it's made her appreciate the comforts of home. No offence,' he added.

'None taken,' said Helen, unable to defend Westbury Park from this broadside. He doesn't even know the half of it, she thought.

On her way back from Morley Holt's locked and empty office, Helen ran into Lionel Frant, who had just caught up with the afternoon's drama from the nurse who had bandaged Gil's head wound.

'Any news of Dr Rudden?' he asked. 'I've only just heard.' There was no edge to his voice.

'No news since he went to hospital. He was conscious and talking when they put him in the ambulance.'

Lionel nodded, looking into her face with concern.

'Are you all right? You were there at the time, I gather.'

She realised she was still wearing the overall with Gil's blood on her sleeve.

'Yes, fine, thank you.' In the absence of Morley Holt, she would have to tell Lionel that Lorraine and William had both decamped, and he would not be slow to apportion blame for the incident. 'Have you got a moment? I need your advice.' Mortification was coming and she might as well meet it as a friend.

'Of course.'

He led her back to his office, which was much smaller than Gil's and less generously furnished. His desk was half the size and covered in patients' files. In front of it were two upright chairs, of which he took the less comfortable. His glasses were almost opaque with smears and she wondered how he could bear to have his vision so needlessly impeded.

'How can I help?'

'I don't know how much you already know, but at the end of today, Gil and I were talking about Lorraine in the art room, without realising she was in the store listening. She got distressed and made a bolt and Gil – rather unwisely, in my view – tried to restrain her.'

Lionel frowned at her over the top of his murky spectacles but did not interrupt.

'Then William came in and thought Gil was attacking Lorraine and waded in to defend her. In the tussle, Gil fell and hit his head. It was all done in a matter of seconds. But the issue now, apart from Gil's injury, of course, is that Lorraine and William both bolted, separately.

'Lorraine has taken herself home, but I don't know where William is. He's hardly competent to be wandering the streets.

He's never set foot outside the grounds before. I don't know what to do.' She offered him a look of helpless apology.

'Quite a lot to consider here,' Lionel said. 'First things first. Neither William nor Lorraine were admitted under a section, so technically they are free to leave when they choose. For his own safety, I might have preferred William to be detained, but Dr Rudden has his methods. I certainly think it would be in his interests to be readmitted as soon as possible, but he's not my patient and I don't know the exact details of his case.

'Now, to Lorraine. I'm not sure why Dr Rudden was involving himself in her treatment.'

'I'm afraid that was my doing. I got him involved.'

'May I ask why?' His polite curiosity made her wince with shame.

'I never really believed Lorraine was ill – she was under pressure at home and I thought it was her way of reacting. I didn't think a diagnosis of schizophrenia would help her. And the drugs have such side effects – her skin is terrible now. I thought Gil might be able to talk some sense into her. Or rather listen some sense into her.'

Lionel didn't interrupt but allowed her to tail off. His brow was furrowed with perplexity and disappointment.

'Wouldn't it have made more sense to talk to me about your concerns? I'm the person treating your niece, after all.'

'Well, yes, when you put it like that.' Bravely, she looked him in the eye. 'But I felt there was some animosity between us. Perhaps that's too strong a word. Awkwardness.'

Lionel was nonplussed. 'There has never been any on my side, I promise you. And, in any case, even if there had been, which I don't admit, you don't imagine it would affect the way I treat Lorraine? I only want what's best for her. If the drugs aren't working or have side effects, we adjust the dose or try something else. I'm not a monster.'

Helen felt wave upon wave of embarrassment breaking over her. To have to abase herself before someone she had considered an enemy, and then to discover he wasn't an enemy at all, was excruciating.

'I know. I'm sorry. I should have come to you in the first place. All this mess is of my own making. Well, mine and Gil's.'

'He's a very brilliant psychiatrist,' Lionel said in a constipated tone that suggested some qualification of this praise was sure to follow. 'But like many brilliant people, he seems to enjoy chaos.'

'He's certainly not afraid to try new things,' Helen conceded.

'I don't mean to disparage him,' Lionel went on. 'I know you're . . . close.'

'We are not actually . . . close . . . any more.'

'And whatever our differences in approach, I've never doubted that Gil's aim is to alleviate his patients' suffering.'

'He said something similar about you once,' Helen replied.

Lionel dipped his head to acknowledge the compliment.

'To get back to Lorraine. It's important she doesn't just stop taking her medication. I'd like her to come back so we can look at a lower dose or an alternative drug. I'm quite happy for her to be discharged back home if she feels well enough.'

'Thank you,' said Helen, ashamed of the grudge she had held against him because of one remark he had made nearly three years ago about the value of art therapy; because she had absorbed Gil's prejudices; because he was stiff and uncharismatic and wore greasy spectacles, and because he had once dared to think he stood a chance with her. 'I'm very grateful.'

'As for William, if you think he is at risk of harm, it might be worth contacting the police and reporting him as a missing person.'

'Oh, not the police,' said Helen with emphasis. 'He'll think he's being carted off to prison. That would be positively dangerous.'

341

'He may not have gone far. If he's never made any attempt to leave before.'

'He'll be thinking he's in trouble. He's spent his whole life hiding from imagined trouble. And he'll have no more road sense than a child.'

'I could get a couple of the night shift to do one last sweep of the grounds before it gets dark,' said Lionel. 'You should go home.'

Helen approached the Tappings' house on foot as dusk was falling. The last time she had visited the place it had been April and the branches of the alder were clad only in new buds and those items of women's clothing thrown from the upper window. Today, the garden was in full leaf and lush with growth, the path occluded by shrubs, sagging under the weight of dense foliage. Brambles with one-inch spikes grasped at the gate.

She wasn't sure why she had come. It was hardly likely that William would have made his way here, almost five miles along an unknown route and without a key to get in. Yet, she felt it had once been as much a sanctuary as a prison and was the place he would make for in a crisis if he could.

Using Louisa's key, Helen opened the front door, which put up a shuddering resistance against months of unopened post. The air was several degrees cooler inside than out and had a sweet, rotten smell that she remembered from the previous visit.

She flicked the light switch; the bulb was dead or the electricity cut off. She had not thought to bring a torch.

'William,' she called, reluctant to venture further into the gloom and doubtful now that he was inside. 'Are you all right?'

As she strained to pick out any sounds above the sighs of an empty house, she became aware of a warmer, fresher stream of air from the direction of the kitchen and noticed a line of dim light at the bottom of the door to the front parlour. Summoning her courage, Helen knocked gently and pushed open the door.

In the candlelight, William sat in the wing-backed armchair facing the empty grate. On the mantelpiece, two candles in pewter holders gave out a faint glow, their flames sputtering and bending. He was so still that for a second she thought he was dead and fear clutched at her throat. Then he turned his head slowly.

'Will I have to go to prison?' he said in his dry, croaky voice. 'I didn't mean to kill Dr Rudden.'

'No,' said Helen, almost laughing with relief. 'No, you didn't kill Dr Rudden and you're not going to prison. He particularly wanted me to tell you that you're not in any trouble.'

'You mean he's all right?'

In an instant, his frown cleared.

'Yes. I mean, he's got a cut on his head, but he was talking quite normally and he told me you're not to worry.'

'Why was he hurting Lorraine?'

'He was trying to stop her from running away or harming herself.'

'Why would she do that?'

'She was angry with us. How did you get here?'

'I ran and then walked. It took me one hour forty-seven minutes.'

'That's very precise. How did you know the way?'

'The old map on the wall in the day room. I've looked at it most days since I came here. It's got all the important places on. This road; Lloyd Park; the corner where the rocket landed; Westbury Park. It was further than it looked to walk, though.'

'Did you break in?'

'No. The kitchen window was all rotten – it just fell in and smashed when I tried to open it. And the lights don't work, but I know where the candles and matches are kept, so that was all right.'

They both glanced at the mantelpiece, where the candles lit up the lower half of the portrait of a man who looked to Helen like H.G. Wells, with a bushy moustache and stiff collar.

'That's my father,' said William, pointing at the corner of the picture.

'Really?' said Helen, thinking that the man looked at least a generation too old. 'He's very imposing.'

'No, not that man,' said William impatiently. '*He's* my grandfather.'

He stood up and held one of the candles so that Helen could make out the signature D.J. Samsbury at the bottom of the painting.

'The artist. *That's* my father. I only found out today.'

'How?'

'I got this letter from Mr Eckerty. That's what I was coming to the art room to tell you.' He passed Helen a folded sheet of paper. 'And it turns out I had a real mother, too, right there all the time.'

September 1937

Dear Billy,

They say I mustn't tell you how you came to be and how Selwyn and Alma got mixed up in it, so I'm writing it all down so that you can read it one day when you are older and it won't get me into trouble. I'm sorry it wasn't the best start in life and I've often asked myself if I could have done anything differently, but I was only young and the others were so unbending.

Sometimes I felt as if you must already know the truth, because we are so close and so similar in lots of ways, but you never said, so maybe not.

344

I met the man who is your father (how strange that sounds!)
when he came to paint the portrait of your grandfather, Ernest
Tapping – the one that hangs over the fireplace in the front
parlour. We were living in Greenwich then, in a big house
near the naval college and the first of the grocery stores, and
it was a time of plenty. Father had been too old to fight in
the war and Selwyn was too young, so we were – uniquely,
it sometimes seemed – spared the losses that other families
suffered and the 1920s were good to us.

His name was Douglas Samsbury, but I don't know if he is
alive or dead, as I never saw him again after that summer and
his name could not be mentioned. He already had a wife or I
have no doubt we would have married. I can only say that, at
sixteen, I thought him a fine man.

Of course, it was then, and I dare say still is, a terrible
thing to discover you are carrying a child with no husband to
make it respectable. But it seems to me there are more terrible
things than this that I didn't do. Anyway, the shame and
the disappointment of the Tappings was very great, because
they always set so much store by what other people, especially
strangers, thought. But they weren't unkind to me, because I
was the favourite. (There is always a favourite child, Billy, and
that is why it is better to have only one.)

It so happened that our brother, Selwyn, and his wife,
Alma, had been married for several years and desperately
wanted a baby. (I desperately wanted this baby, too, but no
matter.) Mother was sick at the time and living away from
home and so of course it was kept from her, and Elsie organ-
ised everything.

Before the pregnancy started to show, I went to live with
Selwyn and Alma at their house in Oxfordshire, and I kept to
myself and practised the piano and read all the books in their
little library. Alma was very good to me, because she wanted

my baby so badly and she knew it would be hard for me to give you up.

It was all agreed that it would be the best possible thing for you and them − and even for me, as I would be able to see you growing up and be your loving aunty, which is more than could be said for many girls caught out like I was. They even let me choose your name and stay for some weeks after the birth to get well again and feed you myself. There was no unkindness about the business − excepting the actual fact of taking someone's baby away and saying they mayn't have it − so I tried to think myself lucky.

When you were six weeks old, Selwyn and Alma went off to the point-to-point at Kingston Blount and I stayed behind to look after you. It was 21 May 1927 − you know the date well from their gravestones and our annual pilgrimage. I'd taken you out in the pram to the village for our daily walk and when we got back, there was a policeman on the doorstep. They hadn't even got to the races.

What happened was this: a delivery van was coming the other way and a bee flew in through the open window. The driver tried to waft it away from the bare leg of the child in the passenger seat and, when he looked up, he was on the wrong side of the road in the path of Selwyn's Bentley.

It was an open car and they were both flung out in the collision, and that is why I will never ride in a sports car, Billy, and neither must you. We had all this at the inquest from the driver of the van, who survived without much injury except to his conscience. The child, his son, was also unharmed, I'm glad to say, apart from a bee-sting.

And so, having gone into Oxfordshire to give you away, I brought you back home again as my nephew, and the part of me that wasn't used up in grieving for Selwyn and Alma rejoiced. It was a difficult time. Father didn't survive many

346

years after Selwyn's death and the business didn't survive long without Father or Selwyn.

It was a terrible reckoning for having come through the war unscathed; suddenly, we were no luckier than anyone else. Fate is very meticulous in the way it keeps its accounts and demands settlement of its debts, and the knock comes when you are comfortable and forgetful of how much is owed.

The three of us had to sell the big house in Greenwich and buy this house in Croydon, where we have lived ever since by the good graces of the trust. It gives me great comfort to think that you have grown up there under the gaze of that portrait painted by your own father.

It is a strange and pleasant feeling to write all this down, as though you now know all of my thoughts, but of course you don't; they will lie in an envelope in Mr Eckerty's office until Elsie and Louisa are no longer here to object. I may no longer be here myself, of course, since we can't promise to expire in birth order, but if I am, I will be able to tell you myself and I hope you will understand and forgive.

Tomorrow, you are off to school and a new chapter of your life is beginning, and I feel hopeful and excited for you, but sad that the house will be so quiet and lifeless without you. I hope that one day all this can be spoken of between us and understood without shame or cross words, but in case such a day never comes, I lay it out here so that you may know how much you are loved.

Your Devoted Mother

Chapter 40

Gil was off work for a week and returned with a shaved patch and a zip of black stitches on the back of his head. The incident had wounded him in other ways not immediately apparent, but Helen could see the change in him. He had lost some of his former assurance – arrogance, his critics might have called it – and greeted colleagues warily, unsure in what terms he was being discussed behind his back.

Helen caught up with him in his office, which looked even barer than usual. Dadd's painting of *Titania Sleeping* had been taken down, leaving a clean patch on the nicotine-stained wallpaper, and there was a gap-toothed air to the bookshelves.

'Are you going so soon?' she asked.

The news that Lionel Frant had been appointed as the new medical superintendent to take over from Morley Holt had been greeted with an audible intake of breath at the staff meeting where it had been announced. Many of Gil's colleagues had assumed the job was his for the taking.

He nodded. 'I always told you I would.'

'Morley's not even retiring for another month.'

'I'm owed holiday and there's no point in delaying the inevitable,' said Gil, rummaging in a deep drawer in his desk and removing a huge onyx ashtray, a leather blotter and a resin model of the human brain to a cardboard box at his feet.

'It was a shoddy thing for Morley to offer him the job while you were still in hospital.'

'Not at all. It was nothing to do with Morley. He doesn't choose his own successor. It was the board. Presumably, I'm no longer considered a safe pair of hands.'

'I don't know why they would think that. Lorraine hasn't said anything, so far as I know.'

As she said this, she remembered her conversation with Lionel himself on the day of the incident and wondered if he had leaked it to the board.

'In the absence of facts, rumours start circulating,' Gil said.

'I've tried to set the record straight, in a way that doesn't compromise Lorraine's privacy.'

'That's good of you, but you don't need to trouble on my account.'

'What will you do?'

'I've still got my private clients. Perhaps I'll take on some more. But, further ahead, I'm looking at a completely new venture.' He had dropped his voice, even though they were quite alone.

'Oh, are you allowed to talk about it?'

'To you, yes. I've been in contact with Ronnie Laing. He's thinking about setting up an experimental community – doctors and patients, living together, exploring psychosis in a radical way, without drugs or ECT. The sort of thing I've been dreaming about for ages. He's got a group of people interested. I'm giving it serious consideration.'

'It sounds rather cultish,' said Helen, making a note to keep Lorraine away from any such outfit at all costs.

'It's a huge gamble. But I think it could completely transform the way we practise psychiatry.'

He had that old visionary gleam in his eye and she remembered Lionel's remark about Gil enjoying chaos. He reached into the cardboard box and brought out a Manila folder.

'I found this, by the way,' he said, sliding it across the desk. 'Case notes for an Eleanor Tapping, admitted in 1911 with neurasthenia and then intermittently until her death from pneumonia in 1932. So, this would presumably be the mother of Louisa Tapping and grandmother of William?'

Helen had told him about the curious provision in the Tapping family trust and asked him to search the archives for a connection with Westbury Park. She herself had no access to patient files without the permission of someone senior. She began to turn the thin yellowing pages, of which there were surprisingly few to account for a residency of over twenty years.

Presented with fatigue, depression, anxiety, irritability, headache on 15 January 1911. Treatment: four ECT and rest. Discharged symptomless on 28 March 1911.

This pattern of admission, treatment, cure, discharge was repeated over the following two decades with shorter intervals of remission and longer periods of sequestration until 1926, when Eleanor Tapping entered the gates for the last time and was released only by death.

'Poor woman,' said Helen. 'With every relapse, her symptoms got worse. And then, in 1927, she lost her son and daughter-in-law in that car crash just after William was born, and not long afterwards her husband. No wonder she never fully recovered.'

'And yet the family must have been pleased with the care she received or they would hardly have made the Park a beneficiary of the trust,' Gil said.

'Yes. Yes, I suppose so,' Helen agreed, taking encouragement where she could.

She closed the file and pushed it back across the desktop.

'You know, you've done a good job with William,' he said. 'I can't take any credit.'

'Not just me. Marion, too. And Lorraine, in a way. Anyway, that's generous of you, considering he nearly broke your skull.'

Gil waved this away. 'He was just defending someone weaker. As any decent man should.'

'One success in three years,' Helen said. 'And a limited one at that.'

'He's re-entering society after twenty-five years. I call that an unqualified success.'

'That has more to do with Marion than me.'

'How on earth did you persuade her to take him in?'

'She didn't need any persuading; it was her idea. It was my job to talk her out of it.'

'How's that?'

'Francis thought she was being hasty.'

'Perhaps it's no bad thing to be in a hurry to do good.'

'She said something very similar to me.'

Helen had kept her word to Francis and presented all of his concerns and reservations to Marion in a long telephone call and she had promised to reflect and talk to him before making her decision. Four days later, she had rung Helen to say that her mind was made up.

'So often it's a choice between the easy thing you'd rather do and the difficult thing you ought to do,' Marion had explained. 'The strangest thing is that as soon as I'd committed myself to doing the difficult thing, a huge weight fell away and I felt completely at peace for the first time in months.'

This talk of William's relocation reminded Helen that there was one other piece of business to discuss. 'I've given notice at the flat, by the way. I move out at the end of August, so . . .'

'Where will you go?'

'Not far. The ground-floor flat has fallen vacant – the old man with the whippet has apparently gone to live with his daughter. It's not as large or as nice as mine, but it's cheaper, so I'll be able to afford it if I make economies.'

'No going back to Mrs Gordon?'

'I did think of it briefly, in a moment of desperation, but no.'

This dissolution of the financial arrangement by which he had supported her represented the final severing of ties. Once he left Westbury Park, Helen could not imagine their paths crossing again. They smiled sadly at each other like mourners at a graveside, between them the burial site of their former passion.

'You know, Helen, I don't regret a moment of it,' said Gil, as though in a last attempt to breathe life into its cold, dead form.

Helen looked into his eyes but refused to capitulate. She *did* regret the wrong she had done Kath and the children; it couldn't be undone, but she wouldn't celebrate it. She thought of something William had said to Lorraine in the art room about rubbing out: even if it's a mistake, every mark is part of the picture.

'I can't say the same,' she said at last. 'I wish I'd got to know you properly as a colleague and a cousin. Then we could have been friends for life.'

'I could never have just been your friend.'

For a second he looked wounded and she realised that, for Gil, intensity had always been more important than permanence, whereas she had wanted something lasting.

A bell rang. Breakfast was over; ward rounds would soon be under way; the first of her patients would be arriving with their unknowable needs and problems, and she would do her best with paper and paint to provide some relief from their troubles.

At the door, she turned. 'Good luck with the baby. Not long now.'

He bowed his head in acceptance of this blessing and turned back to the task of clearing his desk.

Chapter 41

'Mum and Dad are out,' said Lorraine, opening the front door a scant two inches and peering through the chink. 'And I've got my hair in rollers.'

'That's OK,' said Helen. 'It's you I've come to see.'

She had taken a day's leave for this errand, picking a morning when Clive and June would be at work so that she would have Lorraine to herself. On her way she had stopped at Broomfields in Addiscombe to pick up a walnut cake. In her other hand was a canvas bag containing the Anello & Davide shoes that she had rescued from the art room.

Lorraine stood back to admit her, keeping out of sight to avoid displaying her rollers to the empty street. She was wearing a smart new dress that Helen had not seen before and her complexion was a little improved, the remaining spots masked by pale foundation.

'You look nice,' Helen said. 'Are you going somewhere?'

Lorraine spun the slack gold watch on her wrist. 'Wendy's coming round in half an hour. We're going to Martin Ford's in Croydon.'

'Clothes shopping?' Helen was aware of this boutique but had never ventured inside as it was aimed at the young and fashionable.

'No, she's giving up her Saturday job there when she starts her hairdressing, so we're going to see if they'll let me take it over instead.'

'That would be great, wouldn't it?'

'Yeah – twenty-five per cent staff discount,' Lorraine said, rubbing finger and thumb together.

That would make the clothes just about affordable, Helen thought.

'Well, what I've got to say won't take half an hour.'

'It's all right. Wendy's always late.'

'I've only come here to say sorry.'

Helen forced herself to look Lorraine in the eye as she said this. It mustn't be easy, she thought. An apology should always pinch a little.

Lorraine shrugged; she was no more comfortable than Helen.

'I don't know what you've got to apologise for,' she said, turning away. 'I was the idiot.'

'No, you weren't, Lorraine. You weren't an idiot. None of it was your fault. I was the biggest idiot and a colossal hypocrite. But I'm quite cured now.'

They were still standing in the hallway and Lorraine seemed to realise that this was not quite right.

'Do you want to sit down? I could put the kettle on,' she said doubtfully.

'No, I don't want tea,' said Helen. 'Why don't I help you to finish doing your hair before Wendy gets here.'

Lorraine accepted this suggestion with something approaching alacrity. It was easier somehow to talk when they were installed in front of the dressing-table mirror, their hands busy with brushes and pins, their eyes meeting shyly now and then in their reflection.

'So, he's gone back to his wife?' Lorraine asked at last.

'It's not really a matter of *back*. He never left her. I was seeing him on what you might call a part-time basis for three years. There's no excuse – it was terrible behaviour.'

'I don't even think about him now. Not really,' said Lorraine.

'Me neither,' said Helen.

They smiled at each other in the mirror, acknowledging their new, painfully acquired wisdom.

Helen unwound the rollers and brushed out the fat curls and Lorraine showed her the magazine cutting of Cilla Black's bouffant bob that they were aiming for.

'How have things been since you came home?' Helen dared to ask as she backcombed and teased sections of hair. 'With Mum and Dad, I mean.'

'Better,' said Lorraine, turning from side to side to appraise her appearance. 'They seem to be pleased to have me back and Mum doesn't nag me so much. Sometimes I can see her open her mouth to say something and then it's like she changes her mind and shuts up.' Lorraine demonstrated June's sealed-lip grimace and Helen laughed. The likeness was startling, but this was not something that could be shared without giving offence. 'I suppose they're trying to be kind because they're frightened I'm going to go loopy again.'

'Do you ever feel as though you are?' Helen enquired.

She was thinking of the many patients at Westbury Park who seemed trapped in a cycle of recovery and relapse. There were others, too, she reminded herself, with more debilitating symptoms than Lorraine's, who had responded well to treatment and resumed their old lives without further trouble.

'I don't know, really,' Lorraine admitted. 'Dr Frant's put me on a lower dose of chlorpromazine and I feel mostly normal. Sometimes I think I must have brought the whole thing on myself. Like I sort of wanted something to happen.'

'I don't think it's helpful to blame yourself. The truth is, no one really knows where these episodes come from.'

Helen ran the brush gently over the stiff nest of teased hair to form a smooth, plumped silhouette.

'Nice,' said Lorraine, shaking a can of lacquer and spraying the air above her head with clouds of sticky vapour.

'So, what are your plans for what's left of the summer?' Helen said, wheezing slightly. 'Taking things easy, I should think.'

'Mum and Dad want me to go down to the caravan at Pevensey with them, but I think I'd rather stay here. Especially if I get this Saturday job.'

'They're probably worried about leaving you by yourself so soon. It's understandable.'

Lorraine hesitated. 'You could come and stay for the week,' she murmured. 'If you wanted. So I wouldn't be alone in the house at night.'

For a moment Helen was too overcome to speak. She hadn't dared to hope to be so soon and so fully forgiven. 'Of course I'll come,' she said. 'I won't get in your way – I'll be out at work during the day, anyway.'

'OK. I'll tell Mum and Dad. They'll be happy if they know you're staying.'

'Great. I'll look forward to it.'

She hadn't liked to enquire about the future beyond the summer, knowing that much depended on the results of exams, many of which Lorraine had missed, but her niece now raised the subject herself.

'O-level results come out next week. I think Mum and Dad have forgotten – luckily. They never mention it.'

Helen was fairly sure the date was engraved in their memories as another emotional and administrative hurdle to be overcome.

'Will you go back to school to redo the ones you missed?'

'I don't think they'll have me,' Lorraine replied. 'I don't know if I want to go back if all of my friends have left.'

'Maybe you'll have passed enough that it won't matter. You'd got a fair few out of the way before you fell ill.'

'Only four. English lang, English lit, art and geography. And I don't even know if I'll have passed those. Maths was the one I didn't finish and that's the important one.'

'Why don't we wait and see what you get, and then take your portfolio down to Croydon Tech and see if they'll let you do art A level while you resit maths and any others that you need? I've still got all the work you did at Westbury.'

'Do you think they'd let me do that?' A rare tremor of hopefulness passed over Lorraine's face.

'I can ring them up and find out. They've already accepted you to do secretarial. It's only a matter of changing courses.'

Helen felt a crusade coming on. She was a match for any admissions officer – let Lorraine's results be what they were.

'Thank you!'

They hugged at arm's-length and with great restraint, avoiding any derangement to Lorraine's now crisply set hair.

The doorbell rang and Lorraine leapt up, burrowing her feet into a pair of flattened suede shoes worn to a shine at the toes and with a flapping sole, and then looked in dismay at the lowering effect on the rest of her outfit.

'Oh well,' she said.

'You know, I did bring back your grey pumps,' Helen admitted with an air of trepidation. 'I mean, I know you don't want them and you don't want to be reminded, and I can just take them away and put them in the Scouts' jumble sale . . .'

Before Helen had even finished speaking, Lorraine had kicked off the shabby old shoes, leaving them to fall where they would, and was taking the stairs at a run. Helen followed, laughing to herself.

'You look nice,' said Wendy on the doorstep, her glance sliding to Lorraine's feet, with that girlish instinct to find the one thing that needs to be envied. She, too, was painted and powdered and backcombed and sprayed as though for a beauty pageant rather than a mooch around Croydon.

'So do you!' Lorraine cried, and for a moment they squawked compliments at one another while Helen looked on in amusement.

She watched her niece sweep up her packet of Craven 'A' and lighter from the hallstand and stuff them in her shoulder bag. Smoking: a souvenir from Westbury Park, she thought.

They parted on the street, Helen going towards her scooter, the girls heading to the bus stop, with all the swaggering assurance that big hair and new outfits and too-high hemlines and the certain disapproval of their elders can confer.

Chapter 42

A hand-painted cardboard sign hanging over a fence post read NOT THIS ONE, so Helen kept going past the turning, along the sunken lane between the mossy roots. Overhead, the trees had laced their branches to form a cool green tunnel pierced by wands of sunlight.

THIS ONE, said another sign, and there, leaning against the open gate, was William in a short-sleeved shirt and flannels and a green canvas fishing hat. He waved her in with a proprietorial gesture, closed the gate with great ceremony and jogged behind her as her Vespa bounced along the unmade track.

To their left they passed a little close of newish bungalows with a decent tarmac road and then there was the driveway to Brock Cottage, lined with delphiniums and phlox.

'Those houses weren't here before,' he said by way of greeting as Helen parked up and removed her headscarf, shaking out her sticky hair.

The front of the scooter was plastered with mashed insects.

'It used to be all countryside.'

Before they had advanced a few paces, there was a sound of barking and they were set upon by a flurry of spaniels who appeared from around the corner, tumbling over each other in their frenzy to reach William. Receiving them as they leapt at him, he commanded them to get down while petting them, fending them off, putting his arms into the fray and stirring them in frenzied circles.

'I'm training them,' he explained without irony when they had gone tearing off again.

'Are you sure?' Helen said.

Though her only acquaintance with Brock Cottage had been through William's sketches, the two low storeys of flint with a stable door and a roof of neat thatch, its lawns, flower beds and orchard, struck Helen with the force of a memory, or somewhere visited in a dream. William immediately started leading her on a tour, pointing out the rose beds that were now his responsibility and the newly dug vegetable patch, the wild-flower meadow and the view beyond the trees, desecrated now by the grey tiled roofs of a modern housing development. She detected a lordly confidence and pride in the way he showed off his domain, which was quite new.

Marion, in a pair of floppy trousers, a cotton blouse and a straw sun hat with a chewed brim, was arranging the furniture on the small brick terrace. She stopped beating cushions when she saw Helen and raised an arm in greeting.

'Come and have a drink,' she called before William could drag Helen all the way to the stream to show her the fish. 'We've got home-made redcurrant cordial. It's as sour as mis-chief, but what else can you do with redcurrants?'

It was mid-September and they had been installed in the cottage for a month, during which Helen had had no news of William apart from a postcard from Marion saying 'All is well!' and now this invitation to lunch. She was itching with curiosity to see how he had adapted to his new life, or his old life, as perhaps he thought of it.

'How are things going?' Helen asked when they had embraced and were sitting at the weathered wooden table with glasses of the unpromising cordial in front of them. 'William seems very much at home.'

He was out of earshot, dispatched by Marion to fetch a sun umbrella from one of the sheds.

'Very well,' said Marion with emphasis. 'We're getting used to each other's little foibles and I'm sure William has much more to put up with than I do.'

She would never be disloyal, Helen thought.

'He loves being outdoors,' Marion was saying. 'There's no shortage of jobs to do in the garden, but I try not to work him too hard. The dogs take up quite a lot of his time, which is fine. I'm not sure how we'll fare when the nights draw in, but we have our little routines.'

She stopped as he appeared from around the side of the cottage dragging a heavy stone base and a wooden parasol with several broken spokes, the spaniels wheeling around his ankles.

'Where do you want it, Ma?' he asked, sitting down to inspect the various breakages.

'Oh, just so it shades the table, otherwise the butter will melt. I was just telling Helen about our routines.'

'Cake at four,' he confirmed.

'Yes, whatever we're doing, at four o'clock we down tools and have a cup of tea and whatever's in the tin. We've been doing a lot of baking, too. William makes very good scones.'

'And *Sunday Night at the London Palladium*,' he reminded her. 'On Sundays.'

'We like our television in the evening.'

'What did he call you?' Helen asked when William had returned to the shed to collect some tools.

'Oh, he calls me Ma. Short for Marion, I suppose. It was a bit wearing being Mrs Kenley in my own home.' She gave a sheepish laugh.

'Does he go out by himself at all?'

'He walks the dogs around the lanes, along the same route, and talks to the other dog walkers. And he goes to the village shop for supplies. They know him in there. He never ventures far. There's a bicycle that used to be Basil's, but he's not got the hang of it. I think it's something you have to learn as a child. A couple of locals have asked if he might do a bit of gardening for a few hours a week, so that might be something.'

'Has he done any drawing since he got here?'

Helen had sent him away with a set of pencils, Winsor & Newton coloured inks, pens, brushes and sketch pads as a farewell gift.

'No. None. I can't quite account for it. Maybe he will in time.'

'Perhaps it came out of a feeling of loneliness,' Helen said. 'And he's not lonely any more.'

'At the moment he spends most of his time out of doors. Perhaps in the winter he'll go back to it.'

'And how about you? Are you missing your flat and the ballet school?'

'Not really. Thank you for asking. I keep myself busy. I go to choir on Mondays, and William stays in with the dogs and has the place to himself. It's nice not coming back to an empty house.'

Helen was dying to ask about Francis but didn't dare. Marion was so sharp and so knowing; she would make all sorts of unwelcome inferences. In truth, Helen had hoped he might be here today but was not surprised that he wasn't. He had made his opposition to the whole scheme clear and it was understandable that he kept his distance.

William returned with some pieces of dowel and garden twine and proceeded to make rudimentary repairs to the parasol, fashioning splints for the broken spokes. He had taken off the fishing hat to reveal a large sticking plaster on his head, a consequence of his frequent collisions with the low beams.

'Very good,' said Marion, appraising his efforts.

'Shall I show . . . the cottage?' he asked when the job was done and the parasol was standing crookedly in place.

He still had problems with the transition from formal to informal names and it would be a while before he could call her Helen with any conviction.

'Yes, please,' said Helen, jumping up to oblige him.

He made a point of demonstrating the two-part opening of the stable door so that she could appreciate its versatility.

'It's useful for keeping the dogs out or in,' he explained.

The interior was neat and clean, with a mixture of old and very old furniture, and Helen wondered how much of it dated from the period of William's childhood. The kitchen had seen some renovation, as there was now electricity and a modern free-standing oven instead of the old range, but the large wooden table in the middle of the room bore the gouges and scorch marks of decades of use.

The sitting room that ran the length of the house had two plush sofas, three dog baskets and a boxy television in one corner. Above the fireplace with its blackened stove loomed the portrait of Ernest Tapping. It looked much less at home among the dainty chintz of Brock Cottage than the ugly Victorian relics of the Tappings' parlour and Helen marvelled again at Marion's generosity of heart.

'I see your father's work is on display,' she said. 'Is your mother here, too?'

William plucked a framed photograph from a set of shelves in a recess that held a collection of pictures and small ornaments. A sixteen-year-old Rose Tapping, her hair shingled, wearing a Peter Pan collared dress, stared mistily out at her across the vanished years.

'She looks very pretty,' said Helen, which was no more than the truth.

She couldn't have been said to look happy, but then smiling in photographs was one of those things that was not done in the 1920s, like falling for a married man and having his baby, Helen thought.

'That was taken before I was born,' William explained. 'There didn't seem to be any photos of her after that.'

'It was an expensive business back then,' said Helen. 'You couldn't just snap away with your instamatic.'

She thought of Clive and his cine camera, with his confidence in a posterity that would have any interest in his 8mm home movies of the Hansfords.

'I'll show you upstairs now. I have to duck.' His fingers strayed to the plaster. 'You probably won't.'

William led the way, tolling the names of the birds as he passed the paintings. Teal, pochard, gadwall, scaup. On the landing, he pointed to a closed door. 'That's Ma's room. I don't go in there.'

'No,' Helen agreed.

She followed his stooping form into a sunny bedroom containing a small double bed, wardrobe and chest of drawers. On the counterpane was a pile of clean laundry, neatly folded. He pounced on it and began putting it away. From the window she could see over the back garden to the fields and farmland beyond. One of the curtains was kept half drawn, William explained, to block out the view of the new houses. That way, it was easy enough to imagine they weren't there at all.

'Did you bring any of this from Coombe Road?' Helen asked, looking at the brass barometer and horseshoe on the wall and wondering at his choice of decoration.

'No, just some books. I prefer the things that were already here. The bed is new, though. I'd never slept in a double bed before. There's so much space.'

'We all miss you at Westbury Park,' she said as they made their way back downstairs and then realised that this hardly made sense. He had made few friends, being at best reluctant to speak, and of the few people who had got to know him, Lorraine and Gil were no longer there. His absence had gone largely unremarked.

'I miss Smokey,' he conceded. 'But I prefer it here.'

In the kitchen, Marion was taking a cheese flan from the oven with a coarse woollen mitt.

'In case I have given the impression that we are creatures of habit, let me tell you about our latest experiment. We're *vegetarians*.' She pronounced the word with great reverence and precision.

'Goodness,' said Helen. 'Was that William's idea?'

'Yes. He decided he didn't want to eat animals any more. So now we get through no end of cheese and eggs.'

William came in and began rummaging in the cutlery drawer.

'We're getting hens,' he said, having caught the end of Marion's remark. 'I'm going to build a henhouse.'

'It will need to be quite a fortress,' said Helen, thinking of the spaniels.

'It will be.'

They followed Marion out into the garden and he laid three places at the table. He pointed to a rolled napkin in a silver ring with an engraving of a squirrel.

'That's yours,' he said to Helen. 'Not to keep. Just while you're here.'

'Understood.'

The cheese flan, covered in a clean tablecloth, sat on a raffia mat beside a bowl of salad. The jug of redcurrant juice, wearing a net weighted with glass beads to keep off the flies, glowed like a garnet in the bright sunlight.

Marion turned her head, cupping a hand to her ear. 'Ah,' she said with an air of satisfaction. 'I thought so.'

Over the trilling of birds and the hiss of insects from the long grasses in the wildflower garden, Helen could hear the distant cough of an engine.

'That'll be Francis. I invited him a while ago and he was rather non-committal. So I mentioned it again last week and told him you were coming, just to see if it made a difference.' She smiled complacently as the rumbling noise grew to a crescendo and then stopped. 'And it looks as though it has.'

Chapter 43

'Can me and Tapping go down to the stream?' Francis asked his parents within minutes of arriving at Brock Cottage.

They were still unloading the cases from the car.

'Tapping and I,' his mother replied. 'And, Francis, do you think we could dispense with the Tapping and Kenley business while we're on holiday? You're not at school now.'

'Oh. All right. Can "William" and I go down to the stream?' He stumbled over the name and laughed. 'It sounds so funny.'

'Not to me,' said William, who had never quite got used to being addressed by his surname.

'And take Boz with you,' added Mr Kenley. 'He needs a run.'

The dog had spent the journey on a blanket on the back seat between them, barely stirring, and was now a coiled spring of energy. They left Francis' parents to empty the car and ran to the end of the garden, through the gate and into a field of long grass and thistles. Boswell romped ahead of them as though jumping waves. There were still hours of daylight left, but there was so much to explore.

William had been in a trance of excitement for the entire journey. Since the invitation had been formally made by the Kenleys and accepted by his aunts, he had been looking forward to the day almost with dread. It had seemed hardly possible that something so good would happen to him without mishap, but here they were for two whole weeks.

Francis strode just ahead, as eager to show off his domain as William was to admire it. This is the spinney; this is the stile; these are the stepping stones; that's the bridge. When they stood still and listened, William could hear the insects rustling in the long grass and birds chattering from the trees.

'That's a redstart,' said Francis, picking out some high, piping note from the general chorus of sound.

William wished he could recognise birdsong and identify trees. School did not seem to teach these skills.

Back at the cottage, Mr and Mrs Kenley had unpacked the provisions, chased away the spiders and put the boys' suitcases in Francis' room, which had twin beds with blue-and-white counterpanes. It was low-ceilinged, with uneven floorboards and tasselled rugs to trip the unwary. There was a welcoming smell of wood and flagstones and snuffed candles.

For dinner they had a veal and ham pie, brought from home, served with tinned potatoes. Boswell, restored by his run in the fields, lay under the table, his muscular body pressed against William's feet. After eating, they all rolled up their cloth napkins ready for the next meal.

'This is yours,' Mrs Kenley said, passing William an engraved silver band. 'You're the badger.'

Francis had a fox; Mrs Kenley a weasel; Mr Kenley a squirrel.

The dishes were cleared away and washed up by Mrs Kenley in water boiled on the Primus stove as though it were a huge adventure and treat to do her own housework and one of the joys of the holiday. Afterwards, they played a board game and then there was cocoa and biscuits – just like at home, only with more generous helpings of everything.

He had thought Francis' parents might be grand or strict, or just the kind of grown-ups who aren't much interested in children and expect them to keep out of the way. These possibilities had not troubled him much; it was Francis' company that was the prize. It was an unexpected pleasure then to discover that Mr and Mrs Kenley were as keen as any child on having fun – a concept quite foreign to Aunt Louisa and Aunt Elsie.

On the first night, he and Francis were awoken sometime after eleven by a knock at the door.

'Come and look at the badgers,' Mr Kenley whispered, crossing to the window and parting the curtains.

The boys, instantly awake, scrambled out of bed to join him. At the bottom of the garden, just emerging from the trees, were two badgers, snuffing the grass with their striped snouts. Their pelts gleamed silver in the light of a half-moon and a sky spattered with stars. One of the pair had found a fallen apple and was taking tidy bites; the other, frozen and alert, seemed to be staring straight in at the window, fixing them with dark, suspicious eyes.

'Aren't they splendid?' whispered Mr Kenley.

William nodded, holding his breath, willing the lovely creatures to stay. He knew they had come for him – 'This is yours,' Mrs Kenley had said, and he had rubbed his thumb over the engraving and summoned them.

Downstairs, Boswell stirred and let out a gruff bark. The badgers, though far away, twitched and loped off into the undergrowth.

'Do they come out every night?' William asked.

'No, sometimes weeks pass and we don't see them. You're lucky.'

In the morning, he woke up in stages: first aware of no more than a warm stripe of sunlight across his face; then mystified by the unfamiliar contours of the room; and then elated that he was not at school or even at home but here in Brock Cottage. Francis was still sleeping, so William lay for a while, enjoying this secret knowledge, but soon grew restive at the thought of the wasted minutes and slapped his book on the bedside table a few times and coughed until Francis stirred.

For breakfast there was bacon and scrambled eggs. Mr Kenley had been up for some time and had already strung up hammocks between the trees and run the rotary mower over the grass to make a smoother surface for croquet. No matter how early William woke, Mrs Kenley was up before him, cooking, laying the table or enjoying a cup of tea and her book in the sunshine.

Gradually, they developed a rhythm to the days. In the mornings the boys would take Boswell off and go exploring, roaming for miles over the fields or building a camp in the spinney. It was always sandwiches for lunch, which could be taken with them if they planned to stay out. William, who was used to mealtimes at home and school that were predictable to the minute, found this flexibility unnerving and then exhilarating. It was his first intimation that other people's lives were different and not necessarily the worse for it.

In the afternoon, the four of them would play tennis or croquet on the flat lawn at the side of the house, or cricket in the long back garden. Even Mrs Kenley was mad about cricket; she could catch a ball one-handed and crouched fearlessly behind the wicket wearing a pair of gardening gloves to protect her nail polish. In consideration of windows and the glasshouse, they used a tennis ball for batting practice and Mrs Kenley dazzled him by swiping it over the roof for six.

Later, they might go down to the stream for a couple of hours of fishing before dinner and then there would be cards or dominoes. Every night, Mr Kenley would read *Moonfleet* to them by candlelight and with great expression and a different accent for each character. He was a barrister by profession and liked to exercise his vocal cords, even on holiday, his wife explained.

The happiest hours for William were those spent down by the stream. About half a mile from the end of the garden it broadened out into a deep pool shaded by willows and thick with slumbering fish. They had to wade through knee-high grass and wet nettles to reach a suitable place on the bank from which to cast their lines without entangling them in the overhanging trees. Francis showed William how to bait a hook with a maggot or a piece of luncheon meat. Seeing how much his friend enjoyed imparting the ancient wisdom of the countryside, William pretended to be a little slower and more in need of instruction than he really was.

He was relieved when Francis got the first bite and was able to demonstrate how to reel in a decent-sized perch and use the disgorger to free it from the hook. It wasn't the act of catching a fish that interested William; he preferred to see them skulking below the surface than twitching on the end of a line. The pleasure lay in sitting on the riverbank beside Francis, spotting a kingfisher in the reeds, watching the pond skaters and shiny dragonflies darting over the water, but this wasn't something that could be admitted. It needed a rod and line, however ineffectually deployed, for mere idleness to become a respectable and manly pastime. Even so, he admitted a twinge of pleasure when he finally caught a small, perfect dace. Francis had been so encouraging; he didn't want to disappoint him. Its pewter scales flashed in the sunlight as he gently removed the hook and lowered it into the bucket, where they were keeping the perch to take back and show off at the cottage.

Seconds later – William had not even had the chance to wipe his hands on the smelly fish rag – the dace had flipped itself out of the bucket onto the grass. The boys looked at each other wide-eyed.

'Did you see that?' said Francis.

'I didn't know they could jump. Don't put it back in there,' William added as Francis scooped up the gasping fish. 'It must be trying to get away from the perch.'

'They live in the same pond,' Francis replied.

All the same, he returned the dace to the reedy water by the bank, where it lay stunned for a few moments before slithering away.

'I suppose he is quite a bit bigger and mean-looking,' said Francis, glaring into the bucket at the inhospitable perch. 'I'm going to take it back to show Father. I wonder if he'll survive overnight in here. I mean, fish do live in bowls, don't they?'

'We thought we might drive down to the coast tomorrow,' Mr Kenley said one evening over dinner of shepherd's pie. 'Have a picnic, knock a ball around, take a run at the sea to let it know who's boss, that kind of thing.'

'Can we take the cricket stuff?' Francis asked.

'Well, *obviously* we'd take the cricket stuff,' said his mother. 'But what do you think, William? Are you ready to get back in the car again, or would you rather stay here and loaf about?'

He could hardly believe that there was anywhere with more to offer than Brock Cottage and its surroundings, but he had never been to the sea and it held a secret fascination as the setting of so many of his favourite books. It was only when the others had enthusiastically declared the plan settled that he remembered that he had no bathing costume and couldn't swim. The second of these considerations was the greater; if the Kenleys swam with the skill and competitive spirit that they played all other sports, he would surely drown.

He sought Mrs Kenley out in the kitchen while she was drying the dishes. He couldn't call her by her name, so he just coughed and she turned and beamed at him.

'Hello, dear. Can I get you something?' She carried on wiping the cutlery and returning it to the drawer under the draining board.

'I haven't brought a bathing costume.' This sounded better than admitting he didn't own such an item.

'Oh, I wouldn't worry about that. You can swim in your vest and pants.'

'I can't really swim.'

Mrs Kenley looked horrified. 'Can you not? And we've been packing you off to the river every day. It's lucky you didn't fall in.'

'I just never learnt how,' he said.

Try as he might, he could not picture his aunts on a beach or in anything but the tamest of outdoor settings. They were essentially creatures of the house, belonging among furniture, ornaments and clutter rather than wind and sky.

'Basil can teach you,' Mrs Kenley said with massive confidence. 'He's the best instructor you could find. But, the truth is, it's such a shallow beach, you'll have to walk halfway to France before you're out of your depth if the tide's out.' She put a hand on his shoulder and peered into his troubled face. 'Don't worry. You don't have to do anything you don't want to.'

There could hardly be any more welcome words to an unadventurous spirit than an assurance that they will not be pushed beyond their limits and he gazed at her with grateful devotion.

They left the car near a gap in the dunes and floundered through the dry sand in a column led by Mr Kenley, who was laden with deckchair, windbreak, picnic blanket, rucksack and towels. The boys brought the cricket equipment and buckets and spades, while Mrs Kenley carried a canvas bag and her sun hat. Boswell, off the lead, had bounded towards the horizon and was soon no more than a speck at the water's edge.

They set up an encampment, with Mrs Kenley enthroned in the one deckchair. Mr Kenley claimed not to need one for himself as he had too much to do. He was as eager as any child to get digging and had brought along a proper garden spade for the purpose.

William realised with relief that the sea itself played a very small part in the day's activities and he might get away without the humiliation of a swimming lesson in his underwear. For the Kenleys, it was mostly about the sand, as a material for the construction of an immense moated fortress or a smooth surface for ball games.

It was important to begin their excavations just below the watermark, Mr Kenley explained, where the ground was damp but firm and so that the incoming tide would fill up the moat. He rolled up shirtsleeves and trousers and removed his shoes and socks, and with his unlit pipe still clamped in his teeth, set to digging out a deep circular trench, flinging up shovelfuls of sand, which the boys patted and chopped and shaped.

While they were busy, Mrs Kenley had changed into a navy swimsuit with a white belt, exposing her pale winter skin to the sun, and was reclining in her deckchair using the picnic basket as a footstool. She was not expected to take part in the building project, which was men's work, though William suspected she would be quite as efficient as any man if she was interested in something. She bestirred herself from her sunbathing to come and appraise the finished sandcastle and make a good show of inspecting it from all angles.

For lunch there were hard-boiled eggs and tongue sandwiches.

'Why is this ham called tongue?' Francis wanted to know, peeling the meat away from the buttered bread and holding it up so it dangled from his lower lip.

Mr and Mrs Kenley glanced at each other.

'Is it because it's the colour of your tongue?' William suggested.

He had eaten the stuff once or twice at home but had never thought to question its origins. All cold meat was the same to him, neither pleasant nor unpleasant, and bearing no obvious connection to any animal. This was about to change.

'Guess again,' said Mr Kenley.

'It's not . . . made of . . . actual *tongues*!' Francis exclaimed, clutching his stomach.

'Just the one,' Mrs Kenley explained. 'An ox tongue, boiled and rolled and pressed and thinly sliced.'

It took the swearing of a solemn promise on her part before the boys would accept this as fact.

'Oh, look, if you really can't bear it, you'll just have to give it to Boz and eat the bread,' she said at last, laughing at their queasy expressions.

Nothing ever rattled her or roused her to anger, thought William.

In the afternoon, they set up the stumps and played cricket, using similar rules to the garden variant but a bigger canvas. After her leisurely morning, Mrs Kenley excelled herself at the wicket, smacking the ball for miles across the flat sand. Fortunately, Boswell, fuelled by all that rejected tongue, made a tireless outfielder.

There were other families on the beach, jumping the waves and playing games, but it was apparent to William that none were having as much fun as the Kenleys. Other parents sat around too much and left their offspring to amuse themselves. Before long, some of these neglected children began to drift towards the Kenley camp, drawn by the evident superiority of their entertainments, until they had recruited quite a band of eager batsmen. Even then, Francis' parents didn't withdraw to the comfort of their tea flask, pipe or newspaper but continued to organise and umpire until the incoming tide began to encroach on the pitch.

The hangers-on having been dispatched back to their parents, it was now, finally, time for a swim. William had been dreading this moment, but he was hot and the backs of his legs below the hem of his shorts were beginning to prickle. He hung back while Francis and his father changed into their costumes, sitting on the blanket pretending to be absorbed in the job of burying his own feet in the sand.

'Are you coming, William?' Mrs Kenley asked, laying a cool hand on his shoulder. She had protected her hair with a white rubber cap that dragged her eyebrows upwards in a fixed expression of surprise. He shook his head. 'All right, dear.'

He watched the three of them run down to the water's edge and splash through the foaming ripples, wading further until they could at last throw themselves into the waves and strike out for deep water. Boswell paddled out after them and then had second thoughts and turned back to stand sentry on the sand awaiting their return.

The water looked cool and inviting and his skin was so hot and gritty. Glancing around to check that he was unobserved, William quickly stripped to his vest and pants, which were off-white and had his name sewn into the back for school. Aunt Louisa's neat stitching scratched between his shoulder blades. He jogged self-consciously down the sand, feeling the eyes of everyone on the beach swivel to stare at him.

When he reached the sanctuary of the water, he sat down gratefully in the shallows and risked a glance behind him. Parents were calling to their children, drying sandy toes, shaking out wet towels and dismantling windbreaks. No one was paying him any attention.

Far away, Mr Kenley gave him a welcoming salute. A moment later, he struck out for the shore. Behind him, the bald scalp of Mrs Kenley's hat glowed white in the afternoon sun. She has told him I can't swim, thought William, mortified by this deficiency. He stood up and advanced to meet Mr Kenley, who was now wading towards him through the thigh-deep waves.

'Let's get you swimming,' he said with beaming confidence. 'There's nothing to it, I promise you, especially in seawater.'

William gave himself into Mr Kenley's arms and allowed his body to be supported from below as he lay like a starfish on his back. Every muscle was tensed in anticipation of the inevitable moment when the protective arm was suddenly withdrawn and he would sink like a ship's anchor.

'Don't let me go,' he croaked, rigid with fear and shame.

'I won't. Keep your back straight and raise your hips. That's it. You've got it.'

Overhead in the pale blue distance, a seagull cruised effortlessly, riding the breeze. William closed his eyes against the dazzle and orange serpents writhed behind his eyelids. The travelling waves rocked him gently; he could feel the solid bar of Mr Kenley's forearm and then just the flat of his hand at the base of his spine.

'Don't let go,' he pleaded.

'It's not me holding you up; it's the water,' Mr Kenley said. 'You're as buoyant as a cork.'

It was like learning to whistle, William thought, the moment of change from noiseless blowing to that first clean note; from believing you must sink to knowing you will float. There was no physical transformation that could account for it. The water wouldn't support him and then, miraculously, in an instant, it would and did; there was no retreating from this knowledge. It couldn't be unlearnt.

'Good man!' Mr Kenley was saying. 'You've got it. The rest is easy.'

★

It was agreed that they must at least stay to watch the moat fill up with water, which it did stealthily and then in a great rush, engulfing the lower slopes of the castle. There was something about the gradual collapse of their great construction and its reabsorption into the wet sand that was both impressive and melancholy. Even Mr and Mrs Kenley seemed a little deflated as they left the beach and toiled back to the car with the bags and equipment. William's shoulders, nose and ears were pink from the sun; he would need calamine lotion by bedtime.

On the way back to Brock Cottage they stopped to pick up fish and chips, a treat beyond William's imaginings. His aunts never ate any food that they hadn't made themselves. Mrs Kenley tore off the outer wrapping of newspaper and threw it in the waste bin, but not before William had read the headline: 'Europe's Fate in the Hands of Hitler'. She was quiet for the rest of the journey.

Dear Aunt Louisa, Aunt Elsie and Aunt Rose, William wrote in letters that filled half the card supplied by Mrs Kenley. He was used to this chore from Sunday evenings at school, where he would write a brief bulletin about his health and recent meals consumed through a haze of blinding homesickness.

Here, there was no problem in finding things to say – the days were full of new experiences that demanded to be told. But when he pictured home, it was as though through the wrong end of a telescope; his aunts and their influence had shrunk to the point of insignificance. Brock Cottage was the new, the only reality.

I am very well. There are badgers in the garden and a stream with fish. Mrs Kenley is a good cricketer. Today we went to the beach and I learnt how to stay afloat. Francis is a good swimmer. I hope you are well.

It was Francis' idea to sleep out. Mr Kenley showed them how to rig up a bivvy between the trees using a groundsheet and some rope. The night was clear and the sky crowded with stars, hanging as if only just out of reach. Everywhere William looked were the glitter trails of shooting stars; it made him dizzy trying to fathom the size and mystery of it all.

'You see that star there,' said Mr Kenley, pointing into the void, and they laughed, but he pressed on undeterred. 'There's Orion's Belt, look, and there, just above and to the left, is Betelgeuse. The light you are seeing left that star before Henry VIII came to the throne. To see it as it is today, you would have to wait until the year 2368.'

They gazed at the tiny winking speck, stupefied by these unfathomable glimpses into past and future. Then Mrs Kenley came down the garden towards them bringing blankets and a plate of hot sausages, knowing without needing to be told that they would be cold and hungry and that the comfort of a full stomach was the best defence against infinity.

'What do you want to do when you leave school, William?' Mr Kenley asked one evening in the conversational hour between dinner and board games. The room was lit only by candles and a Tilley lamp, and shadows trembled on the uneven plaster walls. It wasn't cold, but at the boys' request a fire burnt in the stove and Boswell was slumbering on the hearthrug, making occasional scrabbling motions in his sleep as though dreaming of the chase.

'I want to be a zookeeper,' said William.

Recent ambitions had included an explorer and aeronaut and an inventor; this one was quite new and prompted by no more than an upsurge of love for Boswell and all other animals.

'Oh, that's interesting,' said Mr Kenley, with his way of respecting even the most banal of the boys' utterances. 'Which

379

bits of zookeeping appeal? I should think it involves quite a lot of cleaning and mucking out.'

'Feeding the animals and looking after them,' said William who, if he imagined it at all, saw himself as a Dr Dolittle figure, surrounded by tame and sociable creatures that would submit to being his friends.

'I'm not sure I like the idea of keeping animals in captivity,' Mr Kenley went on, packing his pipe with threads of tobacco. 'They always look a bit unhappy – especially the big cats.'

'I think it's cruel to keep them in cages,' said Francis.

'Some zoos have very good breeding programmes to return animals to the wild and stop them from being hunted to extinction,' Mrs Kenley said, glancing at William's stricken face.

'When I'm a zookeeper, I'll set all the animals free,' William said.

He hadn't pictured himself as their gaoler. That would be unbearable.

Mr Kenley flicked at his lighter and sucked the flame into the bowl of his pipe. 'I should think you'd be putting yourself out of a job pretty quickly.'

'Oh, Basil, you don't need to be so literal-minded,' said Mrs Kenley with a shake of the head. It was the first time she had ever disagreed with him in William's hearing and her husband was immediately contrite.

'No, no, of course not. William can be anything he chooses. And I'm sure he'll make an excellent job of it.' He winked at William through the smoke.

'Can I be anything I choose?' Francis wanted to know. 'Like a cricketer.'

'Yes, why ever not?' Mr Kenley said. 'You've both got your whole lives ahead of you.'

★

On the side of the bath was a large white tablet of soap. It produced clouds of soft lather and left William's skin tight and shiny and cleaner than it had ever been. He looked out of the warped glass of the tiny window; Mr Kenley was watering the flower beds and Boswell was bounding around the lawn chasing a butterfly. This time tomorrow, he thought, he would be at home in Croydon, and this time next week, he would be back at school. All the happiness of the afternoon drained out of him – he could feel it leaving his body. He closed his eyes and clutched the cold edge of the washbasin in his hot hands to force time to stop moving.

The latch clicked and 'Whoopsie,' said Mrs Kenley from the doorway. She was carrying a pile of folded towels for the airing cupboard. 'Sorry, William, I didn't realise you were . . .' She looked at him more closely. 'Are you all right?' Her voice was soft with concern.

He tried to swallow the treacherous sob in his throat, but it was too late to call it back. He turned away so she wouldn't see the shameful tears. Mrs Kenley crossed the room in two strides and hugged him to her aproned chest. She smelt of the garden, of clean laundry, of the hand cream that she put on after she had done the washing-up.

'Now what's this all about?' she asked, disengaging gently and passing him a folded handkerchief from her pocket.

It was so white he was frightened to use it, so he smeared his arm across his face.

'Has something happened or are you just feeling sad?'

'I wish I wasn't going home tomorrow. I wish I could stay here for ever.' And then the worst, most disloyal thought of all. 'I wish you were my mother.'

'Oh . . . now . . . that's sweet of you.'

She didn't, he noticed, say that she wished he was her son.

'But I'm sure your aunties do the job of three mothers. You're not unhappy at home?'

'No. Home's all right. Not as good as here, though.'

'But even we can't stay here all the time, and it would soon stop being fun if we did. We have to go back to normal life – school and job and housework and so on.'

At the word school, an involuntary shudder ran through him.

'And while we're away we keep ourselves cheerful by thinking over all the good memories of this holiday – I'll remember that cricket game on the beach and eating sausages down in your camp. What about you?'

'The badgers,' said William, knowing he must pick on something to please her, when what he really meant was *all of it*.

'There you are!' exclaimed Mrs Kenley. 'When you feel a bit out of sorts, you can think of the badgers. And any time you see one in future, it will be like a secret message from Brock Cottage.'

'What will it say?'

Mrs Kenley screwed up her face in a mime of someone communing with spirits. 'I don't know. Something like, "Everything will be all right."'

William gave her back a watery smile. He liked the idea of these messenger badgers, though he thought the chances of seeing one in Croydon were small.

'Anyway,' Mrs Kenley went on, encouraged. 'There'll be other holidays. We usually come down for a week at Easter. You can come with us, as long as your aunts don't object.'

His heart quickened, and then he remembered that these were just words and that the invitation, if it came, would have to come from Francis, who knew nothing of this conversation and might by then have another best friend. Mrs Kenley might forget and he had no way of prompting her. Easter was more than half a year away, as remote as adulthood or death.

'Do you promise?' he asked, knowing that this was somehow rude.

He sensed that Mrs Kenley was a person who kept promises and wouldn't say something untrue just to slam the door on a conversation.

'Yes, of course.' She put a hand on his shoulder and gave it a strengthening squeeze. 'You'll go off to school and work hard and in no time at all you'll be back here again.'

From downstairs came Francis' voice calling impatiently. There was time for one last run down to the stream before tea if they got a move on.

Chapter 44

1964

William carried the plates in from the garden and put them beside the sink, where Marion was washing-up using a cloth of knitted string. Helen and Francis had left at the same time and the house seemed to exhale with relief at the silence. It was good to have friends, but conversation exhausted him, however little he took part, and it was a wonder to him that two people who hardly knew each other could talk so much and so easily.

As soon as they were alone, Marion had turned to him and said, 'She'll do *very* nicely,' and when he asked, 'Do what nicely?' she had just laughed and shaken her head.

The dogs had been fed and were lolling in their baskets, replete. Later, he would take them out for a last run in the dusk: his favourite job of the day. Tomorrow, he would dig over the neglected vegetable patches and plant spring cabbages. The farmer who owned all the paddocks to their west had given them a trailer of logs that needed splitting and stacking against the shed. The grass at the back of the house was due for cutting with the same old rotary mower that Mr Kenley had used. The croquet lawn was now given over to weeds and wildflowers – he had tripped over a rusty hoop while walking there on the first day he had arrived. If there was time, he would start working on plans for the new henhouse. He knew exactly how it should look and could have drawn it in every detail, but creating this vision with wood and wire netting was a very different prospect.

Now, though, he picked up a tea towel and began to dry the dishes that Marion had piled on the draining board. She had snapped off her rubber gloves and flung them in the sink, where they lay palm to palm in an attitude of prayer.

Later the two of them would watch television, the miraculous machine, and she would doze in her chair. He always nodded a goodnight to his father's painting of Grandfather Ernest above the fireplace and the photograph of his mother before going up to bed.

For the first few weeks after his arrival, as he'd stood at his bedroom window watching for badgers in the dark, his head nearly brushing the low ceiling, he could feel himself shrink back through time until he was the child William again, parched with grief at the thought of the holiday ending. There was something luxurious in revisiting an old sorrow from the safe haven of present happiness, but tonight he was tired and his mind was already crowded with anticipation of the important jobs that awaited him in the morning.

Afterword

Shy Creatures has its origin in a true story. In February 1952, police were called to a house in Kingsdown, Bristol, after reports of an altercation – raised voices and items being thrown from an upstairs window. Inside, they discovered a naked man with a five-foot beard and waist-length hair, living as a recluse in conditions of some squalor with his elderly aunt and sundry dogs, cats and birds.

The forty-year-old Harry Tucker had not been seen by neighbours for over twenty-five years. He was admitted to Glenside Mental Hospital (as it was then called) and treated for schizophrenia. The story was repeated in several newspapers, with sensational headlines like 'House of Secrets gives up lost man' and some inconsistency as to details; sometimes it was the man's hair rather than beard that was five feet long. His age was given variously as forty, forty-two and forty-six.

A search of the newspaper archives yielded further information and conjecture: the surviving aunt was one of five sisters, three of whom had once lived in the house, the descendants of a prosperous Bristol grocer. Harry was believed to be the son of one of the unmarried sisters and had attended a local school before disappearing from public life.

There were no more accounts of his progress until May 1953, when the *Birmingham Gazette* reported his death by drowning in the river Frome, not far from the hospital where he was a resident. I became preoccupied with his sad, solitary fate and decided to imagine him a past – and a more hopeful future. It should go without saying that apart from the details of his discovery given above, my version is pure invention.

I transplanted the story to 1964 – an interesting moment in the history of psychiatry (and of society itself). R.D. Laing had published his groundbreaking work, *The Divided Self*, in 1960, but his controversial and short-lived experiment in communal living at Kingsley Hall was still to come. Art therapy was in its infancy – or its adolescence, perhaps – and some of the more invasive treatments for mental illness – insulin therapy and leucotomies – were no longer in common use.

Westbury Park, though occupying the site of the vanished Warlingham Park Hospital in Surrey, is a fictional hybrid of more than one of the large, progressive psychiatric hospitals of the 1960s. For my research into the history of these institutions and the theories and practices that underpinned them, I tried to read only as far as 1964 and no further, so that I would not have the advantage of knowledge unavailable to my characters – making a virtue of my ignorance, if you will. However, the subject was just too fascinating and I found myself unable to adhere strictly to this rule.

Of the books and articles I read for background – and fore-ground – I am particularly indebted to the following:

Nathan Filer, *This Book will Change Your Mind About Mental Health* (London, 2019)

Simon Garfield, *Private Battles: Our Intimate Diaries: How the War Almost Defeated Us* (London, 2006)

Erving Goffman, *Asylums* (New York, 1961)

Richard S. Hallam and Michael P. Bender, *David's Box: The Journals and Letters of a Young Man Diagnosed as Schizophrenic, 1960–1971* (London, 2011)

Katherine Killick and Joy Schaverien, *Art, Psychotherapy and Psychosis* (Hove, 1977), in particular the chapter 'Art, madness and anti-psychiatry: a memoir' by John Henzell

David Kynaston, *On the Cusp*: *Days of '62* (London, 2021)

R.D. Laing, *The Divided Self* (London, 1960)

R.D. Laing and Aaron Esterson, *Sanity, Madness and the Family* (London, 1964)

Peter Nolan, 'Mental Health Nursing in the 1960s Remembered', *Journal of Psychiatric and Mental Health Nursing* (June, 2021) Vol. 28, Iss. 3, pp.462–68

Thomas Szasz, *The Myth of Mental Illness* (New York, 1961)

J.K. Wing and G.W. Brown, 'Social Treatment of Chronic Schizophrenia: A Comparative Survey of Three Mental Hospitals', *Journal of Mental Science* (1961) p. 107, 847

Acknowledgements

My acknowledgments grow longer with each book, which tells a story either of declining self-reliance or of improving manners; perhaps both.

Thanks are due to my agent, Judith Murray, for all her support and to the whole team at Greene & Heaton. Thanks also to my UK editor, Alexa von Hirschberg, for her many helpful suggestions and to Rachel Kahan in the US; to copy-editor Claire Dean and to the brilliant team at W&N and Orion, including Jenny Lord, Virginia Woolstencroft, Esther Waters, Cait Davies, Ellie Nightingale, Jo Roberts-Miller, Chevonne Elbourne and Steve Marking. They are all you could hope for in a publisher and I am in awe of their commitment and energy.

I am indebted to the Royal Literary Fund for the wonderful fellowship scheme, and in particular to the Director of Education, Steve Cook. This organisation really is the writer's best friend.

For memories and memorabilia from 1964, I am grateful to Jane Peacock and John Rowley. Dr Richard Hallam, the co-author of the immensely informative and moving *David's Box*, mentioned in the Afterword, was kind enough to answer my specific questions about clinical practice in the 60s and 70s.

Dr Gordon Cree also provided further invaluable insights on this theme. All errors, anachronisms and wilful divergence from expert opinion are my own.

Special thanks to my husband, Peter, always my first reader and my greatest cheerleader.